ZOMBIE FALLOUT 9

TATTERED REMNANTS

MARK TUFO

DEVILDOG PRESS

SWANVILLE, MAINE

Discover other titles by Mark Tufo

Visit us at marktufo.com

and http://zombiefallout.blogspot.com/ home of future webisodes

and find me on FACEBOOK

cover art by Dane@ebooklaunch.com

editing by Lisa and Tommy Lane

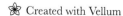 Created with Vellum

To the wife: I don't think the missus gets it. Without you woman, none of this is possible. I love you.

To my beta readers: Kimberly Sansone, Vix Kirkpatrick and Susan Di Muzio, words really only scratch the surface. Your attention to detail and your unique approaches to my books help me put my best foot forward and for that, thank you.

To Laura Blair and Richard Ilsley their vivid imaginations have brought to life some of the worst pop-tart flavors imaginable!

To all the first responders and members of the armed forces. You help to make our country the great nation that it is, the Tufo family will forever hold you in our thoughts and prayers. (To those three cops that let me slide after my recent bout of speeding violations, the barbecue starts at two)

ACKNOWLEDGMENTS

This is just a small token of appreciation for my fans and those that have helped out along the way, whether through helping to fund our Kilts That Care fund raiser or leaving responses on our podcast! And also a small shout out to the admins for my fan pages in the US and the UK, Pauline Milbourn, Kathy Pippen Turner, Jeff Smith, Baylie Poller and Richie LoBo Edgar Shiers, you guys do a bunch of work and I just wanted to let you know I greatly appreciate it!

A hearty thank you to everyone that donated on the GoFundMe campaign. The families that receive your donations will be most appreciative!

John Cox, Ginny McGee, Malinda Gibson, Gary Reilly, Carol Brunnert, Karen Carbonell, Jennifer Erickson, Vix Kirkpatrick, Jenny Clark, Chuck Lentz, Walter Arnold, Jan Buhagiar, Lori Safranek, Tim Scott, Peter Kirby, Barbara Ferrenz, Jack Hager, Jaz Mixer, Shawn Chesser, Frank Edler, Amber Mohler, Kimberly Calhoun, Baylie Poller, Stacey Buhagiar, Michael Milazzo, Charles Rutledge, Nicole Platania, Liz W, Timothy Gildea, Amber Fallon, Brian K, Heather Scott, Eric Shelman, Stephanie Daly, Rob Ritter, John James, Sean Runnette, Alicia Stamps, Lisa Williams, Megan McLaughlin, Jason Teasdale, Dana Ottwell

PROLOGUE 1

Mrs. Deneaux felt pretty good about herself as she exited the Demense building. Tommy hadn't necessarily been her enemy, but he was aligned with Michael, and that bastard had a way of inspiring those around him to be relentless in pursuit of his adversaries. She walked into the garage. She would have preferred one of the Cadillacs or Mercedes Benzes parked there, but instead settled for one of the military trucks, knowing that it would not need keys. She started the engine before lighting a cigarette. She let her head rest against the back of the seat while she exhaled a large plume of smoke.

"There were times, Michael, I did not believe I would beat you. You were a worthy adversary." She took another drag. It was lost on her that Mike didn't consider this survival of the fittest but rather survival of them all. "I will miss you." Then she cackled, "Not really." She was half way through her third smoke when a zombie smacked up against her window. She calmly rolled the window down just far enough to put the barrel of her firearm through before placing a round neatly between its eyes. She backed the truck up and pulled out of the garage.

"Now where, Vivian?" She drove a block away and parked

in the parking lot of a long-disused electronics store that had closed its doors a few years previous. "First things first. I'm going to need more cigarettes and bullets." She'd checked the stores for both, and they were dangerously low. "Should I go back to the Talbot stronghold? Those twits would let me back in. How rich would that be to find refuge among them!" The truck was in drive, and she was just about to get going when the first shells rained down upon the building she'd just vacated.

"What's this? A cigarette and a show, how nice." She sat back and reveled. Her icy blood ran colder when she saw the van barrel out of the building from the same egress she'd used. "It can't be!" she shrieked. A small coughing fit erupted as she swallowed an intake of smoke incorrectly. "You cannot have lived, not after that!" But she knew better. Michael fucking Talbot had once again cheated death.

Vivian couldn't remember ever being so angry and enthralled at the same time. She held some self-directed anger for ever allowing herself to get on the other side of such a fierce enemy, but even more for not just ending it. Never before had she allowed such a threat in her life to go untended for so long. "Only one of us can be standing when this is all over, Michael, and I fully intend on it being me. We'll meet again, someday. I'm sure of it. But for now, I'm going to dig my toes into the Pacific Ocean as far away from you and yours as I can possibly get." She drove off.

PROLOGUE 2

Dᴜʀɪɴɢ ᴛʜᴇ ʀɪᴅᴇ ʙᴀᴄᴋ ꜰʀᴏᴍ Nᴏʀᴛʜ Cᴀʀᴏʟɪɴᴀ, I ᴡᴀs ᴀs emotionally high as I could remember being since the zombies had come. What I would feel going forward would always be tempered with the losses we'd suffered along the way. So the baseline would be a lot lower to start with; it was an evil born from the devastation. Still though, to feel elation, love, accomplishment, just the mere fact of being alive, healthy and among friends and family was nearly beyond words. Of course it was short lived and false, but we had it in our grasp, if only for a moment. We did not tempt fate much on that trip. We topped all the vehicles off with gas and filled everything else that even remotely resembled a liquid container so we would not have to stop again. We took shifts driving, and in twenty-four hours, we had gone from our own reunion to pulling into my brother's long, lonely stretch of dirt roadway for another.

There was a moment when we were coming in that I thought I was hallucinating. My Jeep, my awesomely beautiful fire engine red Jeep, was parked off to the side. But that wasn't possible. There was no way in hell anyone would risk their lives to go cross-country to retrieve it. As nuts as I sometimes could get, the thought of doing this would never cross my mind. Okay wait, that's a falsehood. I have thought about it. Although for the sake of fairness, I've also thought about riding a whale and eating thirty-six hot dogs, none of which I would actually carry out due to the potential liability. And to be honest, I would be pissed at whoever had done it here. To what fucking point?

"Mike?" Tracy had asked as I walked around the Jeep.

"Yup, it's mine."

"You sure?"

"Well there's still Henry drool down the back windshield, I'm sure I could get that DNA tested. But unless someone is really into master pranks, I'm not sure how they could have known what license plate to put on. I had Marine Corps plates. When the state of Colorado offered them I was like "Hell yeah!" Figured I was even going to get a little discount on them for my time in the service. Gotta admit I was a little let down when they charged ten dollars more for them. I opened up the side door; dog smell came out. Henry barked like mad as BT took him out and placed him on the ground. He rushed over to me and placed his paws on the running board. This was my cue to pick his ass up and place him inside. He started sniffing like someone had rubbed bacon all over the back seat.

His stub of a tail would alternate from swinging back and forth wildly to going stiff as a board when he came to certain scents he wasn't sure about or did not like.

"Who did this?" BT asked.

"Someone that knew it was at the sheriff's in Vona." I looked up to Ron's house. It was just then I noticed how dark it was, and I also saw no movement. We hadn't come in beeping horns and playing rock music loudly, but still it was three cars in a world gone silent. We should have been heard for miles. I got a sick feeling in my stomach. Had my Jeep been used as a Trojan horse? But those particular enemies were dead. Weren't they?

1

MIKE JOURNAL ENTRY 1

"WEAPONS," I SAID AS SILENTLY AS I COULD WHILE MAKING sure everyone heard me.

The mood changed suddenly and without question. Within a few seconds, everyone was on high alert. We had a loose circle formed and our complete perimeter covered.

"Dad, what are we looking for?" Travis asked.

"Anything out of the ordinary."

I could feel his questioning gaze without even turning to look. The entire world was out of the ordinary.

"You know what I mean," I barely explained. "Let's move closer," I told the group. "Be careful for booby traps or land mines."

"Hand mimes? They're the best. One was so good I actually walked into the wall he was trying to get around." Trip was, for some reason, carrying Henry, and given the dog's size, Trip was struggling.

We were a good twenty yards from Ron's house. We had already gotten by the thick, sharpened wooden poles entrenched into the ground at a zombie-piercing angle. Next came a heavy chain-link fence. Beyond that were the deep and narrow death trenches we'd carved into the ground. Then was

Ron's house. From our angle, we were staring into the gaping wound that was the burned-out basement. Above that was a deck, and it was from there I saw my first bit of movement. I gripped my rifle tighter, if that was even possible.

"Ron?"

"Mike?" We almost asked our questioning greeting at the same time.

"Is it safe?" I asked, pointing to the ground to get to him. He looked sad, defeated maybe. I hoped it was just tiredness. He smiled when he saw us. We climbed up to him. He hugged and kissed everyone, but I noticed the warmth never reached his eyes. He was holding onto something that had an icy grip on his heart. It was Justin that got the first hint of what was going on.

Two dogs I'd never seen before came onto that deck with us.

"Riley?" Justin asked. "Riley, is that you, girl?" He got down on one knee, gripped the dog's head in his hands, and patted her furiously.

"Justin?" I asked him.

"Dad, this is Jess's dog, Riley. You remember right?"

I remembered once I rambled through the shambles of my less-than-perfect memory. I'd always liked Jess. Thought she was a sweetheart of a girl. Justin had been devastated when she moved away. I remember meeting Riley once or twice. Jess had apologized profusely when her dog had jumped up against my Jeep door, I would imagine to get a smell of Henry, who although he wasn't in the car at the time, tended to leave heavy essence trails of himself wherever he went.

Henry wiggled in Trip's arms until Trip figured out the dog wanted down. I don't know the conversation Riley and Henry were having, but they seemed to be getting along pretty well, and generally, my dog didn't play well with others. I was curious to see how he would react to the little dog my brother called Ben-Ben. Thing looked like he was hopped up on sugar shooters.

"Where's Jess?" Justin had stood up and was waiting for the girl to appear. By the way everyone had filed out of the house and was on the deck with us, I didn't need their sullen faces to explain. I already knew the answer, and soon, Justin would as well.

"Jess?" He stood on his tiptoes trying to look over the burgeoning crowd.

Ron hugged him.

"Goddammit," I said. "When is this shit going to end?"

"Dad?" Justin was choosing not to put the pieces of this particularly bad puzzle together.

"Come here, son."

"Jess!" he yelled out again.

He was rooted to his spot, so I moved to him and wrapped him in a hug he could not break loose from, though he tried. To be in my arms was to come to a horrible realization, and he wanted no part of it. He struck out, punching me in the sides. At first, they were hard hits, but they softened as he began to cry into my shoulder. Tracy wrapped herself around his back.

"I'm so sorry," she said over and over.

It was maybe twenty minutes later when he'd spent himself. Ron ushered us to a place I could have him lay down. He fell into a fitful sleep about a half hour later. I lightly touched Tracy's arm and pointed to the doorway. She looked back at him one more time before I softly pulled the door to the bedroom shut.

"It's good to see you, Mike." Ron said. He sat at the table. Gary had been filling him in on everything that had happened.

"Yeah, it was touch and go for a while, that's for sure. Where is everyone else?" I asked.

"Tommy has them outside doing his best to distract them from everything that's going on."

"Do you have it in you to tell me what the hell happened and how my Jeep got here?" I knew now that Jess had somehow miraculously stumbled upon my cherished ride and brought it here. But then what? Had she been injured beyond repair when she finally got here?

"It was a damned zombie, Mike, a smart fucking zombie. It traversed every obstacle we had out there. Made it through the basement, found Jess sleeping and … and…." He broke down. I didn't need the blow by blow at this point; easy enough to figure out.

I let him get it out of his system as best he could. He would carry the guilt of her death with him for the rest of his life. She'd been under his umbrella of protection, and he had seen himself as failing. It did not matter that he had no fault in this. He would never come to see it in that light, and for that, I truly wept inside. Humans carried guilt with them like luggage, and he'd just thrown a fully stuffed duffel bag onto his back. It would eventually wear him down.

"She showed up a couple of weeks ago. Nicole recognized her. Said she'd been to Little Turtle looking for Justin, and when he was gone, she lived in the clubhouse. She said there was enough food in there to last them for years."

"Right. That's where we stashed everything from the supermarket when we were still able to defend our home." I had a pang in my chest for all that could never be recovered. "Lucky find for her. That still leaves a mighty big gap for her to get to Vona and stumble across my Jeep."

"She had help. A man named Alex."

"Alex, as in Carbonara?"

"Yeah, I think that was what she said his name was."

My moment of elation at potentially seeing an old friend was quickly dashed. Ron did not appear to have ever met the man. "What happened to him?"

"Zombie attack, actually not too far from here. A fucking bathroom break, Mike. They were just trying to make a quick pit stop, that's all."

"There's no rhyme or reason brother; we both know that. Your marker comes up, and that's it. Doesn't matter where you are or what you're doing. I mean, I hope there're certain things that I'm doing when I die, but there's no guarantee." I was trying to find some levity in the heaviness of our conversation. Either way, Ron wasn't in the mood. "There're some holes in this story. Do you know how Alex and Jess got together?"

"It doesn't get any better."

"Not sure if it could. But he was a friend I'd like to know."

"Well, I guess Alex's family had met with a fate much like the rest of the world."

"Aw fuck." I slammed my palm to my forehead. "Those poor kids. Poor Alex. Fuck."

"Yeah, so he got it in his head that he was going to go back to where it had all started and end it. If you know what I mean."

I didn't, not at first anyway. "Suicide?"

Ron nodded.

"He was going to kill himself? I guess it makes sense. At that point, what are you living for?"

"Then he met Jess."

"Something to live for. Unreal how some things come full circle."

"How so?" Ron asked.

"Alex came back to Little Turtle in that semi to save us on Christmas Day. Maybe somehow he knew he had one more person to save back there. Otherwise, why wouldn't he have just done himself in wherever he was? Why make a specific trip to your final destination?"

"Sometimes you actually make sense, brother," he said with a smile that did not have enough power to touch his eyes.

"Every once in a while, I suppose I get my due."

"What now?"

"I'm done, man. I'm just fucking done. There's no one out there anymore that needs my help. They're dead, they're all fucking dead." The gravity of that reality slammed into me. We were now a very small island of the living in an ocean of death.

"Going to be nice to finally have you stick around for a while."

"Yeah, that's something new for me."

"How are you going to sate your hero complex?" BT had come back in and sat at the table.

"I'm good, as long as I've saved your life more times than you've saved mine," I told him.

He smiled again. Much like my brother, it did not have the temerity to travel to his eyes, which were now downcast. "Hell of thing about Alex."

Gary had got up at some point and come back with some beers. I held mine up. "To Alex." We all took a drink.

"To Jess." Ron said as we took another drink.

"To Dad." Gary said.

By the time we'd gone through the list of all the people that meant something to us that had died in this shit fest, I was hammered. I admit I'm a cheaper date now that I've gained a few years under my belt, and I'd never been much of a heavy drinker. But, yeah, I was fairly drunk. Probably didn't help that by the end, we were repeating names. I probably toasted Jen three or four times. Paul five or more. How does one deal with the accumulation of loss? It is a cold, heavy feeling that settles into the bottom of your heart where it grows sharp barbs that take root and will not release its icy grip. It slowly chokes your system, making even the most basic and simplest of tasks brutally difficult.

2

MIKE JOURNAL ENTRY 2

I AWOKE THE NEXT MORNING WITH A MODICUM OF PRODDING from Tracy.

"Any fucking chance this is all a bad dream like some shitty TV program?" I asked, placing my hand against my splitting head.

"Here, take these." Tracy handed me a couple of aspirin and a bottle of water.

"How about I just lie here a few days longer?"

"Your son needs you."

"Yeah, I get that." I sat up with some difficulty and took the pills and water, swallowing them both as fast as I could get the muscles in my throat to move. "I hate this part," I told her as I stood.

"The hangover?"

"Naw, I know that will pass. It's the crushing weight of loss in my chest."

Tracy kissed the side of my face. What can one really say to that? I know she felt it as well. She was just less inclined to wear it on her sleeve, where I tended to show it for the entire world to see.

"Where is he?" I pulled a shirt over my head. "And why am I naked? Did you take advantage of me?"

"Yes, Michael. Haven't I told you how hot, drunk, stumbling men make me?"

"Hell, you must have been on fire last night then."

"Just get out there. He's at the grave site."

Another unfortunate development of the apocalypse was the need for us to revert back to the ways things used to be done early on in the country's formative years. Out of necessity, we'd had to dig graves on our own land, and that we'd already gone past the original capacity was another unfortunate byproduct. Sure, we'd been more hopeful than practical that we could keep the plot small. Worth a shot, I suppose.

I walked out of the house and made my way to Justin. I saw him about twenty yards away, his back to me, his head bowed, and his shoulders slumped. He looked so small, like all the spirit had been ripped from him and all that was left was his battered, bruised and misused body. I approached. When I was next to him, I reached out and wrapped my arm around his shoulder. He said nothing; he did not stir, in fact. I wasn't sure if he even knew I was there.

We stayed that way for a good, long while. A cold breeze started in the woods off to our right, picking up a swirl of leaves that swept around our feet before going about their way.

"I loved her," he said with a croak. It was such a strangled sound I thought at first maybe I had imagined it.

Words eluded me. It wasn't like this was a high school crush (which it had been) and I could tell him that he was young and there were plenty of fish in the sea. And all that stuff parents tell their kids in the vain attempt to make them feel better. It doesn't work; we know it, they feel it, yet we do it anyway.

"She loved you as well. That's why she came."

"Dad, she made it. She made it, and I wasn't here." He turned, and I saw the pain etched deeply on his face.

I hadn't taken this angle into account. I should have—ignorance on my part. It just never dawned on me that he would feel guilt as well.

I squared his shoulders so he had no choice but to look at me. "This is not your fault. This is nobody's fault. This is a war. People die in wars."

He turned away so I couldn't see his tears.

"You will see her again. I promise you that."

"You talking that reunited in Heaven bullshit? It's a lie, Dad. There's no Heaven, only Hell and we're in it." He looked at me defiantly. He wanted a battle I would not give him. He was full of grief, and he needed somebody to lash out at.

"The pain diminishes." That was the best I could offer him. "It will never go away. There will always be a dull ache in your heart when you think about her, but it won't be as debilitating as it is now. I promise."

"You don't know me!" he shouted, twisting his torso so that my hand and arm fell away. "How the fuck do you know how I'm going to feel!?"

"You're right, how could I know how you'll feel? I'm just using myself as an example."

"Go away." There was no vehemence in his request; he just wanted to be alone. What I wanted was to hug him tight and chase the demons inside of him away. What I ended up doing was walking away. Another chill wind whipped along my side; frostiness blistered up my spine. I looked up to the house. Tracy was on the deck, her arms folded. She had a look of concern on her face as she looked down at me. It was Tommy, though. He was the source of the cold dread that was spreading through me. He stood five feet to her right, staring off to the east. He was looking at nothing that I could discern, other than the direction of the ocean, which was about five miles from here and definitely not visible.

"How'd that go?" Tracy asked as I got within range that she didn't have to shout.

"Oh, about as well as you would expect. Tommy, what the hell are you doing?" He had not shifted his gaze in the least.

Tracy turned to apparently see the boy for the first time. "Tommy?" There was concern in her face. She walked over and placed her hand on his arm.

He shuddered and jumped an inch or two, shook his head, and then appeared to be trying to orient himself to his surroundings. He said nothing while he turned and strode back into the house. His terror-filled eyes the only clue he'd left to how he was feeling.

"What's the matter with him?" Tracy asked as I came up the stairs.

"I think he ate some of my sister's cooking."

"Michael."

I shrugged. I told her, "I don't know," but I did. Company was coming, and it was unwelcome.

It's been a week since I've touched this journal. I've oftentimes thought of just not writing in it anymore. Putting the monsters to page seems to only summon my nightmares. Maybe this was the way I could end the cycle. I found the call to write what was happening almost as powerful as a nicotine addiction. Stopping had made my head light and my thoughts scatter. Panic attacks threatened me daily; it was a week later that I finally put the reason to why I was feeling so shaky, with a cause. Writing was my way of dealing with our new world. For good or bad, I was stuck recording my personal history.

The week had not been completely unproductive, as we

worked long and hard at repairing the many areas that needed help. The defenses around the house were as near to impenetrable as we could make them. A fucking whole day and definitely a non-inflated dollar short, but at least we could prevent what had happened before from happening again. Fuck the whole "history repeats itself" shit. Once we were done there, we turned our attention to the destroyed basement. We did some heavy framing and boarded up the massive gap in the wall caused by the bulkers. It wasn't pretty, but it was effectual. Like placing a Band-Aid over an ugly wound. When we'd finally finished, I pulled up an old La-Z-Boy chair and sat down, facing the boarded up wall.

"Fuck, this is a comfortable chair. I could stay here forever. Screw it, maybe I will." Sucks when you realize how right you just might be.

Tommy, who had been picking up something off the floor, looked over to me. He seemed to have something to say on the tip of his tongue, but he kept it to himself. The kid was beginning to freak me out. Like he knew all sorts of nasty things that were about to happen but was hesitant to tell us as if he were protecting us from their exposure.

"What's with him?" BT dragged a huge couch over to me. I don't even know where he got it from.

"Beats me." But again, I kind of knew. In my head, I was berating Tommy for not cluing us in, and yet here I was doing the same damn thing. Frigging irony is a bitch, nope wait, it's karma that's a bitch. So what's that make irony? An asshole, perhaps?

BT dropped the couch and sat down heavily, Gary next to him, Mad Jack taking up the far end. Ron and Nancy started dragging in folding chairs and barstools and basically anything someone could sit on including a bean bag that had been around since the Nixon era. In an impromptu gathering, the entire household save one was present. I wrote out the list of people for a couple of reasons, the first I guess is just historical fact and second because it would never happen again. Not with this cast of characters anyway, and those that died they at least deserved this small mention. Ron; Nancy; their three kids, Meredith, Mark, and Melissa; Gary; Mad Jack; Trip and his wife, Stephanie; my sister Lyndsey, her husband Steve, and their kid Jesse; Tracy's mom, Carol; the four kids we'd saved from the convenience store, Dizz, Sty, Ryan, and his sister Angel; me; Tracy; and a very pregnant Nicole, along with Travis and both of our adopted kids, Tommy and Porkchop; plus Dennis and Jess's baby brother, Zachary. The only noticeable absence was Justin, who had not said more than a handful of words to anyone in the last week. Even Henry and his new friends were with us. I noticed he was very cozy with the female dog, though I was having a hard time remembering her name for some reason. The cat, Patches, thankfully stayed away from me as if she knew that I was not all that fond of felines and may never again be, given my exposure to them. I'd talked to Ron a couple of times about her suddenly finding herself out in the woods *really* far away from the house, but he would hear none of it.

I think it was Trip that cracked out the beer. "Let's get this party started!" he shouted right before lighting his bong, taking a huge hit, and then downing the "water" which was actually beer that he'd used as a filtration system. Ron could only shake his head. Normally, he'd kick the stoner outside to do it. But right now, we were all together. Living, laughing, and loving, and in reality, that's all that life is about.

3

MIKE JOURNAL ENTRY 3

It was another week. The most exciting thing that had happened was that the damned cat had killed a mouse and left it by my bedroom door. I swear it was a warning. Like she was saying, "Talk about getting rid of me again, and this could be you." We both steered clear of each other; seemed safer that way. The more seemingly secure we were, the more anxious I felt. I had been burning at such a high intensity for so long, I didn't know any other way. I didn't consider myself an adrenaline junkie; I didn't want to bungee off anything. I didn't know what my problem was. I kept waiting for something to happen. More times than not, Tracy would wake to find me peering out the window at the yard below and the woods beyond. Something was fucking out there; I knew in the depths of my ragged soul it was, and its black beady eyes were peering back at me.

"Mike?"

My chest rose and fell at a rate that belied the stillness of the night.

"Mike, come back to bed," Tracy entreated.

"There's something out there."

"What? Where?" She got out of bed and joined me at the

window. She was none too pleased, and also alarmed, when she realized I was talking about the abstract. "We've been through this Mike. There's nothing out there. We haven't seen a zombie in weeks now. Maybe it's over. Maybe we're finally safe."

"Safe?" I scoffed. "Naw, baby, this is just the eye of the fucking storm. The shit is still swirling all around us, waiting for the right time to strike."

"Wouldn't Tommy say something? And what does it matter? The fences are up. We have ammunition and a secure location. Haven't we done enough? Haven't we won?"

"Won? Won what? Unending damnation and imprisonment? Surviving isn't winning."

I caught a flash of light off her engagement ring in the corner of my eye as her hand flew up and struck me across my cheek.

"Shut up!" she admonished me. "Our children … we've saved our children. They're alive, and that's all that matters."

The slap, instead of snapping the dismal qualities of my thoughts away, seemed to crystallize them. My shoulders sagged, and I turned away from the window. "I … I don't know what's wrong with me." I was close to tears. "I can't focus my thoughts. I'm always on edge. My chest constantly hurts. I can't sleep. Fuck, I can't even rest."

"Do you have PTSD?"

And just like that, I at least had an answer. Why that never crossed my mind, I don't know. They used to talk about it all the time when I was just about to get out of the Corps. I blew it off back then. Could I blow it off now? I pondered how I was going to answer her query. Sure we had a probable cause. So what? Now what? We didn't have the right drugs or the right personnel to deal with it. And I sure as shit wasn't going to make it common knowledge. The weak and the infirm are discarded in this world much quicker and with more prejudice than perhaps at any other time in history save the Ice Age. BT would be supportive. I know he would. But I'd always know that in the back of his head, he'd be wondering when I was going to lose my shit. I couldn't bear the thought of any of them thinking less of me. And what of my new found "power"? I spat that last thought out. I'd given up part of my humanity; I was no longer tethered to a soul. How far could I go adrift? Pretty fucking far was my answer to that. And again, we didn't have anything that could help me with that. No medicine men, no priests, not even a witch—she'd walked out on us.

"Nope." I told her firmly. She was going to question me on it. I was about as good a liar as I was a singer, and on the latter, I was so bad that I generally hummed the words to a song I was listening to, even if I was alone.

Her mouth opened, and I was saved. Although, being let off the hook by an alarm is kind of a funny way to be rescued. We'd installed panic switches all throughout the house in case someone was in trouble. It wasn't going to help with resale value having buttons and wires going everywhere, but we'd stapled most of the cables to the ceiling in an effort to keep them from being a tripping hazard. Hadn't had a qualified buyer come by in a while anyway. It had been Mad Jack's idea after what had happened. In all likelihood, it wouldn't have helped. But who knows, maybe Jess had cried out for someone that wasn't coming in those final awful moments.

Soft red lights glowed, and the trill of an alarm blurted out three times then was silent. I ran next to my bed and grabbed my gun with Tracy close behind. Now we had a new problem, one we would deal with after tonight, should we make it. The alarm had been sounded, but where was the problem? Ron's house wasn't a mansion, but it was good sized and there were three floors, any one of which could be where we needed to be in a hurry.

"The deck!" It was my sister. The crack of a rifle spurred me on. Floodlights bathed the entire yard in their glow.

"What is it?" I was third onto the deck after my sister and Gary. I had my rifle up to my shoulder, and I was trying to acquire a target.

"There's something over there!" Jesse looked excited. He'd definitely seen something, or at least thought he had. The coincidence that we shared the same view when I was upstairs was not lost on me.

"Who shot?"

Gary meekly raised his hand.

"This isn't Catholic school, man. I'm not going to hit you with a ruler. Did you see something?"

"No," he said in a subdued voice that matched his demeanor. "Don't tell Ron." he pointed to a freshly made hole in the deck.

Of course, it was one of the freshly replaced boards. We'd done a good job destroying most of the deck in our final battle with Eliza. I did a quick head count as everyone started pouring through the door and onto the deck. Again, only one was missing. I had a mind-fearing moment where I thought that perhaps it was Justin that had been spotted out in the woods.

"This better not be a drill, Talbot." BT had come out only in a Speedo and flip-flops. Somehow, the man looked even bigger wearing hardly any clothes.

I brushed past him quickly to go check on Justin's room.

"What's wrong with Mike? He's not even going to say anything about BT's golden underwear?" Mad Jack asked.

BT grumbled. I half wondered when Trip's screams of "mercy" would begin. BT kind of let me slide with that shit. Everyone else was on their own. I didn't know it, but Tracy must have had the same thought, as she was only a stair or two away from me as I took them three at a time. I burst through his door. It was dark and gloomy, much like his spirit had been. The alarm light had been covered with a towel, not allowing it to relieve any of the blackness present there. Even so, I could see his eyes shine as he stared at the ceiling.

The "Oh, thank God" that was on the tip of my tongue was replaced with "Any chance you could have maybe responded to the alarm like everyone else?"

"What for? You had it all taken care of."

"Get your ass out of bed!" I roared. "You don't know what the fuck is going on down there, all fucking wallowing in self-pity up here!"

"Mike." Tracy attempted to calm me down. My own panic and issues bubbling to the surface. *Physician heal thyself* thumped around in my head. Maybe I couldn't fix myself, but I sure as shit could him, even if it took a good solid walloping of his ass with my foot.

"We've all lost in this war, and we're going to lose more. That's a foregone conclusion. But while we can, we have to make the most of it. We cannot give up. We can never give up!" My throat was raw as I fought to find a yelling decibel I had not reached since the Marines.

"Fuck you, Dad." He said it softly, calmly even, then he rolled away, exposing his back to me.

To "lose it" would have been the mild definition. I'm pretty convinced BT had saved either Justin's or my own life, as someone would have to have put me down before I got a chance to hurt my son. Rage took over. My psyche was covered in a deep blood red as all rational thought was ejected from my mind. It was the steel cable vise grip of BT's arms around my body that prevented an irrevocable outcome. He physically removed me from the room.

"Fuck, Talbot, calm the fuck down!" He struggled to get me into a neutral corner. We'd attracted a fair amount of an audience. I could feel veins as thick as my fingers pulsing on my neck and forehead. "It was nothing, false alarm. He missed a false alarm, man. Stop struggling!" I had a modicum of dark joy knowing he was having a difficult time wresting me under control and that if some deep recessed part of me didn't want this, I could have actually torn free. "How the fuck are you so strong?" he asked.

"Insanity," Trip chimed in. "Can't know you have a finite strength. Or maybe it's because he's not all human. *As-par-a-gus, as-par-a-goose.*" I guess he was shooting for the *po-tay-to, po-tah-to* analogy.

"Shut up, Trip." BT grunted as he finally got me downstairs.

The red cloud was passing, but it wasn't taking my anger away with it. My chest heaved and my arms and legs were corded in a tight flex. I looked to the staircase that BT was effectively blocking.

"You don't get it, man!" I shouted at him.

"I don't, Mike. I don't," he said, putting his hands up in a gesture that pleaded for me to stop.

I looked past BT and up to the top of the stairs. Justin was standing there dressed all in black. The light wasn't good enough, but I think he was smiling. I was convinced it had been him outside; he'd probably beat me back to his room by a couple of footsteps.

"He's trying to get himself killed. He's checked out," I said pointing. Everyone turned to look, but he had faded back into the shadows.

"He's just depressed; he'll snap out of it." Tracy had slowly approached.

I knew she was wrong. He'd fallen over the edge. I could see him spiraling away as I myself pin-wheeled my arms on the lip of that same precipice.

I relieved Jesse of his watch. I sat stewing on that deck the entire night. I got to watch a beautiful sunrise that could do little to shine on me, try as it might, as if I had my own personal rain cloud above my head. Unbeknownst to me, BT had spent the entire night on the stairs.

He came out with the sun, an extra-large mug of coffee in each hand.

"Here," he said before sitting down.

I think I mumbled, "Thanks."

"Some night, huh?"

I said nothing. We sat for a decent part of the morning.

"Listen, man. Are you going to tell me what is really going on in that head of yours?"

"Tracy put you up to this?"

He looked at me with a fair mixture of shock and hurt then smiled. "Busted. She's worried, man."

"And you?" I looked over and arched an eyebrow.

"You're Mike Talbot. We're always worried about you."

"Fair enough." And it was. We sat longer. Sometimes someone would pop out and say hi, but mostly, we were left alone. "I've got a question."

"Yeah." He seemed to be gazing at a bird that had landed in a tree not too far away.

"What's with them Speedos?"

"I was wondering when we were going to get to those."

"I mean seriously, man. Do you know how disconcerting it is to see a man the size of a minor mountain wearing basically a golden thong?"

"They were a gift."

"I didn't know the Goodwill gave stuff away."

"They're Versace, man." He looked indignant.

"Maybe you should give them back to him."

"You want to know the truth?"

"I think I deserve that, especially after the things I saw last night."

"Fine, but you're going to feel bad about this." And he was right, bastard. "They're from my fiancée, and I feel closer to her when I wear them."

I cannot tell you how fucking brutal it is to constantly shove your foot into your own mouth. Although you'd think after how many times I'd done it, I would have stretched it out by now.

"It's hard being this big of an ass," I said as I let my head hang low.

"You make it look so easy though."

"How you doing?" Tracy had come out. She handed us both some fresh-from-the-oven blueberry muffins.

"I'm fine; your husband is an asshole, though." BT stood and placed his hand on my shoulder, gave it a light squeeze, and then went inside.

Tracy sat and looked at me.

"Thanks for the muffin." I took a bite.

She was still looking at me.

"I'm not going to be able to eat this if you keep watching me."

"I wondered how long it would take that Mike to surface." She turned so she was looking out to the sky. "Beautiful day."

"Beautiful muffin. You do this?"

She shook her head. "Your sister."

I tossed it off the deck and started rubbing my tongue. "I'm going to be sick all damn day now!"

"She's getting better; she's been practicing."

"A spider can practice looking cuddly its entire life; still not going to change anything. I can't believe you're trying to kill me."

"Who's trying to kill you?" My sister came out onto the porch. She carried a muffin tin. Flour streaked the side of her face and doused her hair. A burn mark was on the back of her hand and what looked like blueberry pulp hung out of her right ear. "Want a muffin?" she asked.

"Already ate one! Thank you so much." I stood, hoping to shield her from the one I'd tossed.

She smiled and went back in. I stayed an hour longer only because I wanted to see if the birds, any bird, a single bird, would take that fucking thing off the yard. A squirrel had come up to it and sniffed before quickly making his way away. "He's probably freaked out realizing he was so close to death."

Tracy swatted my arm.

"I think I'm going to get some sleep," I told her as I stood, popped my back, leaned over, and gave her a kiss.

Her hand touched mine; our eyes locked. "It's going to get better."

I believed that she believed it, and that was good enough for now.

I walked into the living room, stretched again, heard something shift around in my back, and started walking to the stairs. The radio that Ron had used to keep in communication with us was still on the living room table as it crackled to life.

Loud static fizzed throughout the space before a woman's voice came through. "...please help ... is any ... please."

I stared at it as if it were an apparition. I tried to convince myself that I had already gone upstairs and fallen asleep, because there was no fucking way Jen could be talking through that radio.

4

MIKE JOURNAL ENTRY 4

"Whoa." Trip said as he came into the room. He reached out, looking like he was grasping at floating dust bunnies. "Is this one in my head too, or can you hear it?" he asked.

Now normally, it's great to have what you think might be a hallucination validated, but this time I had to consider the source. "You hear that? Or you heard that?" At that very moment, the radio had gone silent.

"Yeah, man. Sounded like someone was having a rough time with their peas. I don't blame them, I mean in a world filled with Frito's, who wants peas."

"Not peas, Trip. They were saying please."

"Oh!" he said excitedly. Then more softly. "That makes more sense."

Mad Jack came bolting in from somewhere. Whatever he'd been doing, he'd been working hard at it because he was covered in sweat. "Did anything come over this radio?" he asked breathlessly.

"Yeah a woman just talked. What did you do?"

"Put a box with some new circuitry up on the roof so we could extend and clarify the send and receive signal."

"Like how much range are we talking?" I asked, wondering if he'd somehow penetrated the Pearly Gates.

"Well theoretically, this radio can communicate around the globe, but whoever is sending a message is using something a lot less powerful."

"Did you know someone was out there?" I moved closer to the radio, reluctant to touch something that I thought was now directly linked to the heavens. Who knows? Something like that being touched by someone like me could result in some serious third-degree burns or something worse.

Mad Jack seemed to be getting perturbed with me peppering him with questions while he messed with the dials, pulled off the back of the radio, and then did some techno-wizardry back there. The smell of cooking solder was strong.

"Shouldn't you have maybe shut that off first?" I asked, backing away. The experiments of his that tended to go awry did so quickly and with explosive results.

"I'm an engineer. I think I can handle this."

I swear to God his next words were "Uh oh." I backed up further.

"That's what happens when you start listening in on God." I told him.

He looked up at me like countless others before him had, basically like I'd lost my fucking gourd.

There was a puff of bluish smoke from the back, and then he got back to his work, furiously creating a miniature atom bomb or perhaps wormhole. Who can tell?

"I thought you were going to get some sleep." Tracy had come in.

I pointed to the radio. "Heard someone over the radio." That in and of itself was big news, considering the last voice heard over it was mine.

"You don't look so good," she said, coming closer. I waved her off and pointed to MJ. She got the point and waited for me to come closer to her.

"I know it can't be, but I swear I heard Jen."

Tracy paused. "Maybe you should have gone to sleep earlier."

"Probably."

The radio came back to life in fits of static and bursts of light. "...I'm trapped, zombies everywhere, need help! Can ... hear ... please."

MJ seemed too busy with whatever the hell he was working on to respond, so I ran to the microphone.

"Hello! Hello! Can you hear me!?"

"...hear you ... help!"

I was getting every second or third word.

"Where are you?"

"...reservoir..." The radio cut out like the plug had been pulled.

I stared at the mic. "Get her back, MJ."

"I'm trying, I'm trying." Heavy beads of sweat had broken out across his brow.

"It certainly sounded a lot like her, but you know it wasn't though, right?" She looked deeply into my eyes to make sure I'd not slipped and fallen; we all know to where.

"I know. It just kind of floored me is all. Doesn't change the fact that there's someone out there who needs our help."

"I'm sure there are thousands of people out there who could use our help. We don't have the resources to help them all, Mike."

"I know that. I'm going to start packing some gear."

"And do what? To go where?" she asked.

"She said reservoir clear as day."

"I'm sure there's what? Only one, maybe two, reservoirs in the entire world?"

"She needs our help. Maybe it isn't Jen. Okay, I know it isn't Jen," I amended when she threatened to smack me. "Maybe this is my chance for redemption."

"It's not your fault she died, Mike."

"Part of me knows that; another part harbors deep guilt. If I had just reached out a fraction of an inch more."

"You cannot beat yourself up about everything that has gone wrong. You have done all you could each and every time. I already see your argument. I don't want to hear that crap about your best not being good enough."

Sometimes she made me feel like an open book, and she didn't even have to read it. Like I was being narrated by some incredibly talented narrator with the ability to hit all of my inflections and quirkiness.

Another puff of blue smoke arose from MJ's workstation. He looked up at me with an expression that resembled something one might display when they have a moderate case of diarrhea and just had an accident. The lights on the radio face dimmed and went out. Seemed like a good time to take my leave before Tracy rooted around anymore in my closet and found some old, haunting demons lurking in there.

"I'm going to get some sleep."

She seemed slightly confused that I had yielded so quickly, like I had an alternate plan up my sleeve or something.

"Well, okay, you get some sleep then."

I kissed her on her furrowed forehead before heading up.

5

MIKE JOURNAL ENTRY 5

AS PLAGUED AS MY WAKING THOUGHTS WERE WITH FAILURE AND ruin and the potential for disaster, my subconscious seemed to give me the day off. I dreamed I was a kid and I was flying much like superman. The sky was a purple hue, and the grass below had a distinctive blue tint, yet the flying me did not see this as unusual at all. I enjoyed the splendor of it and the wonder of flight. I suppose Freud or someone like that would tell me I was expressing my desire to be free from the yoke of this new life, or maybe a cigar is just a cigar. All of my dreams revolved around the nonsensical, and more importantly, non-threatening. When I awoke some hours later, it was dark, and I felt surprisingly good for the first time in days.

Tracy was not beside me. The moon was bright enough that I could tell she was not in the room. Either she couldn't sleep or it wasn't necessarily that late. I went downstairs. Nearly everyone sat at the dining room table. Their conversation was hushed, at least until they discovered that I was present, then it just stopped abruptly.

"Yeah that's not suspicious." I said to the myriad guilty looking glances. "What's going on?"

"Mad Jack got the radio working again." It was difficult to gauge Tracy's reaction to this. I sensed more that she was pissed about it. Then she just stared at me along with everyone else.

"Can we maybe pretend I just got up from an extended nap and have absolutely no idea what the fuck is going on here?"

Tracy sighed. "It wasn't Jen you heard, but there's a reason it sounded familiar."

Before I even had a reason, shots of adrenaline started pouring forth from my adrenal glands.

"It was Erin." Before I could ask all the particulars, she filled the rest in. "She's at the Quabbin reservoir along with a small group of survivors. They're out of food, they have limited ammunition, and they are surrounded by zombies."

I was too surprised to do anything, even to say anything. My best friend's wife, who had walked out into a cold and wintry night, was alive and some three hundred and something miles away. What was my response supposed to be? She'd left us; she'd willingly put herself in harm's way. Was I supposed to risk everything *again* to save her? Justin had suffered the worst of it, and perhaps he still was. She'd chosen her path; I owed her nothing.

"Sucks for her." With that, I went out to the deck. Tracy joined me soon enough, after some soft murmuring from the living room.

"That's it? No call to arms? No rallying of the troops?"

"Should there be?"

"I don't know what I was expecting. Maybe for you to care."

"Don't spin this on me. What would you be saying to me if I told you I was going to get her? We both know you'd be digging your heels in and telling me in absolute terms 'no.' Now that I have no intention of going, you're going to give me a hard time about it?"

"You're right. I would be telling you to stay. Most likely you wouldn't. But this, this is scarier, Mike. You not caring."

"Oh, I care." I spun on her. "I care enough that I'm not going to risk anybody who wants to stay with us on someone who chose not to."

"She's pregnant."

The bottom fell out on me like my ass was on a large hinge and it popped open and everything in me just fell to the floor.

"And before you can ask, yes it's Paul's."

My dead best friend's wife was pregnant with his legacy. I leaned far enough down I could place my forehead against the deck railing. "I have to go." I sighed.

"I know."

"That's it? You're not going to stop me?"

"Do you want me to?"

I stood up. "The Quabbin isn't that far. I could be there and back in a day." That was a lie. Even back in the day, it was a seven-hour drive to the reservoir that contained the water for the city of Boston. And after seven hours of driving, I'd be spent, not able to immediately make the return trip. But there was still the small matter of rescuing her from whatever she'd gotten herself into.

"Go get her, Mike, and be safe."

"You're not coming with me?"

"Your daughter needs me; her pregnancy has been difficult. Besides, you'll be back tomorrow, right?"

I lied, "Of course."

I went back into the house to start getting some things together.

"Where you going?" BT asked.

"Was thinking of going to the store and getting a pack of smokes."

"Great, I'll come with you."

"BT, you don't have to."

"Oh, so you're just going to smoke them all up yourself?"

"Someone say smoke?" Trip asked.

"Thanks, man," I told him. "Ron, I'm going to need a truck."

"No fucking way, baby brother. I've seen tornados with less destructive power. If you want one of my vehicles, I'm driving it." This was a shock to everyone including myself and Nancy.

"What do you think you're doing?" his wife asked.

"I'm being irresponsibly responsible," he replied. "I will not have another car reduced to salvage. These aren't in an unlimited supply."

I wanted to tell him that they kind of were; there were vast parking lots full of cars and trucks that would never be used again. Ripe for the taking. Ron had a funny way of looking at things though. If he hadn't earned it, he would not beg, borrow, or steal it. Fortunately, I had no such limiting compunction.

"Are you sure, Ron?" I wasn't sure how I felt about him joining. He was an untested quantity, at least out in the open. Plus, I feared he would start pulling that "big brother" card, like he would always know the best course of action.

He nodded.

Trip began to stand. BT placed a large hand on his shoulder and pushed him back down. "You're staying here," he told him in no uncertain terms.

I looked over to Tommy. "What about you?"

"I … I think I need to stay here." With that, he left the room. That had kind of been Tommy those last few weeks. He said little as he traveled realms only he was aware of.

It was us three, and I was fine with that; we'd be more nimble: quick in, quick out. That was the plan. And right now, that was about as in-depth as it got. Actually, pretty good for me. Within an hour, we had all we thought we'd need. We spent the next ten minutes saying our goodbyes. And just like that, we were on the road, though this time Ron drove.

"You just let me know when you're tired, and I'll take over," I told him.

Ron raised a thermos the size of a traditional pitcher. "Full of coffee, I should be able to stay awake this entire trip."

"Praise be to Jesus," BT said, and not in mockery. He meant it.

We drove in relative silence. There was a little small talk, but we're like most guys—we don't tend to have a lot to say, and now that major league level sports were no longer played, we didn't even have that on the table. There was still the weather, I suppose.

"The Quabbin is pretty huge, Mike. Any idea what to do when we get there?" Ron asked.

"You guys are the ones that heard her call. Didn't she tell you anything else? Not that it's really going to be all that hard to find her."

"How can you say that?" Ron asked. BT got it right away. "The zombies, it's going to be hard to miss them," he said.

"Right."

"You all right, Ron? You look a little green." I laughed.

We made it through the entire state of Maine without seeing a soul. I've heard of ghost towns, never a whole fucking state though. As we passed Portland, the only things we saw moving were small groups of zombies out on patrol. They turned and followed for a bit before they realized we were a meal out of their grasp, and then went back foraging for whatever was left. There had to be holdouts there, or why would the zombies bother? And what could we do about it? I watched the wasteland pass by. It was stranger than I could have ever imagined to be traveling through the end of times. I'd read tons of science fiction and apocalyptic horror when I was younger, always fantasized about a world with little to no people in it. Sounded glorious back then. What a fool I was. As much as people could suck, it was so much better than this.

Some people were good, some were bad, but most of us

had varying degrees of both elements. Did I believe the earth itself would be better without us? Of course, we were a destructive parasite as far as the Great Mother was concerned. Most animals would also celebrate our passing. The lone hold-outs being dogs and rats. Cats didn't give a shit about us when we were here; no reason to believe they would care now that we were gone. I don't want to wax poetic because I very rarely live in the past, and I'm definitely not a poet. The thought of no more music, no more movies, no more books, none of the marvels of man's imagination coming to fruition was damn depressing. Of course, that also meant no more weapons of mass or even minor destruction, no murder, no crimes against humanity, no greed and all the other less-than-fine qualities of our kind. Was the trade-off worth it?

We'd effectively taken ourselves out of the loop. We talked about super-volcanoes and meteor strikes being our undoing, but it really was a foregone conclusion that we were going to pull the trigger that would blow us away. We'd been trying for so long (and man wasn't predisposed to taking "no" for an answer) that he'd finally gotten his wish. I don't know what the tipping balance was that made a recovery for human popula-tion a possibility, but I had to figure we'd long ago crossed over to the other side. As far as I knew, zombies could survive for years without food, going into their stasis mode to preserve resources. Even if we started to repopulate, we would just acti-vate the zombies again to repeat the cycle of devastation. We'd scratched a rut into the record, and it was just going to keep playing the same shitty little part of the tune before repeating. Yeah, that was my mindset as we traveled down the road. Then the truck began to slow.

"Something wrong?" I asked, first looking over to the instrument panel to see if the truck was breaking down. When I realized that wasn't the case, I checked the magazine on my rifle, pulled the charging handle back, and got ready.

"Relax, just some people on the other side of the road.

Looks like they had car trouble," Ron said as he put the hazards on, came to a full stop, and put us in park.

"Are you fucking insane?" I asked. I rolled down my window, ready to get my rifle up and target someone. I noticed that the driver had already gotten behind his car to use as a shield. "This isn't the morning commute anymore. They'll just as soon kill us and take our ride as say 'hello.'"

"I think you're being a little dramatic."

Dramatic had not even got out of his mouth when the first bullet came in our direction.

"Get out of the truck!" the driver shouted. "Or the next one is in your head."

Ron reached for the door handle. "Duck the fuck down and get us out of here," I hissed.

"He'll shoot me."

"He'll shoot you anyway. Fucking do it, Ron. This is my world now."

Ron placed the truck in drive and ducked down just as I brought my rifle up. I peppered their car with rounds, forcing the driver to dive for cover. Rounds were still coming our way, striking the truck with heavy metallic *thumps*. We were picking up speed, getting away from our potential way layers. The rear windshield exploded inward as one of the men ran out onto the highway to get a better angle. I put at least one, maybe two, rounds in his stomach for his efforts. He would die a slow, miserable death.

"Mike, you hit?" BT asked, alarmed. He'd turned to look at me. I put my hand up behind my ear. The bullet had grazed me right behind it, digging a groove into that bony protrusion. Now that I knew I'd been shot, it hurt like a motherfucker. That was the least of our problems as a funnel of steam shot up from the hood in a newly formed venting hole also supplied by our fellow highwaymen.

"Mike, I'm sorry!" Ron looked on the verge of panic.

"Looks like I'm not the only one that can fuck up a truck," I said, trying to stem the flow of blood from my head.

"You are not going to do a 'told you so' right now, are you man?" BT begged.

I shrugged. "Why not?" He's been giving me shit about his precious trucks now for a couple of months, and he destroys the one he's driving in under three hours. "Sorta feels like poetic justice." It's been well documented I use sarcasm and humor as a way to temper the fear I'm feeling. It was not lost on me that Ron was on the verge of checking out. He'd just had his perceived notion of how the world worked knocked on its ass. It's one thing to think about how it is, it's completely another to live through it.

"You all right, man?" BT looked over to Ron.

"I'm the fucker that's shot," I told him.

"Please, everyone knows you're too stupid to die."

"Shit, BT, don't hold back. Tell me how you really feel."

The engine groaned and clanked. It began to sound like loose sneakers in a dryer. Soon, it quit. Ron's dashboard lit up in a variety of stunning colors. We found ourselves on a slowing roll.

"Start grabbing gear, BT. Ron?" My brother clamped his hands on the steering wheel. He stared straight ahead. "Ron!" I smacked him on the shoulder. He responded with an erg or ugh. "*Ron!*" I shouted in his ear.

He turned slowly. "I almost got you killed; I almost got all of us killed."

"Yeah, so?" I told him. "Grab your fucking gear. It's not the last time you're going to almost get us killed. You'd better get used to it."

"Is he kidding?" Ron asked BT.

"Doubtful." BT had begun cramming stuff into a small backpack. Well, I mean it was a big backpack to a normal human, but small in his hands.

"Why were they shooting at us?"

"Ron, man, we don't have time to question everything right now. Either those douche bags are going to be on us, or zombies that heard the party are going to come and try to crash. We don't have time to think, just do. That's our *modus operandi* now."

"Latin, you're using Latin. I'm so proud of you."

"We're losing him, Talbot." BT was halfway out the door.

"Ron, man, listen to me. We need to get out of here and now." I heard the sound of an approaching engine.

"Mike." BT poked his head in.

"Not deaf, BT."

"Want me to drag him out?"

"Ron, this is the new world. It sucks big, thick corn-encrusted shit through a Silly Straw."

"Really, man?" BT chimed in.

"This is what we have to deal with. I'm not an expert. I'm not, but I do have experience, and you need to listen to me."

I got a strangled "ung." Even if my brother wasn't in the process of losing it, he still had the unenviable task of listening to someone's advice, someone he used to torture mercilessly when we were younger. I would always be his little brother and therefore would never possibly "know" more than him. It was a huge bias that he was going to need to overcome, and pretty damn fast, if the sound of the oncoming car was any indication.

"No time. I already got one crazy Talbot. Can't deal with another." BT came around to the driver's door, opened it, and pulled Ron out easier than a toddler from a car seat. He had him all the way to the road edge before Ron finally told him he could walk on his own. I grabbed what I could and joined them. We'd just hit the tree line by the time the car came up over a hill and into view. The throaty engine was at full throttle.

"Get down." Superfluous words. BT knew better and he dragged Ron down with him.

"What if they want to help?" Ron asked.

"Aw he's just like a little, itty baby. Ain't know no better." BT smiled like a proud parent.

"That a fucking rocket launcher?" I asked with alarm. "Motherfucker." We all buried our heads in our arms, thinking that this would somehow protect us should a rocket-propelled grenade make its way toward us. It wouldn't, but luckily they were aiming for the truck. The car may have slowed, tough to tell. Next thing I heard was the *whoosh* of a rocket, the screeching of tires seeking purchase, then the concussive blast of an explosion that rippled past us along with a variety of truck parts. Our eight-cylinder, six-hundred-pound engine came to an earth-shaking landing not more than ten feet from our location.

"Holy fuck," I said, pivoting my head so I could see through my now splayed fingers. I stood up. What was left of Ron's truck was a burning, smoking hulking mess of debris.

"Well, I can honestly say I've never quite done that to one of your cars."

"Just another day in the life of Michael Talbot." BT was now standing next to me as we watched what was left of the truck burn. "That's going to bring every zombie from the state here."

"I'm sure that's why they did it." I turned to retrieve my brother, happy to see he was slowly getting up.

"Why, Mike? Why would they do that?"

"Wanted our stuff, I imagine."

"And they'd kill us for it?"

"Sure, who's going to tell them differently?"

"Morals maybe?"

"Those are in short supply. Anybody who was loose with them when civilization was here has completely let the expiration date lapse without picking up new options to continue."

"How can you be so cavalier?"

"Do I look like I'm having a good time, Ron? Those

fuckers just tried to kill us for a truck, a few guns, and two days' worth of food."

"Umm, Mike, when you ask somebody the rhetorical question, 'Do you think I'm having fun?'" BT mimicked my voice for that last part, though his was much deeper. "Then maybe you shouldn't be smiling. It makes you look duplicitous."

"He's right, you have this weird lopsided smile, like when you were tattling on one of us when we were younger."

"I never tattled. Fuck you both, we need to go."

"What? We just keep going? They shot a fucking rocket at us."

"Not sure what else you would have us do, Ron. If we packed it in every time someone shot at us, I would have laid down and died that time in Korea."

"That far back?"

"That far back."

"You never said anything."

"I killed a man. I never wanted to talk about it again."

"I'm sorry."

"Don't be. It was me or him. More than likely, he'd be dead now anyway."

Ron looked at me strangely, like maybe he was willing to understand me a little more. That could be good or bad. Or perhaps, he could finally see where I was coming from. I had experiences he did not, and he would now need to lean on me for my expertise. I can't imagine it sat particularly well with him. Better that than dead, though.

"Zombies." BT said flatly, pointing to a spot the way that we'd come. They were a long way off, but they were running.

"Into the woods."

"We're not going to kill them?"

I peeked back. "Nope, too many, and they're just like potato chips."

"What?"

"It's your brother's way of saying the more you kill, the more will come."

"We really have been together too long," I said to the big man.

"Yeah, well, when this shit is all over, I'm leaving. Going to find a nice peaceful place, maybe in California or some shit. Gotta get away from all this. Start over maybe."

It pained me to think of BT leaving at some point. I understood the reasons why he'd want to, that's for sure. Well, it was nothing to worry about at this point. It was a good, long while away. The woods weren't too thick; only had to travel a couple of hundred yards through them until we found ourselves in a neighborhood. The greenery had been more of a noise buffer for the residents in this area than anything else. There were cars parked along the road. Most were locked up. A couple were open but had no keys. We were three streets over when we came across a smallish traffic jam. Ten cars had gotten tangled in a rotary, or a roundabout for those of you not from the New England area. A fair amount of shell casings of differing calibers sparkled in the sunlight.

BT and I were on high alert; Ron was still in a daze. His rifle hanging down in his arms. We came upon the scene slowly; whatever had happened here hadn't been recent. Ron turned away when he saw the legs of a woman lying on the roadway. Good thing he had because she'd been devoured from the knees up. Someone else must have come up on the scene because the zombie that had done the damage was lying on top of her, dead.

"BT?"

"Checking." He went around to the cars, looking for something serviceable, while I made sure Ron didn't go further down the rabbit hole.

"You hanging in there?"

"We've been gone half a day, Mike. I didn't think it'd be this bad. I just assumed that if *you* could do it, so could I."

"Naw, I never thought that." BT stood back up, from where he'd been leaning into a lime green Honda. "Mike has a special skill set."

"Here we go," I said, waiting.

"Crazy, your brother is off-his-fucking-rocker crazy, and in this world, that's what it takes to survive. Why do you think he was going even more nuts in your house? Another week, I wouldn't have doubted if he took a radio, drove a few miles away, radioed like someone needed help, and then gone off to save the fictitious person."

"That's not a bad idea."

"See?" BT asked Ron. "Um, Mike." BT pointed to the body of the woman.

"What?"

"Look a little harder."

"Oh, fucking dammit." Where the woman had potentially once birthed children was a silver set of keys. They were mucked up in varying hues of brown red and black. "Why are you looking at me? You saw them, you should get them."

"Hell, no."

We could sit here and argue about it, but I would lose and we would have wasted more time. I'm sure someone already had eyes on us. Stationary, and out in the open, were generally not great options together. "Fug." Something thick and wet got stuck in my throat as I reached into the decomposing reproductive organs. It was worse than I'd even imagined it could be. I had to use force to pull the keys as if they'd been glued in place with pubic hair and ligature. I stood holding them as far from my body as possible.

"Here." I attempted to hand them off. BT threw an old shirt over to me. I wiped the keys and myself down with enough force to rip off a few layers of skin and some metal shavings respectively. "Volkswagen." I could finally see the top of the fob.

BT moved quickly. "Dome light still works; we might be in luck."

"Yeah, this is luck." I said, walking over to the bug. It was a stick. I placed the car in neutral, pumped the gas, depressed the clutch, and turned the key. A slow sluggish whirring relented to a faster power generation, and finally, German engineering kicked in and the car started. And maybe lady luck was looking out for us, at least a little; the tank was nearly full.

"Get in. I need to find some Lysol right quick." Can't even begin to relate to you how I had to pretend my right hand was dead to me. There were so many times I wanted to rub the corner of my eye or perhaps scratch an itch, and I needed to do everything with my left. As far as my right was concerned, I was fairly certain it now housed the plague, and I would not spread the disease any further. Whatever guiding force we had for the day was still keeping watch. We hadn't gone more than three blocks from where we picked up our new ride when we found a small mom-and-pop convenience store. The kind that held on by the skin of their teeth as the Seven Elevens of the world pushed them into the dirt, much like Blockbuster had done to every other video rental place.

"You're going to stop?" Ron asked after I had already pulled up alongside the building.

"Mike you want me to come with you or...." BT nodded his head over to Ron.

"Stay here. I'll be right back." Sure, I could have used BT to watch my back, but if anything happened in there, I, at least, had my wits about me enough to do something. Ron right now looked like he could get rolled by a gang of peace-loving Hare Krishnas. Are they still around? Whatever. I got out of the car and made sure a round was chambered and my selector switch was on fire then headed for the front door. I had not been expecting what I saw when I cautiously poked my head in. The store was pristine, as if this were a time capsule of how things had been before the zombies came.

It was possible someone had truly lost their fucking mind and was attempting to keep one small facet of his or her life as normal as possible. Unlikely, but possible. Then I got my answer in the cloying stench of death. There were zombies in here. The aisle I wanted was past the rows of cupcakes and chips, bread, automotive goods, and candy. I could see the baby blue color of a diaper package, and I knew right next to that would be a blissful box of wipes. I needed those fucking wipes bad, like a heroin addict needs a fix, like a fat kid needs a cupcake, like a skinny person needs a salad, like a white girl needs a pumpkin spice latte. I needed those fucking wipes, and I was going to risk everything for them. I stepped all the way in. Sunlight streamed through the windows, bathing the store in a fair amount of light. Nothing moved except the lazy swirl of dust. The only thing out of place was a little bell on the floor. I imagine that had been used to notify the owner that someone had entered.

I was past the first aisle, still no blood, no bullet casings, no bullet holes, no bodies, no zombies, just rows and rows of merchandise. If I hadn't been so fixated on those damn baby cloths, I would have started shoving shit in my many cargo pockets. I had my rifle up to my shoulder and scanned every place as rapidly as I could, just kept coming up empty. I should have been feeling more relieved, but, if anything, it was starting to make me feel more apprehensive. It was like that build up in a horror movie. You know something is going to jump out—and would they just hurry up and get it over with so you don't choke on your damn popcorn in front of your date. My eyes were beginning to involuntarily water from the smell. Although in reality it's hard to make your eyes water voluntarily, unless you're an actor. More superfluous words I had not yet written down today. At some point, I'd pulled my shirt over my nose—about as effective as you think it would be. Pretty sure cotton was never supposed to filter out the stench of death.

I shoved a box of the wet wipes into my pocket. If I didn't feel like my heart was going to jump up and through my throat, I would have ripped open the package and cleaned up there. I began to back up slowly, once again doing my high-speed scanning. This time, I started randomly grabbing things, without really looking, and putting them in my pockets. I'd tried shoving a box of high-fiber cereal in, and it wouldn't fit. I carefully placed it back.

"What are you doing, Talbot?" I *literally* had to ask myself what I was doing. My backwards progress to safety was halted, and I was once again moving forward. "You cannot really be doing this, can you?" How can one possibly be asking himself a question and simultaneously ignoring himself? Does that qualify as insanity? Was I losing an argument with myself? I think I'd kept it together longer than most would during these types and multitudes of stress. Apparently, even crazy has a finite quantity. You dip into the well too much, and you come up insane. Is that even possible? My world would have been much better off if my mother had decided she did not want to take her accidental pregnancy with me to term. I would have been a happy-go-lucky non-committed soul running around Heaven, oblivious to all the pain and suffering, which was all the world could ever offer.

Unlike the store proper, the storage room was dark, not completely though, no matter how much I would soon wish it were. Two windows high up offered enough light for me to see the horrors within. As clean and pristine as the outside store had been, the storeroom was the polar opposite. At first, I mistakenly thought that the room had been painted a deep red hue. That was not the case; it was coated in the arterial spray of blood from countless victims. Gnawed bones littered the floor, making it impossible to walk through without step-ping on them.

Not that I would have. A red sticky mass, roughly an inch and a half thick, had congealed on the floor like an oversized vat of holiday Jell-O had spilled. That it was the accumulated viscera of innumerable people was not completely lost on me, though I wish that it had been as well. I saw what I saw, and I'll never be able to un-see it. My eyes were taking in things my brain could not register fast enough. I just started instinctually firing. Best to let someone else sort them out. A small stasis pile, that was bad, as bad as they always are, was off to my left. But certainly, not the worst of it; not by a long shot. A group of ten zombies were keeping watch. Yup, that's what I said. Keeping watch over a trio of humans, or at least a reasonable facsimile of what humans used to look like.

The three people were nude, which mattered little as they were covered in enough layers of grime and detritus as to still be clothed. The man and the woman were as malnourished as I had ever seen two living people. The child in the woman's arms had died—not too long ago, from the looks of him. She'd done her best to keep him somewhat clean during whatever had happened. My quick take on it was that the zombies had trapped a decent number of people in this room and had devoured them at their leisure, holding on to the people like stored food products to only be eaten in times of need. When they'd begun to run low on stores, the majority had chosen to go to sleep while those still awake finished off what was left.

The rifle chattered in my hands as I just kept firing. The zombies had spun and were coming at me. I'd taken down six of them before I had to go back out the way I'd come. The stasis pile shifted as they awoke to face this new threat and potential new food source. BT was in the front door before the storeroom door could completely close.

"Tell me, Mike!" he shouted, scanning for threats, approaching me at a decent clip but always aware, the rifle looking like a toy up against his shoulder.

"Zombies … holding prisoners." I gulped.

He didn't say anything. If he had questions, he would save them for later, as the knob to the storeroom twisted and night-mares came free. Between the two of us, we were able to push them back with a curtain of lead. A zombie that had fallen and was keeping the door from shutting properly was yanked back inside. We were once again left in the relatively unscathed store, although it now was not as pristine as it had been.

"What the fuck, Mike?" He had not pulled his gun down yet. "We need to get out of here."

"There are people in there."

"In there? Are you sure?" We heard screams as if to punc-tuate his question. First, the high-pitched shriek of a woman, and then, the much deeper cries of a man. "We need to get them!" He moved forward.

"It's too late." Even when I walked into the store, it had been too late. Their vacant eyes as they stared up at me had told me all I needed to know. They'd checked out from this life a while back, perhaps with the loss of their son. Maybe even longer. "It's a trap, they're killing them hoping we'll go in and help."

"We gotta go then." BT lightly tapped my shoulder, and we tactically withdrew. Ron was sitting in the driver's seat. We jumped in, and he sped off, I mean as fast as a bug will go, anyway. I looked back, and three zombies were outside the door watching our departure.

"What's going on?" Ron kept looking in the rearview mirror at me. I was furiously wiping my hands and face with the baby wipes. If I could have peeled back my skull and wiped my brain clean, I would have done that as well.

I wasn't sure at first, not completely anyway, and then it sprung on me. Fitting, it should happen that way. I let them know what I was thinking. "The store, the fucking store was a trap. A human lure."

"Are you kidding?" Ron kept glancing up in the mirror,

maybe to see if I was indeed crazy or had slipped over the edge.

"They were holding three people hostage when I went in the backroom, had them backed up against the wall. Not fattening them up before the slaughter, but definitely waiting to butcher and eat them. Had to have already done it to dozens, if not a hundred or more, people."

"You said you found them? Why didn't they find you then?" I understood why Ron was questioning me. None of us wanted to believe the zombies were capable of this level of sophistication.

I didn't know why at first. Why make a trap if you weren't going to use it? "The bell, the fucking bell." I said aloud when the image came back to me.

"Things ringing in your head Mike?" BT asked.

"You know those little notification bells they have?"

He nodded.

"It was on the floor. Their signal was broken, and either they didn't know it or they didn't know how to fix it."

"Saved by the bell." BT said.

"Did you really just say that?"

He smiled a little when he realized what he'd said. "Those poor fucking people." What little mirth he had quickly ran away as it was faced with the horror that had been that store. "We can't leave that place there."

I hadn't gotten to that reasoning and not sure if I ever would. I was pretty much happy that I'd left with my life and that of BT's. Does that make me narcissistic?

"Any ideas?" I asked, pretty much hoping he wouldn't have any. I didn't want to go back, ever. The chances I would be able to forget the utter futility I saw in those two faces was slim; to go back would just reinforce the memory.

"Fire? We could burn the place." Ron offered.

"It was made of cinder block, and I don't think we can go

back in without a substantial fight. Had to have been at least fifty or sixty zombies stacked up."

"I've got an idea." BT had a strange look in his eyes.

"Is this an idea like a 'Mike idea' or a real idea?" I prodded him.

"Those asses that shot a rocket at us."

"What about them?" I did not like where this was going.

"I bet they have more rockets."

"Good for them," I told him.

"We need those rockets."

"Listen, it was all kind of funny when we were talking about how being around me could make you catch crazy, but that's all it was ... talk I mean. You want to hunt down some murderous men, steal their shit so we can come back here and blow up a zombie hive?"

"Yeah, that's about it."

"No," I blurted out.

"Who the fuck made you boss?"

He'd gone from thinking in the abstract to looking like he was going to put me in traction in a matter of a second or two.

"BT, that is a lot more risk than I'm thinking we should put ourselves into." It was Ron who decided now might be a good time to interject.

"You saw them, Mike." BT had softened. "You said you saw a woman holding her kid, nobody, fucking *nobody* should ever have to go through that. We have a chance to make sure it doesn't happen again, and I say we take it."

"Having a chance would imply that we have the necessary weaponry with us. We don't; you want to hunt and kill men so we can hunt and kill zombies."

"How old do you think that kid was, Mike? Tell me. What if it happens again? That's on you."

It wasn't really. There's no way I could be held accountable, but that wouldn't stop me from pondering the thought constantly, and most likely while I tried to sleep. I would forever think of some hapless family wandering into that store only to become a human MRE.

I stuck my finger up. "Don't you ever fucking say my plans are for shit again. Do you understand me?"

"We're doing this? You're seriously thinking about doing this?" Ron asked. "Those guys are long gone by now."

"Doubtful, they probably live relatively close by, and these are their hunting grounds. So, in reality, we'll be getting rid of two human traps today. Fantastic."

"Good to have you back, Mike." BT beamed.

"Fuck this, Mike," Ron said. "This is insane. You said so yourself, not ten seconds ago. We just need to get Erin and get the hell back home."

"You know what's insane, big brother?"

He didn't answer.

"Telling that man, 'no.'"

"That's what I'm talking about." BT said.

"Even if I wasn't afraid, he'd twist me in two. He's right. We'd be doing the right thing and saving who knows how many people. We owe it—"

"To who, who the fuck do we owe it to?" Ron was getting angry.

I looked at Ron. My older brother had been delivered a hard lesson this day, and it wasn't going to get any easier.

"We owe it to the next little kid, the next old lady, the next middle-aged man. We owe it to any potential survivor. What if by not doing this, those men or zombies kill the person that has a cure for all this shit?"

"That's a huge 'what if,' Mike. We could play that game all day. How about I go now. What if we get killed today doing this shit? What do you think happens to those we love back home?"

"He plays dirty," BT said to me.

"He never did like to lose," I said. "We very much could

die today, no doubt, but not for a minute do I think those people back home would pack it in. Sure, that's a shitty argument, I know, I know, but this is something we need to do."

Ron let his head touch the steering wheel. "What do we need to do?"

"Didn't think you'd come around to it that quick." BT smiled as he clapped Ron on the shoulder. "I've got to remember you have Talbot blood running through you though."

"Get back on the highway. I want you to go northbound but on the southbound lanes." I said. Ron looked at me in a way I'd become all too familiar with, like perhaps I buttered my toast on the sides. "I know what I'm doing. The idiots traveled north on the northbound lanes."

"At least they have that going for them." Ron replied confirming my earlier suspicion of what he thought of me.

"We're going to have to drive until we see where they've set up shop. Then we need to turn around. If we're on the opposite side of the highway, the chance that they hop in their truck and pursue will be a lot less because it will be that much more difficult to chase us."

"Shit, that's not bad for you," BT said as he reloaded his magazine.

We weren't on the road for ten minutes when we saw them up ahead. Ron stopped the car so quickly I nearly ended up on the gearshift. That's what I got for sitting in the middle of the back seat.

"What do I do?" he almost bellowed.

"Turn the fuck around."

"Won't that look suspicious?"

"So does sitting here. Turn around before they wonder what the hell we're doing." I could just barely make one of them out shielding his eyes to the sun to get a better look. He was motioning for something inside their decoy truck. I had a gut feeling it was binoculars. "Ron, get the fuck moving. If he realizes it's us, they will come chasing."

Ron ground the gears as we got moving. I turned and kept an eye on the truck. By the time we were out of sight, I had no indication that they were following.

"Now what?" Ron and BT were looking at me. I laid out my plan such as it was. Not sure which of them said "absolutely not" first.

"This is the best way. Someone needs to stay with the car as a diversion, and I need fast back-up. I'll take a radio and tell you when I'm in position."

Ron came to my way of thinking, finally. BT looked at me suspiciously, like he could smell around the edges of my lie.

We'd been standing outside the car. I was leaning down, checking the strap on my knife, Ron was pacing back and forth nervously.

BT gripped my forearm. "You be careful," he hissed. It was a strange mixture between a warning and plea.

"Always, man."

"Before, I just thought *maybe* you were lying. Now, I know you are. What gives?"

"It's just like we planned." He kept looking me straight in the eye, hoping I would look away and finally crack. When he realized I wouldn't, or there was a small possibility he was wrong, he wished me luck. "See you soon."

I got back to the highway and quickly crossed all the lanes to get back to the tree line. I jogged for about ten minutes until I could see the truck up ahead. The men were talking but didn't seem too particularly concerned about anything. Now, it was time to go in the woods, only about fifteen feet, far enough they couldn't see me but close enough that the brush wasn't overly thick. I had time to think while I slowed my approach. I would have much rather had BT with me. The man was an incredible ally to have in almost any situation that didn't involve diplomacy. Not that this scenario required it, but killing men affected BT in ways even he didn't understand. He'd do it because it was necessary, but it was poking holes in his soul. I knew because I was watching. Since I was devoid of that particular trait, I wanted to do my best to spare him. I'd like to say it was a completely altruistic action; it wasn't. Sure, some of it was for his benefit; a good portion was for me.

BT's rope was shortening. There would come a point when he would be done with this war, whether it was done with him or not. I would keep him from slipping further down if it was at all in my power. I couldn't imagine a life in which he was no longer around me, and I'd fight for that as I would my own life.

I was within three hundred yards of the men. I could start taking shots, probably take down two of them before they figured out where I was shooting from and either took cover or took off. Neither of those things worked. If shots started, Ron and BT would come, these guys would take off, and we'd be compelled to chase. We would not be able to determine where and when the conflict would resume. I threw my sling over my head and let my rifle sit on my back. I pulled the strap tight so it wouldn't move around, and then I pulled my Ka-Bar free from its sheath.

Knives weren't my weapon of choice. In this case, though, I felt it was the wisest course. I was within fifty yards, and I could hear snippets of the men talking.

"...hope we find some women."

"...could go for some whisky."

They continued in this vein of conversation—basically, what they hoped to find and what they hoped to do. BT was right to want them dead. These were humans who forgot what it meant to be human. Fuck, who knows? Maybe I'm the one who has it wrong, and this was how humans were meant to act. Preying on the weak has always been something practiced in the animal kingdom. Why should we be any different? Of course, animals didn't do it out of malice; they did it to survive. Would it make a difference if you killed someone and took their stuff so that you could survive as long as malice wasn't involved? That was not a path I desired to venture down.

Ten yards, I poked my head around a tree. I could see the truck and two men leaning against it. A third was inside, his legs poking out the open door; looked like he was trying to get some rest. Being a dick was apparently tiresome. A grunting off to my side got my attention and my heart pumping. For a second, I thought I'd been spotted by a wild boar, who even now was measuring me up to gore with his eleven-inch tusks. That would have been a serious detriment to my plans. I got down low when I realized it wasn't a pig (although, I guess I could have called him one without anybody being to offended, except maybe a true swine) but rather one of the men. He was less than ten feet away. The only reason he hadn't seen me was that he was halfway through taking care of a basic bodily function. His pants were down by his ankles, his back was braced up against a tree, and he looked like he was sitting on an invisible chair as he crapped.

I don't know what he'd eaten, but apparently, it had not agreed with him. Squishing wet sounds of expelled flatulence erupted, and diarrhea splashed onto the ground.

"Fuck, Wayne. What the hell is wrong with you?" One of the men asked from the truck.

Wayne's face was red as he strained. "Fuck you, Collin." He managed to get out between squirts. "Maybe if you cooked better, I wouldn't be dying."

There was some laughter, and then the men over by the truck began resuming their conversation. No man deserved to die on the throne, such as it was, but a better opportunity might not present itself. I propelled myself up and was halfway to him before he could even acknowledge my presence. His mouth opened in surprise, and perhaps in preparation of a scream, before I shoved my knife up and into the soft part of his lower jaw. The blade gleamed as it blasted into and through his tongue and lodged into the roof of his mouth. His hands feebly reached up trying to pull the intruding blade away and out. His throat gurgled to match his stomach. I covered his mouth with my hand while I withdrew the knife. I made sure to keep pressure against him so he wouldn't fall to the ground just yet. His eyes looked to mine. Blood poured past and through my fingers. I waited a few seconds. His eyes opened wide in fright and then shut. My grip slipped, and he fell to the ground.

"Holy shit, Wayne, did you just lose your intestines?" There was more laughter.

I grunted. I must have pulled off a reasonable impression of the dead man because the other men laughed. At this point, I probably could have got my rifle, aimed, and easily taken out the three men before they ever even realized what was happening. The thought never crossed my mind. I have a theory of why that happened, and I'm almost ashamed to admit it, even here in my most private of thoughts. It was the flow of that man's blood across my hand, it was so warm it was like a small electric current was being dragged across my skin wherever it made contact. The half of me that wasn't human loved it, reveled in it even, I wanted it. Sure, BT was slipping, but, maybe, so was I.

I crept closer to the truck. My guess was my pupils were dilating and expanding ... expanding at the desire to kill them, to make them bleed, and then dilating at the stress of the task that needed to be done and the concentration needed to hunt and kill. I was as close as I could be without exposing myself. There was a good twenty feet of open space between me and the men. And still, the idea of the rifle never flashed past my brain plate. I could almost feel the heat of the blood as it pulsed just below the surface of their skin. I backed up a good ten feet, made sure I had a relatively unencumbered exit from the woods, and started to run. I wanted to be at full speed before they ever even bore witness of me.

I think Collin saw me first. My lips were pulled back in a silent scream, the knife up by the side of my head. He reached down for his rifle that was propped up against the truck. His friend saw the alarm in Collin's face but, as of yet, had not turned to see what it was. I broke through Collin's chest plate as I plunged the knife into him up to the hilt. He gasped as the knife severed everything in its path. The stench of fear-shit dominated as the third man evacuated his bowels in fright. I pulled the knife free. A gush of tepid air blew past me from Collin's collapsing lung. I wrapped my left hand around my new victim's neck and pulled him close to me as I repeatedly stabbed my knife into his stomach. He cried out with each impact, losing volume with each repeated thrust. I finally stopped when the fourth man sat up, a revolver the size of a small cannon blasting off.

The left side of the man's head evaporated into a spray of brain matter. I tossed him toward the shooter as I quickly moved away, two more shots missing me by scant inches.

"You fucker!" he spat. Another round kicked up dirt as close to my foot as possible without having blown a hole in it. He was completely sitting up now, and he had the oversized barrel pointed directly at me, center mass. I wondered, briefly, what it would feel like to have the crushing blow of a sledge-hammer hit you in the chest. *Click.* He'd pulled the trigger. Five rounds, it was a five round cylinder! Joy, which is a strange emotion to have at this particular time, surged through me.

"Bad luck for you, good luck for me." I was coming toward him as he scrambled back into the truck, and for, I'm sure, an alternate weapon. I grabbed his boot and pulled him out with enough force he cleared the truck completely and bounced off the ground next to his dead friends. The brunt of the fall being absorbed by his back, shoulders and a solid smacking of his head.

"Please mister, I haven't done anything to you!" His hands were out in front of him in a defensive gesture. Of the four men, this one was clearly the youngest. Mid-twenties, if I had to take a guess. His shaggy hair giving him an even more youthful appearance.

"Just got mixed up in the wrong crowd did ya?" I asked him.

"Yeah, yeah that's it. We didn't mean no harm."

"But you caused quite a bit of it, didn't you?"

He was silent for a moment. I guess realizing that anything he said in defense, I would know for bullshit.

"I don't want to die."

"I can't say I blame you. There is a reckoning, you know. Whether you believe it or not, makes no difference. I've got a feeling you've got plenty to answer for."

I heard the approach of a car. Apparently my reinforcements had heard the shooting. The quickening that been happening in me began to subside. I'd killed the three because I had to. Now what? This man was defenseless and begging for mercy.

"Strip."

"What?"

"Take your fucking clothes off."

He went down to his underwear.

"Those, too. I'm not going to make you squeal like a pig. Just take the things off. Get the fuck out of here."

"Where am I going to go?"

"Hell, I would imagine, but right now, I don't give a fuck. Just get away from me." He kept looking back at me as he ran across the median and down the roadway in the direction I'd come from. BT flew out of the car as they pulled up like he'd been ejected. I knew he was pissed, but a part of him was relieved as well. He swallowed whatever bitterness he wanted to direct at me and instead pointed up the road.

"Friend of yours?" he asked.

"We could have been so much more; he wasn't interested. Tell Ron to stay in the car for a second. I'll get rid of the bodies." I couldn't hide the buckets of blood, but *that* you could more easily dismiss than the lifeless fish eyes of the dead and damned. Like they'd seen what awaits them, and it had burned the flatness onto their irises. BT turned away, and stayed away, at least until I'd sufficiently dragged the dead men away. Ron had come out. He was riveted by the blood pools.

"Let's just get what we need and go," BT told him. I silently thanked him for that.

Ron made a wide berth around the stain. He looked into the woods and quickly looked away. I hoped I'd done enough to conceal the men. Who knows, maybe he got a glimpse of the man's soul screaming in terror as it ran from whatever was chasing it, although I had a pretty good idea of what or who it was.

Ron had grabbed a length of rope. "This will come in handy."

"Leave it." I had an uncharacteristic flash of clairvoyance. I knew without a shadow of a doubt what it had been used for, and I didn't want to be near it.

Ron looked confused but put it back anyway.

"Holy shit." BT held up the RPG. It looked more like an ordinary rifle size-wise in his hands.

They had a whole cache of weapons, which we confis-cated. I'm sure most of them had already been used in crimes against humanity, better we had them than someone else.

"How many rockets?" I asked.

"Three."

That worked. Ten, twenty maybe, would have been better,

and there were good odds that wherever the ass-wipes made camp they had more, or else why use one on us?

"What about the truck?" Ron asked when we'd moved everything over.

I opened the hood and cut through every hose, belt, and wire I could get to, then when that was done, I flattened all four tires. "That should put it out of commission for a while."

"You really going to let that one kid go?" BT asked after Ron had got back in the car.

It was never a good idea to leave unfinished business. It somehow always had a way of finding itself back to you. I could use Mrs. Deneaux as the obvious object of that statement. I could only hope the old bat had found a slow and torturous end. Unlikely, but a boy could dream.

"I am. I just hope he doesn't go home and there are thirty more of them that come looking for us." BT didn't like that answer at all. Luckily, it wasn't something we had to worry about.

We were back on the road in five minutes. Naked man had gone close to a mile. We were coming up abreast to him, albeit on the other side of the highway. He barely spared us a glance as he continued to run as fast as his bleeding feet would allow. Five zombies were matching his pace some hundred yards behind. If I were a sicker bastard, I would have made a bet with BT that he wouldn't make it another half mile, and we could use the highway mile markers as indicators. He was leaving bloody foot prints with every footfall; at this pace he'd run out of blood sooner than he would exhaust himself. Ron sped up and we zipped past him. The boy watched. I couldn't be sure, but it seemed his eyes pleaded for help. I would offer no quarter. He was not worthy of saving. I'd let a higher authority deem that possibility. I may have seen him being dragged down just on the edge of my vision; I would have won the bet. I almost questioned why Ron was pulling off the highway again until I realized we'd only done half of the proposed mission.

"What a waste of supplies," I said, looking at the store.

"I don't think you're looking at this from the right angle," BT said while he was lining up the shot. "We close enough?"

"Trust me. We're as close as we want to be. Only a really terrible shot would miss from here."

"Glad to see you haven't lost your inner asshole just yet."

The rocket ignited and blew out, like rockets do, lots of noise and fire. We watched its progress as it spanned the hundred yards or so, and then, like it had been invited, it slid right into the front door of the store and blew beef jerky, motor oil, pretzels, and most importantly, zombies into oblivion. Wood, glass, and cement flew out in a wide arc, coming up short from pelting us but not as far away as I would have liked.

"Whoa. That was intense," BT said as he took the weapon off his shoulder. We waited until everything that hadn't been launched into the stratosphere landed and the major part of the fire burned before we started to get back into the car. This place would soon have its fair share of zombies investigating, and even if they didn't want to avenge their brethren, they'd still want to eat us. Only two zombies came out, ablaze and stumbling. They looked like lone holdouts from a hornets nest after a powerful zapping of bug spray. I got shivers thinking about the burning zombies from Little Turtle, and the idiot who had lit them on fire, he was almost more at fault for the destruction of our homes than the zombies themselves. I put my rifle up to my shoulder and fired. I'd like to say I hit something, but it's my journal. Who would I be kidding?

"Nice shot, Tex," BT said.

"I'm taking a standing shot, trying to hit a person's head from a hundred yards on a moving target. Give it a go, Annie."

"Annie?"

"As in Oakley."

"Just kill them."

The next shot I took my time, controlled my breathing, followed the wavering zombie, and slowly squeezed the trigger, not even realizing I'd done so until the butt stock pushed against my shoulder. A spray of blood flew onto the lone survivor as the zombie I hit crashed to the ground in a flaming heap.

"Damn, that was a nice shot."

"One second you're ragging on me, the next you're praising. You need to stay consistent, or you're going to mess me up."

Apparently, I'd used up all my sharpshooting skills on the first zombie. Three shots later, I had not so much killed the zombie as I had incapacitated it. My first shot was low and to the right and nailed it in the shoulder, the second was a complete miss, and the third was more of a mystery than any of them as I crushed its left knee. The leg bent backward, and the zombie pitched forward, face first. It continued to crawl forward, but it was safe to see that the conflagration was going to get the best of him, melting his brain before he would be able to wander off and start an irreversible blaze.

6

MIKE JOURNAL ENTRY 6

WE'D GONE SOME TWENTY MILES, NONE OF US SAYING MUCH. When I'd adjusted to get a little more comfortable in the small confines of the car, I heard wrappers.

"Oh shit, I forgot I grabbed some stuff."

BT turned to look. The first was a bag of Ollie's ostrich jerky, the next was a package with three bran muffins, and finally, six packs of sugarless gum.

"That's quite a haul you have there."

"Hey, man. I was under a little duress. I didn't really get a chance to pick and choose."

"Obviously, now give me some of the jerky."

I thought Henry had stowed away when he opened that bag. A more foul odor I don't think I'd ever had the displeasure of smelling, and our world was full of zombies. BT couldn't get the window down fast enough.

"I might have to kill you, man," BT said after another five miles. A sufficient transfer of fresh air had cleaned out the car although there was a good chance the smell had been burned into our olfactory senses. "Give me one of the muffins."

"Really?" Ron asked. "He just handed you bagged death, and you're willing to try again?"

"I'm hungry."

"There's food in the trunk. I'll pull over."

"Give me the damn muffin, Mike."

"I guess you would want your fiber. A man as big as you gets backed up, you could destroy a toilet. Make the damn thing unserviceable. Probably shatter the porcelain."

"Shut up, Mike." BT undid the wrapper. We all waited for the stench of odor, like perhaps everything in that store had been tainted from being in such close proximity to the zombies. After a couple of sniffs, he took a small bite. Satisfied he wasn't going to die, he finished the muffin off in silence.

All things being equal, I'd rather have a blueberry muffin, but this was still pretty good and I was happy to have it. Ron ate the third one as BT eyed him jealously.

"Better eat that fast, Ron, or he'll eat your arm trying to get to it."

"I'd eat you if I thought it would shut you up. More than likely, you'd make me sick, and I'd keep hearing from you as you shot out both ends." BT sneered.

"Trying to eat here." Ron's words were muffled as he spat muffin bits onto the windshield. BT and I laughed.

The mood in the car was decent, at least that's how I sensed it. Considering how the day had gone and Ron's initial reaction, we were doing pretty good. There was some small talk, and thankfully, no more life-threatening altercations. The mood changed the moment we got onto the Mass Pike and the homestretch to the Quabbin reservoir.

I could see the tension worming its way through my brother. His fingers gripped the steering wheel tight enough his knuckles were turning white. He leaned forward, his back not even touching his seat. I wanted to offer some words to him, something that would alleviate his anxiety. I was not sure how he would react. I was his younger brother, and I always would be. Luckily, BT was more adept at this than I was.

"You look like you have a stick shoved up your ass. You all right?"

Ron looked over to BT, actually laughed, and physically relaxed, probably not even knowing that he looked like he'd shoved coal up his rectum and was trying to press them into diamonds before we made it to our destination.

"How do you think she got down here?" BT asked, I was not sure if he cared about the answer or if by having a conversation, Ron would not have the time to work himself up again.

"She must have got a car. I mean the night she walked out, it was harsh winter conditions. She couldn't have been out there too long."

"Why, though?" This was my question. "Why leave? I mean, we all thought she left to commit suicide by snow. Then to find a car and drive away from everything you know? How the fuck does that make sense?"

"Maybe she was trying to get back home like Alex," BT said.

That was a distinct possibility. If she had lost her mind after losing Paul, maybe she thought she could get both back in Colorado. "Never thought of that."

"Of course you didn't," he answered.

I gave him the finger, but behind the seat so he wouldn't see it.

"The Belchertown exit is next," Ron said dryly.

This was it, the final approach.

"Any ideas what we're in for?"

"My guess would be zombies. What do you think, BT?" I asked.

"I blame you for this, Ron."

"Me? How is this *my* fault?"

"You could have done something about him when he was younger. You know, maybe taken care of the problem in its infancy. If you know what I mean."

The Quabbin came into view in all its beauty. It was a manmade body of water, created to supply the precious commodity to the Boston area. The entire area had been flooded, completely covering the buildings and towns that had existed at that time. There had been a lot of pissed off residents back then. It was a case of the betterment for the many to the detriment of the few. I thought sourly that if billionaires had lived here, Boston would have been flooded to supply Belchertown with water instead. The poor had been doormats since the dawn of civilization. It's strange to me that we put so much significance into material gains, but then again, it's not. Men, at least, chase wealth because wealth brings a mate. And there it is, the root of all evil isn't money, it's women. But I'm not telling my wife that. Honey, if you read this it probably means I'm dead, so that's a plus for me, I mean. So you can't get mad at me. But I'm just genuflecting here. I love women, and I know without a shadow of a doubt that you are indeed the stronger of the species.

"Now what?" Ron had gone onto the access road. We were now about to start circling the area.

"Not trying to be a smart ass, but look for zombies." That was the best piece of advice I had. She could be anywhere. I'd hiked around the reservoir a few times in my youth, not because I cared about the local history of the place or how it was made. Sure, I could enjoy the beauty of the area. That was nice and all, but mainly it was because Karen Landers liked to hike around the Quabbin, and if I wanted any chance of seeing her scenic beauty, there was a price to pay. I remembered there were a few buildings around, mostly maintenance. We'd used them to shield us as we'd, umm, use your imagination. There's a chance my wife reads this, and even if it's because I'm dead, she may come into the afterlife and give me a what-for upside the head.

"Bingo." BT pointed up ahead. Had to have been at least a hundred zombies surrounding a small stone building. I can't say I knew this place specifically. Maybe if we got around back, it would become clearer.

"Shit, Mike. Get your head in the game," I berated myself. We were about to get into a firefight with a feared, relentless enemy, and I was thinking about a heavy petting session in my youth. "Well, if I'm going to die, it might as well be with a smile."

"What the fuck are you talking about?" BT asked.

"Why can I not figure out when I am talking out loud and when I'm thinking? Forget it. Ron, you want to stop here, and we'll go check it out?"

"I'm coming."

BT and I looked at each other.

"Yeah, I know you two think I'm a liability. I … I just didn't know it was this bad out here. It took me a little while to wrap my mind around that maybe this world is not going to bounce back, that maybe my kids are not going to be able to go out and find their own way. You know what kind of shock that is. Don't you, Mike?"

I had to admit that I did. I'd had more time to come to terms with it, and I still think I teetered on the brink of depression if I dwelled on it. My only salvation was action. Action kept me from thinking. I'd proved that enough times.

"Fine, leave the keys in the ignition." Not sure if he knew the reasoning, but he didn't question it. Obviously, I hoped I didn't have to leave my brother behind, but it's better to plan for all contingencies. We were about three hundred yards off, safe from the zombies seeing us.

"What about a rocket?" There was gleam in BT's eye as he asked the question.

"Don't think the people in the building would appreciate that much."

"Right, right." BT said like he'd already forgotten we were there to save people not kill zombies.

"What about a drive by?" Ron asked. "I'll get as close as I

can with the car, fire a bunch of rounds, wait until they start following, and then I'll head off with them in tow."

"It's a better idea than blowing everyone up," I said, pointing to BT. "Just these aren't the same zombies; they see you taking off in a car, they're not going to follow. Not far anyway. Once they realize they can't catch you, they'll come right back."

"I'll just go slow."

"It's all we've got," BT said.

"Shit, I think even I could come up with a better plan than this," I said.

"Really?" BT asked.

"Yeah, probably not. Don't dick around, Ron."

"I'm sure he needed that added inspiration."

"I'll be fine." He went back to the car; BT and I stayed where we were.

We heard the car start up, and I think so did a few zombies though they did not move. He passed us by, got off the park roadway, and crossed onto the expansive grass lawn, which was nearly a foot long now from being untended. There were no lawn maintenance people during a z-poc. A couple of years, and the forest would begin to reclaim what was always its land in earnest. I got a spark of unease watching as the small car plowed through the grass and how it bunched up underneath. I wondered if it could possibly high center like during a snowstorm.

"I still think we should have used a rocket."

"Those things are really burning a hole in your pocket, aren't they?"

BT was silent. The zombies were now taking a great interest in Ron as he got closer.

"That's close enough, man." I said more for myself. He was nearly on the walking path that encircled the entire body of water. And the path was no more than twenty feet to the door of the maintenance building. "What the fuck is he doing?"

"Stopping, it looks like."

"Thanks for the commentary."

"You asked, plus you're doing it. You can't give me crap if I do the same."

Ron poked his rifle out the window and began to fire indiscriminately. I could see zombies being impacted as a few moved about in violent, random ways, but only one was fatal. I couldn't fault him; one hand on a steering wheel, not properly aiming, he was lucky he got the one. The zombies seemed very interested and a fair number began to head his way.

"Why isn't he moving?" BT asked.

I was thinking it; he said it. Zombies had reached the back of his car, and considering it was a bug, that was way closer than it needed to be. I was beginning to panic, thinking that somehow he did not see them, or he had passed out from fright or he had a damn death wish. I don't know. I brought my rifle to my shoulder and was going to do all I could to prevent zombies from getting to him when his car jumped forward and stalled. He'd had a manual transmission *faux pas*. Something usually reserved for the new-to-a-clutch drivers. Or the drunk... umm not that I know; I read it somewhere.

"This is painful to watch. At least I know what I'm getting myself into with you. I gotta be honest, Talbot. I'm not all that confident in your brother's abilities."

"Come on, Ron. Get the fucking car out of there." The engine cranked and turned over. There was the grind of gears as he must have jammed it into first. The zombies were by his window. At some point, he must have rolled the thing up, good for him. The car lurched forward again, hesitated, on the brink of stalling before he gave it enough gas and got it moving correctly. BT and I both let out heavy sighs of relief. I'd always been confident in what my brother could do; he'd always been older and seemingly wiser. I think that's a perspective most younger siblings have of their older peers. He sure was straining that belief system today.

"It's not working." BT pointed back to the hut. Far fewer than half had taken the bait.

"We can take fifty."

"Yeah, with a rocket."

"BT, you're going to have to get it out of your head. You can't use the rocket."

"Why not, man? We're not even sure there're people in there."

"Does it look like the zombies are having their annual union meeting to you? Why the hell else would they be congregating there?"

"I'm just saying we don't know for sure."

"Blow it up, we'll check the bodies afterwards," I said sardonically.

"Buzzkill."

"Oh, what the fuck is he doing now?" I went back to looking at Ron, who had been barely outpacing the speeders before. Now he was at a dead stop.

"I hear the engine whining."

"Wheels are spinning, too. He's stuck."

"On grass?" The speeders began to arrive, smacking on the sides of the car, rocking it back and forth in their efforts to get the tasty treat inside.

"Has to be a rock or something."

"There're only twenty of them."

I knew what he was implying, that we go down there, kill them all, and then push Ron off whatever he was lodged on. The only problem with that was that the longer he was stuck, the more zombies over at the shed became interested in the goings on. There was somewhere in the neighborhood of seventy-five zombies, give or take a few ugly fuckers. We had a couple hundred rounds each. Theoretically we could do it, but if we failed, we had nowhere to go. Speeders would chase us down. Plus, we had to hope that our fight didn't draw any more to the festivities.

"Yeah, we go down, pick up Erin, be back for dinner, he says."

"You realize you're talking about yourself, right?" BT asked.

"I can be mad at myself."

"Can you maybe have that argument later? Would love to see who wins, though."

"Shut the hell up. You ready?"

We stood. Both checked our magazine pouches. I was OCD enough that I had to check that I'd chambered a round; actually expelled a fresh round in doing so.

"That could be the one round that spells the difference between life and death."

I knew he was screwing with me. I wouldn't have left the round, but now I had to hit the magazine release button and put the bullet back.

"The time you've wasted here could be the difference—"

"I am going to shoot you."

We moved closer. The zombies were still too interested in Ron to even glance in our direction. I wanted to be near enough that headshots were viable and at a high percentage, but leave enough room that when they inevitably turned and ran toward us, we would have time to defend ourselves. BT started to line up a shot.

"What the hell are you doing?"

"Getting ready to shoot."

"We can't afford to spray bullets. Get down into the prone position; there's a good chance they won't even know where we're at for a while."

"I don't want to get down there."

"Man, I know you're a good shot; you're not that good."

"There are ticks, man."

"What?"

"Ticks. They're like spiders, but they suck your blood."

"I know what the hell ticks are. We'll pull them off if they get on you. I mean, someone will, depending on where they are. Get down here, and you're giving me shit about wasting time." I waited until he was down, and I fired.

"I better not get Lyme disease. That's a hiking-honky sickness.... Oh, let's see nature and catch some parasites!" He was still going on as I acquired targets and shot. I watched as heads were laid open and throats cut through. At first, the zombies did not seem to notice, then slowly but surely, they began to look around trying to find the hidden assassins. BT finally stopped talking and started shooting. I did not notice any zombies going down by Ron. I thought he still had ticks on the mind and was about to give him crap about it when I turned to look. The reason that none of the zombies surrounding Ron's car were being hit became immediately evident, the ones at the maintenance shed, which were closer, had already discovered our sniper nest and were coming full tilt.

"Any chance you were going to say something?" I asked as I switched my field of fire.

"I figured you'd get it soon enough."

We were in a spot of trouble. A hundred and fifty yards seems like a fairly long distance, but if something is running at you at full speed, you're really only talking eighteen or nineteen seconds. Most people never realize that the vast majority of firefights are generally over in a minute or under. With one side victorious and the other dead. This battle was going to be no different. Of course, for those of you wondering, that minute seems closer to about a week.

"I'm out!" I shouted to BT, letting him know I was going to need to reload. I'd no sooner released my empty magazine when he stopped shooting.

He twisted his rifle. The bolt was lodged partially open

with a live round jammed into the back of an expended one. "Stove pipe!"

He was out of the mix for a while. I was going to have to be spot on to make this work. At least the zombies were cooperating by coming closer and making better targets. I targeted the closest zombies for obvious reasons, but this also had the added benefit that, more times than not, the ones immediately trailing would get tangled up and go down as well. It bought precious time.

"Hurry up, man." I was killing them, but not fast enough. Even if he got back into it now, it might be too late.

"What do you think I'm doing, man?" He was as nervous as I was.

Blood sprayed, skulls exploded, brains flew, and still they came. Fifty yards. I spared the smallest of glances toward Ron to see if he had extracted himself from his own potentially deadly situation. I couldn't even see the car due to the mob of zombies coming at us from his direction.

"We might need to run," I warned BT.

"Almost free."

"Now or never, buddy." I was still firing, and I instinctually knew I was getting to the end of the magazine.

"I'm good." I heard his bolt close home. "Holy shit."

"No kidding." I switched out while he fired.

He blew through the rest of his rounds in record time. We'd won some hard-earned time just as he shouted "Out!"

They gained ground while I went solo for a few seconds. We could just about keep them in check with both of us going. Of course, our magazines would run dry and, soon enough, so would our supply. It again became a question of when we would abandon our post.

"BT, we're going to have to go." Although, that ship had not only sailed but also was probably already pulling up at its new port. By the time we arose, turned, and got running, they would be colliding with us. There was gunfire happening to our front. I figured it was Ron trying to get rid of the zombies around his car. I believed that right up until I heard multiple reports and from differing caliber sizes. I had to put a hand on BT's shoulder to keep him down as he potentially tried to make his escape.

"I'm going to count that as a lifesaving gesture," I told him, not sure what he was thinking. Bullets were zipping up and over our location. Normally, this would be extremely disturbing. Right now, though, it was welcome. "Out!" I warned, dropping my magazine. We had a thirty-foot cushion drop to twenty before I could start firing again. Zombies were coming to skidding halts less than five feet from our location. We were about as overrun as we could be without getting trampled.

I think I had one magazine left. Wouldn't matter though; I'd never get a chance to get to it. I debated keeping one round to put in my own head. But I'd already lost count of how many I'd shot. Bone fragments and body pieces began to pelt us as those behind kept firing.

"Out!" BT shouted onto a completely silent battlefield. Smoke from our rifles hung in the air. We were the last men standing. Well, technically, there were twelve of us, but I was pretty sure we were all playing for the same team. I took note that BT quickly and quietly, placed his last magazine into his rifle before he stood. Just because we shared an enemy did not make us friends. For all we knew, they were cannibals that wanted us for themselves.

"You all right?" Ron called out to us.

I stood, waved over to him, but kept my rifle by my hip, ready to pull up and start firing again.

"Mike?" Someone called out. It was Erin. I instinctively looked for Paul. Where there was one, the other was close by. It hurt more than I cared to remember when I realized he would not ever be by her side, at least not on this plane. She ran toward me.

"Thank you." She gave me a fierce hug and then pushed back.

"Why?" Was all I could think to ask.

Her eyes became downcast. "You reminded me of him too much. I couldn't take it."

"What were you trying to do when you left?"

"I think you know."

"You did a horrible job!" BT said brusquely.

"I missed you too, BT." Erin slid into an easy hug with him.

"Damn fool," he told her, though he gripped her tighter.

"What's going on here?" I asked, referring to the eleven with her and their locale.

"We were staying in a safe house in Andover, and we were overrun."

"Doesn't sound all that safe," I said dryly, not trying to be sarcastic, just making an observation.

She laughed. "It wasn't. We've been looking for places to stay for a few weeks now. Ended up here. Thought we'd be fine, at least until we got surrounded. What are you guys doing here?"

"Huh?" I asked. "You called us on the radio."

"Radio? We don't have a radio."

"This a joke?" BT asked.

I might have asked the same question if I didn't have a spike of iciness traveling along the base of my skull.

"What's to joke about BT?"

"We … we got a call from you, Erin. Said you were in trouble at the Quabbin. We're not out here by coincidence."

"I can assure you it was not me or anyone I'm here with."

"What the fuck is going on, Mike?" BT looked about as white as his skin tone was going to allow for.

"I think we had a spectral visitor, and he was looking out for someone near and dear."

"Paul, Paul did this?" Erin put her hand to her throat.

"Erin dear, are you all right?" An older woman flanked by two men approached.

"I'm ... I'm fine, I think." She had tears in the corners of her eyes threatening to fall. "Mike, BT, this is Fannie, Brad, and Shemp."

I shook all their hands. "Shemp, as in *The Three Stooges?*"

He shrugged and gave a half-cocked smile. "Favorite show growing up. I figured I had nobody left in this world who knew my name and I could give myself one that gave me comfort."

"Shemp though? Why not Curly?"

"Too much hair." He bent over to show his thick brown moppish topping.

I liked him already.

"Do you guys have transportation?"

Fannie responded. "We do, we just couldn't get to it. Thank you for aiding us."

"Aiding" was a strange word for what had just happened, but since they had saved our lives as well, I was willing to let it slip. I couldn't even blame her for getting us into this situation, as it seemed that Paul had tampered with the boundaries between the living and dead to get something of great importance to him rescued. I had no answers for what had happened and most likely never would. All I could do was move forward.

"Happy to help. Good thing you have wheels. I don't think we'd all fit in the bug."

A couple of people were helping Ron move the VW. He'd put the thing atop a rock.

"Why ever would we do that?" Fannie asked.

"I just figured you'd come with us."

"Oh, heavens no, not unless you're going to Florida."

I swear I was a millimeter away from asking her if she was planning on retiring. At least I kept my mouth shut on that one. "Florida? Why?"

"Fannie, you've already said too much," said Brad, the other man with her.

"This one is always suspicious." She pointed to him.

"It's a good thing to be these days, well probably all days, but especially now," I told her.

He nodded.

"Relax, Brad. These are obviously friends of Erin's, and they went to great lengths to save her and us. I think they at least should know. What they do with the information is their choice."

Brad's look gave me the distinct impression he didn't hold the same sentiment. She knew it too and continued anyway. I liked her as well. Two people in one day, almost a record for me.

"When we get to Florida, we are going to attempt to get a boat and go to Cuba."

I could think of no reason to go to the tiny nation other than to see if some of the cigar tobacco had made it. She must have seen it on my face.

"We've heard rumors that Cuba is zombie free."

Brad walked away, pissed.

"Don't worry about him. If he had his way, it would just be the two of us. I'm his mother."

Now that she said it, I did see the family resemblance, although, where she seemed to always wear a smile, he had a frown.

"Zombie free, is there such a thing?" BT scoffed.

I could see the natural isolation of an island helping to keep the virus away. Was it possible? "Did they ever have zombies?"

"Sadly, yes. They were as bad, if not worse off, than everyone else."

"What changed?"

"The zombies died, from what we've heard."

"Zombies died? How?"

"They're just gone. No more food; they starved."

"Oh, I hate to be the bearer of bad news, but they're still there."

Fannie's disposition changed so fast I thought I was misinterpreting it.

"I said they are *not!*" Her face turned a color of red usually reserved for a crayon, and not one of those multi sixty-four crayon packs, but the traditional eight, where red is damn red and not burnt sienna. "And that is where we are going!"

"Whoa." I now knew where Brad got his sour disposition, little miss polar swing was in full force. "I'm just saying we've never seen zombies die. They do this thing called stasis, basically hibernation until there's more food."

"YOU LIE!" She was shouting so violently that angry spittle flew from her mouth as she screamed. "GOD HAS TOLD ME THAT CUBA IS FREE FROM THE DEMONS!"

Religious nut. I kept that to myself. I saw no sense in antagonizing her. Her group was concerned, and was beginning to head our way. I guess I'd pulled the trigger a little too quickly on the liking part. I was back down to one, and even that was abnormally high.

"We are his twelve apostles, and we will begin our own Garden of Eden!" I guess she was done as well, because she walked away.

BT looked over to me with the "What the fuck?" look. I shrugged. What the hell else could I add?

"Erin?"

"These are the people I'm with now."

"You don't have to be."

"It's where I *want* to be. Fannie saved me. I'd taken a half bottle of pills. Between that and the cold my heart had stopped. I'd killed myself, Michael. You don't go to a good place when you do that." She shuddered as if in remembrance. "She pulled me from there, I can't imagine not going with her. She knows things. She knew where to find me, said she was looking for me. I consider that alone to be a miracle."

I wasn't convinced, although what the hell Fannie and her troupe were doing there I can't honestly say.

"Are you coming!" Fannie shouted. It was not an order, though it sounded a lot like one. And it certainly was not a question.

Erin hugged me again. "I cannot thank you enough for helping us."

"Yes you can. Come back with us." If I had seen any hint in her eyes that she was being held against her will, I would have fought for her freedom, but I wasn't going to risk our lives then kidnap her. That made no sense, plus she seemed a happy, active participant to the group. "You know I'm not lying about the zombies, right?"

"I know that, but do you know for certain that Cuba isn't free of them?"

"How could I?"

"Fannie says God sends her messages."

"Erin, please listen to me. Come back with us; you'll be safe there."

"Are there zombies in Maine?"

"You know that answer."

"I'll take my chances on the unknown and have faith." She hugged us both again and walked away, turning once to wave. Fannie wrapped her arm around Erin's shoulder, and they kept moving. I waited until they were out of sight, one last desperate attempt to catch a glimmer of Erin's desire to be away from them. She never turned back around.

"What just happened, Mike?" BT had been watching as well. Ron had joined us.

"She's torched."

"Fannie?" BT asked.

"Fannie is scorched earth. Erin has snapped. Paul's death

broke something inside of her. She's not the first person to turn to religion in times of great need."

"There's nothing wrong with turning to religion, but not with a blind eye." BT said with a fair degree of wisdom.

"Now what?" Ron asked.

"Now we go the fuck home, I suppose."

"Don't seem so depressed about it, little brother."

"I'm not, just trying to wrap my head around what just happened. Of all the scenarios that played out in my head, this wasn't one of them. And that's not even taking into account the phantom phone call."

"What?"

BT filled him in. I was still trying to come to terms with just letting my best friend's wife go with a religious cult to the God-friendly, zombie-free country of Cuba.

"Phantom, my ass." Ron had gone to the shed after we watched Fannie and her flock leave. An entire wall was devoted to electronic equipment. Must have been some sort of way to communicate with other parks or something.

"Why lie about it?" I asked, turning the power knob just to make sure it worked. It crackled to life like only a piece of equipment with tubes can.

"Come in Talbot household, or I will use the force on you." I used my best Darth Vader impression, which left a lot to be desired. Should have went with Rambo; at least that is passable.

"Uncle Mike?" It was Melissa, Ron's daughter. She was apparently tending the radio.

"Melissa, I am your uncle." I kept continuing with my charade.

"You all right? You sound like you got a bad cold. Maybe you should gargle with some salt water."

"Forget it. Everything all right up there?"

"Yeah, everything is good, although Meredith called me a be-otch, so I was just about to smack her arm, and then my mother came in and she shouted at us to behave like young women...."

I'd forgotten Melissa's proclivity to talk at ninety words a second and for stretches of ten minutes or more at a time. If I didn't sneak in our status soon, I could be here for the remainder of the day looking for an opening.

"Everything's fine. Heading home now!" I shouted and put the microphone down and backed away quickly.

Ron grabbed the microphone. "Love you!" he said real fast and did the same as I did.

We could still hear her talking. "...and then there was the cat. She went...." I walked out of the hut.

7

MIKE JOURNAL ENTRY 7

For all the crap we'd gone through just to get to Erin and then semi-rescue her, we'd somehow been given a pass to get back home. The only part that was relatively disturbing was the large bloodstain and discarded bones of the man I'd previously set free. I could only hope I hadn't sent Erin off to the same fate. It was late by the time we got back to Ron's. I'd say after midnight, if I had to guess. We were halted by a spot light that I'm sure was baking my face and that authoritative voice of Arnold Schwarzenegger telling us to halt.

"It's Gary, right? It has to be Gary," I said.

"It's us!" I said, getting out of the car, making sure my hands were high over my head, although Gary was more inclined to ask a bunch of questions before he shot, so I was somewhat safe.

"Where's the truck?" It was that same Arnold, halting, accented language, and it was amplified to ear shredding decibels.

"Don't ask." Ron had got out as well.

"I did not say move."

"You'd better shut off whatever the hell thing Mad Jack gave you. And that light, feel like I'm getting a sunburn."

"You are no fun." He said into the Arnold translator before we heard the squelch of the electronic equipment being switched off. His spotlight dimmed but had not completely shut down. I shielded my eyes when I saw lights had come on over at the house, so I could see. I noticed a figure on the deck peering our way. Looked about the size and shape of Tracy. I waved and got one in return.

"Where's Erin?" The words drifted over to us.

"I'm fine honey, thanks for asking!"

"Does a person normally wave when something is wrong?"

"Valid point." BT headed toward the house.

"Don't agree with her; she's already always right." I was about to follow him.

"How's it going, brother?" I looked up into the tree stand. Pretty much Gary's favorite hangout. He usually did some guarding up there. I think mostly he went so he could listen to his walkman and sing without anyone hassling him about it. He'd added on to the stand so it was more like a tree house. It had a roof and a small chair inside, a locked cabinet so he could put some food safely away from squirrels and enough batteries to last him the rest of the year. I'd been up there a couple of times. Told him he should expand it so it wasn't so cramped for two. That was when I realized he wanted to be alone. We all dealt in our own ways.

The entire house was awake and wanted to hear what had happened. I let Ron do it. I was happy to just sit back and relish in the moment. We were back and safe. Safe, yeah, what a fucked-up word, full of lies and deceit. If I knew then what I know now, I would have grabbed everyone and headed to Cuba with the church of Fannie-atics.

"You actually kept your word," Tracy intoned as we laid in bed.

"I must be growing up."

"Something is definitely growing." she laughed. If this was a movie, this is where it would fade to black and you may or may not hear a sensual moan before cutting to another scene. Since I am not in the business of writing erotica, suffice to say it was a very tender night.

8

PAYNE STEPPED OFF THE SHIP. IT WAS RAINING HARD ENOUGH that small floods were forming along the sides of the road, the sewer system not able to keep up with the torrent of water. Although by looking at her, you would have thought it was a bright spring day, her long, red hair blowing back behind her. The rain not daring to touch her as it cascaded down. Charity and Sophia trailed behind as Payne walked upon the pier.

What started as a small spark soon turned the SS Cross-bearer into a torch that sizzled hotly as rainwater hit it. The deck had been bathed in blood and discarded bodies. The vampires had eaten well; the crew having served their purpose of getting them across the ocean was given their just rewards for helping evil.

"So this is the New World?" Payne outstretched her arms. "It rains in this *New* England much like it did in the old."

Charity wiped the corner of her mouth where a small pool of blood had collected. She sucked her coated finger deeply and sighed. "It has been a long time since we drank so deeply."

Sophia was doing pirouettes fast enough that she was

beginning to blur. She laughed wildly. "We will kill them all!" she said merrily.

"Yes, we will kill them all." Payne said, much more levelly. "But there are things I wish to find out first."

Charity grabbed Payne's hand and rested her head on the other woman's shoulder.

"What a glorious day!" Sophia had stopped spinning and was breathing heavily.

9

MIKE JOURNAL ENTRY 8

IT WAS TWO DAYS AFTER WE GOT BACK FROM MASSACHUSETTS. I'd come downstairs, sort of oblivious to my surroundings. I know, shocker, right? I was in the midst of a fabulous morning ball-scratching session. Women won't understand that, but men get it. I bet it's sort of equivalent to a woman taking off a bra at the end of the day. There's a satisfaction that is difficult to explain, yet it is one of life's small to midsize pleasures. I stopped what I was doing immediately when I realized I wasn't alone. Although Tommy seemed to be completely unaware enough to my presence, I could have continued unhindered.

"Hey," I said, trying not to look guilty of having my hand firmly entrenched in my crotch. See, this is why I didn't like to shake people's hands. There is no one that ever existed, poet, laureate, model, pilot, author, doesn't matter; within the last hour of you meeting them they have put their hand somewhere gross. I can just about guarantee it, and then they used to thrust that thing out and expect someone else to grasp hold. I can barely handle the disgusting things I do. What makes anyone think I want to add their list of stuff to that? If we ever do revert back to that old custom, just give that thought a go before you blindly reach out and grab that hand. Just imagine where it may have been very recently, and I bet you're right more times than you're wrong. I noticed that I had gone through my entire inner monologue, and Tommy had still not acknowledged my presence. I did think about resuming my unfinished nether region shake down but decided in the interest of civility to let it pass for now.

"You all right?" I asked, getting closer. Gotta admit I proceeded with caution. He seemed to be in another realm right now, and you know how the saying goes: "Don't wake a sleepwalker." Who the hell knows what happens when you wake a territory traveler?

"They're here," he said in a voice I don't think I'd ever heard come from him before.

"Who's here?" I had to ask, but I already knew.

"I thought we'd have more time." He turned to look at me. There was a panic in his eyes. If a five-hundred-year-old vampire is concerned, then it's safe to say there's something to be worried about.

"Here as in *here*?" I moved to the window and looked out. I saw nothing, but that meant nothing. I looked up to Gary's tree house slash fort. A sting of concern raced along my veins and threaded through my heart until I saw him. He was doing a dance that no person should have to witness.

"Hey, man." Trip had come up beside me. "Looks like he's doing Tai Chi."

"I'm more inclined to think that's the Hustle," I told him.

"Oh, I could see that. Do you think he broke into my stash?" Trip watched Gary intently.

"He doesn't do drugs."

Trip looked at me like I'd been swearing at his mother. He walked away muttering something incoherently.

"Tommy, what's going on?"

"We should go outside."

Within a few minutes, we were standing by the garden and a decent crop of tomatoes.

"They're coming, and I don't know if we should stay or leave," he blurted out in a very uncharacteristic way.

"Start over, take a breath, and tell me what's going on in that head of yours."

"They're on the East Coast; that much I know. I don't know specifically where. If I were to take a guess, I'd say Boston, but it could just as easily be Maryland. Pretty sure it's not Florida."

"All right, I get the picture; they are in this country somewhere. Not necessarily here, right now, but I assume heading this way. Right?"

"I don't know. I don't know if it would be better to stay or go."

"Go?"

"They know we're here or somewhere near."

"Like a GPS?"

"Nothing quite that detailed. They'll be able to get close enough though."

"And if we left?"

"They still might make their way here. To see where Eliza died."

"We can't like psychically scrub the area clean or something?"

"Too much happened there between Azile's magic, the Shaman's powerful medicine, and Eliza's distress during her death. It's like a beacon to anyone who can read the signs."

"So we could go across the country, and that might not change anything?"

"Exactly."

"Well, that doesn't mean we can't make everyone else leave here."

"Absolutely not!" Ron said furiously after we went back in and I explained what was happening.

"Ron, I'm not saying permanently, just for a little while."

"And where would you like us to go?"

"Portland," I told him.

"You want us to move two hours away?"

"I meant Oregon." I was serious.

"This is my home." He was getting angrier by the second.

"It's just a place. I promise I'll treat it decently while you're gone. No parties."

"I'm not leaving, Mike. Let them come."

"You say that now, Ron, and I get it, but these aren't just some bad people or some nearly brainless zombies. These are cunning, wicked, and evil vampires who care nothing of our lives. I sometimes wish I'd never come here."

"Don't you say that. Don't you ever say that. Family is the most important thing. Now, even more."

"If I hadn't come, neither would Eliza or now these three."

"Mike, it doesn't matter now. You're here. We'll deal with this like we've dealt with everything else, as a *family*."

Tommy sat heavily in a chair, his head hanging. "This is all my fault. I'm the one that lead Eliza right to you. I just … I just didn't know that she was using me to find you. I thought I was protecting all of you when really I was putting you in harm's way."

"She would have found us on her own, Tommy. You know that. You saved us."

"That's what I'm talking about, Mike." Ron started. "You're not the only Talbot. She would have got here eventually whether you came or not. You just happened to be next on her list."

I hadn't seen it that way. I guess that's the problem with being a narcissist, you think the world revolves around you.

"So where's safer, Mike? Do we send all the non-Talbots away?" Ron asked.

"Hold on, things have changed. Eliza was obviously out

for our blood. But the three coming, I don't think so. We don't share the same violent history. According to Tommy, it's just mostly him, me, a missing Azile, and a dead Shaman they're going to want to see. The rest of you could ride this out somewhere else, and we'll see how this part plays out."

"You make it sound like they're on a sightseeing tour. Is that a realistic expectation?"

I was about to answer. "Not asking you, Mike. I'm talking to him."

Tommy looked up. "I don't know their intentions. They're curious, that's for sure, or they wouldn't have crossed an ocean. But I don't know if it's going to be words or blood that sates that inquisition."

"Inquisition? That's the word you use there? Could you be a little less manipulative?" I asked him. I was angry. It was one thing that I was in danger. There was no need for anyone else to be.

He shrugged.

"Ron, what about the kids? Shouldn't we at least get them someplace else?" I asked. This had merit. If the vamps swept in here and killed us all, which was easily one of the top three outcomes, then no one would be spared.

"And who goes to protect them?"

That made sense, too. Dying by vampire was no better than dying by zombie.

WE HAD A MEETING THAT NIGHT. Tommy laid out the graveness of the situation. There was a fair amount of heated exchanges. The idea of splitting our group obviously was met with hostility, though most agreed it was something that had to be done. If we destroyed the threat, then we would reunite and all would be well in the world, of course, until it wasn't.

But that would be a fight for another day. The idea of the family splitting to me was a hedging of the bets. If we lost, *if* didn't seem so far-fetched, seemed more like *when*, but again something for another day. So, if we lost, the Talbot name at least would go on.

If I had it my way, only Tommy and I would have stayed at Ron's house, as the vampires were only concerned with us. Better we were the sacrificial lambs rather than place so many on the chopping block, as it were. Ron stayed, Nancy was taking the kids, all the kids, Gary stayed, as did Mad Jack, who apparently was working on a vampire repellant. I have no idea what that was, maybe a cross launcher. Is that sacrilegious? I asked him how that would affect Tommy and me. He got vague and quiet, quickly. I did not take that as a good sign. Trip stayed. Said he couldn't leave because he lost his Grateful Dead button collection somewhere in the house and wouldn't leave it behind. Stephanie was going to go. Steve, my sister's husband, stayed, though he looked like he wanted to be anywhere but here. Of us all, he'd seen the least action. He looked a lot like a fresh recruit, shipped into a hot zone, green and all. I obviously stayed, and no amount of cajoling, threatening, or yelling could persuade Tracy to leave. Henry and his new favorite friend, Riley, stayed behind as well, though I wished they would leave. The good part was the psychotic Ben-Ben and the cat went, though I would have to fear for my kids now that there was a feline in their midst.

Now that we knew who was staying and who was going, the problem was *where* they were going. Probably should have figured that out first; seems we'd put the cart before the horse. Now we just had to scope out a place to make sure that where we sent our loved ones wasn't some sort of death trap. A lot of suggestions were thrown out. We scratched anything off the list more than fifteen minutes away. Partly because we honestly had no idea how long this exile was going to be, and we would need to resupply them periodically. Plus, we would all need the assurance of being able to check in on each other repeatedly. We would both have radios, and should a problem arise in their encampment, help could be dispatched immediately.

We settled on checking out Belfast, the next town over. It was close enough, and it offered brick buildings, at least downtown. Although calling the center of Belfast downtown would give you the false impression it was a big city. Big compared to Searsport, but Belfast proper would hardly take up a city block in New York City. Not that it would want to, mind you, just using a comparison. I actually sat this little expedition out. I had a gnawing pit in my stomach that if I left, that would be the time they struck. Luckily, most of my predictions were founded on misconceptions. Travis and BT kept an eye on Steve, Lyndsey, and Gary as they set about their expedition. Although, it was Gary that ended up the hero of the day. It's his story though, so I'll let him recount it.

Gary's Save

"WE WERE DRIVING——"

"That train, high on cocaine?" Trip asked, now excited. "I've done that."

I shuddered thinking about the world I'd been lost in with a man named Jack Walker. If I really tried, I could almost pretend it had all been a dream. Of course, I knew better, but it was still better to make believe it never happened, because if it could happen, even once, that meant it could happen again, and that was unacceptable. I'd seen nightmares there I'd never be able to forget. Had Trip been high driving that train? Better to not find out. The world was already terrifying enough without having to heap on to that particular memory.

"No train, now don't blurt out again. This is a good story," Gary admonished him.

"It'd be better if someone were high." And with that, he pulled out a bowl. Not much of a shock there. At least it made him quiet for the majority of the story, until he started snoring, that is.

"Mike, can you control your friends?" Gary pleaded.

I shrugged. Getting Trip to do something was like trying to hold sand.

"Yeah, Ponch," Trip said during an exhalation. "Your brother is trying to tell us something, and your friends are being total narcs."

I thought BT was going to get up and pitch him off the deck. He stayed calm, showed more restraint with him than he ever did with me. I was going to have to ask him about that.

Gary waited for a second, specifically looking at Trip to see if the man had anything more to say, before he continued. When he was satisfied, he went on.

"So we're in Belfast, and BT says, 'How about a bank?' I didn't think that was a good idea because the whole front of it is glass, and unless they stayed in the vault, they wouldn't be safe. But he's huge, so I decided it would be better to go and check it out, and then he could realize that he'd made a mistake on his own."

"Gee, thanks," BT told him.

"You're welcome. So we go to the bank, and the windows are gone and the place has been robbed."

I could only dwell on the stupidity of the people that steal money during an apocalypse. Food is a much more valuable commodity. Maybe it happened early on, and those poor ignorant fools thought the mess would all blow over and they'd be richer for it. Opportunistic maybe, asshats definitely.

"Funny thing is, there was blue everywhere."

"Dye packs," BT interjected. "Dumb asses must have got coated in it."

"There were two blue zombies out front, dead," Travis added.

"Talk about insult to injury," I said. Poor bastards take stuff that's not worth the paper it's printed on anymore. End up looking like smurfs, get attacked by zombies, then turn into zombies themselves, and are summarily killed, probably for the money they had on them. That's a bad day, right there.

"We still went in." Gary was giving the evil eye to everyone that was talking out of turn, including me. "Safe was open, some of the deposit boxes had been pried open. I decided it wasn't a suitable location and ordered the troops out."

Ordered? BT mouthed.

I placed my index finger up to my lips.

"Travis wanted to go to the pizza place on High Street. I had to let him know that was not an appropriate place, either. I'll give him credit, though, because I started to think about what was across from it."

"The post office," I said without realizing I'd said it aloud.

"You make me shut up, and then you start?" BT looked at me.

"Yeah, the post office, Mike. Were you there?" Gary looked a little perturbed.

"Sorry, just thinking."

"Did you know most people think silently?"

"Sorry, sorry. Continue." Tracy whacked me.

"The building looked like it could still be open for business."

The post office, except for the safe, was a more secure location than the bank. It had three entry points: The front door was heavy wood with a small window; the rear was a metal security door. The only problematic one was the side door, which was made of heavy glass. That could be fixed, though.

"I led the way because that's what commanders do," Gary said proudly.

"I had to make him take his earphones off," BT mumbled.

"That's when it happened!" Gary said, excitedly standing up. "We were attacked by a vicious horde of zombies!"

Nancy gasped.

BT leaned in to me and whispered in my ear. "It was two zombies, and they were in stasis. One of them was old enough he might have died of natural causes before he became a zombie."

"You should have seen it! I saved everyone. I pushed Travis back and then shot them before they could get us. It was close. I was afraid for everyone's life but my own, because I am almost a ninja."

I had to suppress a smile. I loved my brother, and who was I to question his embellishment. We all see the world through our own filtered glasses, and this is the way he viewed his heroics. He did kill two zombies, no one was hurt, and he found a decent location for a Talbot hideout. In my book, that does make him a hero. Maybe not to the epic proportions he sees it, but that's all right.

"Mike, I think one of the zombies was Mike Two." Gary said sadly.

"Dammit." Mike Two was about my age. Worked the counter there. From New York originally, but I didn't hold that against him. I'd met him a few times when I'd come home to visit. Always really nice, and never seemed to mind when I was shipping things back to Colorado that I had no right to. There are just things that you could get on the East Coast that you couldn't get in Colorado. More than once he'd let me know the best wrapping method to make sure bottles would make the arduous journey. Something about illegal beer just made it taste so much sweeter! He had a quick wit, and we seemed to share the same interests. In another world, I'm sure I would have been inviting him over to the house for barbecues. The reason he got the "two" moniker is because, when I'd met him and told him my name, he'd said his name was Mike, too. For some reason, well okay, I know the reason, I was on vacation and smoking some leafy substance. I assumed his last name was Tooh or something, so it just kind of stuck.

"We put them in a car down the road." Travis said. That was about as good a burial as we could offer: entombment by automobile.

"I had my men clean the place up. We aired it out and made sure there were no other surprises. I now deem this place safe for Talbot inhabitation."

"Thank you, General Gary." Ron said, ribbing his brother.

Gary didn't seem to catch it. If anything, his chest puffed out more. When my brother Glenn, Gary's twin, had died, something inside of Gary had as well. I was always happy to see my brother push back the misery that I knew crept up on him from time to time. I've read that the death of a twin can cause irreparable damage to the survivor as if half of them had died and they can no longer function without the other. Gary found his ways, through music and the characters he desired to portray. If one of them was Gambo or General Gary, more power to him.

"Well, I guess we should start delivering people and supplies."

"Everyone but you, Mike." Ron said.

"What?"

"If you go, there'll be a tornado or something like a killer shark will come out of the harbor and—"

"Yeah, we get it."

"I'm just saying. Wherever you go, a storm tends to follow."

"Didn't I say I understood?" I walked out of the room, letting them get to the tasks of getting everything ready to go. Ron had been messing around, but I've got to admit his words hurt more than he knew. Was I the fucking lightning rod for this tempest? Had I placed everything and everyone I loved under a black cloud?

How different would everything have turned out if I'd just let Justin blow Eliza's head off?

"I know that look, Mike." It was Tracy.

"Huh?"

"That *look*. You've got your bottom lip poofed out, your eyebrows are furrowed, and you have a thousand-yard stare. I've seen that before. You're trying to make yourself go insane."

"How do you do that? The only emotion I've ever been able to read off of you is when you're angry."

"Women are smarter."

"Well, I mean, I know that. I guess I just didn't realize how much more."

"So, what's going on? I saw the way you left the room after Ron was ribbing you." She sat down; I, on the other hand, was pacing.

"Is this all my fault?"

She laughed quickly, and maybe involuntarily, it had come so quick. "The zombie apocalypse? I don't think so. That's a little self-centered, even for you, Mike."

"Ha-ha, real funny. Maybe you and Ron should work on your routine. Not the zombies, the rest of it?"

"Eliza? How could you know that five hundred years ago, you were going to have an asshole relative? Although, given your family history, I guess that's a given."

"Are you really here to help?"

"Sorry. It's just so easy when you're all downcast like this, and I'll be honest, I don't like this version of my husband."

"I'm stretched thin here. Justin is slipping into depression. Half of the family has to move away, and the half that is staying might be in more danger than we've ever been in before. I'd say I have good reason to be somewhat downcast."

She stood and came over to me. "I get it, Mike. I do." She caressed the side of my face and leaned in for a kiss, which I hungrily gave her. "But you don't have time to feel like this. These events were going to play out one way or the other. Who's to say what would have happened to those here had you not come? Their defenses were haphazard and weak at best. You've shown them hope in the face of overwhelming adversity, and they thank you for that. You are directly responsible for most of the lives in this place, not least of all, your family." She began to count them off. "Me, your daughter and future grandbaby, Justin, Travis, that dog of yours, my mom, BT, Trip—"

I stopped her. "I get it."

"Do you? All of them, every single one of them ... us. We'd be gone." She touched her hand to her heart. "We'd be dead now if not for you, Mike, for your heart and commitment, for your willingness to do whatever it takes to get us through. That's why we follow you. That's why we would do anything and everything you ask. We know it, and others can see it. The storm doesn't follow you; you are the storm. Nothing can stand in your way."

I let her words sink in. "Wow those were some pretty powerful words. Now when you say you'll do anything...."

"I knew it. I knew when I said it that was where your focus would go."

I wrapped her up in a hug.

"BT, though, isn't he too mean to die?"

"Possibly. I threw him in there to make you feel better." Her head was nestled against my chest, and I loved the warmth that spread out from the contact.

THE TRANSITION HAPPENED AROUND ME. It went fairly smoothly. Half the group moved out, and supplies were sent their way. I took, maybe, my first healthy downtime in six months. I sat on the deck and just pretty much zoned out. Spent a lot of time looking at trees, and I have to be honest, it felt pretty damn good. Worry, which had been a constant gnawing in my gut, took a siesta, and for the first time in years, way before the zombies had come, I found an inner peace. Anger, anxiety, and a half dozen other negative emotions were laid to rest. I'd love to say permanently. Who wouldn't? But even the temporary situation was unparalleled, and I was basking in it. Nothing happened that day, that week, hell, that month. More than once, we'd talked about reuniting the two halves to make a whole.

All it took to nix that idea was a look over to Tommy, who oftentimes joined me on the deck. Although, whereas I looked like I was on a beach in the Bahamas, he seemed to be sitting on the edge of the Grand Canyon on some sketchy ground. He would stand quickly for no reason and scan the tree line, sometimes sitting back down, sometimes walking around the entire deck seeking, searching. Most times, I could not tell if he was using his two eyes or the third. That makes more sense if you are into mysticism. He'd say a few words, I think Latin, and then abruptly leave. We had a few zombie encounters; that was to be expected considering that we now were in two places with constant traveling in between. We were sure to garner attention with all the extra activity and noise.

On one such trip, I was allowed to go. Tracy wanted to see her mom, and we both wanted to see Nicole, who was about to pop. Can't tell you how nerve-wracking that was. Having a baby was stressful enough, but due to current circumstances, this was going to be a natural birth, without the option of having a hospital as a safety net should something go wrong. And trust me, I'd read enough about it to know it was possible for plenty of things to go amiss, including the mother bleeding out and dying right on the table. I did not think I could handle something like that. I would become hollow inside. I was happy that Nancy had taken some mid-wife classes, once upon a time. She'd never used the knowledge in real life, but she was about to be baptized under fire, so to speak.

The post office had turned into an even bigger boon than we'd initially realized. Behind an old series of sorting machines, which looked like they hadn't touched mail since World War II, was a door that looked like it could stop a charging rhino. That was strange enough. What was weirder was where it led. Should have known, but it was an old bomb shelter, replete with army bunks and metal furniture. It was easily four hundred square feet and could comfortably hold twenty or so people, at least for a little while. The door up top could lock as well as the one at the bottom of the stairs. Nothing short of a nuclear strike could take the place out. When I went topside, I went out to the street trying to figure out where it vented air from. I'd figure out later that there were exhaust pipes that went to the roof of the building. That wasn't my primary concern at the moment.

"Zombies!" I shouted, heading around the corner at a run. I wanted to beat them, and since they were already sprinting, it was going to be close.

Travis and Mark, Ron's son, were perched on the roof, and within a few seconds I received some much-needed aerial support. Stephanie had been pulling supplies out of the car and was standing with an armful of stuff when I grabbed her and pulled her inside. I quickly threw the lock and stepped back. Stephanie was still trying to figure out what was going on when the fastest zombie smacked into the door.

"Oh my."

"Yeah definitely 'oh my.'" I wasn't winded, but I felt like I should be. My heart rate was somewhere up in the two hundred beats a minute range. "You okay?"

"Yes, thank you." She seemed like she was still trying to

collect her thoughts from her fright. People were coming out to investigate while I went back into the sorting room where the maintenance ladder was adhered to the wall. It led directly to the roof, and that was where I was going.

I hadn't made it half way up when Travis poked his head down through the access door. "Going to need more ammunition and more guns."

"How many?"

"Over a hundred."

"Shit." We hadn't encountered a group that big in a while. All of our recent activity must have disturbed a stasis hive nearby, and the problem now was the continuous loop we were about to start running. All the shooting would bring even more. In the next few days, we could easily be surrounded by a thousand or more of the beasts. "Hey sis, can you get on the horn and let Ron know we're in a bit of a mess here?"

To compound matters, I heard a blood-curdling scream I thought was going to freeze my heart. "Nicole?"

Tracy, Carol, and Nancy were escorting my daughter to a back office. "Going to need clean towels, Mike!" Tracy called back.

Zombie invasion punctuated by a birth; a strange day was indeed shaping up.

"Mike, come here." It was my sister.

"Little busy, sis."

She called out to her son. "Jesse, get Travis some ammo and get up there. Melissa, get your mom some towels! Mike, get over here!"

Well, since she got all my chores taken care of, it was the least I could do. She handed me the radio. I could hear gunfire in the background over the microphone. "This is Mike."

"Mike, it's Ron. We're under attack."

This was too coincidental. I almost dropped the receiver.

"Need you guys to get back here as soon as you can."

"Lyn didn't tell you?"

"Tell me what, Mike? I don't have time for twenty questions."

"We were about to call you for help. We're in a bit of a jam."

There was silence from his end. "Shit" finally came through, like it always does, both literally and figuratively, during a war. "How bad?"

"Travis says about a hundred. I haven't got a chance to check yet, but we're firing, so I would imagine we're sending out invitations to everybody in the neighborhood. What's going on over there?"

"Couple hundred, maybe more. They are mostly staying in the trees so we can't get an accurate count."

"Where's Gary?" I thought about that damn tree fort of his. It was within the first few layers of the defensive zone, but it was much more exposed than the house.

"He's fine—in the house now. He's the one who warned us. We'll send help when we can."

"You said they're in the woods, not attacking?"

"Yeah, not yet anyway. Why?"

"How often have you seen zombies not attack? I think they're stalling help from getting here. I've got to go." I quickly handed the handheld part to Lyn.

BT was still at Ron's. Had a touch of the flu, or so he said, but he'd discovered my sister's romance novels and was knee deep into the story of Shane McClough, his plaid skirts, sorry kilts and his ladylove, Countess Laurabelle, and their forbidden love. He'd holed himself up with the books all around him like a squirrel would with nuts right before a harsh winter. Tommy wouldn't leave the house, period, which meant right now we were severely undermanned, and right now that seemed entirely on purpose. How the fuck had zombies pulled off a coordinated attack? If they'd peeled off two hundred or so just to keep Ron and the others holed up, that meant Travis' original estimate was....

"Dad, we need you up here!" he shouted down the hole again.

I climbed the ladder as fast as I dared. I was just poking my head through the hole when my nose was assaulted. More like beat mercilessly with the smell of zombies.

"Holy mother of...." I didn't even bother finishing the expletive. We were surrounded. I did a complete perimeter check, and there was not a place where the zombies weren't at least twenty bodies deep. That was bad, no doubt, but what had a strangeness to it was the fact they weren't doing anything. I mean besides reeking to high heaven and blocking sunlight from hitting the pavement, they weren't moving. There was a no-man's land of about thirty feet from building to zombie, depending on the terrain, that was as empty as a box of tissues in a teenage boy's room. Do with that what you will; some kids have allergies.

"Dad, what are they doing?" Travis had stopped shooting. He knew enough to realize he needed to save the bullets for when it mattered.

"They're not getting ready to sing Christmas Carols. That I know." I don't know why I said it; just happened, but as I was saying the words, it gave me pause to think of the possibilities going on. I rushed back to the hatch that led downstairs. Thought my chest was going to cave-in when I heard screams from below, then I realized my baby was having a baby. So yeah, my chest still wanted to cave-in, but she was all right. I mean mostly; childbirth under the best of circumstances is a tough endeavor. I know; I've attended three of them, and usually, they give me drugs to deal with it. This time I had to fly straight.

"Justin!" I yelled, not once or even twice, but three times. I was on the ladder and coming down when he finally responded.

"Yeah?"

He looked as nonplussed, as if it were a lazy Saturday morning and I was about to ask him to rake the yard.

"Get everyone down into the bomb shelter." I headed back up. I stopped at his response.

"Why?"

I let my head rest against the rung for a moment as I reined in my temper, which was threatening to boil over. "Stay calm and Talbot on." I knew the boy was still hurting; how could he not be? "Because I asked you to." My calming technique had only worked so well, as the words came through gritted teeth. Felt like Clint Eastwood delivering a line in one of his spaghetti westerns.

"We're all going to die anyway."

I lightly smacked my head against a rung before I went back down.

"Yes, we are most assuredly all going to die, that's just a basic fact of life. But dying, son, that's fucking easy. Anybody can do it. In fact, you really don't have to do anything at all to die. Don't move away from the speeding train. Don't run away from the charging elephant. Don't shoot back at the enemy. Don't call a cab when you're shitfaced. See how easy it is to die? You don't have to do shit! Now living, ah, living—that's the hard part. The choices you have to make, the actions you have to take. Living is hard. Don't ever let anyone tell you differently. Now I'm sorry about Jess, more sorry than I can ever begin to explain, but she's gone. These people around you, they're here and they need our—your help. You want to check out, the door is right there." It was a calculated risk. I needed to know where his head was. That he actually looked over to the door and contemplated that route did not sit well with me. Felt like someone was leeching air out of my lungs with a straw.

I was pretty sure I could beat him to the door before he could unlock it and head out. Even so, I slowly moved closer. I finally saw his shoulders sag as whatever had been weighing him down had finally broke him or had broken over him.

"Ryan, grab your sister. Dizz, Sty, get some food. I'll get the animals." He started shouting commands.

I smiled and thanked him.

"You want me up there when I get everyone in the shelter?"

"Not yet. Get everyone and everything you can down there, get them locked in, then I want you to stay with your sister, mother, and aunts until they can get moving. And if there's any way to speed them along, do it."

"She's having a baby, Dad, not taking a test."

"I get it, but the zombies have something in mind, and I don't quite know what it is. Things are going to get bad here in a hurry."

Meredith, Ron's daughter, struggled with a large bag that clipped my side as she passed. "Sorry, Uncle." She headed to the ladder.

I was about to ask her what the hell she was doing, that she should get in the shelter with everyone else, but she was an adult, a decent shot, and we could use the help up top. I helped her with the bag as we went back up. I spared one quick look back. Justin was indeed on the move. At least for now, I had pulled him out of his rut. Although, for how long? Once he started to dwell on it again, he would find himself heading back to that abyss of emotion. And it was hard being a hypocrite. If anything happened to Tracy, I don't know what I'd do. Gun to the temple? Death by zombie? It would be easy enough to pick an exit strategy. Amazing how a pungent odor can just scramble every thought in your head. I was back up top and the situation had not improved. On the bright side, it hadn't got worse either. But that's not saying much. I mean, if you total your beloved car in an accident, what's it matter if the mirror falls off?

"We going to start shooting?" Meredith asked as she began to tie a bandanna around her face.

It was shit like this that drove me nuts. How long had I been dealing with zombies? You'd think by now I'd have learned some of the basics. I grabbed the piece of cloth Meredith handed to me. I could tell by the crinkle in the corners of her eyes she was smiling. She passed out a square to Travis and Jesse as well. I was famous for missing the obvious. Sometimes, perhaps, that was why Justin had taken it upon himself to point it out at every turn. When the world revolved on a slightly different axis, I can't tell you how many times after a tough day of working, respite with myriad aches and pains, I would groan and moan as I found my way into bed. This would immediately be followed up with my wife asking me if I'd taken any aspirin.

Of course, the answer was no, it was *always* no. Years, fucking years, I'd done that. It never, ever, dawned on me as I winced, taking half steps to go and take something that might help alleviate the pain. And this coming from a person that had never had a problem introducing any of a wide variety of recreational drugs into his system. Some things I just tend to have a large disconnect with, and no matter how I try to bridge the gap, it falls short. Meredith tightened the knot behind my head.

"We gonna start shooting?"

"What's on these?" I was sniffing vigorously.

"I ground some scented candle wax into them. I think these are coconut."

"That's brilliant."

"I know, Uncle. But what do you want to do about the zombies?"

"Right. Sorry. Just nice to not feel like someone shoved shit stones up my nose."

"You know that's gross, right?"

"Diarrhea dollops then? Fine, we do nothing for now.

They're not moving; it's a waste of bullets. We use them if we decide to find a way out or they start trying to come in. They're waiting for something. I don't know what it is, but I imagine we'll find out soon enough."

I WAS WRONG. It wasn't soon enough. They did have the good graces to let me see the birth of my grandson. And by seeing the birth, I mean, I came into the room after everyone was all covered up and cleaned off. The Talbot family was celebrating the edition of Wesley Michael. I admit I cried when I saw him for the first time, and may have even shed a few tears when Tracy held him up to me. "This, this is what we live for," I said quietly. He wrapped his thumb and forefinger around my index finger.

"Dad! Something's going on!" Travis shouted.

I quickly kissed Tracy. "Everyone all right in here?" I looked at Nicole. She looked tired, but hale and hearty.

"Sore but okay." she said.

"Can you guys get her down to the bomb shelter?"

"We can, but we don't want to; it's not very comfortable." There were actual mattresses we'd brought over here for sleeping. They might be on the floor, but they still beat an army cot any day of the week.

"Take the mattress." That, of course, was only part of the problem. She'd just had a baby, something akin to me pissing out a baseball, and I guarantee I wouldn't want to move for about a week if that were the case, but it was still something that needed to be done.

"Mike, for God's sake," Tracy stated.

Oh? I was about to rail on about what God was and was not concerned about right now. I held it in. Very uncharacteristically of me, if I might add.

"Tracy, please, just do it." And with that, I left. I could feel the dagger-like stares of four women as I hurriedly left. The first stars were beginning to appear as I came back up on the roof. Meredith sighed when she came over and pulled my bandanna back up over my mouth and nose. No one said I wasn't consistent.

I came to where Travis was. He was pointing. "They just started moving." It wasn't much, but an opening was beginning to appear. "It looks like they're making a path. Do they want us to try to go through that? Are they letting us go?" There was hope in his voice.

I didn't want to crush that, but this wasn't the Alamo and they weren't the Mexicans allowing the women and children safe passage. "I think they're making room for something to come in."

"That's what I thought, too. I was just—"

"Yeah, me too, kid." I wrapped my arm around his shoulders. Darkness had completely settled over us before the zombies stopped moving. A large path was nicely illuminated by a half moon and, thankfully, cloudless sky. Perhaps God did have a soft spot for us after all. That was of course until I saw the first bulker. I swear, at first, I thought it was a trick of the light. I was convinced they had helmets on. Their heads were huge, almost looked like a Lego man's, all rounded and out of proportion to the rest of its mass. It wasn't safety gear though. It was bone, thick bullet-repellant bone. Meredith pulled her trigger first. The rest of us soon followed.

"Just the bulkers!" I shouted when I saw regular zombies falling. I heard the ricocheting whine as a bullet, I know, I absolutely know, hit one of the fat bastards square in the forehead.

"Travis, we have anything bigger downstairs?"

"Pop's .308. And Justin has an AK." Both were significantly heavier rounds than the 5.56s Travis and I were shooting. Meredith was basically using a slingshot in the form of a

9mm short-barreled rifle. Jesse was the only one using anything with enough force to crack heads. But a bolt action .30-06 wasn't going to keep them at bay for long.

"Get them!"

He was on the move. The problem was, so were the bulkers and right for the weakest point.

"How are they doing this?" I had the questions, that was for sure; never the damned answers though, no none of those. Much like understanding a woman, some things were hidden completely from me. I turned to yell at Trav. "Tell your mom and the others they need to move into the shelter. *Now!*" I don't know if the bony skulls of the bulkers made them blind, but the beast ran into the building as opposed to the door, and still, I felt the vibrations of the violent collision on the roof. I had gotten down into the prone position and leaned my head and shoulders over the edge so I could swing my gun down. I was basically shooting straight down into the top of his head. The first couple of shots dug deep grooves into the heavy bone. The third broke through, dropping the monster where he was.

It seemed the top of the head was slightly more vulnerable, but still no picnic and not the easiest shot to take, either. Two more bulkers hit the building. One nailed the door. I heard a loud crack, but they had not broken through yet. I moved slightly from the impacts. Travis almost finished the job when he grabbed my calf, making me jump. He handed me a heavier rifle. I thanked him when I was sure the frog lodged in my throat had finally moved.

"The women?" I asked as I flipped the safety off.

"Not yet."

"Motherfucker. The tops of their heads. Shoot the tops of their heads!" I pushed back and went to the access door. "Tracy!"

"We're doing all we can, Mike!" she yelled back. She had Wesley in her arms; Nancy and Lindsey had Nicole supported between them, half carrying, half dragging her toward the stairwell. I was watching their painstakingly slow progress when the radio came to life.

"Mike, you there?" It was BT.

Tracy headed for it. "Don't you dare. Get your asses downstairs." I got into position to go down and retrieve the communication device.

"Hey," I said into the mic. When dust rained down on me from another hit, I waited until the women had shut the upstairs access door, grabbed the radio, and headed back for the ladder. I had a moment to reflect on the brilliance of the zombies, they'd split our forces in half between Searsport and here, and they were once again doing it as some of us were below and some were above. I had no doubt we were about to yield the main floor. BT was asking questions as I climbed. I could tell he was getting frustrated I wasn't responding.

"Talbot, answer me!" I damn near felt the force of the airwaves being pushed by him.

"Sorry man, moving the radio. And stop yelling at me. You should be congratulating me. I'm a grandfather now."

There was a pause. "That's awesome, man! Is that why you took so long to get back to me?"

"Not so much, we're in a bit of a bind here."

"How bad?" He was all business.

"Five hundred or so zombies and a platoon of bulkers threatening to bring the building down. We've got people in the bomb shelter and I'm on the roof with Jesse, Meredith, and Travis."

"You split up?"

"I know, man; we broke the cardinal rule of survival. No choice. Nicole is in no shape for battle. She needs people around to take care of her, and if we're going to have any chance here, we need to do whatever we can on the roof to disrupt their plans. Any chance of help from your quarter?"

"Not any time soon. The zombies seem to be massing, but they're not moving, like they're waiting for something."

"Bulkers, I bet. Use heavier guns. They're adapting. Their skulls are thicker. The 5.56s aren't too effective."

"What the fuck, Mike?"

I know what he was asking. How did this happen?

"Don't know, man. I have to get back in the fight and I guess conserve the battery on this thing. Unless I contact you early, I will only power this thing first thing in the morning and at twilight."

"Good luck, Mike."

"You too, man." And with that, I turned the dial to off. The clicking sound it made seemed like a finality. Obviously, I know that's my own bias being superimposed onto a material thing, but that didn't make it any less true.

We were at the point of firing at will. We'd put a serious dent in the bulker population, laying fifteen of them down for good. Must have been five or six tons of zombie flesh put to rest, but we had received damage as well. They'd just about caved-in the back door. A few more hits and they'd be in, and unless we could get a hold of a certified zombie pest control eradicator, we would not be able to get rid of them. I had a small window to make a call: We either made a hasty retreat and headed for the bomb shelter or we stayed here and fought it out. The pros of going downstairs: We were safe, they could not get in, end of story. The cons: I have claustrophobia and staying in that shelter would certainly bring on debilitating panic attacks. Once in, we could not get out. We'd run out of food and water eventually.

The pros of staying on the roof: We were free, free to starve, die of thirst or succumb to the elements. I was in the middle of a battle for our lives with basically three kids. This wasn't my ideal scenario, but they all could fight; they'd proven it before. The basic question though was *where were they safer?* I was not going to the shelter, but where should they go?

"Who votes for going to the bomb shelter?" I shouted over the gun reports.

Travis stopped and looked at me with a strange expression. Soon, everyone did.

"What did you say?" Jesse asked.

"I want to know who wants to go downstairs and into the shelter," I said again.

"You're putting this up for a vote dad? Really? Weird."

"Yeah okay, funny man. Right now, both choices aren't the best, but at least we have them. Soon enough, we'll be stuck on this roof. If anyone wants to go downstairs, now is the time to do so."

"What are you doing?" my son asked.

"Staying here."

"Me too, then."

"How long could we be stuck up here?" Meredith asked, looking up to the sky. The nights were getting cooler, and rain was always a possibility.

I almost said indefinitely. "Hard to say," I figured was the best compromise. We'd die of dehydration long before exposure.

"If we stay up here, shouldn't we get some supplies?"

"Out of the mouth of babes," I said. Meredith had said something that had resonated within me. She was thinking long game, where I was in the moment. "We gotta move. Trav, you and Meredith keep the bulkers at bay. Jesse, come with me. We're going to grab what we can."

As soon as my feet touched the ground, I started scanning everything. I actually used my brain for once. I know, it was almost as big a surprise to me as it is to you. There were two five-gallon containers of water against the wall. We'd used new gas containers, so at least they had handles, but trying to get something that heavy up a vertical ladder is no joke. There was some ammo, not much. Most of it by now was either upstairs or down. I thought about knocking on the door and confiscating it, but at some point, they might have to fight their way out, with or without our help.

I was on my fourth foraging expedition, Jesse was heading up with an armload of blankets and food. The smashing of material echoed around the room as the building shook. I thought I was in luck and it had held, then I heard the sound of the metal doorframe clanging off the marble flooring. They'd gained entry.

Jesse looked down. "Uncle?"

I motioned for him to go up as I brought my rifle to bear. All was quiet. That same feeling you get in the middle of the night when, for no obvious reason, you've been awakened. Your subconscious, in a valiant attempt to keep you safe from danger, has warned you to a potential grievous harm that your consciousness cannot pick up on. You sit in your bed, doing your paramount to hear anything while simultaneously hoping for the best. Yeah, it was kind of like that, though I knew this threat was real and there really wasn't a happy ending here. Remember how just a little while ago, I was thinking out my plans and ideas? Well apparently, I'd used up all my brain power because, for some reason, instead of heading straight for that ladder and relative safety, I did the exact opposite.

"Oh, so this is what they mean by death wish." I hissed through clenched teeth. "Why do you do this shit, Talbot?" I was berating myself even as I inched forward. "Is it some sort of morbid fascination with death? Is that it? I mean, because I'd really like to know. You can tell me, man, I won't say anything to anyone else." And yes, I was really having this conversation with myself. It was my way of whistling away the monsters and just as effective. I think the only reason I wasn't being trampled at this exact moment was that the bulker that had broken out the door was now wedged tight in the opening, like a cork in a wine bottle, and nothing short of the world's largest corkscrew was going to move him.

He growled this low mewling sound. His fingers, which

were pinned to his sides, flexed and curled. He shook with rage and impotence. I could have played a dangerous game of got your nose, as he was not going anywhere. Just because I dance all around the edges of insanity doesn't mean I have any desire to join her ranks, though. Some might argue I'm already there. As I entered into the large foyer, I looked left and right to make sure nothing had snuck in before this beast had lodged himself. I moved closer. I was now less than ten feet from one of the most dangerous animals on the planet. His red rimmed, thick, broken-blood-vessel eyes watched my every move, never once blinking. A tongue nearly the size of a well-portioned steak flicked out of his mouth repeatedly, though the color was anything but that of a fine piece of meat —more the gray of the post office walls.

He was a marvel as far as zombies go, approaching seven feet tall, a rounded head capable of stopping most calibers of bullets, a bulk that put him in excess of six hundred pounds, making him basically a zombie battering ram. How was this possible? Who could possibly be engineering zombies for specific jobs? Was it something coded into the virus weaponry or was there still a human facility cranking out these things to ferret out the few remaining people, and for what purpose? If it was something like the New World Order, and they wanted to stroke their massive egos by lording over people, then they should be herding them all up, not finding ways to root them out and crush them. I had my rifle less than three inches from the zombie's orbital socket.

"Survive this, motherfucker." He hissed at my words. I was about to pull the trigger when his body started twitching. I thought he was going through some sort of transition, like maybe he was turning into a zombie werewolf or something equally as terrifying. I backed up, maybe the first smart thing I'd done in the last five minutes. Although in hindsight, if he was changing into something even more dangerous, perhaps I should have put a bullet in his eye.

"Uncle Mike?" It was Jesse calling from the roof, trying to figure out what the hell I was doing.

"Coming." But I wasn't, not yet. For better or, the more likely, worse, I was staying until the fat zombie sang. The zombie's eyes rolled into the back of his head and his mouth opened even incredibly wider as if he could somehow unhinge his jaw like a snake. Something like a scream issued forth from his mouth, though it sounded more like giant rocks being ground against each other. It was deep, bassy, and definitely disturbing.

"Everything all right?"

"Yeah, mostly," I called up, still backing away. I could now see Jesse's head poking down through the hole while also keeping the vast majority of my attention on Billy Bulker. I don't know why I give them these Dr. Seuss names. I think it just makes them less fucking creepy in my head, and any advantage I can get in that department is fine with me. I swear Billy's eyes had done the impossible and gone completely around so that his irises were rolling back up. They were distant at first but then began to focus on me. Whatever was causing the incredible pain he was in, I think he was laying that blame completely at my feet.

"Yeah, well, maybe if your fat ass wasn't trying to come in here and eat me you wouldn't be in this predicament!" I yelled at him. He started shaking more, like I'd just rattled his cage or something. That was when the horror really started to kick in, the reason Billy looked like he was having grand mal seizures became clearly evident. It wasn't him doing the twitching, it was the five or so zombies behind, ripping through him to get in. When Billy's stomach began to expand outward, I was thinking of the *Alien* franchise and the little babies shooting through the chest and belly. It was kind of like that, but it was a full-grown zombie head instead, pretty much just as terrifying. It had literally eaten its way through one of its own. That was the first time I'd ever seen anything of the sort. I'd like to say it was because they were now looking at each other as food sources and would continue to kill each other, but I think this had more to do with frustration on the zombie's part. I mean the one stuck behind at least. He was starving for human flesh, and Billy was in the way, plain and simple. And until Eddie Eater could wield a chainsaw, he was using the only means available to him to rectify the situation.

He tore through the abdominal muscles and thick layers of fat, trying to get his shoulders through. Yellow ropes of gelatinous mass hung in his way, giving him a very jaundiced look as he kept gnawing away. The pure visceral horror I was feeling was directly the cause of my inaction. I cycled between running for my life and sanity, unloading a few dozen magazines of bullets into the creatures in front of me, or the more passive, just staring in blazing confusion with my mouth hanging agape. The level of revulsion was far and beyond anything I have seen in all my years, except for maybe the inside of a port-a-potty after a weeklong music festival in the heat of summer down in southern Tennessee, that is.

I did shoot a few rounds into the stomach of Billy, doing my damnedest to kill Eddie. I didn't stick around to see if I succeeded because Billy was beginning to bulge in another couple of places, and I'd taken all the mind-fuck I could for the remainder of my lifetime, no matter how long it may be. I nearly bowled Jesse over as I came rocketing out the sky hole.

"What's going on?" My nephew asked.

"Nothing you want to know, or that I ever want to talk about." I closed the lid, flipped the latch that was designed to hold a padlock, and frantically looked around for something to stick in the small hole to keep anything else from coming up. I ended up pulling out a drawstring from a hoodie and tying it around the locking device.

"Yeah, that should stop them." I said sarcastically.

"Can they climb ladders now?" Jesse looked about how I felt.

"Just being safe," is what I told him, but I was thinking in another week they'd be flying jets. Wouldn't that be fantastic to be hit by zombie strafing runs? Again, with some sort of silent cue, the zombies knew the building had been opened and were amassing around the ingress. They were beginning to flood in. In a perfect world, they all would have shoved themselves in there, and we could have sought help for our loved ones below. My heart panged knowing that zombies were directly above them and we could do little, if anything. I had everyone halt their shooting. At this point, there was no point to continue. They were inside, destroying everything, if the sounds of crashing furniture below were any indication. For a good long while, we watched those still outside, then when it became evident they were not going to give up their vigil, we retreated to the center of the roof where we could no longer see them nor them us. The smell was better, only marginally, but still better. Not much was said. We were all coming to grips with what was happening; then, just as the sun was going down, we got our first cosmic joke in the form of a far off thunder crash.

"Maybe it won't hit us," I said hopefully. That's when I knew weather was of the female persuasion. The wind picked up, and the temperature rapidly began to cool.

"Probably not, Dad," Travis said, good naturedly, just as the first drop nailed my forehead. It was a long, miserable night. Rain fell through its entirety. At first, we tried to use the knee wall that surrounded the building as cover from the elements, but that soon became an exercise in futility as swirling winds carried the water in every imaginable direction. There was not one part of me, or any of us, who was not completely soaked. I was sure that I'd gotten less wet while swimming. Shivering came in uncontrollable fits as muscles rubbed against each other doing their best to create heat from friction.

We amassed as one large ball of humanity in the west

corner, doing our best to share what little body heat we had. Due to my enhancements, I was feeling the effects of the weather less than those around me, and still I was freezing. I must have told them a dozen times I was so sorry for getting them into this mess. Sometime during the night, we'd somehow fallen asleep still huddled together. I awoke to a small songbird sitting on the wall above me. He chirped happily, his head swiveling back and forth while he looked down on me. The sun shone on my back. I could see mist rising up off of the kids as the water began to evaporate. We'd made it through the night. Now, I had to hope none of them had developed pneumonia. I stood. The bird took off. It wasn't the first time I'd wished I'd had wings so I could leave as easily.

I stretched and let the sun touch as much of me as I could allow. If I were alone, I would have peeled off all of my drenched clothes and let them dry. The squishy wet feeling of stuck on clothing was not one I relished. I figured the kids were already traumatized enough without me walking around nude. Oh, to be Trip for just an hour; he wouldn't care. Travis was up next. He stood and yawned then did what I didn't have the foresight to think of. He looked down the side of the building. I hoped that the rain had somehow dissuaded the zombies from pursuing us. From the look of resignation on my son's face, it was easy enough to say it had not.

He peeled off his shirt and laid it on the wall. I followed suit.

He shielded his eyes. "Shit. Dad, you should warn someone before you try to blind them."

"Hilarious. I haven't had much time to get a tan."

He sat back down, undid his shoes, and took his pants off. "That's much better," he said as he laid down against the roof. His boxers would dry soon enough. Jesse and Meredith were awake and noticed our various states of undress. Meredith was down to her bra and panties in under half a minute. I had previously figured her to be the most shy of the bunch. If anything, she cared the least. Jesse seemed slightly uncomfortable in his tighty-whities, but I also noticed he was in no rush to get his wet clothes back on.

"Uncle, there's no need to be bashful." Meredith was poking fun at me for still having my pants on.

"I don't think bashful is my problem," I told her.

"Geez, Dad. Your legs can't be any whiter than your chest." Travis was lying down, but still had it in him to give me a hard time.

"I'm fine," I told them.

"I bet his underwear is dirty," Meredith said to Jesse and Travis who both laughed.

"My underwear is *not* dirty!" I protested a little too loudly.

"Holes?" Meredith prodded. "Didn't your mom ever tell you to put clean underwear on in case you're ever in an accident?"

"She did, and I never understood why. If I was in a bad enough accident, I would need to go to the hospital, I would be covered in blood, and they would just cut the damn things off and start working on me without a care for the state of my undergarments. I was always of the belief that it was best that medical professionals be able to skip that particular step."

Meredith's eyebrows furrowed then spread as she smiled.

"What's he talking about?" Jesse asked.

"Our uncle, in addition to being a Marine, is also a commando," she said.

"A commando?" he asked.

"You know." She pointed down below.

"Oh, commando!" Jesse laughed.

Travis sat up. "Oh gross, Dad."

I shrugged. "It's always been more comfortable, I mean right up until this point, anyway."

"You can strip if you want to." Meredith giggled.

"Umm, no. Some of us are a little more modest."

"You do know things shrink if they stay wet too long, right?" Now she was outright laughing.

"I am not having this conversation with my niece!" I walked away. Okay, so maybe sloshed away is a better word. I ended up taking my boots and socks off and rolling my jeans up as best I could. When I was certain they were all lying down with their eyes closed, I went to the far side of the roof and just gave a quick once over to make sure there was no truth to what she'd said. I mean, I know on a fundamental level she was just screwing with me, but any men reading this know that you just don't take any chances when it comes to your junk. I'm happy to report everything seemed intact, even if there was some water-induced shriveling. Actually, more than likely, you couldn't give a shit, but I was happy, and this is my journal, so the entry stays.

It was about noon when my pants had really begun to dry off. It was at about this time when, ironically, I discovered I was pretty thirsty. We'd almost drowned in fresh water last night, and now, I felt like I was walking in the Sahara. Life is a funny fucking thing, and then you die. The kids were in various states of putting their clothes back on. The day wasn't overly warm, but the sun was out in full force, and we were on a black tar roof. It was plenty warm enough up there. For the first time in a very long time, I was completely at a loss as to what to do. I could tell they were starting to feel the beginning effects of exposure. They were much more lethargic than they had a right to be. I made sure everyone drank some water and ate a little. As I chewed, I looked at the hole to the floor, wondering if we could possibly fight our way out, when I looked up to see Travis grabbing at the electrical cable coming into the building. The parent in me nearly seized up as I saw him doing something so foolhardy, then it dawned on me that it wasn't live, hadn't been for months.

"Dad," he called, but I was already on my way.

"What do you think?" I asked him. The wire didn't look

like it could hold a stuffed teddy bear much less a full-grown man.

He leaned over and started yanking on it. I couldn't help it; I grabbed his pant waist.

"I'm not going to fall, Dad," he admonished me.

"Not with me holding you, you're not." I didn't let go, even though he clearly wanted me to. Hell, I was still holding on when he stood back up and had two feet firmly planted on the roof next to mine.

"You mind?" he asked. That's when I got the hint.

The cable stretched from the post office about fifty feet to a small series of shops—a mini strip mall, basically. It housed a furniture rental store, and once upon a time an awesome Chinese food restaurant, which I would just about give one prune-like right nut for some of right now. I think the other store was like a ninety-eight cent store. Apparently, this is where people went when they were priced out of the dollar store. I once passed this store, and they had a sign on the window advertising ninety-eight cent steak. I had to see it with my own two eyes. At a time when stew meat is $4.99 a pound, what the hell can ninety-eight cents buy you? I was picking up an order my brother had made for us and some other guests that were visiting, and I was starving. But come on, how many times are you going to come across something like this?

There was a huge freezer right by the doors stuffed with packages of this magic meat as if in preparation of hordes of shoppers coming in just for this special. I guess it worked because there I was. I picked one up. My first thought was it was pretty heavy. I was expecting something as thin as a slice of baloney. I was sort of right. The front of the package was a solid white. When I turned it over to peer at the contents, I thought I was looking at one of those old-time oddity displays they used to have for the traveling shows. Some *thing* hung in a suspension of frozen liquid; looked like the aborted fetus of a pigeon. It should have had little hands pressed up against the package in a nightmare inducing "let me out" pose. It was a shriveled up gray wad of a meat-like thing in about a pound of dirty water. I, for the life of me, could not imagine in what scenario this sounded like a decent item to buy. I think I would have picked up the cherry Pop-Tart knock offs, the savory sounding Fruity Squares, before I would have ever touched this experiment gone awry. Funny thing, though, three days later, and the day before I was heading back to Colorado, I went into the store. The fridge was no longer there. I figured the USDA or Inspector General or maybe the CIA, realizing that someone was trying to poison the populace, had removed the offending display.

"Excuse me," I asked the cashier, who seemed to be in the middle of a good-sized meth tweak.

"Yeah." She turned, her mouth flapping as she wildly chewed a giant wad of gum. Her right hand moved extremely fast as it continuously swatted away an imaginary bug by the side of her head. With her left, she was peeling off a series of scabs on her neck. I was transfixed, or horrified, while she pulled nickel-sized hunks of dried blood clots from her body. Yellow pus slowly oozed from the open sores.

I swallowed hard, doing my best to not keep staring at her. "The steaks, are there any more left?"

She snorted. No, I mean she literally snorted, not once and then caught herself like most people do, but rather four or five times, to the point where snot started coming out of her right nostril.

"This was so not worth it." I said, heading for the door, trying to figure out a way to open it without using any part of my body. A store that charged ninety-eight cents for everything certainly couldn't afford automatic doors.

"Mister, them there steaks were gone that very same day. Iffen you want the good deals, you gotta get up early like them birds that like them worms."

And there it was. That was what that steak looked like:

fucking worms. I wouldn't doubt if it was indeed parasites found in the cows and the butcher had found a loophole and was able to sell it as beef because the thing fed off beef or something. Then she completely threw me for a loop when she told me that it was the Chinese food restaurant "that had done bought them all." I maybe would have flipped her off if I wasn't in such a rush to go buy an industrial sized bottle of Tums, Kaopectate, and ipecac.

I came back from my culinary nightmare. By now, we'd aroused the curiosity of the rest of the group. Like we were synchronizing our movements. We looked to the wire to where it connected to both buildings and then down to the horde below, who had as of yet not looked up. I put one leg over the wall and grabbed the line again, expecting some inordinate amount of electricity to stop my heart and burn my hair.

"Wait, Uncle. What are you doing?" Meredith asked.

"Going for help."

"You're double my weight."

"Probably."

"You think that thing is going to hold?"

"Only one way to find out."

"Don't you think it would be better if someone lighter tried?"

I looked to my small group, one of which I was clearly in charge of protecting. "No."

"Dad, I could go," Travis said.

"You could, but I'm the only one doing it."

"What if the wire breaks?" Jesse asked.

"Are you taking over Justin's role of Captain Obvious?" I asked. "Listen, if anyone is going to take the plunge. Shit, wrong word. If anyone is going to walk this high wire, it's going to be me. I'm not going to stand here and put one of you guys in danger. I should be fine. That wire probably weighs over a hundred pounds, and the fasteners should be rated to hold at least double that."

"We've all lost weight, Uncle, but I still don't think you weigh a hundred pounds."

"Don't go using math on me, Meredith. This isn't up for debate. I'm the king right now, and I'm giving the orders."

Yup, I was scared, petrified, in fact; heights and I weren't on speaking terms. We had more like an ass-clenching agreement. I sat on the edge of the wall, my legs dangling over, thinking about how best to grab the wire without jumping on to it and adding too much undue stress.

"You taking your rifle?" Travis asked.

"Hmm, one rifle, three full magazines, that's got to be an extra fifteen pounds." Meredith said.

"Thanks for the update. I'll be sure to tell your dad how helpful you were," I told Meredith as I placed the rifle across my back and tightened the buckle that was resting uncomfortably on my sternum. "This sucks." My hands were shaking. No matter how I tried to concentrate on stopping them, they wouldn't.

"Are you sure about this?" Meredith, ever the constant kidder, was actually serious.

"I wish I talked out loud less," I told her.

"There could be another way," she finished, but I was already on the move. With my right hand, I grabbed the wire right where it went into the building. I put the majority of my weight on the line and scooted my ass off the wall. My legs swung out, and I simultaneously grabbed with my left hand and pulled my body up to wrap my legs around the line. My head was at an uncomfortable angle, being too close to the post office. I was sort of screwed, a surge of panic sent a cascade of needles throughout my body. I was in no position to climb back up, and I was too petrified to move.

"This is fucking great." I moved just enough that my head was free of the building. I turned to the side, noting how far up I was and what waited below in the event I slipped or the bracket gave.

"You should move," Jesse prodded.

"Me and you are going to talk when I get back," I told him. It was what I needed, though. With my hands behind and over my head, I began to push off on the wire, forcing myself forward. At first, it wasn't horrible. Sort of reminded me of my long-ago Marine Corps days. Then, as I got further away from the building, the line began to sag something fierce. The good thing was that if I fell, the odds I'd survive were greatly improved—I mean at least until the zombies started tearing in to me, but at least the meat wouldn't be all bruised up for them. I felt like I was on a damn bungee cord the way the thing just kept dipping down. The zombies still weren't looking up, but we were within feet of each other. If I so desired to hang by my legs, I'm pretty sure I could have dragged my fingertips across the NBA wannabes' heads. Just so we're clear, I didn't want to. I'm just saying I could have.

I was at this lowest point when I felt a heavy vibration on the cord. I bent my head back as far as I could so I could see back the way I'd come. The kids weren't looking at me but rather the building coupling. They were pointing animatedly and reaching for it. That didn't bode well. They could have yelled something to me, but what was the point? There wasn't much I could do. So far, I'd had a little bit of Irish luck going for me as the zombies had still not noticed my high-wire act. That's the problem with having English origins though, us and the Irish don't see eye to eye very often and they were only going to yield me so much good measure. I did the only thing afforded to me, and no, it wasn't vomit. I started moving faster. It got significantly harder now, though, as I was forcing my way up against gravity and at a fairly steep angle.

"When are you ever going to start thinking things through?" I berated myself. I was splashing zombies in fat drops of sweat. All I can figure is that they thought it was raining again. My hands were beginning to cramp up, and the muscles in my arms were beginning to thrum with exertion and the constant push of adrenaline.

"Hurry!" Meredith shouted out. I didn't bother to waste any time looking back, really no sense. I mean, if I were in the middle of a roadway and a truck was barreling down on me, then perhaps it would be a good idea to look back and figure out which way to dive. But really, all I needed to know was that the bracket was failing, and once that did—well, I'd be swinging through the air. I got further than I thought I would when I heard the loud *twang*. Sounded a lot like a light saber cutting through the air. Most of you should get that reference; if not, maybe think of the largest known humming bird whizzing by your ear at near-record speed. I swung for not more than ten feet or so. My knuckles took the brunt of the assault as they slammed into the cinder block wall. The trailing edge of the wire as it whipped down onto the zombies was enough to get their attention. I was now hanging completely upside down *a la* Spider-Man and the zombies were staring back.

"You should climb up!" Jesse shouted.

"I'm going to kill him," I muttered. Unlike Spider-Man, I could not reel myself in. I had to do a relatively ninja-like move, and I was so not feeling it at this very moment. I twisted my torso and unlatched my crossed legs. In conjunction with that, I also released my death grip. My hands slid from the sweat as I repositioned them and once again clamped down. I again twisted my legs around the line, clamping a piece between the bottom of my right heel and the top of my left foot. It afforded my arms a small respite. I was by no means out of the woods. My bleeding knuckles were doing what they do best: bleed. The blood was bringing zombies in my direction. I had another eight or so feet to climb, which wasn't bad, but now there was only one cable bracket left, and it was holding me and the weight of the dangling cable. My life clock was rapidly draining down to zero. The way I saw it was

I had two options: Climb down quickly and deal with the zombies down below or go up and get on the roof to reweigh my situation.

For right or wrong, I chose up. I was happy to see that the bracket on this side was still holding perfectly. Figured this one was made in the good old US and the other in China; biases die hard. The relief that spread over me as I placed my arm on the roof was palpable. I just wished there was a handhold, something I could pull myself up with. I had to keep using my legs, feeding more cable through and then pushing up. Eventually, I had my chest on the roof and was able to get into a push up-type position and pull the rest of me over. Once I was certain I was completely on, I rolled over.

"You all right?" Travis asked.

I had enough energy to give a thumbs up, and that was about it. I caught my breath and stocked back up on my psyche reserves before I once again stood. On the far side of the little mall was a cluster of trees, close enough to the edge of the building that I should be able to reach over and grab a decent enough branch to aid in my descent. I really wanted to take a moment to figure out what I was going to do when I got there, though. Of course, I was on the move almost immediately. Crossing over to the area devoid of enemies.

"You're about as smart as a gravy boat, Mike," I said while I grabbed a branch that had the decency to almost be resting on the roof. I thanked the oak profusely as I climbed out on the limb. "I do this a lot, don't I?" I mean figuratively, although I guess literally now as well.

The obvious choice was the firehouse, providing that it still had ladder trucks in it. It did not. We'd checked when we were looking for suitable locations to move the family to. I started thinking about going to a hardware store and getting a cherry picker, as they are sometimes referred to, or a bucket lift. Good idea in theory, but they are slow and not defendable. Then the idea that should have been the first was the last. I needed a utility truck. It had the cherry picker built in. I turned to look at the kids, who were watching me. I wanted to tell them what I was up to, but I was in a zombie-free zone, and I really wanted to keep it that way. I was going to be gone for a while. The utility company was a good four miles from my present location. I'd jog for a bit, but even if everything went as smooth as silk, I'd still be an hour. And considering nothing had gone smoothly in a good long while, I wasn't too firm on that timeline. I waved and was gone.

I moved stealthily for a good block or two, just to make sure that I was putting some distance between the zombies and me and that I didn't stumble onto or into another lair. I was at the empty fire station when I came back out on to the roadway and decided to beat feet. I took a right up a ramp to get onto Route One and was now a half mile closer to my destination. A cool breeze was coming off the ocean and directly into my face. It was welcome after the foul odor I'd been smelling for the past twenty-four hours. I was in fairly good spirits as I ran, that was until I came into view of the bridge that passed over the Passagassawakeag River. Yeah, I sure as shit didn't make that up. Means something like, "You fish on your side and I'll fish on mine." Even the Native Americans weren't too fond of too many people crowding in on their space. People haven't liked people since there were people. I find it strange that we as a species feel the need to congregate in large groups like cities but then make sure we have our own space clearly delineated from others. With doors, fences, and locks. What other proof do you need to realize we don't like each other?

Sometimes it's a blessing to have a mind that wanders. Makes focusing on any one problem a difficult feat, which means I generally forget what's wrong. Then sometimes it's a curse because I can't concentrate on fixing any one problem. There were zombies on the bridge, ten as a matter of fact. Then as if to reiterate my point, I started singing the schoolyard song, "Ten Little Indians." Not politically correct, but pretty sure the zombies weren't going to have a protesting demonstration any time soon. I kept jogging, getting closer with each footfall. I weighed my options: take up position and remove them with extreme prejudice or merely go for the outrun mode. It had to be by bullet. Sure, it would draw more zombies, but if I tried to get past them, they would just follow me forever.

I put my rifle up to my shoulder and began to sing softly. "Ten little zombies standing in a line. One shuffled home then there were nine." I rocked back just as the top of the zombie's head exploded in a plume of red and white. "Nine little zombies, screwing with fate. One fucked off and then there were eight." I once again rocked back. I'd spoken too soon. I clipped the zombie on the side of the face, shredding a hole through a fair amount of its teeth and maybe part of its jaw. He turned and was looking straight at me. As if on cue, they all turned. Yup, they definitely talked. My next bullet was pretty close to dead center in his forehead. He was down, but the eight little zombies were now running my way. It was okay, though. I had time and bullets. "Eight little zombies, abominations of Heaven. One went to sleep and then there were seven." It was slightly low, as it obliterated her nose, but the effect was the same: She went down in a tangle of arms and elbows.

I was about to start the next line when I heard something behind me. I almost blew it off. It was far away and sounded like a muffled slap. In this world, it wasn't a good idea to ignore extraneous noises, though. I turned, pretty sure I blanched—didn't have a mirror so I couldn't tell for sure—but my head got light for a second, so I'm thinking it's safe to assume my blood was running cold. There were enough zombies coming up on my rear they could have filled the bleachers for the high school football team's homecoming game. That was something I did not have enough bullets for.

It was time to run. I went toward the seven, keeping my rifle up, hoping I could diminish the threat to the front. I had a good quarter mile on those to the back of me and a rapidly closing hundred yards with those to the front. I thought about diving into the water once I got on the bridge, but it was at least a hundred-foot drop, and at that height, it would be like swan diving onto concrete. And then, well there's that whole scared of heights shit, so that probably wasn't going to happen anyway.

I killed one more and sufficiently wounded another by cracking its femur as to be out of the picture. Five was still plenty enough to do the damage. I hopped over the concrete barricade that protected pedestrians from some of the worst drivers: you know, drunks, texting teenagers, and women. I got as close to the metal barricade that signified a suicide leap as I could while the zombies and I came into close proximity. They slammed into the barricade, some with enough force to break toes or crack kneecaps. With their hands outstretched, they clutched at my clothing. Fingernails snapped off, fingers broke, and still they grabbed at me. When I broke free, the chase was on. Two figured out the barrier and got over it. Two more kept pace on the outside. The one that had shattered his kneecap was still trying, God bless his diseased little heart as he limped along.

The ones to my immediate left were keeping pace easily enough. Probably could have passed me by at any time if this were a road race. Extremely difficult to outrun an opponent whose whole strategy is sprint, continually. I was coming near to the end of the bridge and the slight protection the barricade afforded. Didn't matter much. The two behind me were close enough that if I passed gas they would get a little payback for all the olfactory damage they'd given everyone else. The larger group to the rear halved their gap. I wasn't winded, not yet, but it was only a matter of time. I shook my head when, with my rapid look back and evaluation of the trailing group, I saw a woman. Had to have been somewhere north of eighty, easy. She was hauling ass next to what looked like a man a third her age. How the fuck is zombie-ism the fountain of youth? Her blue curly hair swayed atop her head. A tattered gray shawl flowed behind her like Super Grandma's cape. Surreal didn't even begin to describe the scene.

I thought I might be in luck if she caught me. With her mouth pulled back like it was, I think she'd left her dentures on her nightstand, forever trapped in a glass filled with effervescent cleaning bubbles. I had somewhere in the neighborhood of a mile to get to the Central Maine Power yard. There was no way I could make it, not in a straight shot. I took a hard right as soon as I was over the bridge. This led to a nursing home, or assisted living facility as our new politically correct world liked to call them. Fucking stupid. So when I was filling holes for the state, I wasn't a ditch digger; I was a roadway engineer. Not sure why people are so hung up on labels, or how it could possibly matter. The bigger question right now was why did I even care? Zombie fingertips were scraping against the base of my spine seeking purchase. It was a moderate slope down to the house that had an impressive view of the ocean. Although my mother never gave a shit about that, she was always too busy berating the staff for being too fat, too lazy, too slow. Why anyone would want to give the very people that controlled every aspect of your life grief was something that will always amaze me.

I was heading toward the home my mother stayed at until the end. Would it be irony if I were to die there as well? No, I had nothing to do with her fate; the pack and a half habit for sixty years was more likely the culprit. Although there was the argument that my behavior was what pushed her to that practice of lighting up. I shook my head. "Mom, I know we didn't always see eye to eye. Shit, I don't even think we looked at each other's faces much. Still, you're family, though, and I could really use a solid right now."

One of the zombies had taken a fall right behind me. I couldn't chance looking back to see if he'd wiped out any others. I saw his arm slide past on the wet grass before I left him behind with a grass-stained shirt—and no matter how much Tide he used, it would never come out, no matter what the commercials said. It did indeed seem as if my mom was looking out for her wayward son. The door to the facility was propped open with a turned over wheelchair. There were a couple of bonuses to this. First, and foremost, I could get in, and second, and maybe just as important, the previous occupants who weren't already food but zombies could have gotten out. Last thing I wanted was to be gummed to death. It would be incredibly embarrassing because, first, I'd start laughing as the sensation would have a tickling quality. This would change when their jawbones finally worked their way through their rotten gums and I was starting to get torn apart by bone instead of just teeth. Yeah, it wouldn't be so funny then.

There were a lot of actions that had to happen nearly simultaneously in order for my continued survival to continue. I bounded up the three steps on the front porch in one leap. My living-challenged friends had a little more difficulty. I heard knees, elbows, and chins smack off the wooden decking as they collided at high speed. A few ejected teeth flew past my head and landed on the polished linoleum floor of the home's foyer. I vaulted over the wheelchair. My hope was that, with my trailing leg, I would push the chair out of the way and the door would close behind me, having the closest zombies smash face first into the heavy wooden door. Want to know what really happened? I jumped too high. The top of my head struck the doorframe, abruptly ending my short flight. My head lost all its forward momentum but not my legs; they kept sailing into the house. I looked like I was getting ready to slide into second base. I was horizontal to the ground and maybe two feet off of it. Want to know what saved my life? Got to imagine it was Benny. You see, Benny was the maintenance slash janitor of the building, and he had a serious case of obsessive-compulsive disorder. I'd met him a few times. I don't think he liked me much. I always tended to walk over his freshly scrubbed floors after tracking in all manner of debris from outside. I swear I would come down the sidewalk on a warm dry day, wipe my feet extensively on the welcome mat outside, and yet, as soon as I walked in, branches, rocks, small mammals, and their offal would fall off my shoes.

And no matter when I came, he was right by the door, with mop in hand, to scowl at me as I passed by. If he could have beat me mercilessly with that stick and gotten away with it, I believe he would have. It was the high gloss that he had to have on that floor that ultimately saved my life. When my hip, foot, and head smacked off the floor, I just slid—I mean to the point where it looked absurd. Almost like a movie parody, I just kept going: through the foyer, through the receiving room, and halfway into the back hallway. Might have kept going if I hadn't been placing my hands down, trying to get traction so I could get back up on my feet. Going back to shut the front door was out of the question. Zombies were already streaming inside. I had an equally, if not better, idea now anyway. For the quickest of seconds, the early praise I had for Benny turned sour as my feet rapidly moved in place while they sought a friction they could not find.

It was the door to the bathroom that proved my salvation as I grabbed the handle and pulled myself forward. I took a left when I got out of the hallway. I was now looking at the back door and the ocean. I opened the door, making sure to close it tightly before I started running down to the shoreline. I flipped a bird over my shoulder.

"That's right, Talbot. Piss off the natives." I headed to the ocean. I'd like to say beach, but those are few and far between in Maine. Sure, there was plenty of coastline, but very little of what you would call a traditional beach. It was mostly *slippery as wet rubber, sharp as razor blades, hard as my head* rocks on the shoreline. This was punctuated with slimy seaweed and sand fleas. Yup, that generally made up the Maine coastline. No white sand beaches or little umbrella drinks here, not that you'd want to go in anyway. The water, even in the middle of August, was cold enough to freeze a witch's ti—. Well, you probably know where I was going with that.

My plan was to follow along the edge of the water. With Maine's propensity for corners and crags, the journey would most likely be triple the length but uncontrolled by zombies, and that was just fine. I slowed down to a slight jog, allowing my body to catch its breath. I had a hitch in my lungs and a stitch in my side from the earlier pursuit and a constant nagging worry for those I'd left behind. It was hard to look out at the sun kissing the water. The scenery was beautiful, and I could appreciate it to a degree. It's just that I wish the world wasn't so tainted. It was impossible to stop and smell the roses when the air had an inclination to smell like dead animals shoved up randy assholes. And it was difficult to take the time and appreciate things when you were constantly being pursued. We were steadily moving from true living to merely surviving. It was not a shift you were cognizant of, but it changed everything. Regular life, which was already fraught with its inherent pitfalls, was now tenfold as hard.

I might have devolved into a small pity party if I hadn't taken that opportunity to take one quick glance back at the nursing home. I was too far away to make out any particulars, but it was clear enough to see that the zombies had busted through the door and maybe even some of the big picture windows. The pursuit hadn't started yet; I got the feeling that zombies had a difficult time seeing things far away. It was about time they had some sort of limitation. Although burning in the sun like some other monsters I'd encountered would have been more preferable. I wondered how Jack was doing with his particular type of monster. The gods really must get a kick out of all the alternate realities they toss out there. I wonder if they have brainstorm sessions where they just start naming horrible creatures and see if people can deal with them. We must be an atrocious species that they're in such a rush to end our lives. Or who knows, maybe it's fun as hell for them to watch us run around like idiots. I mean, I used to think it was fun to cook ants under a magnifying glass. Most likely the same thing for them. Would I have unleashed zombie ants on the ant hives I've terrorized if I could? Sure, I would have. Kids are nearly insane. Doubt me? Think of all the asinine things they do. What won't they put in their mouths? What won't they dive off of? What situations won't they put themselves in? Why do you think parents go prematurely gray or bald? Because it takes a lot of effort to keep crazy Cathy and insane Isaac from running into traffic with nothing more on than a pair of wet diapers and sand pails on their heads.

Good to know that gods are juvenile. Where the fuck are their parents to tell them they're little assholes! I started running again, partly to forget about the pain I was in both internally and externally. I didn't know then, but I'd already been spotted and the chase was afoot again. I was starting to wonder how much farther I had to go and had even begun to slow down before I realized I was no longer alone. The shore was getting crowded like tourist season had officially begun and the visitors needed to claim their square footage of beach before there was none left. They were coming out from the yard to my side and some were behind. I didn't know if I had enough left to outpace them. My options were limited: stop and make a destined-to-fail stand or head into the water. I didn't think zombies swam, but they would follow into the water. I'd have to go far enough out that they would not be able to reach up from the depths and pull me down into a watery grave.

It's fairly well known, at least in my head, that I have a dislike for water that is not in little cubes cooling my iced tea or coming out of a showerhead. The odds that there were sharks in this water were negligible. Stupid *Jaws* for putting that imagery into my head. Even so, it was fall. The water was frigid. There were tides and currents. I was fully dressed, and I was only a moderate swimmer.

"Fuck" was my resignation word as I took a sharp right and headed straight in. The water wasn't horrible as it slapped around my calves and thighs. When it hit my nether regions, it felt like someone was snapping my balls with rubber bands. If you're a guy, I'm pretty sure I have your attention right now. I began to take in quick, unfulfilling breaths as I dealt with this most unwelcome sensation. If there was any hesitation on the part of the zombies, they didn't show it while they splashed in, the closest less than twenty feet away when I was nearly at nipple-shattering level. I had to keep my jaw clenched to keep my teeth from breaking against each other like rogue waves against a cliff. Before I needed to start swimming, I once again cinched my rifle against my back. I could only hope the water didn't foul it up beyond being able to use it. If I knew for sure that it would, I'd just let it go. Between it and the weight of the bullets, my pants, and boots, this was already going to be an arduous journey.

I had a slight panic attack when I felt something rub up against my leg. Fuck it. There was nothing "slight" about it. I started smacking the water and pushing away. Actually fell over into the water, submerging my head, and got a briny solution up my nose and in my mouth. I stood back up and spat out the water. I wanted to laugh, I'd damn near pissed myself because of seaweed, but I had other real problems. The zombies were advancing, and the thought of being eaten in the water, for some reason, seemed more terrifying. I swam, putting as much depth as possible between me and my pursuers. As I hoped, most of the slimy bastards went under, although on retrospect, that was pretty scary as well. I was shooting for the whole "out of sight, out of mind" perspective but not knowing where they were was worse. As fate would have it, some of the zombies had positive buoyancy and were able to stay afloat. I'm sure their legs were still moving, but the arms had not got the message and floated uselessly out in front. I had a feeling they were going to bob in the ocean like message-laden bottles for a good, long time. I felt sorry for the people where these things finally made landfall. The message they were delivering was not one anyone wanted.

I was leaving the bobbers behind, and that was good. I could not see the bottom dwellers, and that was good as well, at least for a little while. My marathon sprint and my less than smooth swimming skills were using up my reserves, which didn't run too deep thanks to the events of the last few days. I started to angle back so that I could at least walk on the bottom. The problem was somewhere along my wet jaunt along the coast the ledge had dropped out where I was. I dipped down when I thought I was in safe range of the ocean floor, and my head went down. In fact, I sunk like a stone for a good ten feet. I had still not made contact by the time I began to panic and flail about spasmodically. By the time I broke the surface, I'd taken a decent-size swallow of whale piss laced with squid shit, yes that's what I feel the majority of ocean water is composed of. Think about it, everything, and I mean *everything*, is done in the ocean. Animals crap, urinate, they fertilize their eggs, they have sex, they have babies, they die, they decay, all in the very substance I was now desperately trying to dispel from my lungs. Yeah, you should have maybe packed that thought along with you the last time you went to the beach with your picnic baskets and kids. You'd basically been telling your kids to go swim in a cesspool.

I'd been hoping to cycle through better thoughts as I drowned. I just kept moving my legs and arms, not always in a coordinated manner but at least in the general direction of the shore, which had a *Twilight Zone* thing going on: No matter how hard I tried to get closer, it moved farther away. I knew I should have begged off those last twenty or thirty times I'd dosed on acid. Yeah, it must have just been those last few times that had fucked with my mind. I was coming to my furthest limits of what I could endure. The back of my left leg had seized in a mind-numbing charley-horse. I had to keep it as straight as a board or the muscle would seize up, and in all likelihood, unravel from either the back of my knee or the top of my ankle, or maybe it would unravel from both ends at the same time. Wouldn't that be special? I was down to kicking out with one leg, desperately keeping the other still in the hopes it would stop feeling like a taut rope getting ready to break, when finally I felt the toe of my boot scrape bottom— at least I hoped it was. If I went down in search of a bottom-less pool again, the odds were good I wasn't coming back up.

I stretched out as long as I could and let my weight sag. I was spent. My mouth was about the width of my lip above the water. Just about every time the wind blew or a minnow left a wake behind his swimming body, water would flood into me like the side of the Titanic. I started hopping farther in. My arms were so sore, just getting them up was a chore. Some-where in the back of my head, I was sure that a large part of my problem was the hypothermia leeching off all my energy. If I stayed in much longer, it wasn't going to matter if the zombies caught me or that I'd contracted a serious case of dysentery. I'd die of exposure, and dead was dead. It didn't much matter how you got there. If I died, my son, nephew, and niece's chance of survival became grim. Those in the vault would fare better, but for only so long. As an adult and a parent, and maybe just the figurehead leader of the Talbot household, life was already stressful enough. I did all in my power to provide a better life for my offspring, but now, well now, all of my actions had to be weighed with how it would better their chances of survival. I did not envy anyone, espe-cially me, in that position.

The panic had abated. The water was now about chest

high. I took in long breaths and relaxed as best I could. Wasn't necessarily easy, as the zombie bobbers were constantly turning their heads so they could keep their eyes on me. Didn't matter to them they couldn't get to me. It was unnerving, but it was all right. It wasn't the first time I'd be the center of a zombie audience. I could feel goose bumps the size of engorged ticks forming on the upper half of my body. I needed to get out of the water and soon. The problem was the zombies on the shoreline that were perfectly content to walk along on the warm, dry edge of the water. They knew, they fucking knew my path involved going back that way, and now that I was able to keep my head above the water line, some of the zombies joined me in the water. The chase was back on, definitely at a slower pace, I was already tanked, the zombies easily kept pace they were not at all concerned with their non-existent stamina issues. Maybe at some point they drop and die from exhaustion like an over taxed horse. Although I'd yet to see it, and I'd fall long before they did.

I moved closer to shore. I was about waist high. I was afraid if I went in any closer, those on the beach would come out. The only piece of decent news in the whole damn thing was that there had to be a current or something because the bobbers were heading out, and good fucking riddance. Of course, that did little for the ones behind me struggling to catch up. The hindrance of pushing through the water seemed to be messing with their motor skills. I could stay ahead of them, but I'd never be able to outdistance those on the shore, who seemed to be out on a leisurely stroll. I was in a bit of a pickle, and I hate pickles. I have my reasons. There was a craggy knoll about a quarter of a mile up. The outcropping of rock was where I was going to have to marshal all my strength and make a run for it. While they were struggling to get over the rocks, I hoped I could make enough distance to get to the Central Maine Power yard. Most of the zombies to the rear were falling behind, but there were always a few smart ones in the bunch. The brainiacs, which had been a sort of aberration in the beginning of the z-poc, seemed to be getting more and more common.

I hate to beat a dead horse, actually, screw him; why would he care? It bears repeating that the zombies were becoming smarter at a geometric pace. I had no doubt in my mind that eventually they would learn how to use tools to their advantage, maybe even guns. Then what? How could any human holdouts survive? Would roving bands of zombies be able to drive and fire out the windows? Humanity wasn't even on its last legs; we were now low-crawling our way out into a footnote of history. Would zombies start opening schools and teach about the vanquished humans? I guess it was possible. Not sure what the fuckers were going to eat when we were gone, but shit, man had been plaguing, ravaging, destroying (you chose the appropriate verb) the planet for ten thousand years, so maybe the zombies should have a turn. Yeah, I actually had that thought. You have all sorts of sour thoughts when your nuts have crawled up inside your belly, seeking some sort of internal heat, and you're pretty sure you're about to become a meal for an opponent that you sort of hoped would finally show so you could get out of the doldrums of an ordinary life. Fuck, I've always hated that saying, "Be careful what you wish for." Now even more so.

I stopped about a hundred yards from being parallel to the rocks. I needed to give my body just a second or two to recoup. The zombies on the shore stopped as well, not the waders though. I bent at the waist as a wave of nausea passed over me. Pretty sure that was a slight case of dehydration letting me know it was lurking in the back corners of my body as well.

"Enemies from within and without," I said as I stood. "You asshats ready?" I started a slight jog at an angle to the beach that I hoped would bring me just past the jetty and into the clear. As I came abreast of the rocks, my plan mostly worked. A good number of them struggled to get over, but of course, I had a few Zeinsteins that figured it would be better to get in the water and around that way.

"I hate you guys," I breathed out. I was about knee level and pushing as hard as I could to get into shallower water. I was high-lifting my legs, which wasn't doing any wonders for my energy level. Ankle level, then just the soles of my boots, and then a semblance of sand. I was free of the ocean. That was a start. I needed to get back on the roadway. I had no idea of exactly where I was in relation to where I needed to be. This wasn't my typical view of the area. I had a good hundred-yard lead. I was just stepping on to someone's lawn as they were about to get out of the water; those on the rocks had still not appeared. The cramp that had threatened to drown me earlier came back with a vengeance. I immediately let go any thought of bending my leg. If I did, I would feel compelled to stretch it back out, and I would tear it, plain and simple. I was hampered. I looked like any heroine in any horror movie, although I didn't have a twisted ankle. I was dragging my useless leg behind me in that classic pose. Now all I needed was some blond hair, big breasts, and maybe a world-class scream and we'd be all set. And maybe a director to yell "cut" at any fucking moment would be epic as well.

I needed a break. There was no way I could outrun them now. Apparently, I had a god or two on my side. The zombies in the surf were now fighting a particularly nasty set of waves that had picked up seemingly from nowhere. I'd take it; I'd take help from anywhere at this point. Who knows, maybe they just wanted me to survive just a bit longer so I could die in a more horrific manner. Fine, every second was already precious, I'd take what was given. Even got a grim smile when I watched a zombie get bowled over by a decent four-foot wave. Two minutes earlier, and I would have been in those and I wouldn't have fared as well. I didn't like my prospects as I looked into the small yard. It was a vacation cottage. It was nice enough, and had I been able to afford it when the world was normal, I would have loved to stay here and enjoy the views it afforded. But it was small and looked to only be one floor.

"Beggars can't be choosers," I mumbled through gritted teeth. My leg would not loosen up, no matter how much I reached behind and tried to untwist the knot my hamstring was in. The door was locked; so was the window right up until I put a rock through it. I was so tired and in so much pain, I didn't even bother to announce myself. I realized this as half of my body was inside and my legs were outside. If I was intruding on someone's abode, I was about to become the human version of Swiss cheese. I kicked out with my legs when I had no handholds to grab onto. A scream forced its way from my throat while I fell to the hardwood floor. My left leg was bent so tightly I thought my knee was going to pop. Tears of pain leaked from the corners of my eyes. Every instinct of mine begged me to force my leg open at all costs. Instead, I vigorously rubbed the muscle, doing my best to coax it free. I was in danger of cracking my teeth, they were slammed so tightly together. I don't know how long it took to ease my leg down. Time seemed to have stopped as I breathed through every agonizing second.

When I could finally get my leg straight, the next thing was to get the rifle off my back and then lie on the floor with my quivering arms stretched out so that I could stare at the ceiling. Maybe it was tears of joy now, but they were still coming out. Of course, they were manly tears much like the scream had been; I just wanted to get that part out there. This was one small victory in what needed to be a long string of them. When I was sort of certain I could move without my leg once again binding like a Chinese woman's foot in the 1800s, I pushed myself up off the floor so I could get a quick assessment of my surroundings. First things first though. I dragged the kitchen table over. It was made of a good, strong oak. I only noted that because it was as heavy as you might expect, and my weakened condition made it more difficult to wrestle into place in front of the broken window. It wasn't perfect, but it would have to do. A card table would have been a pain in the ass for me to maneuver in the bad way I was in.

I moved as far away from the window as I could. Zombies relied heavily on their sense of smell. Luckily, they weren't bloodhounds. They couldn't trail me like that, but if they caught a whiff of me on the wind, they would investigate. A quick check of the kitchen revealed it had all the amenities one would expect from a rental: mismatched dishes and glasses, even some old jelly container glasses, a drawer of beat up silverware that had not a trace of silver, and absolutely no food. I was about as close to shouting out a swear as I'd ever been when a form passed by the kitchen window. The zombies had found their way. I ducked down, making sure to keep my left leg stretched out in front of me. Looked like one of those crazy Russian dancers. It was not a pose I could hold for long. It was easier to get all the way down onto my butt. I scooted out of there like a dog with worms, back into the living room. If any of the zombies took a second to look into the windows, I would appear like a prized jewel. There was a small hallway that led to what I imagined was a bedroom. I hoped it had a closet. I moved over to my rifle, placed it on my lap, and kept moving.

"Well, I wasn't expecting that." I was constantly looking over my shoulder to navigate as I dragged myself along. There was indeed a small bedroom at the end of the hall, but off to the right, where I figured there was a bathroom, was instead a ladder that led to a small deck, and there was a door off of that. I was intrigued. Felt like a seven-year-old discovering a fort. A leg on the verge of quitting and two arms that had as much substance as wet spaghetti, check. Going up the ladder to investigate? Double check. It's amazing how you forget about all that ails you when you start to tap into the inner-child part of yourself. I still wasn't going to move my left leg anytime soon, but the other three extremities made the climb up fairly easy enough. When I got to the top of the ladder and onto the landing, I realized that standing would only be achieved in a stooped fashion. I reached up and back to turn the handle to the door. I was rewarded with a small bed, a single by the size of it, actually just a mattress on the floor, but it was made and it looked like a nice comfortable albeit dusty quilt was on top of it.

A small nightstand with an artfully arranged bunch of seashells and an unadorned lamp were the only other furniture in the room. It was clear you could not do much more than sleep in this room, and right now, that was exactly what I needed. I usually have a problem with sleeping in a strange bed. This time though, I was too tired, wet, and hurting to give a shit. I shut the small door and stripped down completely, just now realizing how cold and clammy my skin was as I crawled underneath the covers. It wasn't immediately that I fell asleep, but it was pretty damn close.

10

MIKE JOURNAL ENTRY 9

I AWOKE THE NEXT MORNING WITH A START. NEARLY TOOK OFF the top of my head when I sat up quickly. I was trying to figure out where the hell I was, and more importantly, why I was naked. Figured BT was trying to take advantage of me. That gave me a smile. I missed the man. Then everything crashed back into me: the kids, the roof, the zombies, my leg. I was pretty sure I hadn't slept for two days because my clothes were still slightly damp, though I sort of wished I had. The idea of putting them on while my skin was salted over from the ocean was not all that appealing. The choices were limited. Pretty sure the kids wouldn't want to be rescued from me in that condition. I could see my son, saying "pass" when I showed up in the truck. I grabbed my damp clothes and opened the door.

"Zombie." I said softly. It was the smell. It wasn't overpowering, not at all, almost a ghost of the scent. Like I'd been visited by an ethereal living dead one. I placed my clothes down and grabbed my rifle, hesitant to use it even if I needed it. If I was feeling sticky from my time in the water, how was my rifle faring? I wasn't going to do anyone any favors if the damn thing blew up in my face. I listened intently for a sign of anything out of the ordinary. Nothing. That didn't necessarily mean too much though. Zombies were generally stationary when they were trapped, at least until something caught their interest. I pushed the rifle through the railing, but there was no target.

I climbed down the ladder, clearly aware of just how naked I was. Something about nudity displayed just what frail and fragile beings we were. On the plus side, my left leg was completely behaving itself, sore but otherwise moving like it should. I made it all the way down the ladder without any problems. It was when my right foot touched down that all the festivities began. I don't know where the fucker was hiding. She scared the shit out of me when she turned the corner and ran straight at me. Barely had enough time to turn around and get my rifle in front of me. As for the shit thing, I want to be clear that this was more an expression than a reality, although at least I was appropriately undressed if this were to have happened. The barrel of the rifle struck her belly as she forced herself forward. The barrel twisted up, and just as I lost my grip, a round went up and under her breastplate then the rifle fell to the ground.

She didn't care, even as the round exited somewhere around her collarbone and slammed into the ceiling. I had her at arm's length. She was slimy, sort of like month-old deli meat. With one hand, I tried to fend her off while also trying my best to punch her into oblivion. I'd hit her enough times in the temple to make that happen. I was sure she had to be feeling some effects. She drove my back into the ladder, and for one disgustingly gross encounter, my best friend for most of my teenaged years collided with her midriff. Let me make this clearer: My penis smashed up against her greasy, oily, dirty, diseased and sore encrusted, gray, brown, dead, pus-covered skin. I damn near froze up. Felt like I was trying to hump a beached tuna or something. I mean not that I'd ever done something like that. Was just letting my imagination run wild with that one. At this fucking point, I'd do the fish a couple of times if it meant I didn't have to touch this thing. I attempted to push off, with extreme prejudice, but my hands sunk into her sallow and rotten flesh.

"Oh, come on." I looked at the gelatinous mess hanging from my right hand. It looked very much like an overabundance of dog snot. This I was all too familiar with. Henry could manufacture it like no one's business. She came back for more. I made sure to turn my hips to the side to avoid a repeat of our earlier encounter. She turned her head when I punched. She couldn't have been any closer to biting down on my knuckles if I'd purposefully inserted them in her mouth. She snapped at air, her teeth making an awful clacking sound. I just kept jack hammering the side of her head. There was a loud *crunch*, and either my knuckles had given or her skull had. There was enough pain in my hand that it could have been the latter. Her eyes were beginning to lose focus as I somehow went faster. My arm was a blur as I cocked it back and just kept pummeling. I had my left hand wrapped around her throat. I was clutching so hard that if she had any humanity in her, she would have been fighting for air.

My chest was heaving with exertion while I forced her to the ground, my umm, my junk dangerously close to circumcision by zombie. Luckily, it hadn't dawned on me at the time. Her eyes rolled back in her head, her skull was caving, as I forced shards of it into her brain. My knuckles were bruised and bleeding by the time I finished. My shoulder and bicep were sore, and I'd dislocated two fingers.

"Fuck!" I yelled. When I let go of her neck, she collapsed to the floor, shaking violently. I kicked her once in the midsection for the pain she'd inflicted on me. That's when I remembered I was barefoot and that hurt as well. So being the brainchild that I am, I hauled off and kicked her with my other foot. I cried out in pain again. "You're an asshole!" I told her. She didn't care as she passed over to wherever they go. I stumbled to the bathroom, my limbs now dangerously heavy as the adrenaline dose dissipated within me. Pastel blue coated the walls along with a plethora of seashells. It looked like a third grade art experiment in there, with shells glued to the mirror and the toilet. All I could think was they looked like damn barnacles. I tossed the lid off the tank reservoir and plunged my hand in, a swirl of sludge drifted off. I cried out again when my disjointed joints bumped up into the toilet innards. When I pulled my hand out, it was reasonably clean, but I looked like I had a severe case of crippling arthritis. My pinkie and "fuck you" finger were bent at unnatural angles.

"This is going to suck; this is going to suck" was my mantra for the moment. Must have repeated that phrase twenty times, psyching myself up to do what needed to be done. I dipped my toe into the pool (figuratively) with my pinkie. It was smaller, so I figured it would hurt less. Side note: It didn't. Sounded like two pieces of wet, heavy-grit sandpaper rubbing against each other when I grasped the tip of my finger and pulled straight outward. For five brutal seconds, the knuckle did not pop back into place but rather sat atop the hand as if to get a better view of the world. A flood of relief passed through me when it slid back into place. Sweat flowed from every pore within my body. So much so, it was pooling at my feet. If I hadn't known any better, I would have thought the toilet had a leak. I danced around until the pain abated. The thought of going through that again did not sit well with me. Usually, you can do something once because you just don't have any idea how bad it's going to be, but once you have the experience, do you really want to give it another go?

Case in point, my sister had a dog, Talon, beautiful German Shepherd, but he fancied himself a hunter. His quarry was a porcupine. He ended up with a mouthful of one hundred and twelve quills. An emergency visit to the vet and three hundred and thirty-six bucks later, he was cured. At three bucks a quill, I would have done it. You got to believe any sane dog would have said, "Yup, lesson learned; that slow thing with the funny spiny looking fur is a definite no-go." I guess this was a poor example. The very next week, he came home with ninety-eight. I think my sister got a volume discount at the vet the next time, though. Much like Talon, I was compelled to go back for more. I grabbed the tip of my middle finger and danced around that small bathroom like I was being stung by a nest of hornets. I was yelling all sorts of obscenities, a fair number of them made up on the spot. Instead of wet sandpaper, this one sounded like an old rusty door that hadn't had its hinges oiled since the New Deal era. Before I popped that finger in, I wouldn't have thought the human body capable of making that sound.

Maybe I had enough endorphins flowing through my body this time, or it just wasn't as bad, but the pain was almost manageable. I dropped to my knees, gripped the edges of the toilet bowl, and wretched. There wasn't much to it besides some long strings of bile-laced drool. I stayed that way for a few minutes, my head hanging low. I was again wiped. When I felt certain I could stand without swaying, I did so. I went back out to the hallway. The zombie was still twitching like she had a small electrical current being pushed through her body. I stopped and stared at her. She couldn't have been much older than twenty, maybe even late teens. Almost done in by a female teenager. She tried to finish what my daughter had started. I think a grim smile forced my lips upwards. I wasn't sure, and I definitely didn't want to see that expression in the mirror. I looked up and scanned the rest of the cottage, a little late in the game. If there had been another zombie, I would have been screwed. It wasn't like they were wallflowers and would wait until someone came up and talked to them, even then avoiding eye contact. Nope, they were all teeth and fingernails.

I was as gross as I can ever recall being. A fair part of me including my nether regions and thighs were coated in a thick viscous solution I decided to call body gel. I'll deal my way, you deal yours. I had blood all over both arms, some gray matter and bone bits as well. Add to that the general overall stickiness of my forced swim the previous day, and I could barely stand my own skin. There was no way I could put my clothes back on. I didn't have the intestinal fortitude for that. I went back to the bathroom. I'd completely spoiled the water in the toilet tank and had sort of puked into the bowl, so yeah, the toilet was definitely out. I flushed and heard a strangled cry of air-logged water pipes attempting to do something they hadn't been called on to do in some time. There was some gurgling: my belly and the toilet. I jumped back when bright, blood red water flowed into the toilet. It looked like I'd severed the thing's artery or something. I'd seen rusty water before, but this looked like paint and was nearly as thick.

"Take pity on me!" I wailed to the gods. I could see the fuckers now, and they were laughing at me. I started mimicking them, "Yeah, let's get the automysophobiac as disgustingly dirty as possible without any chance of cleaning himself, and we'll see if he breaks down or not." I think Zeus was giving ten-to-one odds I wouldn't make it through the morning. Oh, and just in case you ended up in your shelter without a dictionary, automysophobia is the fear of being dirty. I had that one in spades in addition to the rest of my issues. I turned the shower on as well as the sink. Whatever sludge was working its way through the system, it had completely fouled up the showerhead because only drops of blood, as if the thing had sliced itself with a razorblade, were making it through the small openings. The sink spigot, though, was gushing the vile fluid that I noticed had a very distinct and disgusting odor, like rotting fish.

The bathroom was looking like a serial killer's headquarters. I backed out and closed the door behind me, not even bothering to shut the water off. Well, fluid, I didn't shut the fluid off. I thought I might have more luck in the kitchen. I didn't. This I did shut off, though, when the foul smell began to assail my senses. I got down on my haunches to check the cabinet under the sink. There were your typical cleaning supplies. I wondered if Drano would hurt too much if I lathered it on my skin.

"Ah dish soap!" I hadn't even begun to think this through as I squirted copious amounts on my body. Dish soap in small amounts in a perfect world takes a few gallons of water to wash off, I didn't have so much as an ounce. I was wondering how much saliva I could produce in the next few minutes. I now had a rapidly thickening congealing mess of soap holding all the other things I had on me, onto me. My arms were outstretched. I didn't dare move for fear that something would get stuck.

"What have I done?" I lamented. I pulled everything out from under the sink; anything in liquid form went into the "maybe" pile. Lysol, carpet cleaner, lighter fluid, you name it. I'm crazy, not quite insane though. I looked out the window and to the ocean. That was my play now. Sticky was leagues better than whatever I was now. Hell, I wouldn't care if a school of haddock pissed on me right now. Anything was better than this. I was heading for the back door when a small door to my left caught my attention. I opened it up just to make sure there were no zombies. It led downstairs. No smell; that was encouraging, and it gave me pause to reconsider my ocean swim. I was heading outdoors without clothes but, more importantly, without my rifle. I had to check the basement. Maybe I would luck out and there would be a hot tub.

The basement was more of a crawlspace, just tall enough that I could stand, but it wasn't much bigger than the bathroom upstairs. Shelves containing large jars dominated the whole wall to my left. At first, I mistakenly believed that this was indeed the home of a deranged killer and the jars were full of various body parts he used as trophies for his sick fantasies. Then it dawned on me that these were pickling jars full of mostly cucumbers. Some had beets and other things I wouldn't have eaten when other fare was available. My repulsive self was forgotten for the moment as I opened a jar of pickles and took a sniff. Why I was compelled to place my nose a quarter inch from the top of the jar is beyond me. A strong scent of vinegar burned through my olfactory nerves before I could pull away.

I looked around, pulled a large nail out of some rotten wood, and used it as a skewer. There was no way I was touching potential food the way I was. I hadn't taken a breath until the tenth pickled cuke touched down into my stomach. As I emptied the jar, I realized that I now had a viable solution to cleanse with. Sure, it smelled horrible, but vinegar was a powerful non-lethal astringent. I tipped the remaining contents, pickles and all, over the top of my head. The smell was horrendous. I did get a laugh, though, when a couple of the brined vegetables got stuck on various parts of me. Brought me back to what at the time I thought was a dark period in my life. I would go back to that just laid-off self in a heartbeat if it meant I got to avoid this time and place. Two jars later, I had gotten a fair amount of the soap off of me, though I'd traded one repellant for another.

"Just get most of it off, man, and then you can take a quick dip." I was trying to soothe my neurotic half. Okay, neurotic two-thirds. Three-quarters?

A serial killer would have been repulsed by what I left on that floor. I looked better though, even if I had traded my scent away. I was fairly convinced that it had permeated my skin and I would smell like this forever. Would Tracy ever want to lie with someone who smelled like this? Wouldn't doubt if I sweated vinegar for the next few months.

"It's better, man. Right? It has to be." I checked again for the tenth time, hoping maybe I had somehow glanced over a case of bottled water or something, then I headed upstairs. I was going to get my clothes, rifle, take a quick swim, get the damn truck, save my kids and wife in the vault, and then maybe drive out to the hot springs in Colorado, where I would see if I could melt off the top few layers of my skin. I'd gathered my things and had my hand on the door handle as I stared at the ocean and what I now considered clean water. Perspective is an amazing thing.

"Dammit." Ten zombies were milling about at the shoreline, not doing much of anything really, just being a nuisance. I could take care of them from here, but the noise would bring others. That was assured. I would have to forgo the water. The litany of swears I spewed out as I dressed far surpassed that of those I'd said when I was popping my knuckles back into place. I was as mad as a pit bull with its balls stuck in a vise as I headed out the front door. I didn't stop mumbling swears until I saw the sign for the power company. The gate was closed and locked. Again, this was good and bad. Good because no zombies could get in; bad because no zombies could get out. I climbed over. It was as I was sitting atop in that precarious position that I saw them. Zombies had discovered me, probably not all that hard considering the scent of me was as potent as a skunk and half as appealing. They'd probably like me this way. My meat would preserve longer. I risked injury to flip them the bird before I went down the other side.

Twelve trucks were in that yard. Four were dead. This I knew after trying to turn the lights on, batteries having given out at some point. I had eight chances. Now I just needed to find some keys, and that meant going into the building. I'd been avoiding that because if there were any zombies here, that was the most likely place. As unattractive as I was feeling toward myself, I still had to go into combat mode as I approached the door. Rifle to my shoulder, my gaze fixed and focused looking for targets. I banged on that door like I was selling used vacuum cleaners, then stepped back to see if anyone would come to greet me. No one did, which I found just outright rude. The door was locked. I went over to the side, where some offices were. I grabbed a good-sized boulder and hurled it at the window, where it bounced back, nearly crashing into my shins.

"Stupid safety glass." I was reluctant to shoot, but I wasn't going to keep messing around here. I'd already spent far too much time away from those who needed my help. The first shot left a nice hole about the diameter of the bullet I'd fired. "Perfect. Couple of hundred more shots, I'll make a hole big enough to fit through," I said aloud. Two more shots.... The second didn't do much more damage than the first. The third, however, starred that glass from corner to corner. "That's what I'm talking about." I grabbed the boulder again. This time, I was rewarded with the satisfying crash of glass breaking up into nearly a million pieces. Still no zombies coming to investigate. Didn't mean I was free and clear. They could have been stuck on other floors or in offices. Just as long as they weren't having an after-hours party in the key room on the night the zombies came, I should be all right. I waited a few extra minutes, just in case there was a slow zombie, then I climbed into the building, quickly coming up with my rifle at the ready.

"Three stories. Think, Mike. Where would they keep the keys?" There was a garage bay off to the side for maintenance. That was on my short list. I didn't think the boss would have something so mundane as key watch duty under his care but his receptionist would; odds were she ran the show anyway. "Okay, but the boss is most likely on the third floor. Probably don't want the help going up to the classy part. That leaves the front desk." I was confident I had reasoned this out correctly. It really is mind-boggling when I use my brain. The things I can do. Maybe I was learning; maybe I could actually look before I leapt. I was feeling pretty damn good about myself. Then I ran into another cliché: pride cometh before the fall. I ran down a hallway to a large open area where a huge oak semi-circular counter dominated. This was the nerve center of the building, where all the communications, rosters, and most importantly, keys were housed. Of course they were in a small, steel case, but that was fine. What was not were the zombies staring back at me as I got behind her desk.

"You're shitting me, right?" They'd waited until I had made it inside. That was the only reason they'd not come to check out the noise. This getting smart shit was beginning to become unnerving. How much was it going to suck when they became smarter than me? Wouldn't be that long either. For hell's sake, I was in remedial English for much of my high school career. Then, when I let my reasoning catch up, I realized they weren't moving. Well, I mean they were moving, just not toward me. They were struggling against their bonds. Looked very much like electrical cable. Made sense considering where I was. But who had done this? Eight zombies were tied up. Tethered together, and to a large steel beam that was a support column for the building. I don't know who the person was that had wrangled them up, but I silently thanked him or her. At first, I had a hard time concentrating on the steel box. I was dividing my time looking up and to the zombies, where I was sure they were going to break free and rush my location.

If the box hadn't been bolted to the wall, I would have taken it with me outside where I could have busted it open. I could hear the rubber insulation of the wire squeak and squeal as the zombies rubbed against each other and strained against their constraints. Most of the time, their gaze was upon me, their arms upraised, their mouths open in silent screams of rage and desire. But every so often, they would turn to each other as if they were discussing something like a plan. Trying to open this box with them there was like trying to take a piss with someone watching. Sure, it could be done, but who the hell wants that kind of pressure? They got a little rambunctious when I started slamming the phone against the lock. I wasn't even watching where I was hitting when the phone shattered much like the window had. I ended up holding a jagged piece of plastic with some circuitry attached to it. I had not wanted to use my rifle, but I was running out of options. It was two bullets later when I noticed the receptionist's top drawer was slightly open and there was a key that looked like it would have easily fit into the lock.

"Yeah, Mike. Weren't you *just* talking about thinking before doing?" The repercussions had stirred the natives up something fierce. Two male zombies had dropped to their knees and were now gnawing on the heavy gauge wire that bound a female zombie, who apparently was in charge of this small troop. So they now had a pecking order. Well, wasn't that special? Still had to work at prying the box open, and of course, I'd damaged the thing enough that the key no longer worked. After a torn fingernail and two significant scratches and one tear deep enough to draw blood, I was staring at a panel of keys. For a brief second, I panicked, thinking that this just might be the receptionist's storage panel for some cherry granola bars or something equally as disgusting. Like maybe some of Tommy's Pop-Tarts. No one had quite experienced food until they'd had a mayonnaise-filled and cinnamon-topped pastry. That was easily one of the most disgusting things I'd ever tried. When he'd handed me a piece, it looked like some sort of vanilla-frosting filling and the cinnamon smelled pretty good. The combination of the wet tart mayo mixed with the spiciness of the cinnamon was one of the most disgusting melding of flavors I'd ever been exposed to. There are foods I hate: cherry, ham, green vegetables … those are all known. But I like mayo and I like cinnamon; however, the two together are horrendous, about as appealing as peanut butter and tuna. Two great tastes that suck ass together! It can't be normal to digress like this. Can it?

Seven sets of keys. I almost hate to admit this, but I was debating on which ones I needed to take. Hey! Don't fault me.

I was stressed out and was feeling the time crunch to get back to my loved ones, and in the end I figured it out anyway. I took them all. I'm smart like that. I was feeling pride at my accomplishment, of figuring out my little conundrum, when I heard footfalls of someone (thing) rapidly approaching.

"Shit, I never knew the fall cometh so quick after the smugness."

They'd worked together and had got through her bonds. My rifle strap was over my shoulder, and I had two handfuls of keys, not yet transferring them to my pockets. I let them fall to the ground. They hadn't yet hit the floor when she launched herself. Yup, this one was no dummy. She wasn't going to run into the desk like the vast majority of her brethren would have. She was going over it.

I ducked down as she went over. She had caught some serious air and launched right over me. Her right hand reached out and grabbed hold of my left ear. I thought she was going to rip the damn thing off. She didn't let go until her head hit the wall. I'd been bent back at a wholly unnatural angle before losing my balance and falling over. My head was next to her abdomen. Her hands reached for me even while I struggled to right myself. Getting the gun was out of the question. It had fallen off and was mostly under her. There was a screech emanating from her that I could just make out on the peripheries of my hearing range. If I had two guesses, one would be she was calling for back up, or two, she was wondering what wine would go with her upcoming meal. Her hands were desperately seeking purchase wherever they could land while she moved her torso to get her mouth into position.

Her face was gaunt, her cheeks sunken, her teeth rotten. It was clear to see she was starving. I just didn't want to be the one to cure her condition. Not sure why this group hadn't chosen stasis. Perhaps the bindings had something to do with it. Didn't really have the time at the moment to dwell on it. She landed a bite on to the bridge of my hat. She twisted her head back and forth, triumphantly thinking she was getting sustenance. It gave me the moment I needed, allowing me to get a leg into her mid-section. I pushed her along the floor and away. She was resilient if nothing else. She twisted, coming back again for the next round just as I reached behind me, getting my arm up on the desk so I could hurry myself along. I don't know if I had the Lords of Combat on my side or they were doing an experiment. My hand touched a tool I thought was long ago forgotten in this modern era. My hand closed on a letter opener. Maybe the average Joe had no use for one, but I'd imagine someone who had to open a hundred letters a day might appreciate the knife-like apparatus.

It must have been a gift. The metal itself seemed made of silver, and the handle was a burnished walnut or equally expensive wood and was also engraved. I'm sure that the person who got it would have appreciated a bonus or a gift card more. This was akin to getting your wife a vacuum cleaner for Christmas. Sure she might need one, but what the fuck, man. Do you never want to get laid again? Wow, serious departure from the subject at hand…. I brought the impromptu blade past my face and lodged it deeply into the zombie's cheek. I could see the glint of the blade through her open mouth. It was about as appealing as it sounds. It got worse when I skewered that little hanging thing in the back of her throat, you know, the thing that makes a normal person want to gag when you touch it? Not the zombie though, she didn't even flinch. I withdrew the blade and went to drive it deep into the side of her head, and may have succeeded if she hadn't thrown up her arm in a defensive gesture.

A large portion in the very heavy majority wanted to, almost needed to, forget the blood that ran through me. I knew I recovered better. I knew I ran faster. I knew I was stronger. I knew all those things on a fundamental level, though I did not acknowledge them. I didn't want to because of what it entailed. Because of all the negativity that surrounded these enhancements. Right now, this zombie had me in a precarious position. Her block of my strike had me falling over to the side with her coming down right on top, and I was in much need of help. I reached out with my mind, something I hadn't done in a long while, something I'd never wanted to do again. This made my genital glazing earlier feel like a sponge bath in natural spring water by comparison. The mind I touched was as black as her teeth and as fathomlessly evil as one without a soul could be. I would not turn that mirror on myself, not now, not ever.

There was a hesitation in her movements as she felt my presence. I didn't get the feeling it was one lone thought but more of a collective, like there was a vast committee in her head, all with one goal, with one purpose, but many entities trying to bring this about. And even as I formed a thought, I felt other presences in there as well … the same but different. I was seeing multiple views from the other zombies. Most were looking at the desk and desperately wanted to join in the feeding. Others, I saw them as they were chewing through their cables. She'd have help and soon.

"Stop!" I forced through our mind waves, or whatever the hell the link we talked on went over.

Again, she hesitated. The downward pressure she was forcing on me eased up just the slightest amount. I didn't wait for her response before I began to use this to my advantage. After my earlier encounters with Re-Pete my fully remote-controlled zombie, I expected more of the same. When the resounding "No" came through our connection, I've got to admit I was more than a little surprised, shocked, and scared. And probably some more "s" adjectives. It hadn't bought me much time, but enough that I could change the momentum of her downward push. We were nearly face to face, and unlike others of her kind, she wasn't blindly chomping at the bit, hoping that something got stuck between her chompers. She was waiting for an opening, greedily eyeing my forearms. My left hand was trying to close around her neck. My right was pushing on her side. I still clutched the opener tightly. She had more coordination than most, but at times, it still seemed like she was a toddler trying her best to figure out how all the parts worked independently and in unison.

I brought my right hand up. She was defending her vulnerable temple, and then it dawned on me because, well I'm just that quick, that she knew what I was going for because we were still linked. I severed the connection. The damage had been done, for her at least. She over-committed to her temple, leaving most of her face completely exposed. I shoved that opener as deep into her eye socket as I could. I just nicked the side of her orb, cutting into it like it was a soft piece of cheese. As I pushed the blade in deeper, it forced her oozing eyeball out, the optic nerve holding it attached. It swung like a pendulum down by her ample breasts. Yes, I noticed them; being a guy can sometimes be one of the easiest things in the world. We are so hardwired for certain things as to become predictable in our behavior. I'm not saying I found her lust-worthy; it's just that I couldn't help checking out her breasts, which signified her ability to simultaneously attract a mate and feed her children. Although in her case, she could have kept a daycare facility amply supplied.

There was a shriek of pain from her as I pushed deeper, and then she was still. I hadn't realized it at first, but the cry wasn't auditory. She had passed that signal through the link we had in common and that I'd thought I had previously disconnected. Maybe strong emotions could override the off switch. When I was certain she would not stir, I let her drop to the floor. I let her have the wooden handled skewer, my gift to her. I didn't screw around. I braced on the top of the desk, and shot the fish in the barrel. I was fine that they couldn't move much; made my job easier. When it came to zombies, I was under the personal opinion there was no morality involved. These weren't fathers, mothers, sons, daughters, brothers, sisters—not black, white, Hispanic, Asian, Muslim, Catholics, Hindu—they were just fucking zombies. In some ways, they'd figured out how to create peace and unity by stripping away all of those man-made designations. Of course, it could have been that they all had a common enemy: us. Who knows, maybe when we were all gone, they would break down into their own groups, shufflers, speeders, bulkers, and brainers. That would be great if they'd start killing each other now, make my job easier.

I'd killed all but one zombie. He looked to each of his fallen comrades and then to me as I came from behind the desk and approached, my rifle still upraised and against my shoulder. His lips pulled back in a snarl, exposing all of his teeth. He pulled against his restraints, not to run away but to run at me.

"Fuck you," I told him evenly. I don't believe it was the words that worked him up into a frenzy but rather the sound. He was rocking back and forth, violently trying to shake loose from his bonds. I think I could have told him I'd bought him a flying pony for his birthday and he would have been just as crazed. "Sucks to be you." I was within a foot of him. He stopped moving. He growled and leaned forward, desperately trying to rest his forehead against my barrel. I fired. His feet slipped out from under him, and he cracked down onto the ground with a skull-shattering impact.

I grabbed all the keys and headed outside of the building. There was a line of zombies at the fence. I felt like a captive lone wolf at the zoo who had finally come out from his hiding den and four classes of excited fifth graders on a field trip had just spotted me. They all moved down on the fence, bunching up so they could get a better look.

"Yeah, that's not creepy." It was, but not as creepy as it was about to get. I'd hopped into the nearest truck, pulling the door shut. I was more than a little concerned when I tried all the keys and none of them fit. "The next will work." I wasn't totally confident, but what the hell was I going to say to myself? "You can always hitchhike." When I stepped out of the truck, I took note that some of the zombies weren't completely fixated on me but rather looking to the building, actually up at the building.

"What's that all about?" I came a little closer to where the zombies were pressed against the fence. I had hopes they would press hard enough to make zombie play-dough push through the diamond shaped wedges. It would have been gross, no doubt, but highly satisfying. I tilted my head up. I was looking at dozens of zombies looking down at me. They were trapped on the second and third floors. Had to have been at least fifty of them. "Don't you dare!" I shouted at my nuts. They wanted to migrate back up into my stomach, where they could safely hide. My mouth went dry as I looked up. It took me a moment to realize that some of the zombies up there were beginning to leave. I wanted to believe that they were getting bored and were going back to their desks to go play a rousing game of solitaire or something, but that wasn't it. They were looking for a way down, and if they had any brainers in their pack, odds were they'd figure it out.

"Next truck." I rushed off. The third key slid in effortlessly. There was a chime and a slow steady *whir* then the triumphant cough of an engine firing. "Thank you," I said, momentarily letting my head rest against the steering wheel. I wanted to thank God, but I was still holding a grudge for all the things that had befallen not only me but everyone. Of course, I knew it was the hubris of man that had done all of this, but as our overseer, He should have maybe been a little more diligent, perhaps giving a healthy case of leprosy to the originator of the virus. Then I realized that might not have been such a great idea since my lineage was tied to it. "Umm, we good?" I asked looking up. I'd not been hit with an errant meteorite, figured that was as clear a message as any.

"Gonna have to get out and open the gate." I laughed at

myself as I pressed down on the gas. I really wanted to plow into the part where all the zombies were congregating, but I tempted fate every day that I awoke. Maybe right now was not the time to keep pushing that envelope. Instead of folding over, the gate actually swung outwards. I was relishing in the small victory when it scared the shit out of me by swinging back and smacking hard into the side of the truck. Didn't do much except scratch the paint and give me a coronary; other than that, we were good. I beeped the horn as one final "fuck you" and took off back to town. For as long, arduous, and dangerous the trip to get the truck had been, I was literally back to the post office in under ten minutes.

Unfortunately, the zombies had not departed during my absence, although I think I would have been severely pissed off since this would have made necessitating getting the whole truck thing a moot point. Three heads popped up on the roof as I rolled in. I waved up. They waved back. Pretty sure we were all feeling high levels of relief at this moment. Now came the tricky part. Just because I had a means of escape did not mean the zombies were going to allow me to use it unhindered. I slowed way down, put the truck into low, and powered forward. The zombies that were coming to meet me were greeted with a few tons of steel. The first lucky few were pushed over, and I ran over them, leaving them relatively unscathed. That was, of course, the ones that didn't end up under the wheels; they were crushed like giant cockroaches. The resultant spray out of organic material was hideous, to say the least, as it splashed against curbs and buildings, some of it going as far as twenty feet to red wash walls.

Then as more zombies began to strike the front, more and more flowed around the sides, some reaching out and grabbing hold. The engine, although not quite taxed yet, was beginning to feel the accumulated effects of all the zombies as the RPMs nudged up. Although I was going no faster, I'd actually lost a mile per hour or so. Two zombies were on the running board next to me, one holding on to the mirror, the other the door handle. They weren't beating on the glass, which would have been better than the stare they were giving me while they pondered their next moves.

"Think all you want, assholes. I've got a little surprise for you." I hopped the curb with the truck, shook a couple of the other bastards off like a dog does fleas. Not my new buddies though; they were stuck like barnacles. The mirror was the first thing to go as I scraped up against the building. The zombies were leaving a trail of shredded clothing and then finally skin and blood as I rubbed against the coarse brick building. Still, they held on.

"You're grossing me the hell out," I told them as they shook from the contact and the ass sanding they were receiving. The one holding the door handle was finally scrubbed away like a bad toilet stain. He rolled down the whole length of the truck before dropping off the end. My mirror guy was much more stubborn. I realized I was going to completely pass the building by. I put the truck in reverse. I finally loosened the stubborn bastard. As he rolled along the hood, I could hear the sound of heavy bones grinding together while he was wheeled away. For good measure, once he'd fallen to the ground, I went back into drive and ran over him. I stopped the truck—you can believe this or not, but for some fucking reason, it was at this very moment I decided to check the fuel gauge. Yeah, I already know that's pretty irresponsible of me. You don't need to remind me. Apparently, my appeasement to God had worked because I was sitting comfortably at three quarters full.

I again thanked Him. You could say that He had nothing to do with it, that a person had filled this up. Sure, I can agree with that. I can also agree that I could have picked out another truck that was running on fumes. Listen, I'm not a wise person, a diviner or sage or anything. I do know there are plenty of things in this world I have no clue as to how they operate or why. But when you can use all the help that you can, why close any prospective doors just because you don't think there's something on the other side? If a great brown-green crocodile alien warrior arose and wanted to give me help right now, you can bet your ass I'd take it. Sure, I'd be scared as hell of it, but one thing at a time. I'd deal with the walking luggage when the time came.

I was as close to the building as I could be and still allow myself room to get out of the truck using the window. Couldn't be the door. If I could fit, so could the zombies. And I could not have them in between the truck and the wall. That needed to be a zombie-free zone for our escape. The window sloped away from the wall, and this was the only reason I could wriggle out. Felt like a newborn seeking release from the womb. It was a tight fit as I pulled myself free. I'd no sooner got on the roof of the truck than a couple of zombies got on the hood.

"This is just so much fucking fun!" I booted the first one that tried to run up the windshield. Must have been a hell of a kick because I saw at least three teeth go to the right as his head spun to the left. His head took the rest of him spiraling off and into the crowd much like a stage diving rock group lead singer. Although instead of crowd surfing, he kind of just hung there in the air. I had to twist too far to get an effective kick on the next zombie. A glancing blow on the shoulder paused his progress. I was done playing king of the hill, and I ran for the lift. The only way to be safe was to get out of their range. When I hopped in the bucket, this was another of those moments where I maybe should have taken a moment in a less hostile environment to familiarize myself with the controls, and maybe even more importantly, make sure the damn truck wasn't in service for the hydraulics.

"Okay God, I know I'm kind of overusing the 'I'm Your child and all' card, but fuck, just this one last time, I mean, for this minute anyway. I can't speak for the next minute. Could

You just maybe let this thing work?" I didn't bother with the safety door as I jumped into the small booth. I hadn't been expecting it to move the way it did. Gotta tell you it didn't leave me feeling comfortable. There were three controls, a green push button labeled "Power," a small joystick for moving the arm around, and under a clear plastic cover, a red button labeled "Emergency." Not sure exactly what that did, but if depressing it made some machine guns or flame throwers appear, that would really help with this emergency. I was pretty sure that was not what would happen, but in that very moment, you have no idea how much I wanted to give it a go.

The green button backlit when I pressed it. I took that as a good sign. Then I nearly tossed myself out of the bucket when I jerked the arm to the right. "Holy shit!" I shouted when I realized that less was definitely more. The controls had a feather touch. Damn near cracked my neck from the whiplash. The only decent thing that came out of it was that I sent three zombies airborne off the truck, and at least two of them had smashed their heads hard enough they were going to be out of the fight. I'd not yet learned the finesse of the stick. I swung back and missed crashing into the post office by inches.

"Dad, up! You want to come up!" Travis urged.

I mumbled a few choice swears under my breath, having still not learned anything. What can I say? The pressure was making me freak out a bit. I pushed the stick forward. I heard hydraulics whining and the truck engine taxing itself, but I was not moving. Somehow, I figured pushing it harder would make something happen. Still nothing.

"The stick toward you, Uncle!" Jesse yelled.

I mumbled more expletives. I yanked the stick back. I was nearly propelled out like I was wearing boots made entirely of Mentos in a container full of diet coke. My knees were up above the lip before the arm caught up. I landed with a grunt. I eased up just as I got to the height of the kids.

"Someone call for a lift?" I asked, doing my best to not make my ascent look like the cluster fuck that it was.

"I'm not getting in that thing." Meredith said, backing away. Couldn't really blame her; the operator was not very good.

"I'm getting better," I told her.

"When?" She backed up another step, like I was going to reach out and force her in.

"You can't stay up here."

"Dad." Travis pointed down toward the truck. It was then that I noticed the arm I was riding was swaying. At first, like I was in a small breeze, and then more like I was at ground zero for a decent-sized quake. Zombies were swarming on the truck.

"Well, that certainly makes things more interesting." My heart felt like it was fighting to get outside of my chest. It was beating against my rib cage so violently. "Come on, we're going to have to fight our way out of this, and the sooner the better." The fish weren't biting at all. The roof was safe. Sure, it was a slow death, but that was preferable to the insta-death below. "Travis."

"Yeah, Dad?" He knew what I was saying. He just wanted no part of it. He wasn't backing up like Meredith, but the thought was crossing his mind.

"Tell me there's a cheeseburger in the truck," Jesse said.

"Huh?"

"The only way I'm coming down is if you tell me there's food and preferably a cheeseburger in the truck."

I'm not the brightest bulb on the string, and sometimes, I even flicker like I'm gonna go out, but I figured this one out quick enough. "Sure, I stopped at McDonalds before I came here. There's a bag of quarter pounders and like nine orders of large fries."

"The quarter pounders have cheese?"

"Sure." I said as convincingly as I could, now that the bastard had made me hungry. In fact, the more I dwelled on it, the more I wanted it to be true. I was half-tempted to go down without them and eat in peace before they found my stash. Jesse hesitated before moving closer. I helped him get into the bucket. Not to be outdone, Travis got in next. It was crowded, but we'd make room for one more.

"I can't leave you up here, Mer," I pleaded.

"Sure you could. I'll keep a watch out for the flying zombies. They're next, you know."

"Take it back," I told her. With the way they were evolving, I wouldn't doubt it as an eventuality.

I think she realized how serious I was. "Uncle, they're not going to sprout wings; that's crazy."

"Yeah, well, so is living dead roaming the earth in giant hordes, eating everything that gets in their way."

"Oh ...well when you say it like that. I take it back; there will be no flying zombies."

"Damn right. Now get your ass in here or I'm coming on that roof and tossing you head first into the bucket."

I think she realized I was serious about that as well because she did it without any more qualms. I was pressed tight up against the front of the bucket. Good thing we were stuck in there like a cork too, because once again I had yet to find the *feel* of the controls, we dropped a good ten feet in a half second. My stomach hovered above my head for a bit before settling back down.

"You suck at this, Uncle." Meredith said what the rest of the group was feeling. I turned my head to give her a little crap, but the green tinge in her face signified that I already had.

"All right, I'm going to go down another five feet then we're going to blow some holes in these zombies. Jesse you're closest; you go straight for the window and in, then Meredith, Travis and I'll follow. Understood?"

I got nods from all of them. I think even some of the zombies got in on the plan, because they nodded as well. Pretty sure they were just waiting in extreme anticipation, though. I was so paranoid about dropping us right into the waiting arms of the zombies, I wasn't even applying enough pressure to get us moving. The kids were ready to fight; apparently, I wasn't.

"Dad?"

"Yeah, I'm working on it." In contrast to my earlier movements, right now a snail could have outpaced us. I hoped I never got enough practice with this contraption to get the gist. When we were close enough, I gave the word. Zombie hands were halfway up the exterior of our ride, pushing against it from all angles. If we weren't so close to our targets, it would have been more difficult to hit them. As it was, we were carving slices through them. Bodies fell away from the truck. At first, the destroyed zombies were resting atop the heads of the others that had not yet figured out how to climb aboard or could not find a place to perch. We already looked like one of those crazy overcrowded train cars from India. You've seen the photos, people camped out on top or hanging from windows. Can you even imagine having a mild case of claustrophobia and being the first poor son-of-a-bitch that got in that car in the morning? The press of that many bodies would be debilitating to one with a condition. There is not a call center job good enough that I would make that trek every day. Yeah let that one sink in for a sec. There you go, you got it! I dropped the bucket a little lower once we'd made some headway; that was as literal as it was figurative.

"I think I can make it!" Jesse said excitedly.

I wasn't too keen on "think." But like a typical teenager he didn't wait for my response before jumping out. Hands reached and fell short as he quickly moved for the window. I covered his progress. I blew the side of the head off of a boy that looked like he could be delivering newspapers in 1850's London, not sure who wore knickerbockers in this day and age but I didn't stop to think about it for very long. Another zombie was trying to come up onto the hood and cut off Jesse's egress. Travis moved quickly to shoot a zombie coming from Jesse's vacated spot, and his hip hit mine, which in turn knocked me into the controller. We swung a foot or so to the side. I blasted a hole in the hood of the truck. I prayed to the truck gods that I had not damaged anything important.

"Sorry," Travis said. I don't feel he had the appropriate inflection to express the apology with enough genuine concern. It was bad enough I'd hit the hood; it would have been much worse if I'd hit my nephew. The truck rumbled then sputtered. I was holding my breath, and then it quieted down and purred normally. So far, everything was still working.

"Meredith, you're up." She moved without saying a word. That might have been a first. The truck was nearly devoid of the zombies. Blood and gore caked everything. What I had not taken note of until this very moment was that there was now a small empty perimeter around the truck, I mean, except for the broken and nearly decapitated bodies of dead zombies that is.

"What the hell?" I asked the question as I fired. "Go Travis!"

"Meredith isn't in yet," he said, looking over his shoulder.

"We have a window here, let's not lose it. Go! I'm right behind you!"

Much like Meredith, he went without another word. I was thankful for that. Whatever the zombies were doing, I didn't know how long it was going to last.

"Meredith's in, Dad!" Travis yelled from the window. I spared a quick glance. All eyes were on me, from the cab of the truck and the zombies around. There was this expectant air, like we were all waiting for what would happen next. I took three quick un-aimed shots, using them as a deterrent and also to maybe bolster my courage. I placed my hand on the lip of the bucket and started my jump over. That seemed to be exactly what the zombies were waiting for. As one giant, disgusting organism, they moved. My trailing foot caught the lip of the bucket as the sheer weight of zombies caused the truck to move aggressively. My rifle went flying from my bracing hand while I tried to catch myself from falling completely on my face. I smashed my knee across one of the hydraulic pistons. This sent me tumbling, luckily toward the post office, where the wall kept me from heading off the side. My knee was battered, as was the side of my face where it collided with the brick. Zombies were making a mad dash for dinner. The rifle was a lost cause; it rested neatly on the hood before a zombie stepped on it and sent it to the ground. I wasn't going to make it. Not a chance in hell.

"Travis drive! Just drive!"

There was a slight delay while he moved into position, and then the truck started rolling forward. The grind of metal on brick was ear splitting. I scrambled back up on my feet and hurried into the bucket. It was my only chance. At least a dozen zombies were on the truck with me, and more would be joining them. Travis turned the wheel enough to get us off the curb, and we lost a couple hangers-on, but they were quickly replaced. I hoped there wasn't a safety device on the boom arm that prevented it from moving while the truck was in gear, or I was basically a human taco in my own plastic shell. For good or bad, the bucket moved up a little with a jerk. At least five zombies had grabbed hold of the lip of it and tried to keep it in place. I went a little higher. The arm groaned in protest from the multiple forces being applied to it while Travis laid bare just how inexperienced he was behind the wheel.

When the zombies came, he had been in the midst of

learning how to drive with his learner's permit. Once the shit hit the fan, we'd seen no reason to continue teaching him. I was just now realizing how large of an error on my part that was. A vodka-logged Russian on a three-day binge could have driven straighter. I didn't know if he was doing the wet dog routine and trying to shake the zombies off or this was really how he drove. I remember fearing for my life a few times while we were out learning, but nothing quite this bad.

"Middle of the road! Drive down the damn middle of the road!" I had no way of knowing it, but at the time, the windshield was coated in a thick layer of viscera, making it nearly impossible to see anything, and right now sticking your head out the window was not advised, as the animals in the park were hostile. He jumped another curb, came back down, and clipped the fender of a Honda. Something in the bucket linkage was not a fan of all the stress it was receiving and broke free, I now spun like the damn teacup ride at the carnival. You know the one. You tell your wife you'll take the kids on it because it looks like the most innocent thing that the fair has to offer. Then while you're evilly laughing on the inside, you tell the rug rats to hold on tight while you proceed to crank that inner wheel for all its worth, turning the kiddie ride into a spinning torture chamber of doom with centrifugal forces threatening to pull your eyeballs into your skull.

The funny part is that the kids are scared shitless for the first few seconds, and then they're laughing their asses off, begging for more. Then I would get off the ride, my stomach would be junk for the next twenty-four hours, and they'd be begging to go back on while eating fried dough, French fries, corn dogs, and cotton candy. By the time I would get home, I'd be lucky if I could hold down some Alka-Seltzer. Every fucking year I would do it, thinking that this year it would be different. Pretty sure that's the definition of insanity; good thing I barely know how to read. Got to the point where my wife would bring a couple of tabs with us so I could take them as soon as I got off the ride. Want to know what's even funnier? Even when the kids were older and too cool to go with dad to the carnival, I would still get on that fucking ride, even though I wasn't trying to scare a kid anymore. I'd try to spin that damn thing off its axis. Same results, too.

That's what I had going on here as well, although I don't remember ever having to worry about smashing into telephone poles. The truck swerved hard to the left, the bucket whipped that way, just clipping the pole with a fingernail's width of the bucket. The resultant crack sounded thunderous, like the heavens were getting ready to open up. The only thing I could think to do was raise up higher so there would be less arm to swing back and forth. There were a couple of things wrong with this. I was changing the center balance point of the truck, making it much easier for it to flip, and there was also a good chance I was going to clothesline myself on a phone line crossing the road. The way I was manipulating that control, I looked like a kid desperately trying to get a prize on those stupid claw games. Luckily, we were in the center of town, so there were no lines to be concerned with, but that good fortune was only going to last another couple of hundred yards, and we would not have lost our pursuers by then. At least, the twisting was acting like a windshield wiper, pushing the zombies off like the unwelcome bugs they were, and much like an old windshield wiper, it was leaving a heavy, sticky residue that would never come off without a sandblaster. The problem was I was doing enough revolutions to throw my equilibrium into the shitter along with achieving a hellacious gut ache.

I knew I was riding lady luck hard, bouncing up and down on her shoulders while I pulled her hair back and asked her, "Who's my bitch!?" She was only going to take so much before tossing me off. The front of the truck was clear enough that Travis and Jesse were able to stick their heads out. Travis's driving improved, but it still wasn't anything that was going to get him his license anytime soon. It was already too late as far as the arm was concerned, that whole, "a body in motion will stay in motion," and that was most certainly true for that bucket I was riding. It was turning like a ballerina in the midst of a pirouette. At least I wasn't quite at a figure skater and a front-toe spin speed, not yet anyway. The telephone line was fast approaching. I dropped the bucket as fast as the mechanism would allow. I spun far out to the right, and I had to hold on to the bucket to keep from being pitched out by the forces. Jesse's eyes got huge as I swept over his head, the front of the truck next, then I came back around to sweep over Travis, who I don't even think saw me. We were down to three zombies on the truck and a horde behind. I needed off of this contraption before I ended up splattered across any number of immoveable objects.

I needed to time my jump out just right, so let's get all the facts straight here: I needed to time my jump with the speed of the moving bucket, the speed of the truck moving forward, the inertia of drag times, the coefficient of time and space displacement calculated by the fractals ... yeah I was airborne by now. I jumped out of the side that was already damaged, hoping this time I wouldn't catch my foot. So far, so good; I made it out scot-free. Now, I just had to hope my momentum didn't send me off the truck and onto the pavement, where the trailing zombies would make short work of me. At some point during my flight, I heard the fracturing crash of my home away from home coming to a violent end. The problem of such a destructive hit was that it had the effect of sending the arm back toward me a lot sooner than I'd anticipated. Oh, who am I kidding? I had no idea how any of this shit was going to work. I had jumped and hoped for the best. I was so low on that truck body I could have been considered a second coat of paint. I was grabbing anything that remotely resembled a handhold to slow me down. When I finally came to a stop, I dared not raise my head.

It was like I was stuck under the blades of a helicopter as that arm continuously whipped by overhead. I don't know what Travis ran into this time, but whatever it was, it twisted the entire aperture to the point where the bucket slammed into the side of the truck with enough force to lift us onto two wheels. I was now looking down at the roadway as I held on to a hydraulic hose for all I was worth. A platoon of angels must have sat down on the far side, because somehow the truck slammed back down onto all our wheels. My jaw bounced off the truck body, and I'm pretty sure I chipped a tooth. For the briefest of seconds, I wondered if there were any dentists still around. The arm was imbedded in the side of the truck— well, more like the truck body had melded around it. I pushed away from the edge and got onto my hands and knees. One determined zombie still shared the exterior with me. He wasn't moving forward; much like me, he was holding on for the ride. The trailers were losing ground as Travis was now somewhat driving a straight course.

"Dad, you all right?" he shouted back.

"Fine! One zombie to your six!"

"Should I stop?"

"Not yet! In a couple of miles!"

The ride was somewhat enjoyable after the previous few minutes. I kept an eye on the zombie, as he did me. Neither of us moved, which was fine with me. I was still trying to get my adrenaline levels down to an acceptable level. If a cop gave me a sobriety test right now, I would look like a meth addict in the midst of a giant tweaking. That always goes over well with the cops. The truck started to slow. I took a quick glance behind me. I was happy to see that we were out of sight of our pursuers. I raised up at the same time as the zombie. I waited until we had almost stopped before I hopped off the truck. It was nice to have regular old ground under my feet. I staggered a couple of steps. Apparently, my inner ear had not yet completely stopped its spin cycle. The zombie got down as well, in a very athletic predatory jump if I had to admit it. Back when this started, it would have just walked off the edge of the truck, fallen into a heap of deadness on the roadway, then pushed himself up to a standing position before once again coming at me. Not this one though. I had a start as a rifle report rang out. The front of his head bulged out as the bullet struggled to get out of its encasing. The zombie fell forward.

"Thank you." I told Travis.

"Where's your gun?" he asked me.

"Get back in the truck."

"You told me that my rifle is the most important fighting tool besides myself and that I should never leave it behind. But yet here you are, Dad, without your rifle."

"You're really going to give me shit after that bumper car excuse you call driving? Get in the damn truck before the zombies catch up." I smiled. It was easy to smile when you'd flipped Death off and were still standing. Of course, he'd be back, but for now, it was Mike four hundred and seventy-two to Death's zero. The sucky part about that was Death only needed one to win.

"Where to, Uncle?" Meredith asked. "Oh my God! Is that you?" she cried as I got into the truck. "You … you smell like maybe bad pickles or something. I thought, like, maybe it was something in the bucket, so I didn't want to say anything. It's horrible … I thought Henry was the worst thing I'd ever smelled. You beat him." She yanked her hoodie above her nose and drove her face deeper still under the makeshift nose cover.

"Okay, I get it. I stink."

"Understatement, Dad."

"Listen, you guys have no idea what I've been through!"

"Yeah, well, just think what we're going through right now." Meredith's voice was muffled. "I think maybe you should tell us. You owe us at least that much. I think I'm going to vomit."

I couldn't help but notice her eyes were watering from my stench.

"It's not really that bad."

"Uncle, just because you've burned a hole in your nose doesn't mean the rest of us have." Jesse added.

Travis was turning different reddish shades as he tried to hold his breath. Meredith was threatening to shoot out the windshield to get more air in.

By the time I'd recounted most of my tale, they'd made some sort of peace with my funk, or more likely, I'd caused some serious permanent damage to their olfactory senses. When I was done, I circled back around to Meredith's original question, because it was a hell of one. Most of my family was stuck in a bunker under the post office. They were safe, though, and that was something. We needed to regroup. I needed a weapon, and we could definitely use more ammo. Then my thought was to go to Ron's and assess that situation. If we could help, we would. Problem was the easiest store of guns was at Ron's. Maine was a gun-friendly state, but we'd proved over and over again that going into someone's home to look was not a great idea.

"We need a bigger truck." I headed for a rock quarry a couple of towns over. It wasn't quite the Tyrex' that Eliza had used against us, but I hoped the zombies would have a hard time getting on to it. The trip ended up being half a bust. There were two trucks there. One had its engine out and the other was dead, and dead like not moving, not undead or living dead, meaning it would move. There is a huge gun store in Holden called Maine Military. We stopped. Had to. It's a requirement of all rednecks to stop. It's in the *Redneck Nature Guide* right after the discussion about beer-can chicken. They had been cleaned out like the store had closed and the inventory sold off at auction. Someone had even taken the fake prop guns hanging on the far wall. I felt bad for the idiots that thought those were going to do anything to the savage lines of enemies coming their way. Well, I guess you could always go *pew, pew, pew* really fast in mimicry of a machinegun.

I was saddened by so much nothingness. The people who came through here had been thorough. I would love to see their hideout. I could guarantee they were doing all right. They had enough ammunition that they could hand it down from generation to generation. I was at a loss as to what to do. We were a mile down from the gun store, heading to Ron's, when Travis pointed to another store. It was a fireworks place.

"This is no time for bottle rockets," I told him right before I locked up the brakes, having all the kids brace against the dashboard in an effort to keep from ruining their expensive dental work. All of their responsible parents would have been pissed at me if I had busted anything.

"And you say I drive bad? Plus, you can't get bottle rockets in Maine."

"What?" That sounded like blasphemy. One of my favorite Chinese-made products of all time, and it was banned?

"Something about unknown flight path or something."

"Well, that's the damn point of them." I drove backward up the road so I could turn into the parking lot. Unlike the cleaned-out gun store, this place looked like it had just been freshly stocked; if not for the heavy coating of dust I would have assumed it was getting ready to open for business. Any other fucking day of my life this would have been like letting a monkey loose in a chocolate covered banana factory. Right now, all I could see were large noise makers. I mean they had rockets, but the odds that these would hurt mass amounts of zombies was minimal. I wished I had Justin around; the kid had the uncanny ability to take some of the most harmless of fireworks and turn them into small bombs. Then I was walloped with that "a-ha" moment. I ran over to the sparklers.

"Which ones, Trav?"

"Which ones, what?" he asked. He was looking at the mortars.

"Remember a couple of years back. July Fourth. Justin had us come outside to check something out. Blew a trashcan to shreds, broke three of our neighbor's windows, and apparently, made Mrs. Durphy's dog so scared he shit all over her expensive couch."

"Oh yeah, I forgot about that. Didn't you have to go to court?"

"No, I paid for the windows and told Mrs. Durphy if her dog hadn't been on the couch to begin with he wouldn't have shit up there. She only threatened me with court. She did move out soon after. I always meant to thank Justin for that. She was a pain in the ass."

"Because she didn't want her windows smashed or her dog to suffer near coronaries?" Meredith asked.

"Was anyone talking to you?"

She raised her hands in an apologetic manner.

"It was sparklers." Travis was thinking. "Colored sparklers. I remember him showing me. He grabbed a handful of them and wrapped them in an entire roll of electrical tape."

They had a bunch on display and even more in the back. The beauty of having an energy truck was the overabundance of electrical tape they had onboard. We made over twenty handmade bombs before I decided we should check out just how effective a weapon we had. We used one of the sparklers itself as a fuse. I lit the sparkler, and like a seven-year-old, I got transfixed by the shower of blue sparks.

"Dad, throw it!" Travis backed up.

Thing had to be a pound by the time it was all wrapped up. I tossed it a decent distance away and even backed up a few steps. We all waited. I could still see sparks shooting on the ground, then nothing. I was not liking our chances of dispersing a zombie horde with pretty colors. I started walking forward. I about halved the distance when I was rocked by an explosion. A peppering of small rocks and clods of dirt struck me, but that was nothing compared to the concussion that felt like it was shifting my internal organs around.

"Fuck me!" I laughed, brushing myself off.

"You're bleeding, Uncle," Meredith said as she ran up next to me.

I had an inch long splinter, which looked like a piece of chopstick, wedged in my forearm. I didn't care. If the divot in the ground was any indication of the damage we could do, then I was all in. Actually, I did kind of care about the chopstick, if that was indeed what it was. Who knew whose mouth that thing had been in? I pulled it out. It came loose with a sickly wet smacking sound. When I felt like my organs had slid back into place, I caught up with the kids, who were looking at the eight-inch-deep carve out in the ground.

"I think that will work," I said while we all looked down. "This time though, we're going to wrap some shrapnel up inside as well." Again, we had more than we needed in the truck: screws, staples, nails small hand tools … we didn't care as we bundled everything up. By the time it was all said and done, we had nearly a hundred of them.

"Let's go get the Talbot compound back!" I was happy. It was the first modicum of hope I'd had in a while, and I was going to enjoy it. The truck sounded like rocks going through a cement mixer by the time we pulled up to Ron's. That we had everyone's attention was without a doubt. We'd known this was a one-way trip with the truck, so I'd made what sounded like a decent plan on the go. It had more holes than Trip's underwear and smelled as bad upon closer examination. I had let the kids out before I drove closer. Their job now was to creep as close as they could to the horde and climb a tree. I had to hope that zombies hadn't thought to post sentries quite yet. That was a comforting thought as I rolled on. I lit a makeshift fuse, fixed the bungee cord on the steering wheel to keep it straight, and popped a heavy rock on the accelerator to get it closer, then I bailed.

"No, no, no." I'd gone face first into a poison ivy plant. That was not the greatest way to start a mission off. The truck plowed into and through quite a few rows of zombies before it succumbed to the terrain and the sheer press of dead people around and under it. Zombies swarmed around and even in it looking for a meal. I'd gotten off the long driveway and into the woods. I got to the very outer edges of the zombies before finding a decent-sized tree to climb, and one that actually afforded some cover when the debris started to fly. I was not more than ten feet off the ground when the tree vibrated. A wash of heat and bits of metal blew past me. Then came the wonderful smell of burning corpses. I was downwind, fantastic. I got up higher, hoping to out climb the stench. It sort of worked. I was damn near thirty feet up. I scanned the tree line to my left. Travis was waving his arm back and forth. I acknowledged him then raised my shoulders in a questioning shrug. He pointed to where Jesse and Meredith were. I could barely make them out through the cover of branches, but that they were safe, that was all I needed to know.

I finally got a decent look at the truck, or at least what was left. The heft of the body was fine, but the cab had been shredded, peeled back, in fact—looked like a giant pissed-off ape had stripped it back thinking a banana was inside. Dozens of zombies laid around the wreckage in various forms of body-frayed disarrayed states. Those that weren't outright dead were missing limbs or had large swaths of muscle torn from their bodies, making any form of decent locomotion out of the question. Arms hung at odd angles, legs were bent awkwardly, torsos had gaping holes; it was all the carnage one would expect from an IED, or improvised explosive device. A couple of zombies were even ablaze, which worked in our favor as they sought to share their body heat with others.

"Who's out there?" Ron called from the deck once the

truck simmered down from blazing inferno to camp fire. Meredith called out.

"It's me, Daddy!" she said triumphantly.

"Mer?" he yelled out. I caught the hitch in his throat. I'm not going to lie; I teared up a bit as well. Who wouldn't? His daughter, who he had no idea how she was doing, suddenly shows up and is right as rain. "Who's with you, honey?"

Zombies were beginning to meander over to the sound of her voice, looking around for the source. "Jesse, Travis, and Uncle Mike!" I watched a flare of flame come up from her spot then drop down close to the base of the tree, closer than I would have liked it. I didn't think the bomb had enough power to knock the tree down, but that wasn't a risk one took. If the ride to the ground didn't kill you, then the zombies would take up the slack. I could see her leaning over to watch the explosion.

"Meredith, hide!" I yelled, using as much force as I could. She peered at me for the briefest of seconds, and then I think it all kind of dawned on her. It was a damn shame that she had a fair amount of Talbot running through her as well. The explosion was glorious. There were vivid reds, deep blues, dark greens, and purply purples. Ran out of adjectives. It ripped the entire layer of bark off the bottom three feet of tree. Its days were indeed numbered. Although, odds were it wasn't going to fall today. Disease, rot, and ruin would be its downfall. The nearest zombies were propelled in the air along with various body parts. If it were people, I would have been sickened. That it was zombies only made it that much better. I conveniently forgot the simple fact that they once were human.

I was easily over fifty yards away from her, and still, I found a two-inch nail embedded in the tree not more than a couple of inches from my head. "Damn." I used force and pulled a good half inch of it from the tree.

"Talbot where you at?" It was BT.

I made sure I had my voice under control. If it hitched while I replied, he would rib me mercilessly. It wasn't just that he was my best friend. It was now I felt like I could share the burden I'd been shouldering the last three days alone. Of course, the kids had been holding their own. It was just, at the end of the day, their safety was my responsibility. That was tough enough, but that two of them were my sibling's kids made it that much more difficult.

"Over here, man," I said reaching as deep down as I could for my baritone.

"Good to see you. About time, man. Where the hell you been?"

"What are you, my mother?"

"I missed that." I think he was talking to Gary.

"Me too, man." I said softly. "We've come to rid you of your infestation!"

"Mike, I'm not thrilled you gave my daughter explosives."

"Relax, brother. They're fucking sparklers. Fire in the hole!" I yelled before lighting one and ducking behind the trunk. Leaves rained down on me as my tree shook. It was twenty maybe twenty-five explosions later I called a cease-fire. I wasn't sure anybody would hear me, as I could barely hear myself, and I was the one doing the talking. My ears were ringing, and my eyes were bouncing. The zombies had taken hellacious damage, but even more importantly, they'd yielded ground. In all likelihood, we'd only killed ten percent or so of the horde, but they'd had enough, at least for this round. At some point, gunfire had erupted on Ron's deck. They were making the tactical withdrawal of the zombies a full-on retreat. I climbed down off the tree to see if it was any type of ruse on their part. I made sure to keep an eye out on the too-maimed-to-walk zombies that could still inflict a deadly wound. So far, so good.

I went over to each tree and waited for the kids to come down, urging them to run for the house while I watched their backs. It was while I waited for Jesse to get back safely when I thought about how I didn't have a weapon—well a rifle, anyway. I still had plenty of bombs, not great for in-close combat though. Meredith was the last down, and I ran with her back to the house. BT wrapped me up in a huge bear hug when I got to the top of the deck. I didn't have the heart to tell him I was covered in poison ivy oil. It wasn't a long hug anyway, once he got a big strong dose of me.

"You fucking reek, man! But it's still awesome to see you!" I noticed he was backing away before coming forward to grab me.

"Thanks, man," I told him as he placed me down. He had a big grin on his face. "Before you go asking, everyone else is all right. They're in the bunker." I consciously moved closer to him, just to screw with him.

"Want a sandwich?" Trip had come outside in nothing more than his underwear and mismatched socks. He held up what looked like three pieces of bread. "I always get hungry after sex, man. Me and the missus were going at it so hard the earth moved. A few times!" He smiled then proceeded to scratch his nether regions before once again thrusting the sandwich under my nose. "Whoa, man. I just realized I should have put pickles on this thing," he said as he sampled the air and headed back into the house.

"Your wife isn't even here!" BT called him out.

"Whoa, man. Then I guess I rocked my own world." He held up his right hand and looked at it with an awed expression.

BT walked away, disgusted. Muttering something about crazy whiteys. I too walked away when he grabbed his sandwich again and started eating. Unfortunately, Trip decided to follow me. Finally, I stopped and just started talking, trying to distract myself from him. I told everyone what was going on at the post office and about the new development with the zombies, although they'd witnessed some of that first hand.

They were still out there, but they'd pulled back completely out of arm throwing range. We went into the house. I needed to get cleaned off and hydrated, and a little food wouldn't hurt, either. Especially considering that Trip's bread sandwich was starting to sound better and better. When I was done, Ron sat down at the table next to me.

"Now what?" he asked. "And yes, you still smell a little like vinegar—well a lot like vinegar, actually."

"Must have soaked in. At least I'll preserve well. As for the post office, I guess we mount a rescue. Maybe it was a mistake to separate," I told him.

"You think?"

"Hey Ron, I know you're worried, but I didn't come to that decision on my own. If you remember correctly, I wanted to take my family who I mistakenly thought was the source of this newest threat as far away from here as possible, and it was you that maintained, fervently, I might add, that we had to stay."

"I'm sorry, I'm sorry. I've just been so worried."

He felt even worse after I told him what the kids and I had been through the last couple of days. He kept refilling my water and offering to make something for me to eat.

Gary came into the room decked out in all the football gear he must have been able to round up in the tri-county region. A *Star Wars* storm trooper would have looked under-dressed next to him.

"Going somewhere?" I asked him.

"Aren't we going to get everyone else?"

"You're going like that?" BT had finally got some distance between himself and Trip. For some reason, Trip followed him around incessantly, and BT couldn't stand it. He would peek around corners in the house making sure Trip wasn't in the room before he would enter. More times than not, though, the perpetual stoner would be behind him, wondering what BT was looking at. You could oftentimes find him peering underneath the bigger man's shoulder and arm.

"The question you should be asking is, 'Why aren't you going like this?'" Gary replied.

"I could round up five hundred brothers, and I guarantee I would not find as many crazy motherfuckers as are in the house."

"That's true; the average rate of insanity is higher among whites than non-whites." Trip had ducked under BT's outstretched arm and walked into the room. "Although, if you can believe it, Genogerians actually have the highest rate of all at a staggering two-point-three percent within their general population. Wait ,,, is that this world?"

"Did he just say old people are insane?" Gary asked.

I shrugged. Sometimes you could only take a stab at what Trip was talking about.

"I'm not sure if I should agree with him or not." BT looked confused.

"I wouldn't. He'll just change his mind about what he said later." I figured this for sage advice.

Ron wanted everyone back on track. "We need to figure out how to get them back."

"Through the use of overwhelming force," Gary said.

"Nice." I could get onboard with that plan.

"Not very helpful," Ron chided him. Gary looked slightly deflated.

"He's actually on to something. You've seen it yourself; these new zombies aren't big on taking casualties. They are apparently becoming self-aware. Wow, I did not realize just how scary that sounded until I said it. Fuck. Anyway, umm … where was I? Yeah if they're getting routed, they will withdraw. We just need to show them the door so to speak."

"Do we leave the house?"

"We can't leave it completely unguarded, but I think if a

few of us head out now, we could be back before dark with the rest of our families."

"I've got something that might help." Mad Jack beamed. He handed us small boxes about the size of a garage door remote.

"And these are?" I asked him. He looked at us like we were supposed to know what they did.

I noticed Trip was repeatedly pressing the green button on the side. I was thankful it was not a personal detonation device used to blow yourself up in case of an emergency.

"Zombie repellers shrunk down!" He beamed.

I was skeptical. We'd had mixed results thus far. I mean sure, practice makes perfect, but when a failed experiment could lead to death, one got wary.

"I improved the battery life and the odds of a fire have been halved."

"Halved you say? And what were the odds of a fire before the improvements?"

He didn't look too particularly pleased to answer that question. He turned his head and mumbled a number.

"He said sixty-three percent." Trip was drinking something that looked like ice cream.

"We have chocolate chip ice cream?" Travis asked.

Tommy pulled him away when my son reached for it. He shook his head. "It's milk."

What I thought had been a whiff of zombie wafted by my nose. I now realized it was old and curdled milk, with some sort of foreign object in it, probably fly larvae.

"We need to save them, if only to get Stephanie back and rein his fool ass back in." BT could not get far enough away from Trip. He covered his nose with his hand.

I nearly forgot about the box in my hand. "Wait, sixty-three percent chance of bursting into flame, really?"

"Yeah, but I halved it."

"Oh great, so there's only a one in three chance of this thing bursting into a white phosphorous grenade then?"

"Thirty-one point six seven is not one in three," he said indignantly. "And it does not burn like a phosphorous grenade. The wearer would suffer no more than a second-degree burn roughly the size of a bowling ball."

"Oh, is that all? And what of the bite marks from the zombies nearby?"

"Well, that would be an unfortunate side-effect."

"Did he just call getting eaten by zombies a side-effect?" BT looked like he was about to take up arms.

I smiled. Sure, it was serious business, but the sight of BT about to lose his fucking mind was priceless.

"What if I were to wear two; that way if one burned up, I'd have a spare?" I asked.

"Oh, I wouldn't do that." He sounded very troubled by that thought but did not elaborate before leaving. He oftentimes did that. I don't think he meant it as a slight. I just think he had the social graces of a pre-pubescent boy suffering from crippling shyness mixed in with the attention span of a moth.

"He's a weird bird," Trip said before taking in his last big gulp of whatever the hell he had in that glass. Hearing the thick liquid slide down his throat threatened to loosen my lunch's hold within my stomach. He smacked his lips and rubbed his belly. "What did I just eat?"

"Are you seriously thinking about using these things?" BT looked on the verge of smashing his against the floor like a television remote after his favorite team lost in the playoffs because of a bad call.

"It still works two out of three times." I said, thinking I did more to rev him up than calm him down.

"We still need to get out of here." Ron brought the discussion back full circle. "Just because they've withdrawn doesn't mean they've given up."

"That's why I'm wearing this!" Gary thumped himself in

the chest with a hockey stick I'd yet to have seen. He winced from the strike.

"You all right?" Meredith asked him.

"I'm fine," he forced out.

This was not a good scenario. We had already split the group, and we were going to do so again. The house would be undermanned while we made our rescue attempt. There was no doubt it had to happen. We just couldn't go about this the traditional Mike Talbot way.

"It might be better to leave them where they are?" Tommy paced around the room, not focusing on any one thing, at least not in this realm.

"What the hell does that mean?" Ron was not too thrilled with the prospect of leaving his wife alone.

"They'll be fine for at least a week," he said, never looking at anybody.

"And then what?" Ron asked.

"Then? Then they might be on their own." Tommy left the room.

"Duh, duh, duh!" Trip sang the words. "That sounds ominous! They usually play that music in the movie when someone is about to jump out of a closet." Trip's gaze immediately went to the outside door. He stared at that thing longer than I figured he could until what I thought would happen happened. "Are we waiting on pizza?" he asked. "My stomach hurts. I maybe shouldn't have had that second blueberry and mayonnaise smoothie." He went in the same direction as Tommy, although I think he was heading for a bathroom. I had no idea where Tommy went, probably the roof to get better reception for whatever signal he was tuning in to.

"Okay, so we don't need them to leave. We just need them to clear a path. We mount a few of these incendiary devices on the car."

"They're not incendiary devices!" Mad Jack yelled.

"Shit, when did you come back in?" I'd been busted.

"Okay, we mount some of these zombie repellers-slash fire bombs."

"Talbot, why are you prodding the genius? This is what makes them evil." BT was getting in on the goading.

"You don't understand the load the circuitry is under for the signal that needs to be produced. The right components for this job haven't even been made yet. I'm working with prototypes here. That any of them work is a testament to my...."

"It's okay, Mad Jack. Don't get your pocket protector all twisted in knots." I walked over to him. He was not a fan of good-natured ribbing, and I'd be damned if I indeed made him an evil genius and awoke to see that he had teleported me to an alternate realm where maybe aliens ruled or I was haunted by ghosts. Zombies were bad enough; I'd leave it at that. "Listen, these boxes have saved our ass a couple of times, and we appreciate the hell out of them. Okay?"

He nodded quickly and pushed up on frames for glasses that weren't there. "Okay," he echoed. I looked sternly over to BT, who I'm sure was about to undo my gesture of good will.

"Ron, I'm going to need a truck."

"Of course you are." He sighed.

"I'll be gentle."

"I'm running out of trucks, Mike."

"We'll get more."

"It's not the same thing."

I get that there's a certain satisfaction to going and buying a car that you've worked hard for. You appreciate something more when you've earned it. But there was this little button in my brother that no matter how hard I tried to press it, it would not depress. The world was different. A lot of those old ways of thinking were no longer relevant. Sure, we still needed to hold on to faith and morals, compassion, the things that made us decent human beings, but the other shit, the pursuit of material things, appearances, keeping up with the Joneses

... those things made no sense anymore. Everything we did was purely about survival. Being the first child, he'd always been an overachiever, and his hard work was supposed to mean more than just "making it." I could see his angle. It just wasn't valid anymore, and that pissed him off to no end.

"It's the truck or our families; what's more important?" I don't think I meant to strike that quick and hard at his jugular. Maybe I did. His eyes shot to mine, full of anger and resentment, and then immediately cooled to reason. Now that I had him, I was going to go full bore. "I need the Gatling gun as well."

BT's air sucking-in sound wasn't helping my cause. I pressed on.

"I need to plow the field so to speak. I need it to mow down all the zombies in the road leading up here. I don't make it out of here, they're all screwed."

Ron stood, pushing himself away from the table. "Fine, Mike. Take my truck. Take my gun. Why don't you take my Rolex as well? Make a clean sweep of everything I've worked for in my life. That's what you do, isn't it? Just take? You've been doing it your entire life. Why work hard when people are just going to hand you shit? Isn't that your motto? Oh, Mike, he's the baby of the family. We have to look out for him. We have to help him. Look how far that got you in life. Couldn't hold a decent job to save your life, could you? Just a couple of years ago, you had to call Mom and Dad and ask for money so your family could eat. How pathetic is that? Forty and can't provide for his own!"

"Ron, that's enough." BT stepped closer.

"You don't know shit, BT," Ron spat. "His entire life, he's skated on the backs of those carrying the rink. And it's never enough. He always wants more, and somehow us idiots keep giving it to him. My father worked his ass off providing for our family. He did an admirable job. We ate and we had a roof over our head. But you don't know how many times those basic necessities were threatened by Mike. His legal expenses siphoned off a good portion of our parents' savings. Or how Mike defaulted on his car loan and my parents, being the good little co-signers that they are, had to foot the bill. Mike has always been about Mike. He places himself above all others, no matter the cost."

"You're a damn fool," BT said, pointing a meaty finger in Ron's face. "I've personally seen him put himself in harm's way more times than I can count to save someone."

"Yeah?" Ron questioned. "Did he do it for him or for them?"

"What the hell are you talking about? He saved them."

"I'm saying, 'Did he save them for himself or for them?'"

"What you're asking makes no sense."

"Sure it does. Mike would save his family and friends at all costs because he would not want to put himself through the pain and suffering of watching a loved one die."

"That's not always the case. I've seen him risk his life for those he barely knows."

"And by doing so, it fans the flames of his ego, which burns as bright as the sun. He does what he does so that he appears as if legend. Isn't that it, Mike? If you can't actually do in this life, then there's always the smoke and mirrors routine."

I'd had enough. I can absorb a few punches if it allows someone the opportunity to vent, but Ron looked like he was just getting started. "Let's get a few things clear, brother." Ron was about to speak. "No, it's time for you to shut the fuck up while I say my piece. You got yours; I get mine. Yeah, was I a dumb kid? Sure was. Did I cost Mom and Dad a shitload in legal fees? Again, a big yes. In fact, close to thirty grand, which, if you had bothered to ask, I had paid back all but five grand before I got laid off the last time. As for the Jeep, after Dennis totaled it, I had two options. Either have him thrown in jail for drunk driving and stealing my car or pay for the damages out of pocket. Yeah, Mom and Dad paid for it up front, then Dennis and I paid it back. You do realize at that time we were both working for Dad's construction company? No? You missed that part? As for asking Mom and Dad for money when I got laid off, yeah I did.

"We were in fucking trouble. I couldn't make the house payment. I was doing odd jobs and spending every waking hour looking for work. Do people sometimes need help? Yeah, man, they do. We're not all born with a silver fucking spoon in our mouth. Oh, don't go giving me that butt-hurt expression on your face. You were always the golden child, the one that could do no wrong. Everything you ever received growing up was brand fucking new. You ever get a fifth-generation hand-me-down bike that's about ten years out from the newest version? It had no fucking pedals, Ron! All I could do was walk the thing up hills and glide down. As for saving my family and friends, why the fuck would *anyone* want to go through the pain of watching someone they cared for die? That makes absolutely no fucking sense. Am I being selfish because of that? I don't know. Maybe that's the defini-tion of it, but sure, I'd rather die trying to save them rather than be safe and sound while they were in danger. As for saving those I didn't know, I don't know what skewed version of me you have, but I don't do it because I want to be written about in textbooks. I do it because it's the right fucking thing to do, you asshole. It's not my fault your expensive college degree isn't worth too much in this new world, not my fucking fault at all. Speaking of which, Ron, how much did that degree cost? I don't seem to remember you having to repay your college loans like I did. Was that a gift from Mom and Dad? You know what? You can shove your truck and your gun up your ass. I'll walk out of here. I'll get your wife and your kid back here, and then I'm leaving. I honestly didn't know you thought so fucking little of me. I've always looked up to you. I should have realized you were looking down at me." He reached over; this time it was my turn to leave the room.

"Shit." I was outside Ron's storage area. I truly meant what I'd said about walking out of here. But I still needed a rifle and a ton of ammo, and there really wasn't a way for me to ask for it.

"Hey, Dad." Travis came up by my side.

"Hey, Kiddo."

"You all right?"

"I'm good," I told him, putting my arm around his shoulder. "I'll be better when we have you mom, brother, and sister back, and I guess nephew now. Hey, while you're here, I don't think your uncle will have any problem with you maybe getting that rifle over there along with those magazines and that can of ammo." I pointed to places all over the room that I didn't dare enter. When we went out to the driveway, BT was behind the wheel of a brand new Dodge Ram.

"Just because he thinks you're an irresponsible, immature, capricious, thoughtless, harebrained individual doesn't mean he feels the same way about me."

"Feel better now?" I asked him.

He nodded. "I'd beep the horn if I didn't think the zombies would come."

Mad Jack's head popped up from the other side of the truck. "Magnets!" he said excitedly.

"Okay? Should I be happy about that?"

"Oh very much so. I'm sticking the boxes all around the truck."

"Could you maybe not put it there?" I asked as he stuck in on the little door that covered the gas cap.

"Oh that would probably be a good idea."

"How can you be so smart and so oblivious?"

He didn't seem too happy with my observation.

Tommy had two large duffel bags, one of which was suspiciously moving. At first, I thought it might be Henry, then I saw smoke leaking through the heavy material.

Tommy shrugged. "He said he couldn't be seen entering the truck."

"So you carried him in a duffel bag? Now you're just being an enabler." I told him.

Tommy shrugged again. He did, however, toss both bags up into the bed of the truck like he was a disgruntled airline employee.

"Hey, man. I dropped my jay!" came muffled through the bag, then there was a harsh coughing scream. "I'm burning, man! I'm burning, man!" Then a pause. "Wait … am I at Burning Man or am I a man burning? That's deep!"

"I can't take this." I strode over and unzipped the bag. I backed away, quickly fanning clean air to my nose. "Nope, you're definitely burning. So that's what old patchouli smells like when it cooks. Damn."

"This is my best shirt!" Trip sat up and was quickly patting down the front of his Hawaiian print shirt that looked like it had been made before the small island chain became the fiftieth state.

"Why is he here!?" BT roared, stepping out of the truck.

"He's why I couldn't be seen," Trip said in hushed tones.

Now I got it.

"He's just going to screw everything up!"

"It'll be all right. He knows what he's doing. You ride up in the front, Trav, with BT. Me, Tommy, and Trip will hang out in the back."

"You sure?"

"Yeah, we're fine. We got the boxes. Oh hey, MJ, what's the battery life on these things?"

"If they don't burn, about an hour. Considerably less if they do."

"Great. Where's the on off switch."

"Switch?"

"Fuck. BT we have to roll while we can."

"I'm not happy about this, Mike." The truck dipped down as he got back in.

"When's the last time you were happy?"

"The minute before I met you and every minute before that."

"He's funny," Trip said.

"Trip, what the hell isn't funny to you?"

Travis opened up the small window. "Uncle Ron is on the deck." Travis waved. I didn't turn around. My wave would have included a couple of universally offensive gestures and maybe a few newly invented ones. We were rolling along at a blistering five miles an hour. We were all locked and loaded, even Trip. Tough to take a man serious with a joint hanging out of his mouth, but he looked all business, right now. Zombies started flooding out of the woods and directly onto our path as we rolled closer.

MJ's boxes might work just fine, but I've always been a bigger fan of eradication rather than deterrent. "Kiss my ass," I said, lighting a sparkler fuse. I jumped when I felt something brush up against my hindquarters. "What the fuck, Trip. I didn't mean literally! And definitely not you, man!"

"Oh, he knows what he's doing. It'll be all right." BT was mimicking me.

I've been proven wrong plenty of times, but usually not so quickly. Didn't have too much time to worry about it, though, as the bomb exploded off to our front. Luckily for us, BT was going slow, because the truck veered to the side, almost putting us in a ditch.

"What the hell!" he shouted. "Who throws bombs and doesn't tell people!"

"Maybe if you were paying more attention to what was going on in front of you rather than watching a grown man have his ass kissed, you would have known about it."

He grumbled a bit but didn't say anything else.

"Yo Daisy, I'm throwing more bombs."

"If you are referring to *Driving Miss Daisy*, she was his passenger. The chauffeur was Hoke Colburn."

"Never saw it. Just figured you looked like a Daisy."

With the truck still rolling, BT got out. I mean all the way out.

"What are you doing, man?" I got over to the far side of the bed. Trav reached over to grab the wheel.

"I'm doing something that should have been done a long time ago. I'm gonna beat your ass."

"Wait, man, this is crazy, we're in the middle of zombies and...."

He wasn't listening. He was still coming closer. I jumped out and ran to the front of the truck, making sure to keep as much of the truck between us as possible.

After a few attempts at trying to catch me and a slow rolling approach to the zombies who seemed mighty interested, BT finally got back in the truck. "You're lucky you're fast for a white guy."

Oh, I had all sorts of responses, but I wisely let them sit and stew in the sarcastic batter of my brain where they belonged. The beast had been sufficiently poked. I quietly climbed back into the truck. BT reached behind him and pulled the window shut.

"That guy's crazy," Trip said, swirling his finger around by his neck. He was also rolling his eyes, sticking his tongue in and out, and rubbing his belly.

"Yup, he's the crazy one, Trip." I guess at least Trip hadn't jumped out of a moving vehicle with zombies all around us to seek revenge. I didn't throw any more bombs, although the zombies seemed to have gotten the picture or MJ's boxes were working better than expected. Fifteen feet was still entirely too close; seven miles would have been better. We'd just turned off of Ron's small approach road when I smelled burning paint. At first, I thought it had something to do with the sparklers and maybe Trip had inadvertently lit one and now we were sitting on a rolling bomb, then I saw the smoke coming from the side of the truck. I leaned over.

"Shit." I tried to kick the flaming box off, but MJ must have used superglue based magnets because the thing didn't move, and I was afraid to keep hitting it for fear my boot would catch fire.

"What is that? What is that?" BT screamed. It didn't sound the least bit muffled through the glass, and it sounded like it came from a bullhorn when he slid it open.

I didn't say a word. It was Tommy who spoke. I think even Trip knew he was on BT's short shit-list and figured he might not be fast enough to get away should BT charge again. "Mad Jack's box is burning a hole through the quarter panel."

"Not a phosphorous grenade, my ass." I watched as paint and steel dripped down onto the ground.

BT slammed his hand down so hard on the steering wheel, he bent it. "I promised him I wouldn't wreck the truck!"

"At least you got it out of his sight." I was being sincere. The look he turned back on me showed that he didn't share in that sentiment. The box fell to the ground. A plume of flame and cloud rose, looking very much like a miniature nuclear bomb.

"You think that's like Hiroshima to the ants?" Trip asked me. He looked pretty upset about that prospect.

"Let's hope not. It looked like an unpopulated area." He perked up at my words.

"We don't have much time." Tommy said, not sure if it was to me or not as he wasn't looking my way.

"How do you know?" I knew what he was talking about.

"They're actively looking."

"Haven't they been for a while?"

"Sure, but they're a lot closer now, and that makes the link that much stronger. You should be able to feel it, too."

"Hell no, I've been ignoring that half of me as best I can. How much time do we have?"

"Unsure. Vampires don't live on the same time schedule as we do. They look at things in terms of decades where people look at things in terms of days. Soon though. That they already acted so quickly on my sister's death speaks volumes of their curiosity."

"And what of their intent?"

"Vampires aren't very social creatures, Mr. T."

"So we can reasonably assume it won't be good?"

"That's a fair assumption."

One more box caught on fire before we got to town. BT started swearing again. I was just happy it missed the tire, or we would have had to stop to change a flat, and I was already feeling the pressure of our time constraints. A lot of the zombies had peeled off with me from my first escape and then again with the kids, but like the good little zombies that they were, there was still plenty of them to go around. The seventy or eighty that were outside immediately started running in our direction. Slowly but surely, the ones inside the building started to trickle out as well. I stood up and leaned against the cab.

"Loud noise." I said just as I started lining up shots and pulling the trigger. I was so abundantly sick of zombies. I didn't enjoy killing them. I just wanted them dead. I wanted them extinct like I wanted mosquitoes extinct. Just seemed that right now, at this very moment of the earth's history, they were a part of the ecosystem and would be as difficult to get rid of as the damn pesky bug was. Tommy got next to me and started as well. After Trip lit another joint, he stood too, although I don't think his verbalizations of *bang, bang, bang*, as he pulled the trigger on an unloaded rifle were quite as effective. Tommy and I were doing a decent job of slaughtering the zombies. But even so, without MJ's boxes, we would have not been able to keep them at bay just by ourselves, and I think they knew that at first. That was why they kept coming. When they couldn't make those last few tantalizing feet, they lost heart and began to disperse. I didn't let them. Even though Tommy had stopped, I kept firing away. Cracking and splattering the backs of their exposed skulls like eggs. To let one go now only left an enemy for later, and that enemy could potentially spawn others.

I told BT to pull up as close to the broken down door as possible. He stopped and backed the truck up so that I was just about even with it. I poked my head in. Four zombies were huddled against the far side of the room, apparently feeling the effects of the boxes. The one snarling at me was the first to have his brains forcibly removed from his head. I jumped down out of the truck and into the building. When I went to kill the second, I realized my rifle was empty. Tommy handed me a magazine as he came in behind me.

"I'm going to get ahead of you on the kill total." I said as I slammed the magazine home.

"You could do this every day for the next ten years and you still would not have killed as many things as I have. I'll let you have your turn." He walked over to the doorway that led down the stairs. I finished off the remaining zombies and joined him.

I wondered if he had a tally, and if he did ... did I want to know? He said "things" and not people. Had he perhaps killed an elephant? A narwhal? Maybe even a yeti? Tommy smacking on the door pounded me out of my present thoughts.

"It's me, Tommy!"

There was a muffled questioning of "Tommy?" on the other side. I heard the door locks being turned and, when the door began to slightly open, there was some crying, not tears of sorrow or joy, just the kind of crying infants make. I looked in as the door was opened all the way. Justin was first at the door holding a rifle making sure we were who we said we were, and behind him was my wife holding a baby.

"Say hello to Grandpa," she said, smiling.

My first reaction was to turn around and look for my father. I'm pretty quick like that.

"You, Talbot, this is your grandson. Wesley Mike Talbot. Remember him? It hasn't been that long. Maybe you should stop hanging around with Trip." She held him up so I could get a better look. I went toward them in a slow-moving daze. The women folk were beaming. The boys looked like they'd seen every cootie a girl had to offer. Nicole was on a bed, she looked relieved and happy to have had the baby. My baby had had a baby; my heart skipped a few beats.

"You want to hold him?" Tracy asked tenderly.

"Umm... fuck no."

"You're not going to break him."

"Have you seen me not break anything?"

"Hmmm, you're probably right. Maybe I'll just hold him a little longer."

I thought I was going to melt into a puddle of man goo when he wrapped his tiny hand around my pinkie finger.

"He's so little." I moved in closer.

"Tracy, say your last words to your husband. I'm going to kill him!" BT boomed, coming into the small space. Wesley cried out in alarm and fear. I turned to watch BT's eyes grow wide. His mouth opened even larger. He shook his head and immediately left the shelter.

"Well, maybe I'll hold him. If an infant can scare that man, then he should be all right if I hold him." I was smiling like the village idiot with the baby in my arms. The baby's wispy eyebrows furrowed while he searched a brand new database for some information regarding me. He was coming up woefully short and probably would for many years to come.

"Whoa." Trip said as he came to a sliding stop. "This

seems a little early; does this baby have blue eyes or brown?" he asked as he came closer.

Tracy intercepted him. He seemed to get confused for a moment. Stephanie came over and lifted him up easily. She would have spun him around like a top if she had the space. She kissed him a few times before placing him back on the ground. "I missed you." She brushed his hair back from his face.

I waited for him to ask who she was. That wasn't an unreasonable response from him. What he said gave me chills instead. "Wherever I go, whenever I go, I guess is a better way of saying it, you're there and you're always as important to me then as you are now." He kissed her. Then in an instant, he changed the tone. "Did you pick up my dry cleaning? I have an important meeting on Thursday. And, oh yeah, the funkies are getting closer." He said when the cobwebs lifted from his mind.

"Hour, my ass. MJ and his machines, everyone up." I handed Wesley back to his grandmother. Gotta admit that was truly weird. Was it going to be weird having sex with a grandmother? I'm a little ashamed that thought went through my head at that moment, but not really. Then she turned to help Nicole, and I realized I was not going to have any problem with calling her granny. She was more fit and toned than when we got married. Everything was going to be A-okay.

"You have a funny expression on your face. Are you high?" Trip asked.

"What? No," I told him.

"You wanna be?"

"Is it easier holding a head up with no brain in it?"

"You should know," he shot back.

"Wow, can't say I was expecting that from you. Good one. Come on, let's help everyone get out of here."

He smiled for a sec, and then I could watch as he forgot completely why he was smiling. He looked around, maybe hoping to rediscover why. I couldn't decide if Trip was blessed or cursed. How awesome would it be to forget all the bad that happened in the world? I'm thinking pretty damn good, because the man was everlastingly happy, but that could be because he was unendingly high.

"Good job," I told Justin as we shoved everyone into the truck. Nicole, the baby, and Tracy were in the cab with BT. The rest of us were stuffed in the back of the bed. Tommy, Travis, and I stood to make room for the others. Travis and I leaned over, holding on to the roof of the truck. Tommy stood straight up as if he'd been rooted to his spot. The zombies were within five feet of us when BT pulled away. I think, at first, he was afraid someone was going to fall out, but he wasn't even going fast enough to outpace them. He sped up when I yelled at him. I think he was hoping that if anyone fell out, it would be me.

We were about halfway back to Ron's when BT began to rapidly slow down. I stood up straight to try and get a better idea and view of what I was looking at. Even then, that didn't help much. There were heads, dozens of them, young, old, women, men, children, arranged in perfectly formed rows across the entire two-lane roadway. They'd been whole zombies first. At least, I'm pretty sure, there were no tortured screams for mercy as they'd been twisted from the shoulders of their original holders. These had not been severed by an extremely sharp melee weapon. They'd been ripped clean free. Some heads sat askew with some spinal cordage still attached.

"We've been gone less than forty minutes. Who could have had the time to do this?" I asked no one. Of course, someone could have already had a bag of heads for some reason and now put them out there to screw with us, but these were fresh if the blood trails running down the slope of the road were any indication. I caught movement to the right side of the road an instant after Tommy's head swiveled in that direction.

A cartoon character pajama-clad boy of about five had his back to us as he dragged something through the brush. I knew what it was before it ever became visible. When her hair became visible, it only confirmed the nightmare. She was nude, save the oversized t-shirt she'd been wearing. Mother and son had been sleeping when whatever had come for them had indeed found them. He had his small fists wrapped in her long blond hair as he struggled to pull her onto the roadway.

The boy didn't look our way until Stephanie gasped. He snarled, exposing impossibly long teeth and blackened blood shot eyes. There was a ring of red around his mouth, most likely that was from his mother. I didn't need to be as smart as Mad Jack to figure out who had visited these horrors upon this family. The trio was close. This had been a small message to inform us of their arrival. It was Tommy that put a bullet into the boy's chest, exploding his heart, and then before the boy could even fall over, he put one in his head. Even if I wasn't shaking nearly uncontrollably, I'm not sure I could have pulled that trigger.

"Get us home!" I slammed a fist on the cab.

"The heads, Mike!" BT yelled back.

"Fuck the heads; get us home! They're in danger!"

The truck lurched forward. BT did his best to skirt around, but they were unavoidable. The loud crunching was as disturbing as it was deafening. Not deafening in the traditional sense but rather it was the only sound that could be heard. Neither the thunderous roar of the engine nor Wesley's cries could drown out that sickening resonance. For some reason I'll never be able to discern, I turned around. It looked a lot like you would expect truck-crushed heads to look like, eyeballs, brain, blood, and skull fragments respite with tufts of hair littered the road behind us.

"I think I swallowed my jay." Trip looked a little rough around the edges.

Travis had his head down, as did most everyone else; it

could have been in silent prayer or in effort to hold down gorge. Either had its merits. BT had thrown caution to the wind. He was driving like Tracy now. If he hit anything bigger than a castaway nickel, then a fair number of his passengers would be airborne. Maybe it would be better to be left by the side of the road here rather than go back to what I perceived was going to be a slaughter at Ron's. They had no idea what was heading their way. We were a mile out when we could start to hear the pop of faraway shots. Somehow, BT coaxed the truck a little faster.

"Mike, what do I do when I get there?" he yelled.

I knew what he was asking. I just had no way of knowing what to tell him. Should we crash through everything and let the chips fall where they may or did he stop for us to make a tightly knit killing formation move to the house?

"Wing it, man."

"I'm not you!"

"Thank God." Trip muttered.

"What?" I asked him.

"Oh, I'm just happy. I didn't swallow my bone. It's right here." He pulled a still lit marijuana cigarette from his pocket. He had a crinkle of a smile pulling up the corners of his eyes. I knew he'd been talking about me, but right now, I'd have to give him a free pass. BT was going so fast the press of zombies didn't have enough time to let MJ's boxes take effect, if they even still worked, that is. Zombies and parts of zombies started coming up and over the hood. We all had to duck down to keep from getting rained upon. I thought Ron's son, Mark, was going to pass out when a hand with three fingers landed in his lap. His mother quickly picked it up and tossed it over the side. She was not going to be able to get rid of the perfect blood outline left behind though. If we made it through today, those pants were going to end up on the burn pile.

The sheer press of the zombies was beginning to slow the

heavy truck down. Ron might not trust me with his toys, but BT had set a record for time lapsed until complete destruction. Radiator fluid was blowing straight up like Old Faithful. Tires were hissing as the two on the left side were blown out from some foreign object. We were listing heavily. Those of us not smart enough to hold on for dear life were firing. It was a race to the finish line, our lives the prize. Thick smoke poured from Ron's house, some from gunfire some from the burgeoning fire. The shit had started; it was all or nothing. The Talbot last stand was in full effect. Fire erupted from under the hood. Bullets blew from the cab and the bed as we tried to keep the zombies as far from us as possible. Hands slapped at us while we whipped by. Teeth bit down on air. Yelling and screaming was coming from so many directions I couldn't even begin to track it. I did what I could do in my personal circle of hell. My barrel was beginning to glow a dull red as I tossed rounds through it at a rate it was barely rated for. Didn't matter if the rifle made it through the day if we didn't.

The war was on; the zombies were in it for the win. There was a line of Talbots on the deck and none of them were shooting in our direction. We had no cover. The threat to them was closer and more real. Somehow, we were the cavalry in all of this, and I didn't think we were going to make it. At some point, Travis had grabbed the bombs; Justin and he were lighting multiple fuses. The truck rocked from the closeness of the explosions, we were now being pelted with debris, much of it zombie rubble. So much was going on, my mind was in hyper-drive. I had my zone of influence, and that was all I could control. I don't know when the barrel of my rifle split or when fragments of the bullet splintered into my forearm, never even felt them. It was Trip who ripped it from my grip and sent it off into the crowd, where the smell of cooking flesh erupted when it stuck to the side of a zombie man's face. He thrust his own, and a magazine that he had in a pocket, into my hands.

I didn't even think to thank him as I hit the bolt release button and started savagely meting out justice again. There was no one in or on that truck, save Wesley and his mother, who was crouched protectively over him, not fighting desperately for their lives. BT even had his rifle resting on the door-frame while he pulled the trigger. Aiming was not necessary.

"Hold on!" I yelled when he approached the first zombie channel dug into Ron's yard. I lurched forward, barely catching my head from bouncing off the roof. I left a bloody wake where my arm had hit. Tracy's scream flared through my mind. I didn't even think about what I was doing when I got on top on that roof, down the hood and jumped onto the zombie who had grabbed her hair and was trying to pull her from the window. I slammed the butt of my rifle so many times into the side of his head it collapsed under its own weight. He died with thick swaths of her hair in his hands. I'd bludgeoned him to death. The truck was still moving past, and I turned the rifle back around. I was yelling so loud, I could feel my vocal chords being shredded.

Nancy was ripped from the back of the truck.

"Mike!" BT yelled when he saw me.

"*Go*! Get them inside!" I launched, slamming my shoulder into the zombie's head, pushing him over. Blood spurted from a bite-sized wound in Nancy's cheek. Teeth cracked around my hand guard as the zombie bit down in an attempt to keep feeding.

I reached down, pulled her up, and tossed her into the outstretched hands of Stephanie, who was still within reach. Mark grabbed onto his mother's side and helped to pull her aboard. I caught a glimpse of a wide-eyed Tracy in the side view mirror before she was obscured. Zombies pressed in from all sides. The end was nigh. Don't listen to the fucking bell because it's tolling for thee. Not quite the poem but fitting. I was out of rounds, my hands blistered as I grabbed the barrel, but that mattered little. Just giving the zombies a little char flavoring if they got to eat them. The rifle held up for the first half dozen or so smashes, then there was the unsatisfying crack of plastic giving way. Soon, I'd be swinging just the upper receiver, and that wouldn't have enough heft to do the damage it needed to. I had just enough time to see a trio of women dressed in heavy gothic garb not more than fifty yards to my side before I was swarmed over.

11

THE VAMPIRES MOVED FORWARD, THE ZOMBIES THEY PASSED completely ignored them—actively avoided them, in fact, as if they were a black hole upon the fabric of reality and to approach would sweep them up into an alternate reality where zombies were hunted for sustenance.

"I smell them! I smell them!" Sophia had gone ahead of the two women and came back running. A large smile dominated her delicate features. Within the hour, they came to a large, gated community. A ten-foot-high, steel-plated door on a track led into the housing area.

"Do not come any further!" a man guarding the gate said in an authoritative voice. He stood inside a small shack built a few feet taller than the fence.

"Sir, but we have come so far and we need help!" Sophia said, stepping out of her dress as easily as if it had been a wrapped towel. She stood there, placing her left index finger on her bottom lip. Her lithe form accentuated in all the ways a man could find attractive. The guard started stuttering.

"Humans are so predictable," Charity said when the gate began to roll back. "And delicious." She cut open her tongue dragging it across her teeth.

"Be careful. They may be predictable, but they are still dangerous. Let us find out how this place works before we feed."

"You are right." Charity sighed, letting her canines slide back.

"You should cover up, ma'am." Another guard had come out. He looked embarrassed to be gazing upon Sophia's nude form, yet he could not take his eyes from her.

"Dangerous? Look how stupid they are. Ruled completely by their groins. I could rip his throat open and he would still be looking upon her breasts," Charity whispered to Payne as they strode closer.

"Please forgive my sister; the zombie invasion has not been kind to her mind." Payne said.

The guard's eyes grew wide for a moment as he seemed to see the other two women for the first time.

"There's … there's children here. She can't be seen like this. Decent folk just trying to um…." He lost his train of thought when he looked over to Sophia, who was running a finger along the inside of her thigh.

"Even now, he is among the most evil presence he will ever encounter, and yet his manhood grows engorged. They are fools."

"We will dine, Charity, but I want the entire feast, not just the side dishes. Sister, please put your clothes back on. The fine citizens of…"

"Umm, of New Lynn."

"New Lynn citizens are more sensible than this. They have small children that will be frightened of your attributes."

Sophia licked her lips, bent over, picked her dress back up, and refastened it. When she was done, she caressed the sides of the man's face. His eyes upturned at her touch. Then she let him go to join the other two as they strode in.

Children were at play on the far side of the street. Women and men were busy, some chopping wood, others hanging laundry. At least one seemed to be trying his hand at furniture making with varying degrees of success. If the pile of broken wood in his front yard were to be used as an indicator.

"I think I'm going to like it here." Payne said while they strode in. More people turned to watch as the women walked past. Some had a niggling in the back of their minds that something wasn't quite right. It was the children who saw through the facade the vampires put on. The women were consumed by curiosity, jealousy, and like the men, by lust. The vampires had long ago honed their abilities to manipulate the emotions of their prey. Even men who had a proclivity for other men found themselves desiring the trio. Lust and desire, the most base and debased of human emotions, had long been used in the seduction of their feeding. It was the children that had no such craving and could get past that. The game of soccer had stopped. One of the younger children had started to cry about the monsters. Charity turned and smiled, placing her finger up by her mouth in a shushing sound. Warm urine ran down the small girl's leg.

One of the small boys went running for the leader of their community, hoping that somehow he would once again be able to keep them safe. Within a couple of minutes, a tall, white-haired man strode purposefully toward the women who had stopped by the center of the town.

"Welcome, welcome to New Lynn." He led with his arm outstretched. As he got closer, he pulled his hand back in. His jovial smile faltered for a moment before he plastered it back on. "My name is Earl Blackstone, but most people just call me Judge."

"A pleasure." Payne held her hand out to be grasped.

Judge looked at it like it was a serpent wrapped around a spider.

Payne looked at him curiously when he did not take her proffered hand. She smiled as she withdrew the offer.

"This is a fine community you have here," she said.

"It is. We've worked hard to make sure we're safe." Earl looked over the women, curiosity turning to unease.

"Is there ever such a thing as safe? There are so many monsters in this world."

"Monsters in this world!" Sophia giggled as she echoed Payne's words. She did a small spin before sitting down on a park bench, still giggling, heady from the intoxication of so much food, so close.

"Are you three just passing through?" Judge asked, a cold chill caressing his shoulders and trickling down his back. He rarely carried his weapon within the confines of the wall. Now was one of those times he'd wished he had not left it atop his dresser.

"Oh, I do believe we plan on staying for a little while," Payne said.

"He does not look at us the same way as the others," Charity said as she studied his face. "Are we not lust worthy?" she asked him directly.

"It's clear to see that you have all the necessary parts to make most swoon, but I can see a little deeper than that. There is something lacking, lacking in all of you. I don't know quite what it is, but I would rather lie with a sow than with any of you."

"Did you just compare me to a pig?" Charity intoned.

"No, I think you misunderstood me. I like pigs."

"Are you a religious man, Judge?" Payne walked completely around his body, looking intently at him as if for some sign of his divinity.

"Do I believe in the good Lord? Is that what you're asking? Let's just say our relationship is a difficult one."

"This is truly strange … only those with strong beliefs or an innocence of age can get a sense of our trueness."

"I have strong beliefs, maybe not necessarily the ones you are talking about. As for innocence, well, we've parted ways a long, long time ago."

"We should kill him. He'll warn the others," Charity said.

"I'll do it!" Sophia stood up.

Judge wanted to run, run as far away as he possibly could until his aging heart finally gave out, but he couldn't. He found himself rooted to that very spot as if his boots had been nailed in place. He struggled to move every, and any muscle, and found he could not do so.

"What have you done to me?" He grimaced.

"One does not like one's food to run away from them, do they? I have caged you much like you would a rabbit."

"Food?" He labored to get out. "You're not zombies."

"Oh, I can assure you, we're worse."

"Much, much worse." Sophia giggled.

"Come, lead us back to your home. We have much to talk about."

Judge was manipulated like a marionette. He desperately tried to give a signal to those who watched their departure. Try as he could, he could not erase the idiotic grin he was wearing. If someone had taken a moment to look into his eyes, they would have told an entirely different story.

"Interesting, I would have expected something more grand for someone calling himself Judge." Payne was looking at a small Tudor-style home. It was kept in immaculate condition.

"I lead a small community; I'm not a pretentious asshole."

"It's a pity you're not younger, I may have kept you around for a little while."

When they got inside, Judge found that he was finally able to move his arm. He swung it, violently striking Payne on the cheek. Moonlight Serenade played in the background.

"Oh yes, indeed, I would have loved to have gotten to know you better," she said as she wiped the blood from the corner of her lip. "I will lay waste to your virtues. You will die needlessly in hate." She said those words as she descended on him. Though he could not move his vocal chords to cry out, his screams threatened to blow out his lungs. Great volumes of air blew past his lips. Payne dragged her teeth across his carotid artery, puncturing it every so often to take a small sampling of his blood. "You are a unique one, Earl Blackstone. Perhaps if your relationship was not so cluttered with your God, you could have been a very important holy man. I suppose it is bad for you and good for me that this is not the case." She laughed as she ripped a hole out of his neck. Blood arced like a water fountain. Sophia immediately moved in so that her mouth was under the downward trail of it.

"There are people gathering on the lawn," Charity said, peering out the window.

"Splendid. Invite them in," Payne said as she stood.

"Are you sure?" She looked over to Judge's still-twitching body. "Most of them are carrying weapons."

"Yes, but first start the record over." Payne stood and absently brushed at the copious amounts of blood running down the front of her dress. Within ten minutes, Payne had torn the townspeople asunder, rending souls from bodies as easily as she had their blood. Their cries for mercy fell upon deaf ears. Within a week, the fifty residents of New Lynn had been reduced to twelve, and most of them were children. Two women had been allowed to live to keep them from crying uncontrollably.

"I do not believe I have had so much fun since Bonaparte's reign." Payne stood on the porch overlooking the children, who were made to sleep on the grass in front of the house.

"Perhaps we should not have gorged as we did. We could have made this community last for months." Charity stood next to her.

Sophia ran around the children, tugging on their hair, laughing in delight when they squealed.

"We could not have culled the herd. There are not enough of them. They would have gotten suspicious, and then we would have been in danger."

Charity scoffed. "From cattle?"

"A bull has been known to gore an unsuspecting rancher from time to time."

"I suppose there is some truth to that."

"There is also the Tomas affair. It has been a very long time since something has intrigued me to this degree, and I wish not for our quarry to make their escape. Although, I do not sense that. Tomas, and possibly the other, know we are coming, yet they wait."

"That's good. Is it not? We catch up to them, decide what manner of punishment we wish to inflict, and we travel this new world seeking out more food."

"It does not concern you at all, sweet Charity, that they are not on the run?"

"Should it?"

"Tomas, at least, knows exactly who we are, and even though he does not possess a soul, he still carries the great burden of morality. He believes what we do to be great atrocities toward God's children. He knows we will most likely kill him, yet he waits."

"Maybe he has struck his descensus."

"It is possible he has outlived his time, but he is still young as far as our kind go. Perhaps he is unafraid."

"Unafraid? Of us?" Charity was upset at the notion. "How dare he! I will give him something to be afraid of!"

"Yes, we will, but we must be smart about this. There are unknown elements."

"We are the unknown elements!"

"I do believe you may have dipped a little too deeply from the human well, Charity. Your emotions are getting the better of you. Tomorrow we will take the children and women, leave this place, and make our way to Tomas. Perhaps I can gain some more understanding as we go."

"Will we find a coach or some other suitable method of travel?"

"I think walking would be more beneficial."

"The young will not make it."

"We will feed on the weakest as need be. I am going to use the 'sight.' I do not wish to be disturbed."

The next morning, Payne was even more confused than the night before.

"Get them on their feet," she ordered one of the children's watchers.

"It's still early. They have not rested proper—"

Payne reached out, quickly ripping the woman's head down by the ear, tearing it halfway off. Blood poured from the painful wound. "We leave when I say we leave. Meat has no opinion in this matter."

Sophia began to lick at the tear on the side of the woman's head. Payne held the woman in place a few moments longer, even twisting the ear from side to side.

"Are we clear?"

"Ye-yes. We're clear." The woman had her hands halfway up. She knew better than to reach and grab the vampire's hands though.

"I said meat has no opinion. That means no voice. Nod meat, nod your acknowledgement."

The woman nearly imperceptibly moved.

"I don't know what that means. Nod more."

The woman screamed out as she bobbed her head. Payne kept her arm steadfast and the ear in a tight grip.

"I will tear your fucking head off if you don't answer me properly."

Her shrieks pierced the veil of the early morning as her movements ripped her ear completely off. Payne threw it by her feet. "Good."

Sophia hovered around the woman for hours, constantly drinking of the blood that fell from the jagged opening, until finally she could take no more and ripped through her neck. Sophia held her firmly in her grasp as the woman's legs danced about wildly. Fear had caused her eyes to open wide;

blood loss and shock made them close slowly. When Sophia was done, she let go. The woman fell to the ground considerably lighter than she'd been only a few moments before. Two children wailed for their mother before the lone remaining woman gathered them up.

Three children had died by the time they'd gotten to the New Hampshire border, two by natural causes as exhaustion and exposure took their toll. The third the vampires had shared, drinking hungrily in front of the other remaining ones. The lone woman had sobbed.

Sophia looked up. "It will be over soon," she said in a sing-song voice almost tenderly. "I will save you for last, though, so you can watch each of the young die first." The woman sobbed harder, clutching one of the younger children tight to her breast.

"You're worse than an animal!" she shrieked.

Sophia laughed. "You are food. What do you know?"

"Animals don't torment their food!"

"Well, what fun is that?" Sophia asked.

"What you do not know, human, and what Sophia may only know on a subconscious level, is that fear produces subtle changes within your physiology which make you taste even better. Why would we not want to eat the finest?" Payne scratched a long nail down the side of the woman's face. "That is why we are saving you for last. You will have seen so much that the fear will have worked itself deep into your marrow. We are aging you like a fine wine, and when the time is right, we will drink deeply."

"I'll kill myself first!"

"No, you won't." Payne smiled. "The boy you hold before you reeks of your scent. He is your offspring, and you will do all in your power to protect him. It will be for nothing, of course, but that will not prevent you from trying." Payne plunged back down into the rapidly cooling body of the twelve-year-old they'd been feasting on.

Sophia tossed the husk into the woods like it was a used up juice box before they resumed their walk. By the time they'd reached the Maine border, they were down to five children and the woman.

"Something is coming." Charity had turned first.

They turned to the approaching sound. A large motor coach began to shimmer into sight a few miles in the distance and then took on more substance as it moved closer.

"A lunchbox!" Sophia clapped her hands and twirled twice.

PAT EVERFREE HAD BEEN TOURING the highways and byways ever since his wife of forty years had died of pancreatic cancer. He'd been in a sparsely populated town in Kansas when the zombie outbreak had started. For two months, he had stayed in the trailer park until he'd awoken to realize he was the only one still there.

"You're seventy-three, Pat, you can't live forever," he'd said to himself in the small bathroom mirror. He and his wife, Patricia, (they were known as the Pats) had talked about touring the United States for more than half their marriage. Work, kids, more work, and then grandkids had kept them fairly rooted to their hometown in Kansas. It was three years to the day that his wife had come home from the doctor and told her husband that they should buy that Coachmen motor home they'd been looking at for the past six months. He knew without her saying another word she was dying. They signed the papers the next day. Patricia's first and only ride in the behemoth was to the hospital as she began to cough up blood. Pat had begged to call an ambulance. Patricia had told him she wanted at least one go-around in their dream. How could he deny her that?

It took him another week before he built up enough courage to leave the campground. He had a difficult time reconciling the world he was seeing now with the world he'd known his entire life. The dead littered the streets. Buildings were reduced to ashes. Society had crumbled as had his desire to live. That all changed the day he saw her by the side of the road. She had on a yellow dress and scant else. Her feet were bare and bloody; her face was bruised and battered. She did not look over to him when he approached. Tears flowed down her face and fell to the roadway in front of her.

"Honey, are you all right?" Pat had asked, looking down at her from his window. She didn't stir. "Would you like a ride?" Without looking at him or saying a word, she stood and came around to the passenger door. Pat hit a release button, and it swung open. She climbed in past the passenger seat into one of the beds in back and was fast asleep before he got the door shut.

When she awoke later that night, Pat had told her how to work the shower. He apologized that all he had for clothes was his wife's, and though she was a beautiful woman, his wife was slightly curvier than her. He'd smiled at that last. For the first couple of days, Pat tried to get her to talk, or at the very least, to tell him her name. When he realized that was not in the cards, he'd stopped trying.

She'd completely exhausted Pat's water tanks before removing herself from the shower. She'd dressed in Patricia's faded blue jeans, which were eight sizes too large, and a sweater that she could have swam in. She'd sat in the passenger seat, rolled down her window, and threw the dress out on to the roadway.

"If you want to sit up here, you need to put on your seatbelt."

She did so without hesitation. Every so often, she would look over in Pat's direction. If he turned to look at her, she would immediately stare straight ahead.

"You look about eighteen. I have a couple of grandkids, boys though, that are your age. I don't exactly know where though. I always thought it was foolish when my oldest son, Reggie, talked about survival prepping, and then they went and blew their entire savings on a bomb shelter. I was so angry at him, sacrificing their future like that. Who knew? When he tried to show me where it was, I told him I wanted nothing to do with his foolishness. Who's the fool now?"

For a week, they'd fallen into a routine. He'd drive most of the morning, staying away from major cities. For lunch, she would make them macaroni and cheese, apparently her favorite. Pat didn't have the heart to tell her he couldn't stand it. He'd only bought it because it was Patricia's favorite. Then, when she was done cleaning up, she would sit next to him while he drove. The difference this day happened right before he was about to pull over for the night.

"I'm glad you're a fool," she said. It had taken him a moment to put that into context.

"Me too, honey. Me too." He'd smiled.

"My name is Tiffany."

"A pleasure to meet you, Tiffany." Pat smiled, extending his hand; she hugged him instead. "Patricia would have loved you: the granddaughter we never had."

Pat had the uncanny ability to avoid trouble, and they'd stayed mostly unscathed right up until the Maine border. Tiffany had soon after learned that mac and cheese was not on Pat's preferred list of edibles and moved to his much more eating-friendly beef stew. She was preparing it when she felt the large vehicle slow down. She went up to the front to see why. A couple of hundred yards away was a small group of children and four women. The woman by the children looked scared. She was dirty and had dried blood over most of her while the other women looked like they were out for a nice stroll.

"Something's wrong here, Pappy." Tiffany had started to

call him what she'd called her own grandfather years ago before he'd died in a construction accident.

"They need help, like you did, is all."

"They need help." Tiffany was pointing to the woman and children. "Those others do not."

"Nonsense, they're just women."

"Lizzie Borden was a woman."

"Good point. There is something strange going on here." Pat put the RV in reverse. He looked at the small backup screen and kept going until he could no longer see the strangers.

"What are you doing?"

"You need to get out."

"What?"

"You're right, something is wrong up there, and I would not feel right if something were to happen to you."

"Let's just leave."

"I need to see if I can help them. What if I had not helped you?"

"It's me and you Pappy, please don't make me get out."

"It's just for a few minutes. I'll go up there and see what I can do, and then I'll come right back here for you."

Tears began to form in her eyes. "We should go back to your house in Kansas. Maybe your son left a message; you said so yourself. We could go find them, and you could be with your kids."

"I'm with one of my kids now," he said affectionately.

"Please, Pappy. There's something wrong with those women. I can feel it; just looking at them makes my stomach hurt."

"Probably just that last batch of stew you made. I think it was expired." He tried to make light of the situation, but it wasn't working. Tiffany was trembling and tears were falling.

She started heading for the door.

"Grab the rifle and some food and water first."

She turned. "You don't think you're coming back either, do you?"

"Nonsense, it just might take longer than expected, and I don't want you out here without protection. And I know teenagers; they eat and drink constantly."

"I'm barely a teenager anymore."

"Nineteen is still not twenty."

She kissed him tenderly on the cheek before departing with the bolt-action .308, forty rounds, a canteen of water, and two MRE packets. She got to the side of the road and ran as quickly as she could so that she could watch.

Pat closed the door and reluctantly pressed on the gas. He could not remember being overly altruistic in the past, and he was still fumbling around with these new feelings as he once again approached the original point he had been before backing up. As he rolled closer, the small pit of unease that Tiffany had put into him had flowered and began to bloom into a full-fledged bout of apprehension and nervousness. Two of the women on his right watched his approach with a mild look of curiosity. One looked genuinely pleased. On the left, there was a slender woman holding an even smaller child. She looked beaten and defeated until something flickered across her face. Hope, maybe?

Pat could not fathom what was happening here. For the fifth time, he looked down to his lap and the .357 Magnum revolver he'd placed there. When he looked back up, he saw the woman with the child running toward him. None of the other women made a move to stop her. She was screaming though, he could not make out her words over the loud drone of the diesel engine and his own failing hearing. When his wife died, he'd not seen the reason to go through with the hearing aid appointment he'd scheduled. Without her to talk to, there was hardly anyone he wanted to hear. Selfish ... he knew it then, and he knew it now. Her death had killed something inside of him as well, at least until Tiffany had reawakened it.

How he wished she were here now. Tiffany or Patricia, both, either.

"Help me; help us!"

"Well, that was as clear as day." Pat said.

Pat pulled up alongside the woman.

"They're…" She had to pause to catch her breath. "… insane! They're killing everyone!"

"Them?" He was about to point far up the road to where *they* had been not a moment before. His heart jumped in his chest. The trio was not more than ten feet from the front of his RV, motionless except for a small breeze that was making their garb stir. None seemed to be out of breath from exertion.

TIFFANY HAD BEEN WATCHING through her scope and still could not believe what she'd seen. She thought that possibly it had been her mind playing a trick on her or maybe something was wrong with the optics or maybe the shimmer on the road had given the illusion of unnatural speed. Her instincts were demanding action, most were telling her to run far away and never look back. Another was telling her to line up a shot and keep shooting until those things stopped moving. Pappy had taught her how to shoot. She was decent, but she knew her limits. She'd never hit them from this distance. More than likely, she'd put one into the side of the RV.

"Leave, Pappy. Please leave." Even from her spot, she knew the woman with the child was begging for help. What kind of monsters were those women? She'd been personal witness to the brutality of man, and they did not hold a candle to what she figured those things were capable of. She scanned over the children with her scope, and all of them had checked out. There was no hope in any of those dead, flat eyes. They'd seen things that had stripped away who they were. Parts that could never be replaced. There were long moments where nothing happened. She couldn't see him from her angle, but she could see the brightness of the brake lights he depressed, and she could imagine him behind the impossibly large steering wheel. Everything happened in a flash as the woman and her child headed for the passenger door. She jumped when she heard the explosion of his revolver.

Pat's heart was working harder than he could ever remember. Pain began to shoot down his left arm, exploding into bursts of pain along his fingertips.

"A fucking heart attack? As crazy as this world is right now, I'm going to die from a heart attack?"

He could feel the constriction as the muscle began to seize into a spasm. He didn't know if the change in his expression got the woman moving or not, but she had circled around the RV and was coming up to the passenger side. The trio in front of him seemed almost bored with the whole encounter. Two of them, anyway. The one in the middle with the red hair, she seemed fixated on him. Concentrating hard. Then it dawned, he wasn't having a natural heart attack. She had somehow psychically reached in and was crushing his heart with her mind as effectively as if she were using a sledgehammer.

"Eat lead." He used his right hand to pick up the revolver, which seemed nearly ten times its normal weight. He pulled the trigger, blowing out the windshield. The red-haired woman, who had been smiling, ducked to the side as the round scraped against her scalp. He'd not hit his target, but it had the desired effect as she'd released her death grip on his ticker. He whipped his head back and forth, looking for them. When an incredibly cold hand reached up and grabbed his shoulder, he knew it was the end. She pulled his arm out of his socket. His seatbelt performing its job admirably. He undid the restraint before she removed his arm completely. He hit the ground hard when she effortlessly pulled him through the open window. He was certain his shoulder was broken along with a couple of ribs. None of that mattered as long as Tiffany got away. He hoped with all his being that she had left when she heard his gun go off. He was sure she hadn't, but he truly wished she had.

"Hello," Sophia said, staring down at him. "Do you come here often?" Then she laughed.

He coughed. "It's poor form to laugh at your own jokes." He was trying to gauge exactly what he was dealing with here. He knew his life was forfeit. He would just have liked to know what had done him in. "What are you?" He thought to go for the direct approach.

Payne heard his question and came forward. "The devil once said that there were great and terrible things that needed to be done on earth. He asked who would go forward and accomplish these deeds. I raised my hand and told him I am here."

"You're a demon?"

"Of sorts, I suppose. Though demons cannot roam freely in this realm." Payne implanted in him what he needed to know to understand what had befallen him.

"Please, that's all I have left to me."

"I have not let a soul escape in centuries. Why would I start now?"

Pat grinned. "I'll tell you why." He placed his gun up against his head and pulled the trigger.

Payne screamed in rage. Tiffany shuddered from her hiding spot.

"That was *my* soul to collect!" She moved closer, reared back, and kicked, sending Pat airborne for ten feet. He landed in a broken heap.

"His soul will still be lost, Payne," Charity offered.

Payne spun. "It was mine to collect, not his to lose. And the all-merciful God may still allow his passage if he but asks for forgiveness!" She sneered.

Tiffany watched in horror as Payne bent down and lifted Pat by his head. With one hand around his neck and the other under his jaw, she tore them apart and threw both halves away.

"Oh, Pappy," Tiffany cried, letting her forehead rest against the ground.

"Round up the meat. We will take the vehicle." Payne strode inside.

"There appears to have been another here," Charity said once they were all onboard. "Should we go and look?"

"I am not in the mood. Bring me something to eat." The screams were muted within the confines of the RV, but Tiffany could still hear the pleas from her location. She did the only thing she could think to do when the vehicle pulled away. She stood and followed. She didn't know exactly what she was going to do when and if she ever caught up to them, but Pappy had been nice to her, and he deserved her effort at least. She didn't look down when she passed the shell that had housed him. She kept repeating that what was there was not him. "It's not him. It's not him." She was a mile away before she let the tears fall in earnest. She left the highway and went into Portsmouth in search of a car to either head to the West Coast, where she might try and find a way to drive to Hawaii, or continue north and catch back up.

Tiffany had never thought much on religion. Her parents were good people, but they weren't religious. The topic rarely came up in the circles she lived in. But as she walked into Portsmouth, she would have sworn there was something, some unseen force at work. A guiding hand. Something or someone that had seen the evil and sought to right the wrongs. She cleared her thoughts, focusing her white-hot anger on those who had taken Pappy's life. She took lefts and rights, not looking at street names or even knowing where she was. She heard sounds all around her, some human, some zombie, though she never encountered anything. She found herself standing in front of a house at 777 Highgate Drive. The gray Victorian looked slightly out of place in a neighborhood dominated by ranch style homes, but it wasn't garish.

Tiffany walked up to the detached two-door garage. The side door was unlocked. When she entered, there was a vehicle covered in a large off-white canvas covering. She pulled it off, raising thick plumes of dust and exposing a 1969 white Shelby fastback Mustang.

"Is this thing going to work?" she asked the thick ribbons of swirling dust. "This is insane." She looked inside, and the keys were sitting on the driver's seat. She got in, took notice that she did not need to adjust the seat, placed the key in the ignition, and turned. The loud *thrum* of the high performance engine was nearly deafening in the small garage. "This isn't an escape vehicle; this is for pursuit." She knew what she had to do. Now, she made up her mind to do it. "Lead the way," she said once she got out onto the road. "I'm not going to lie and say I understand what's happening here, but if you've chosen me for this, then who am I to argue?"

12

Tiffany found her way back to the highway. The speedometer stopped reading at 120. She had it so far drilled to the right she thought it might break out of the small circle it was housed in. It took her an hour and a half at her break-neck speed before she finally caught a glimpse of the recre-ational van far up ahead. Fear crept up her neck and wrapped around her skull when she saw the brake lights come on. She thought she'd been discovered. She let out a sigh of relief when she saw that the van was getting off the highway. She slowed down to something less likely to end her death by fiery twisted metal. By the time she hit the off-ramp, she had slowed to forty.

"Augusta Route 3. What are you guys doing?" she wondered aloud. She slowed even further, making sure she did not come up on them again should they be parked. After a half hour more of driving, she didn't know if she was relieved or not that she had not come across the van. Whatever was in that vehicle was not human, and she would be better off never encountering them again. But if she did not, she would never be able to give Pappy the payback he deserved. She could honestly not tell which side of the fence she wished she would fall over onto. She was thinking on this when she had to press the brakes hard, thankful it was not enough to lock the wheels and start a tire-squealing skid. As it was, she pulled over to the far right and shut off the engine.

She was close, too close. Not much more than a quarter of a mile away. She could see light coming from the inside of the vehicle. There was no activity outside, which was a good thing. She opened her door, grabbed her rifle, and then quietly exited. She'd not gone more than a hundred feet when she began to hear the screams. Someone's suffering was the reason she'd not been heard. She froze. The screaming was coming from a woman, or at least she thought so. She couldn't imagine a man being able to reach that falsetto, although all things were possible under the knife and where that knife made contact. The sun was quickly setting. Even in the burgeoning darkness, she felt completely exposed and afraid. She headed for the large culvert that ran the length of the roadway. At first, she moved quickly, with the hopes that she would be able to aid the victim. She slowed as she got closer, knowing in her heart whoever was in there was long past the point of being able to receive help. Inconsolable sobbing was met with unbridled laughter.

Tiffany's heart raced as she got up next to the vehicle. She didn't know what to do. Those things that looked like women were in there, but so were the innocents. She couldn't just start blasting away, hoping to avoid the former while hitting the latter. Little did she know she would have been doing them a great service if she had cut their lives even shorter. She backed away when she heard whimpering and what she could only think of as loud slurping sounds.

Deep down, she knew they were vampires. It was just that her consciousness would not allow her to believe something so insane. As if her mind were trying to protect it from itself. She hardly remembered her walk back to the car or falling asleep exhausted in the back seat. When she awoke the next morning, she thought perhaps it was all a dream. The RV was gone and all her problems could be as well if she but merely turned around. She started the engine and drove forward. Within an hour, she once more came across the RV, nearly slamming into the rear end. It had been left in the middle of the roadway. She waited for someone to come out and investigate. When no one did, she got out, this time leaving the car running in the hopes she would be able to get back in and make good on an escape attempt if it came to that.

She walked around the entire vehicle, hyper sensitive to any noise. It was quiet, save the flies buzzing around the roof, looking for a way in through the vent system. When she felt fairly confident no one was inside, she did another loop around. This was her life she was playing with. She felt the extra carefulness was warranted. The next part of her plan involved knocking on the door and stepping back. If any of the gothic looking women answered, she was going to start shooting and at no point start asking questions. She knocked and jumped back, catching her right foot on her left and going down in a tangle, hard on her ass.

"Stupid, stupid," she berated herself as she dusted off and stood. Had anyone answered, she would have been dead. If she lived to be a hundred, she'd never be able to give a satisfactory answer as to why she decided to go inside. It was the smell that assailed her first—the thick aroma of iron, sweat, fear, and something else. She thought if evil had its own scent, this would be what it was like. She expected blood to be running down the center aisle, to be splattered across the ceiling and be pooling in the beds. She was surprised at first to barely find a few droplets. She was more horrified when the reason of why this hadn't occurred struck her. Apparently, even vampires adhered to the policy of waste not, want not. Children sucked dry were placed almost tenderly in the small RV beds. She thought she was going to be sick as she quickly exited.

After ten minutes, she was able to get herself back under control. "Now what?" she asked as she shielded her eyes from the sun and did a complete 360. In the end, she decided to walk in the direction the van was pointed. She hid in the brush when she heard the sound of an approaching vehicle. She looked up to see perhaps the biggest man she'd ever seen in her life driving, and in the back was an older man with a long goatee, laughing. By the scowl on the driver's face, it appeared he was the butt of whatever was making the man in the back laugh. They looked friendly enough, but she'd learned the hard way that looks could be deceiving. This world brought out the worst in some of the best, and it was better to avoid than encounter. She thought a man in the back of the truck had spotted her, but the way his head was canted to the side and smoke was emanating from his mouth, he looked like he was smoking something that held way more interest for him than anything surrounding.

"Safe to say they haven't come across the trio yet," she said as she extracted herself from the bushes. She stayed on foot, going in the same direction as the truck had been. She couldn't be sure, but it was safe to assume that vampires would look for humans, and a truckload of them had just whisked by. The sun was high overhead by the time she came across what had to be a trick of the light or the first signs of dehydration or just a major stroke. She stopped fifty yards away, unsure as to what to do next, when she looked upon a roadway littered with zombie heads and the body of a dead boy and a woman that looked a lot like the person that had been running toward Pappy's truck. She looked around wildly, fully expecting monsters to jump out from all around. The heads were almost as effective a roadblock as a twenty-foot wall. She lost more than a fifteen minutes, transfixed by what she saw.

That it was zombies made it marginally better, but still. "Who takes the time out of their day to do something like this?" she said aloud. "It's a message. The women are sending someone a message. Is it to the people in that truck? But why?" She could see that this train of thought was going to produce more questions than answers. She might find what she was looking for if she kept going, or she could stay alive and just turn around. She knew the events were bigger than her and could easily roll her over. She continued on when she remembered something her father had told her many years previous: "Honey, it's the smallest splinter that causes the most pain." He'd been laughing as he looked upon the living room she had absolutely destroyed with her toys, five rolls of toilet paper, and what had previously been a full container of baby powder.

"I am that splinter." She kept repeating those words as she skirted the beheaded roadway. She did her best to push the imagery from her mind as she walked, but the darker it became outside, the darker her inner thoughts became. It helped little that a gusty chill wind had begun to kick up.

13

MIKE JOURNAL ENTRY 10

THE ONLY GOOD THING ABOUT BEING COVERED BY A HALF-dozen slimy zombies was that, for the most part, they were in each other's way and none able to get a clear bite on me. It was impossible from my angle to tell what was going on considering I was flat on my back under a pigsty pile of putrid flesh. The load was becoming lighter as zombies were literally being flung off of me. Only two people I knew could pull that off, BT and Tommy. Bullets whined all around me, hitting the ground not more than three inches from my head. Whoever was shooting was getting a wee bit too close for my comfort.

"Get up!" Tommy shouted. There was a true look of terror on his face, even more than the clusterfuck of zombies around us would account for.

"You make it sound like I've been sunbathing!" I smacked the butt of my rifle against the jaw of the last zombie pressing down on me. Teeth flew out of her head. Didn't matter, the jagged ones she had left still looked like they could do enough damage. Tommy ripped her so violently upwards she pulled me with her. I found myself in the much more desirable position of standing.

"Fuck! Who's shooting?" A bullet grazed across my thigh.

"Sorry, man!" It was BT. He stood atop the truck that was parked half inside of Ron's house.

Tommy had a bar of iron. It looked like a damn car axle, especially when he swung it. He mowed through zombies as easily as a scythe through wheat. The muscles bunched on his arms as he heaved through every swing. I'd taken one step to stay in behind him when I felt something penetrate my chest and wrap coldly around my heart. It felt so real, so physical, I actually rubbed my right hand over where I figured the entry wound was. When my hand came away clean, well I mean, without any fresh blood or gore, I figured it was a heart attack, a sort of a payback for all the shit food I'd eaten growing up. One can only scarf down so many French fries before they catch up.

"It's Payne!" Tommy huffed out. He was tiring from his attempts to keep the zombies from biting distance.

"It is painful." I told him, thinking he somehow knew what was happening inside my chest cavity. Then I figured that he, indeed, did know what was happening, and he didn't say painful, he said pain, as in Payne the vampire. I didn't do anything consciously because, well, I didn't consciously know how to deal with this particular problem. I turned to her and just struck out with everything I had, hoping some of the pellets from my psychic shotgun would hit home. Won't lie, I grinned when she staggered back a step and the vamp next to her reached out to keep her steady. The amount of energy I'd expended on the one hit threatened to cave my legs in. I reached out with my right hand and grabbed hold of Tommy's shoulder, letting him make a path for us. It was all I could do to hold on. I turned to get a quick look at our new adversary. She'd recovered much quicker than I had, but she did not reach out again. I took that as promising sign.

14

"WHY ISN'T HE DEAD?" SOPHIA ASKED INNOCENTLY. "I thought you were going to kill him." Her head was tilted to the side slightly as she asked the question.

"It is not for lack of trying." Payne smoothed her dress as she stood. "He is a strong one. The bloodline runs deep within him."

"He is but a halfling, and a newly created one at that," Charity said in a probing tone.

"He may be new, but the blood running through him is an ancient one. I should know, considering it is mine."

"How far removed from the source is he?" Charity asked. There was concern in her voice.

"The same as myself, two."

"That cannot even be possible!" Charity cried out.

"And yet it is. Come, we will leave them to their devices for now while I dwell on this new development."

15

MIKE JOURNAL ENTRY 11

I WAS SPENT. FELT LIKE A RAG DOLL WHILE FIRST TOMMY AND then BT manhandled me around and into the house. I caught a glimpse of Nancy on the floor, Tracy and Stephanie at her side trying to stem the tide of blood. I would have pointed out the fact that it was too late, but they knew that. They were offering comfort in her final moments. Besides, I was having a difficult time keeping my eyes from crossing and passing out. I'd once gone to a party and someone pulled out an Apogee bong, or something like that. Thing was four-feet tall. Someone actually had to hold the flame in place, burning the weed while you sucked for all you were worth. I filled that thing up, looked like downtown LA during rush hour inside that glass tube.

When I felt like I couldn't pull any more in, I let go of the carburetor. For those of you smart folks who are not savvy to the ways of a bong, this has the effect of releasing all the stored up smoke into your lungs in one fell swoop. I was no virgin to joints, pipes, or normal bongs. But this thing was like the nuclear bomb of bongs. That smoke hit me like I'd been punched in the head. My eyes crossed, and I fell over on my ass. Someone caught the bong before it could fall over as well.

Unfortunately, I'd not been treated with the same respect, although I did receive a chorus of guffaws! Where was I? Oh yeah, that was basically how I was feeling after my encounter with Payne. I couldn't see straight, my brain was clouded over, and my chest felt mule-kicked. I'd said back then, I'd never do it again. Looks like I'd lied.

BT put me down on a chair. Unlike the bong encounter, which took me a full ten minutes to pick myself up and two hours to stop drooling on myself, I was feeling better after about five minutes. I mean physically I was feeling better; mentally I was a fucking mess. Nancy, my brother's wife, was lost. I began picking up her screams as my senses started to return to equilibrium. Ron's basement looked like a war zone triage, respite with all the sounds. I don't even know if he had a clue his wife was dying. What am I saying? Of course he didn't, or he'd be down here by her side wailing at the heavens. Would he though? He fancied himself an agnostic. He believed in nothing but the here and now. I'd always thought that a pretty narrow view of the world previously, and my idea of that view had been broadened in the last year or so. Who did you blame when things went wrong? The nothingness?

I was having a difficult time getting my bearings, but we were still in the middle of a war. Just because I was out for the standing eight count didn't mean everyone else had stopped. Tommy, Travis, and BT had gotten in front of the women. Meredith was urging them to grab her mother and go upstairs. I honestly didn't think bringing her deeper in was a good idea at this point. I don't want to sound callous, but she was a handful of breaths away from playing for the other team.

I reached out. I looked more like I was trying to keep from falling over when I grabbed Meredith's shoulder. "Get your dad," I urged her.

"We have to take my mom upstairs."

"Meredith, get your dad."

She got it at that point, whether she wanted to or not. Tears were falling by the time she got to the steps.

"I need a gun!"

BT looked over his shoulder and to the women behind. There were three there. I grabbed Tracy's. She'd been using a 9 mm carbine. Not the optimum weapon, but it beat using my hands and probably the slingshot that Trip was wielding. I'm not sure when he got that. I certainly don't recall, although something niggled in the back of my head in regard to his projectile launcher. As if he knew I was thinking about him, he turned to me and winked then started whistling. Again, I don't know why, but my bladder threatened to loosen. It was just that whistlers, all of a sudden, had sparked a fear in me.

He stopped as suddenly as he'd started, or maybe I couldn't hear him anymore because I was firing a gun. Don't know, don't care. After a bit, I heard the heavy sobbing that had a distinctive male timbre. Meredith had indeed gotten her dad. I'd been through a lot, I'd seen a lot, even done a lot, but I don't think I've ever heard a more deep and mournful sound coming from a person. If I didn't know better, I would have thought it was from some wild animal. My heart broke. I did all I could think to do, which was keep pulling the trigger and hopefully drown out that sound. He was living a reality I never wanted to be party to.

16

MIKE JOURNAL ENTRY 12

We won the day, whether the zombies had been spurred on by the Gothic Girls and had faltered when they left or the new survival instinct within our enemy had finally decided that the losses were too great and had withdrawn. Didn't matter. They withdrew, although, to call today a victory was a gross distortion of that word. Nancy Talbot had died. Four of us had had to wrestle Ron away from his wife before she could do her resurrection thing. Tommy gave her the last rites: one she deserved in the form of prayer and one she most certainly did not. This involved a long metal spike driven through her temple and a quick spin to make sure no synapses could keep firing. I watched out of respect and guilt. Of everyone who had died since this had started, I felt like her demise was the one that most deserved to be laid at my feet. Ron spiraled from fits of rage to wails of the damned. My heart lurched with each pounding or cry out. I noticed more than one person keeping an extra eye out on me, expecting me to do something stupid.

In fairness, I was never too far from doing something stupid. I guess I just looked more apt to do something at that moment. I didn't do much of anything actually. I was kind of half-expecting Ron to shoot me in the chest with a shotgun for bringing this grief upon him. That he didn't just showed how broken he was. What didn't dawn on me, and perhaps maybe never would, was a simple fact that Tommy brought to light. It played out a couple of days later. The house was as quiet as one might expect. Although this wasn't the peace of a mausoleum, it was more an expectant type of silence, as if a fuse had been lit and everyone was waiting for the resultant explosion. It came soon enough. Instead of a shotgun, it was Ron's fist. I'd come in from the deck, my turn on guard duty. My head was hanging down, like it did a lot those last couple of days. The smash hit me like a sledge on my right cheek. Hard enough, my head hit the frame of the door. There was a little buckling to my knees, but I stayed standing. I think mostly because I did hit the frame. I instantly knew what was happening. There was no need for me to look into the mask of rage my brother wore as his blows rained down on me. I did not move. I did not try to deflect the hits or inflict my own damage. I stood there as if this were my own personal penance.

Again, it was Tommy who interceded. "Stop!" he shouted as he lifted Ron and chucked him halfway across the living room. It had happened so fast Ron was throwing punches into the air before he realized his target was out of range. He quickly started to make his way back to me. Blood ran down my face, some from open wounds on me, some from Ron's knuckles where he'd split them. I think my nose was broken, I had a tooth or two loose, and my jaw hurt like hell.

"He brought this upon me, upon us all!" Ron could not have yelled any louder. "I need to kill the cancer before it destroys us all."

My head came up at that; he wasn't just getting frustration out, he planned on killing me. Would I have defended myself if I'd known that? I decided I wouldn't have. I could be killed —there was no doubt about that—but odds were he'd break all of his knuckles and both hands before he'd be able to do that with his fists. Sure, I'd look like a bloody pulp. I'd feel like shit, but I wouldn't die. Besides, I felt like I truly deserved it.

"What exactly did he bring upon us?" Tommy asked. In contrast to my brother, he was calm. Stern, but calm.

Ron had no desire to match Tommy's demeanor. If anything, he raised it up a notch. "Are you serious? He's brought death to us. Not just zombies but vampires. Everything he touches dies on the vine. He's killed my brother, my father, my daughter, and now his plague of existence has killed my wife!" He lunged, nearly getting past Tommy. I stood still, awaiting my fate.

"He has killed none of them. The zombies are no more his fault than they are yours."

"And what of the vampires!?" Spittle flew from his lips.

"They are as much his fault as they are yours."

Ron struggled against that iron-like grip of Tommy for a few moments before he finally turned and looked at the boy. Rage faded to confusion.

"Eliza, my sister, was a product of a Talbot."

I'd never told anyone that. I guess it really wasn't my secret to harbor; not sure why I kept it in. Guilt, shame? When she died, I figured, wrongly, that the secret died with her. Or at least one more witness was gone. The truth had been down to Tommy and me, and apparently, he thought it was time to share.

"What the fuck are you talking about? He led her straight to us!"

"That is not the truth, Ron. If she had killed Mike, she would have made her way to your home soon enough. If anything, your brother bought you a chance. Would you have been able to defend against her had you not known?"

What Tommy was neglecting to say was that I wouldn't have stood a chance, either, if not for him. I knew what he was doing, though, trying to put me in as bright a light as possible.

"Half of my family is dead!"

"Yet, half is alive. Nothing can be done for those who have left. Those that are still here will need you now more than ever."

"It wasn't Eliza that took my wife away from me."

"And it wasn't Mike, Ron. It was the zombies."

Ron didn't seem to like the fact that the focus of his anger was misdirected. That in all reality, there was nothing or nobody that he could turn that intense hatred onto. It was a feeling of utter impotence, one in which there was no blue pill big enough to get rid of. By this time, my nose had stopped bleeding. I could even feel the cartilage begin to slide back into place. It sounded like someone was making popcorn on my face. I was starting to garner attention, and I'd had enough for the rest of the day, week maybe.

"We done?" I asked my brother. He said nothing. That was about as good as it was going to get, at least for now. Just about all of the inhabitants of the house were there with a couple of exceptions. Of course, it had to be Trip that broke the silence while I left the room.

"Bravo, bravo!" he said, stepping into the middle of the room. "They just don't put good drama like that on television anymore. The acting, the make-up, the scene ... perfection. I predict a couple of Bonies being awarded for this performance."

I was nearly out of ear-shot as I heard Tommy talking about Victor Talbot and how he changed over Eliza. When he'd done that deed he'd then indoctrinated her into an existence of cruelty.

BT followed me out. Tracy, thankfully, had not been one of the people present. I think she was out by Nancy's grave with Ron's youngest. No saying how it would have turned out if she had been there. Either she would have urged him on, getting in a few licks for all the shit I'd done to her or, more likely, she would have tried to stop him. I've taken a beating or two before, and I'm sure this life hasn't quite finished doling them out for me, but if he had ever touched Tracy in anger, his children would be orphaned; I'm not sure I could have stopped myself. So I knew the place he was coming from, even if it had gone astray.

"Your face looks like hamburger. You all right?"

"I'll be fine," I choked out. I was as close to tears as one could be without actually producing fluid.

"I came late, man. I would have stopped him."

"He needed to get it out."

"Jesus, not on you. Not that way. He's your brother."

I walked into the bathroom. BT stood in the doorway. He was right, my face indeed looked like torn up, bloody shreds of meat. I turned the faucet on and did my best to get my swollen countenance into the stream. It stung before freezing under the cold. It's worth noting because not all of you will have been this lucky in the apocalypse. We got our water from a well, and it was pumped by a generator that used a variety of fuels including solar power to operate.

"You should put some disinfectant on that."

I stood up to look at him.

"Right, forgot."

I was in about as much danger of getting an infection as I was of being dragged off by faeries. Wait, I take that back; little miss demigod doesn't need any more fuel for her imagination. I stripped off my shirt. It did not have the recuperative powers I had, and if Tracy saw the copious amounts of bloodstains on it, she'd have a fairly good idea I'd gotten into some sort of trouble.

"You know you really don't need to be in here with me. Right?"

"What if you need help finding something?"

"Did you really just make a dick joke?"

"I thought it might help."

"You have a skewed version of altruism." I showed him the exit before closing the door.

"What now, Mike?" he asked.

I examined a deep bruise on my right side. Ron may have cracked a rib.

"I don't know, BT. I have no idea what happens next."

"I meant with you. Are you going to stay? Whatever you decide, I'm with you. I want you to know that."

I winced as I raised my arm over my head. Definitely cracked.

"You all right in there? Sounds like you just found it and you're not too happy with the results."

"Really, man? Again?"

"I'm sorry. I'm stressed out, and I learned this stupid tactic from you. If there's anyone to blame, it's you."

"That seems to be the theme of the day."

"Aw shit, man. I didn't mean it like that."

I gripped the sides of the sink and let my head hang a bit. "I know, I know. I'm sorry."

"Where is he?" I heard Tracy asking from the next room over. Apparently, news had traveled down the grapevine.

"If you say, 'Looking for his penis,' you and I are going to have words."

"Why would I say something like that?" BT asked innocently. "He's in there."

"How is he?" I heard her whisper.

"Not too good." BT answered.

"He's fine, and he has bat fucking ears, remember?" I opened the door.

Tracy winced when she saw me. "Does it hurt?" She reached a tentative hand up.

I instinctively pulled back. "I don't think touching it is going to make it feel any better." I told her, tenderly grabbing her hand to stop its progress.

. . .

***

THE NEXT FEW days were somber. According to Trip, the next episode in the Talbot saga was just as gripping, as Tommy discussed Eliza's origins with Ron and what would have happened had I not shown up. And even if Ron had somehow dealt with her, Payne and her cohorts still would have shown. Nothing would have changed except the death count, which Tommy told him would have been considerably higher. If the damn vamps weren't still out there, I would have gathered up my family and left. On an intellectual level, Ron had heard and even understood Tommy's words. On an emotional level, I was the portent of death for his family. No matter how much time passed, he would always harbor some resentment toward me. The only thing that could alleviate some of that would be my departure. I'd give him that relief in a heartbeat if I didn't think my actions would bring more harm to those who stayed behind. And life on the road was no place for Nicole, especially since there was now a baby to deal with.

We'd stay; I'd stay. I could deal with his glaring eyes and hateful stares for the added safety I could offer. At least that was what I hoped. If push came to shove, I don't know who was going to stop them if they decided to come in. I'm convinced there isn't anyone mortal, or nearly immortal, that Tommy couldn't take on, one on one. Three on one is a different matter. BT and I, for all our strengths, were amateurs at best, stepping onto a pro field. All of us together, maybe we stood a chance, maybe. We'd get an idea soon enough about that though. The day started off as putridly disgusting as the previous one, smell-wise, I mean. The zombies had pulled back. They had not departed. It was a siege of sorts. I mean, we had plenty of resources to hold out, but they could do so indefinitely. Advantage: zombies.

It was warm for a late fall day. The trees, oblivious to the carnage around them, were a spectacular variety of hues. Deep ambers, lush reds, golden yellows. Tourists would be about losing their minds right now with the views while local gift shops and motels dotted along the coast raked in the last real seasonal money of the year. Oh, to be one of those people with hardly a care in the world, except where to take the kids for dinner. I was standing on the deck, looking out to the trees, not really seeing anything. It was quiet. I'd like to say too quiet, or I sensed something. But nope, I was drifting around lazily in the ghost of vacations past. Tommy caught the scent of something amiss.

"Mr. T, where's your brother?"

It took me a moment to shake away the sight of my eight-year-old daughter waving around a huge overpriced stuffed animal moose and begging if she could have it. Forty dollars had seemed a steep price to pay for momentary happiness. Right now, I'd pay forty thousand for it.

"Ron? He stays as far away from me as he can." I don't even think it was anything conscious on his part. I walked into a room; he walked out. If I was there, he wouldn't be, simple as that. I'd taken to eating outside so that he could have people around him during meal times.

"I'm asking about Gary." Tommy said.

"I haven't seen him. You check the basement?"

"I've checked everywhere. I need to know where he is."

Tommy seemed panicked, and if he felt the need to panic, I think I did as well. It didn't help when Riley came out on the deck with us. She was looking off to the side. Her fur was bristled, and a long, low growl rumbled through her chest, into her throat and out her muzzle. We'd discussed the need to stay inside the house or on the deck and always visible to another person while the vampires were around. They were supernatural beings; we needed to be on a constant vigil. We'd had to double the guards and stay on high alert. I'd known through previous combat that it is difficult to keep up this level of security. Sure, for a little while you stay on your toes, a mouse farts a hundred yards away and you grip your rifle expecting trouble. After a week of pulling extra shifts and nothing happening, a bear could drop a difficult deuce ten feet away and you'll yawn. We'd definitely entered the complacency stage of danger alert.

My heart sank when we heard the opening chords to "Living on a Prayer." Not that I didn't enjoy the song, but it was coming from Gary's tree stand, a place we'd expressly forbid him from going. It had not been a fun argument, and apparently not an effective one either.

"Mike, it's my for*trees* of solitude. It's the only place I can get away and pretend none of this is real." he'd argued.

"For*trees?*"

"My home, my spelling."

"I get it, Gary, I do. I wish we all could do what we wanted to. But it's too dangerous right now." He nodded at all the appropriate times, so I'd thought he was listening. Now, I'm not so sure. Was probably bobbing his head to a tune playing inside of there.

Tommy, Riley and myself rushed over to the far side of the deck as more of the song drifted over the landscape. It was nearly impossible due to leaf cover to see much of the tree stand. That was another thing I'd asked him to do previously —cut back some of the branches.

"How private would it be if everyone could see?"

"What the hell are you doing in there that you need so much privacy?"

He'd shrugged, looking slightly embarrassed.

"Just use the bathroom, like everyone else." I'd said bluntly.

"I'm not doing *that.*"

"Ummm, yeah, me neither," I'd assured him, saying it like he'd brought up the subject and not me. "Then what the hell *are* you doing?"

"I like to sing"

"Okay."

"And dance."

"Now you're getting a little weird."

"It's what I like to do."

"Any chance you dance better than you sing?"

"Doubtful, that's why I like—"

"To be in private. Yeah, definitely get that. Us Talbots have about as much rhythm as sneakers in a dryer."

"Mike, that doesn't even make sense."

"Sure it does. They just randomly clunk around inside there."

He stopped to think about it for a second. "Oh, okay, I guess you're right."

"Gary?" I called out tentatively for my brother.

There was no response except for an increase in volume to the song. Drifting among the treetops like that, it was creepier than I would have imagined a Bon Jovi song could be. As per usual, multiple things happened at once, although, knowing our adversary, that had been the design. I could hear Henry barking loudly downstairs and then a scream, Meredith maybe. I was half turning when Tommy's hand shot out and grabbed my shoulder, turning me back around. Gary was visible; he was being held upside down by his ankle, below the canopy. He was limp as if he were unconscious. I refused to believe it was because he was dead, but he was pale, oh so fucking pale. The screams downstairs grew in pitch. I was torn in indecision on where to go first.

"I'll handle her." Tommy said, pointing to the tree stand. He hopped over the railing and landed below. I was back in the house and heading to the basement. BT was on the staircase just ahead of me. We didn't bother to ask each other what was going on. Someone needed help, and that was all that mattered at the moment. I'd like to say I was prepared for what I saw, but really, why would you ever have scenarios running through your mind where two vampires are terrorizing your family? I mean, if you did, then you have other issues. Meredith was with her brother, Dizz and Sty were on the far side of the room. Monopoly pieces were strewn all over the place. Meredith had a hand cannon out, waving it back and forth between the two women. Henry was in between the kids and the vamps. I gotta admit the dog looked savage with his head hanging low, a growling so deep I could feel it in my chest. Long ribbons of drool hung from both sides of his snarling mouth. Long, glistening canines were exposed.

BT and I pulled up short right at the entryway. The room was locked in an electrically charged atmosphere, and we were both afraid that adding our presence would alter the dynamics in an unfavorable way.

The red-haired vampire turned to me. I'd forgotten the ethereal beauty they possess. My mind, I think any mind, has great difficulty correlating how something so intensely magnificent could be so utterly devoid of goodness. But what better way to hide a predatory evilness than through a mask of magnificence?

"Victor?" she asked, her eyes clouded for a moment, a look of ecstasy and confusion comingled for a moment. "No, alas no, but you are of the blood." She smiled.

"Of the blood," the other echoed.

"Meredith, you guys need to come this way." I had my rifle out and pointed. I did not look away from who I imagined was Payne. I was pretty convinced that to do so would spell my doom.

"Meredith? You are of the Talbot bloodline as well. Yes ... I can feel it as it beats quickly through your veins." She licked her canines.

"Through veins," the other vampire said.

"Who's the parrot?" I asked, trying to get Payne to stop thinking about blood, but that was like getting Henry to stop thinking about cookies.

The parrot-y vampire hissed at me.

"Do not move!" Payne shouted to Meredith, although she never took her eyes from me. "You killed our dearest Eliza?" she asked.

"She had it coming," I told her evenly, wondering if she could feel the thrum of my blood.

"I expected more."

"He gets that a lot," BT said. He was as tense as I'd ever seen him. I swear I could hear his muscles rippling in preparation for a fight.

"Meredith and the kids and the dog have nothing to do with this. Let them go, and we'll deal with this, whatever *this* is." I thought about saying "fight," but if they weren't here to kill us, I had no desire to put the thought into their head.

"That is where you are wrong, spawn of Tomas." Her face took on a scowling countenance. "There is a price that must be paid."

"Must be paid ... in blood," the other said, licking her lips suggestively.

"I can get you some chickens or something." I was stalling. I was terrified. I no sooner wanted to get into a melee with them than I wanted to get into a shark tank with chum as clothing.

Henry had upped his game and started barking. He must have sensed something was about to break; that, or he was getting tired and he needed this to all be over so he could take a nap. The spell was broken as she looked to Henry. Sly dog, he knew what was up.

"Kids, run!" I yelled, firing even as I brought the rifle up. I blew massive holes in the drywall as I sought vampire tissue to sink my lead into. Things slowed down to agonizingly frustrating slices of moments. Meredith turned to the others and started shoving them along. Payne moved with a speed I hadn't seen since Eliza. Her hand wrapped around Dizz's neck, and his eyes bulged as she applied extreme force. BT fired on the other vampire, who had not moved. She almost looked indignant that someone would even have the nerve to do such a thing.

Meredith and Dizz were off to our side. Henry had somehow sunk his teeth into Payne's calf. BT had put two bullets into the vamp I would find out was named Sophia. I grabbed my Ka-bar, letting my rifle fall to the floor.

"He is *mine!*" Payne shouted. "He is the first in a long line of recompenses."

Where my knife should have struck temple, it whistled through the air, the memory of a laugh the only thing there to let me know she'd ever even been here. Henry had been wrenched free from his tooth hold, he came to a yelping stop against the far wall.

Sophia moved a step closer to BT before turning to join Payne, who had departed. BT swore as his rifle jammed. He got so pissed he hurled it at Sophia's head. She turned back around and swatted it away as if it were an errant hair on a slight breeze. The smile that pulled her lips back and revealed her fangs, will forever be etched in my memory. No one in the history of the world had ever gazed upon another with such malice. Psychopathic murderers had more mercy harbored within themselves. Sophia did not kill to sustain her existence; she killed for the sheer pleasure she derived from it. The food source was just an added bonus. Payne and Dizz were gone, so I went toward the only other target I had left. There was not one part of me that didn't think she was going to crumple me like an old soda can. Didn't stop me though. I'd not gone more than a step when I heard the explosion; the side of her closest to me blew out as her pelvis was destroyed by a twelve-gauge shotgun slug. Travis stood in the frame of the outside door, the smoking gun in his hands. Sophia screamed out in a savage guttural sound that reeked of pain and fury. Vampire or not, she was going to need some time to recover from such a grievous injury.

"*Again!*" I screamed to Travis. Her hip was basically a mosh pit of loose parts gliding around in a stew of meat, and still she stood. Her leg collapsed when Travis fired again. Her eyes rolled back even as she went down. The smart thing would have been to start sawing through her neck as fast as possible, removing her fucking psychotic head. I didn't—for two reasons: one was Gary and the other was Dizz, both of whom I had to believe were still alive. I didn't know if vampires negotiated, but I had to try. BT had come up along-side me, his barrel nearly touching Sophia's head. I grabbed it from him. Trading my knife, I turned it around and pummeled the butt stock into her, seven or eight times until she fell over unconscious. Her beauty had been diminished significantly with her nose lying flat against her cheek and at least one orbital socket broken. Her lips were split and bleed-ing, and I'd started the scalping process, as her hairline was beginning to separate from her head. A normal person wouldn't make it, but already I could see the healing process beginning in her.

"Nice job, Travis. Grab something to tie her up with."

BT propped her up in a folding chair, and I wrapped her in over three hundred feet of rope. She looked like a mummy by the time I was done. Hardly any of her showed through the blue nylon of the repelling line. The stuff was rated at over 1000 pounds of tensile strength, I had to believe this would hold her. Tommy came back just as I was finishing off the last knot.

"Charity got away."

"I don't give a shit about Charity. Where's Gary?"

"She took him." His head hung low.

"Is he still alive?" I nearly choked getting those most distasteful of words out.

"I believe him to be."

"Well then, we have something to bargain for."

"What happened to Sophia?" Tommy lifted her head up.

"She's a Yankees fan. I had to." I told him. "Will these ropes hold?"

He pulled on them. "For a while. She's awake."

I stepped back once I realized just how close to her I was. I didn't notice any change other than her nose was straightening back out.

Tommy slapped her hard enough to rattle my fillings.

"Tomas!" She hissed. "Sister fucker! Sister fucker!" She said it two more times before I brought the rifle above my head.

"Say it again, and I'm going to keep hitting you until your head looks like gruel."

She laughed. "My sisters will not fuck me, they will save me."

"Helping others is not a strong suit for them." Tommy told her. "They will leave you here to rot."

She started to laugh. "Those they took will rot much faster than I."

BT placed the edge of my blade against her neck. "I will saw your head off."

"Please," she said in the high-pitched voice of a little girl. "I'm so afraid." And then she started laughing again.

"What's the matter with her?" I asked.

"Not everyone comes through the transition intact." Tommy said.

"Shit, Talbot, you're proof of that." BT said.

"You're holding a knife against a vampire's throat and you still have time to give me crap?" I saw his shoulders shrug.

"We should just kill her," Dennis said, he had come to join us.

"And what of Gary and Dizz?"

He wanted to say "they're already dead," but he just didn't have it in him.

"I bet they're delicious!" Sophia licked her lips.

I backhanded her hard enough to break two knuckles. Her

255

blood sprayed against the far wall, and still she laughed. I walked away, wincing at the pain in my hand.

"What do you want to do?" BT had come up next to me and spoke softly.

"I want to go and get them. You need to stay and watch that crazy one."

"Guard duty? Come on, man." BT said.

"I need Tommy with me, if anyone can find them it's him. And I need someone here that has the mental and physical abilities to do what needs to be done if we don't return."

"Mike, you know they're not going to trade out. Let's just be done with her, and then we can all go."

"And if they get past us, who defends this household … Trip?"

"Fuck you, man. You really know where to hit a man. I wouldn't let that man guard an anthill. Probably bring it inside so he could watch it from the comfort of his couch."

"Tommy, we need to go," I said, turning back around. He didn't ask where; he already knew. His body language showed that he thought this a futile effort, but he did not say "no."

"They're already dead, and soon you will be as well." Sophia said, her manic laughing finally stopping. "You do know what happens to those that die without a soul, do you not, Michael of the Talbot line?"

"I'm not a hundred percent sure, but maybe you can tell me when you join us. BT, we're not back in an hour, cut her fucking head off as painfully as possible." Maybe it was the flat way I delivered the words or just what the words intoned, but for once she shut the hell up.

It was easy enough to follow the blood trail as we left Ron's property. I tried not to think about what that kind of blood loss would do to somebody. I was convinced if we could get to them soon enough, we would be able to save them. I believed that very thought right up until I saw a body impaled against a large oak. A branch as thick as my forearm was protruding from his chest. The fact that he was upside down only added to the horror of the moment.

"He was dead before this was done to him." Tommy stepped closer.

"Is that supposed to make it better?" It was a rage-filled question. If Tommy said anything, I think I would have jumped on him both literally and figuratively. Instead, he tenderly reached up and pulled the boy free and then laid him down on the leaf-strewn ground.

"Let's go," I told him, trying to shut out the cold wind that blew within and around me.

"He must be buried."

"And he will be. He's dead, he can't get any deader. I want to try and make sure that doesn't happen to my brother."

Tommy took one long, mournful look at Dizz before we departed. We pushed on, moving faster through the Maine woods than we had a right to. Tommy pressed on hard. Everything looked the same to me; I was not sure what trail he was following, but as long as it wasn't a blood one, I was okay with it. I was so intent on staying on Tommy's heels I never even realized when it had become difficult to see them. Darkness wasn't creeping up on us as much as it had enveloped us completely in its gloomy embrace. A horror director would have lost his shit with how perfectly this scene was setting itself up. Clouds had covered the stars, and a small sliver of moon peeked through a thick fog that had rolled in. I could hear the ocean off to our right, lapping against the rocky coast. A lighthouse should have been blaring a warning to wayward ships. The night was still; the only thing moving was the heavy mist around us, the only sound that of the tide.

Anger still burned brightly in me, but I'd be lying if I said fear wasn't wriggling its finger around inside my skull. They could be within an arm's length, and at least I'd never know. Tommy with his va-dar (vampire radar) most likely could tell.

So when he answered, "Not sure," when I asked, "Where to?" I was more than concerned.

"Help" floated through the air much like the fog around us. The sound diffused and spread among the water droplets, making it impossible to tell from which direction it had come. I wasn't even sure if it was Gary's voice. That was answered soon enough when we heard a snippet of Bon Jovi.

"What are they doing?" I turned quickly around, trying to locate the source of the sound.

"They're playing with us. They know we're here. They're trying to scare us."

"Trying?" I said to him. "Where's Sophia?" I shouted. Funny how quickly they stopped playing the music. The resultant quiet was even more terrifying.

"Help!" That was indeed Gary. I was somewhat relieved because he was still alive. But that was like being happy for a mouse in a cobra enclosure. It was only a matter of time.

"Gary, we're going to get you out of this mess."

There was cruel laughter in response.

"What is it with vampires and laughing? Sophia stopped laughing when we were through with her!"

"Liar!"

"That's Charity." Tommy said. There was a downward lilt to his voice as he said her name.

"That's her name?"

Tommy sighed, "Yes."

"Yeah, that's like naming me Tactful," I said to him. "I've killed one vampire, what's another?" I shouted out.

"I will rip you from the heavens if you have harmed her!"

"That is a threat you cannot keep!"

A sound came from her that could have curdled sour milk. Apparently I was getting under her skin, although, all things being equal, I was definitely more scared. I don't know what sway the vamps held over the elements, if any, but the clouds split to reveal a crescent moon and a sprinkling of light dusted us just as the mist in front of us began to swirl independent of any sign of wind. It pulled back like a curtain on a stage to reveal a major player in this drama. Payne in all her magnificent, evil glory stood before us. Tommy grabbed my arm as I began to raise it.

"Where's my brother?" I tried to push past Tommy. He would not allow me any closer.

"Tomas, it is so good to see you after all these years." She smiled at him. It looked genuine enough. If given a different set of circumstances, I could almost believe that they were friends long ago and that had not seen each other in many moons. "I was saddened to hear of your loss. Your sister was a special vampire. Did you take it hard, especially after having devoted so much of your life to protect her?"

"I realize now that I should have spent more time trying to end her suffering than to let her inflict it upon so many others."

"You have been washed out by walking among the chaff, dear Tomas. Your sister was wrong in letting you stride the world so long with one foot in our world and one foot in theirs." She scoffed at that last part while pointing to me. "And now you honor her memory by protecting the one that slayed her? You have betrayed yourself as well as us all."

Tommy seemed to sag under the assault of her words. I took that as my opportunity. "I am going to shove my fist in your mouth." I got past his arm bar.

"There is much resemblance in you to my dear Victor. The fire of humanity burned so brightly through him. I was curious to see what would happen when it mingled with my lineage. He hated me for that." She reached out and ran her fingers along the side of my cheek. "I think he would have rather died violently that day rather than have the life I gave him."

"Life? You call this life? Watching all those I love around

me grow old and die and knowing I'll never be able to join them in the afterlife?"

"Love? Love is a myth. You have been granted immortality, the chance to shape your destiny as you see fit."

"Destiny? You don't shape destiny."

"Oh, my foolish child, you have so much to learn. You are like a babe playing with his blocks for the first time."

"I would like my brother back." I was fighting to keep her out of my mind. No matter what she said, her words had a soothing effect as she attempted to control me.

"He is no longer your brother. You belong to another world now. Join with me. I could show you so much that you have missed."

"I have no desire to see your world. I caught a glimpse of Eliza's. You can keep it."

"It is true Eliza had a different take. She let her past dictate her future. There is so much more than endless revenge and retribution. There are places that mortals cannot travel within this realm, grand things they cannot do. I am offering you the opportunity to bear witness to it all."

"At what cost?"

She smiled.

"The cost of my family? You want me to just hand them all over to you?"

"That would be easier on us and on them, yes. There is little you can do to prevent it."

"You killed a boy, a fucking innocent boy and then stuck him on a tree like a fucking ornament!"

"I was proving a point: the hopelessness of your situation. Your family will be treated with more respect if they are given over willingly."

I forced her from my head. I was happy to see a glimpse of a wince on her face as I did so. "Don't be trying your mind voodoo shit on me."

"Is that your doing?" She turned to Tommy.

"It was not. He has more power than he knows or is willing to tap into."

There was concern in Payne; I could feel it coming off of her.

"I could kill you both where you stand."

"Probably could, although Sophia won't live another half an hour if you do." I told her.

She looked on the edge of rage.

"Didn't think immortals could die. My friend has this huge blade right now stuck in the crook of her neck. I don't check in, and he just saws through that flesh like he was butchering a hog."

"You cannot!"

"Sure I can. I hate what I've become, but I hate you and your kind even more. If it were the last thing I did on this planet, I would consider it a victory."

Charity came out from the shadows. "Let me kill the impudent one, and we will go and save her." Much like Tommy had done to me, Payne reached out and halted Charity's progress.

"I want Gary back, you want Sophia. We can exchange them and then you can continue on with your little fact finding mission. Then you kill us or we kill you. Personally, I like our odds; we're not some little village in 1760 France that has no clue the monsters you are. Each of us is armed, willing to fight—and more importantly, we know how to fight."

She went exactly where I'd hoped she would not. "How long do you think it would take for me to create an army of vampires? We could tear through your paltry defenses before the sun sets. You have to think bigger than survival in terms of days, Michael. You do not understand the vastness of the universe, the secrets awaiting your exploration. It is so much bigger than the life you are so reluctant to let go of."

Now it was my turn to laugh. "I know how well your kind plays with each other. That three of you are together is a rarity, and you want to let loose a few dozen? And then what? You're going to try and rein them in? I already know man is becoming a rare commodity. How are you planning on feeding all those mouths? And new vampires, they are oh so very hungry, they'll mow through the population like hungry teenagers through a refrigerator stocked with snacks. Raise an army, my ass. You'd no sooner do that than you would suck on a rat for a meal."

"He cannot talk to you like this!" Charity chided.

"Ah, perhaps you do know us better than I had given you credit for. I sometimes forget that those who share the blood can see down the line of past events."

"Sophia for Gary, then you three get back on your little boat to China, or however the fuck you got here, and leave. You are no longer welcome on this continent."

"He has no right!"

"No right? You have my brother, bitch. I have every *fucking* right. You so much as break his Walkman, and I'll parade Sophia's head around on a fucking stick so that the crows can feast on her God forsaken eyes!"

Charity moved past Payne almost quicker than I could track. She was not used to a lowly half-breed squaring off against her, and she certainly wasn't used to Payne telling her what she could and could not do. She had her own agenda, and she was going to play it out. That was, at least, until Tommy sprang into action. She'd been so focused on me she barely took note of the downtrodden boy. His punch started somewhere in downtown Seattle before it connected with the side of her head—the temple, to be specific. Her legs were buckling even as she slid sideways in between me and Payne. She fell to her knees a good five feet to the side, her head lolling about like a bobble-head mounted on a Jeep dashboard on a particularly rocky trail.

Inside, I was jumping around like a little kid. This was

almost as good as watching the Red Sox beat the Yankees in the playoffs. I tried to stay as calm as I could on the outside.

"You still feeling pretty confident about your odds of taking us down, Payne?"

She said nothing.

"I think, if we put our minds to it, Tommy and I could kill you, and then, when we were done, we'd take care of Concussive Cathy over there before my buddy finishes off Sophia. By tomorrow morning, you three and all your illusions of grandeur are but fucking dust."

She still said nothing, weighing her options, I guess.

"Makes no difference to me if you spend all of eternity wandering the vast wastelands of purgatory."

She looked at me with surprise.

"Oh yeah, I know all about that place, too. You have to wonder what's worse, being forever alone in that gray world or having to pay for all your transgressions with the source spring of evil. I suppose Eliza knows. I sense confusion on your part. Did you not know that we reunited her with her soul before we killed her?"

"You lie; that is not possible."

She said the words, but she didn't seem overly confident about them.

"It's the truth." Tommy told her. He was looking at his knuckles that had swelled from the hit.

I wasn't going to tell her that we'd had the help of a burgeoning witch and a spell-trapped Shaman. It was better if she somehow thought we could do it again.

I felt bad for Tommy, and I'd smooth things over later. Right now, I needed to do all I could to convince Payne we were not adversaries she wanted to have.

"She screamed for mercy at the end. Begged me not to do it. What came for her was unimaginable. Can you imagine being tortured in a place where every second can be dragged out into a lifetime?"

Charity wobbled her way to a standing position. She had to reach out to a small tree to steady herself.

"Please, Payne, give us Gary, take Sophia, and go home," Tommy pleaded. "Make something good come out of my sister's suffering."

"Your traitorous ways to our kind disappoint me, Tomas. Although a lot of that fault lies at your sister's feet for letting you stay half turned for so long, you belonged neither to us nor to them. You were forced to find your way as best you could. You had the chance to be a great ally to us, yet you align yourself with the lowly humans."

"You were human once," he said to her.

"For merely a speck of my existence was I saddled with that burden. Does a butterfly feel for the caterpillar when it sprouts its wings?"

"Fuck the metaphors, Payne. I want my brother. Your lives depend on your answer, right here, right now. We either leave with him or you die. It's as simple as that."

"And what of Sophia?"

"We get home with no further problems, and I release her."

"That is your word?"

"Scout's honor." I told her flashing a "v" sign.

Payne thought on it for a moment. "Very well."

That seemed to snap Charity out of whatever stupor she was in. "You cannot!"

"Oh, I can and I have. We have found out what we came to find out. To do more is to risk too much."

"You are worried about a broken vampire, a halfling, and some human food? Perhaps you are not the illustrious vampire we all thought you to be."

Payne hit her with a backhand that dropped her once again to the ground. Charity moaned in pain.

"Do not doubt my resolve, Charity. We did not come to seek retribution for Eliza, we came to see the force that had her removed from this world. We have accomplished that. I did not like Eliza. I respected her, though, and I have done what I have set out to do. I have no desire to join her as a plaything for the Dark One. Release the human."

"Whoa, whoa, whoa. I don't trust this one. I think maybe you should do it."

"Perhaps you're right."

"Oh, I know I'm right. She'd cut his fucking throat and say oops. Vampire or not, she's still female and I've seen that look before."

Charity looked like she was going to explode. Tommy stood over her, making sure she did not attempt to stand again. It was a couple of minutes later when I finally heard them coming back through the woods.

"Where are you taking me?" Gary asked, the fear evident in his voice.

"I am releasing you."

"Releasing me how? Like letting me go, releasing? Or releasing me from my earthly tethers, kind of releasing?"

Well that was definitely a Talbot-esque type of response. If I wasn't so fucking nervous, I would have smiled at it.

Gary looked about as pale as the mist that surrounded him. He seemed to have a difficult time reconciling that Tommy and I were ahead of them.

"Are you real?" he asked.

"Pretty much," I told him, stepping forward. I gave him a quick embrace. "Are you all right?"

"Mostly. They can get in your head."

"Yeah, I know. Get behind me. We're going to leave now."

Payne nodded. "It was a pleasure meeting you."

"Yeah, not so much on this end."

"You will do as you promised and release Sophia?"

"I swore to the scouts. They take their oaths seriously."

And with that, we turned and left. We'd not gone more than a couple of miles when Gary asked to stop and rest. He was drained, Payne had pushed him hard to get away.

"You weren't in the scouts," he said, sitting on a downed tree.

"Yeah, I know."

Tommy looked over to me.

"Relax."

By the time we got back, the morning sun was beginning to spill over the horizon. I thought I was done with the weird sights for the immediate future, but in fact, I was kind of just getting started. Sophia and BT were still together, although he looked like shit, and MJ and Trip were with him. So far not too strange, but Sophia had on a patented tin foil hat as did Trip, although hers had electrical wires running from it, leading to some sort of box that MJ was fiddling with. Trip was doing various yoga poses. I knew what they were, but in the off chance that I can keep my man-card intact, I'm not going to name them.

"Oh, thank God." Tracy had come out. "Oh, you poor thing." She grabbed Gary and ushered him inside. "Where's Dizz?" she asked before she followed my brother in.

I pursed my lips and gave a small, terse shake of my head.

"I'll talk to the kids," she said.

"Thank you." I leaned in and kissed her quickly. "What the fuck is going on here?" I asked, looking around. "Are you all right?" I focused on BT. He was sitting in the corner with an ashen look to him.

"Gary? Dizz?" he asked, looking up for the first time.

"Gary's fine. Dizz didn't make it. What's going on, man? You look terrible."

"She … she got in my head, Mike. She made me believe she was my fiancée. I had started to cut through the restraints."

I think I may have gasped. Does that sound too much like a nineteenth-century female? I thought I saw my man-card floating off on a small breeze. If she had gotten loose and BT was under her control, she could have sliced through the rest of the household in no time. We could have come home to a much different, ghastly, and gruesome scene.

"It was Trip, fucking crazy-ass, stoned Trip, saved my life."

"He saved more than just you, man." I pulled up a chair to sit down next to him. Now that I'd stopped moving, I found just how tired I was. It was part that, and it was part the stress of realizing just how close to disaster we'd all come.

"I guess you're right. She was so far down inside of me I probably would have helped her."

"It's okay, man. It's not your fault."

"Mike, I almost let her go, and on top of that, I have to reconcile that it was Trip that prevented that."

"You feel like talking about it?"

"No."

I sat back. It took about five minutes less for him to start speaking than I thought it would.

"I'd swear, even now, Mike, that it was my Linda sitting in that chair. Down to the smallest detail, she looked like her. I don't know why Trip came here."

"Was looking for leprechauns!" he shouted out in a horrible Irish accent as he moved into the child's pose. You should just pretend that you have no idea how I knew that.

"He came in, Mike, with his stupid little tin foil hat, and then he stuck it over her head. Things started to get fuzzy, you know, like shitty television reception back in the antennae days. Linda's face was blurring with Sophia's back and forth until finally it was just that bitch's. I almost stuck my knife through the side of her skull."

"Kind of wish you had." Sophia glared at me. At some point, someone had been wise enough to place duct tape over her mouth. "What the hell is Mad Jack doing? Was he looking for leprechauns too?"

"Pshhh, as if he could see them." Trip moved into downward dog.

"Trip said I should go get him, so I did. He grabbed some of his equipment and came down here after I told him what happened. He's been working ever since. Keeps saying things like 'fascinating' or 'incredible,' though he never explains further than that."

"You bother to ask? Guy likes to talk about his experiments."

"Never thought to; been a little preoccupied after having a conversation with my dead fiancée."

"Understood. I'm sorry, man." I brought a fist down on his thigh and tapped him gently. As I stood, he looked at me gratefully. "Whacha got going on?" I asked MJ. It looked like he was getting ready to fry her brain like an egg and then maybe decorate it for Easter.

"She's incredible!" Mad Jack said before dashing off to look at another piece of gear.

"She in your head too?" I kept a close eye on him.

"My head? No, no. I have signals interfering with her broadcasts."

"Broadcasts? Like television signals?"

"Sort of. Let me see if I can dumb this down."

"Oh, thank you for that. If you could use words with no more than two syllables, that would be fantastic as well."

MJ looked at me funny. "I'll try, but that's a tall order."

"Just tell me what the hell is going on. If I don't understand it, I'll just nod and say uh-huh at the appropriate time."

"Okay, the human body has low levels of electrical current that run through it at all times. It controls nearly everything we do, perception of pain, muscle contraction and movement, nerve function, healing, and definitely brain activity."

"Okay, so far, so good on my side."

"Well, the brain is the super highway for these signals, and measurements have been done that show the typical human can power a 15 to 20 watt bulb. Some people more, some less." He made sure to look at me directly when he said "less."

"You're not even trying to be funny right now, are you?"

"Huh?" He looked puzzled. "Can I continue?"

"Go for it."

"There have been medical studies where sent small currents that were sent into a person helped correct all manner of brain disorders, including Tourettes. There have even been studies that show people can and do emit these signals."

I saw where he was going with this. "So our friend over there, she can do this?"

"She's not my friend," he said, as if it needed to be clarified.

I pinched the bridge of my nose. "Figure of speech, MJ. Just keep going."

"Well, you know how I said people can power a small bulb?"

"Yup." I was trying my best not to show him how much he was beginning to aggravate me.

"Mike, she could run a toaster … on the other side of the room."

"That a lot?"

"About a thousand watts. She could completely fry the circuitry in someone's head if she had a mind to."

"She can reach out with her mind and just kill people?"

"Yes."

"How far?"

"I can't really pull off Trip's impromptu shield to test, but I don't think a hundred feet is out of the question, maybe as much as three hundred."

"Are you shitting me? She can kill someone from a football field away?"

"I am most certainly not 'shitting' you."

"Can you scramble her up a bit with this gizmo?" I swirled my finger around his electronic wizardry.

"This is test equipment. It's for measurement purposes."

"I get what test equipment is for."

"Then why are you asking if I can zap her?"

"She can't leave here." I looked over to Sophia. She could hide in the woods and silently destroy everyone.

"Gary's asleep. He should be fine, Mr. T." Tommy had joined us.

"You know about her?" I asked almost in an accusatory tone.

"I knew of her. I'm not sure what you're asking. What's all this?"

"Apparently, Sophia here is like a mini Tesla, only she's deadly."

"What?"

"MJ over there seems to believe she has the ability to send electrical currents out that can either control or kill a person."

"And you believe him?"

"Yeah, I know what you mean. Mad Jack is pretty two-faced and deceitful. I haven't trusted him since we found his van filled with Pabst Blue Ribbon. I mean, who drinks that shit when just about any beer you want is available?"

"You know what I mean."

"Yeah, I know. I might be more suspect if our big sad friend over there hadn't spent the night with his fiancée."

"She's dead."

"You catching on yet?"

"What? Oh. Holy crap."

"Yeah, that's pretty much what I said. Is this something all vamps can do?"

"To a degree, we all have the ability for mind manipulation. In varying degrees, some are better at it than others. I'm better at it than my sister was, but I'd never be able to convince a person that I was someone else."

"Well, it seems Sophia is training for the Olympics with her skills. I know what I promised Payne, but we can't let her go."

Tommy frowned. "I wondered why she even agreed to do it. That's not really her style. You want to keep her captive."

I said nothing.

"You want to kill her?" he asked, astonished.

"What other choice do we have?"

"In cold blood?"

"Her blood is already cold, and it's not like she's an innocent. How many deaths can be attributed to her over the centuries? Five hundred? Five thousand?"

"Still, Mr. T."

"Tommy, do you really believe Payne is just going to walk away? In your heart, is that what you believe?"

He said nothing for a good long while. "No, I don't. She'll kill us all just to do it."

"MJ, you're a hundred percent sure on what she can do?" I asked.

"I'm as sure as I can be given the data I have. The only way I could be more certain is if she killed something. But I wouldn't recommend that type of real-world test."

"Thanks, I needed that warning, kind of like someone telling me that the contents of a cup of coffee are hot, or possibly, not to hold lit fireworks in my hand."

"Yes, like that."

"I'm going to lie down." BT stood.

"You cool?"

"As cool as I can be. Stop looking at me like that, Mike."

"Like what?"

"Like the way everyone is usually looking at you. I'll be fine. I know what she did, but I have to admit it was still nice seeing Linda, and I'd like to hold on to that for a little while longer."

"Enjoy your rest," I told him.

He turned before he walked out of the room. "Don't let her go." Then he left.

"Anything else you can learn from her?" I asked MJ.

"Encyclopedias could be written about her."

"What are you going to do?" Tommy asked when I reached for the knife sheath attached to my calf. "You can't just kill her like this!" He blocked my way.

"Are you kidding me? Did you see what they did to Dizz? What they would have done to Gary? What they would have done to us all? What they will do to us all."

"This is different."

"No, it's not. This is a war. Our side prevails or theirs does. She's not a bystander or a casualty of war. She's an active participant."

"She's a prisoner."

"Get out of my way, Tommy."

He stood his ground.

"Mike?" Tracy had come in. "Is there a problem?"

"Mind-melting Maggie over there is a danger to us all, and Tommy is of the ilk that we should let her go and deal with her at a later time. That about an accurate portrayal?" I asked him.

"That's fair," he responded.

"Mind-melting?"

"That's not a truly accurate description, but she can indeed send an electronic signal with enough power to stop all function within a human being." MJ said.

"From a distance." I added.

"How far?" she asked.

"Well, the experts haven't come to a decisive conclusion, but at least a hundred feet, maybe as many as three hundred." I told her.

Tracy looked concerned, and she had every right to be. It got worse real quick.

"They're out there." Tommy said, looking to the yard.

"In the abstract?" I knew he meant close. It's just always nicer to hope for the best. His look to me was all the answer I needed. "Listen, we both know how this is going to play out."

"Please, let me know the future." Tommy said wryly, not a tone I was accustomed to hearing from him.

"Fine, here goes my prediction. You untie her. She reaches up and pulls off her little hat. Then she immediately begins to mind-fuck me. I drop to my knees with blood leaking from my ears and nose. You realize you made a horrible mistake, then you dash in and shove a huge knife into her skull. She's dead but it's too late for me. The damage has been done. I'm now basically a slobbering vegetable."

"Much like now."

"Gee, thanks wife."

"So we're now in the business of doling out punishment for a crime that has yet to be committed?"

"Fuck, Tommy, when did you become a liberal? Does she look innocent? What about Dizz, doesn't he deserve some justice?"

"She didn't do it."

"Guilty by association."

"That's not a thing."

"Sure it is. There were plenty of states that had that on the books."

I had no idea what was about to happen while Tommy and I were verbally sparring. I would have fought to the death to make sure Sophia did not walk free. Tracy avoided the middleman. I'd not been prepared for the sound of her pistol going off in the enclosed space. Sophia's head sagged forward, a nine-millimeter hole neatly punched into the back of her skull.

"Nobody threatens the lives of my babies, no one! If you can't handle that, then get the fuck out of my house!" She looked over to Tommy, the barrel of her gun still smoking.

The look of shock on MJ's face would have been comical under different circumstances.

Trip stood. "Whoa, I don't think this was how this was supposed to play out."

Tommy looked like he was about to blow like Mount Vesuvius.

"Everyone out. Now!" I shouted when it looked like no one was going to move. I had a pretty good idea the bullet had done enough damage to kill the vampire, but I wasn't completely sure. There was a tried and true method; nobody needed to be there to witness it. I wanted to pretend I was cutting up some chicken breast sections and not decapitating someone. It didn't help that she stirred as I first put my blade against her skin. Something wriggled around inside my head. At first, I thought it was my conscience for what I was doing, then I realized it was a foreign body invading and trying to make a beachhead. Even with her mostly destroyed, I could tell I was no match for Sophia. I would not be able force her out like I had Payne. Sophia would wash over me like a tide to a sand castle. I dug deeply with a sawing motion, easily cutting through her skin, larynx, windpipe, cordage, and muscle, finally getting to her spine. The serrated edges caught in the dense muscle and cartilage, at least until I applied more force, and still she tried to destroy me from within. Most likely would have succeeded, if her thoughts weren't so scattered. If she had a cohesion to them at all, she would have crushed me.

I was panting from the mental and physical strain by the time I lifted her head clean from her body. That didn't even take into account the spiritual strain. Killing something is bad enough; removing its head is quite another. I just had to remember that she was no more human than a fish.

"I wonder what deep-fat-fried vampire tastes like." I placed Sophia's head in a trash barrel.

"You did *not* just say that." It was Tracy. "I wanted to see how you were doing. Now I'm not so convinced that was a good idea."

"I was trying to persuade myself she was a fish. Forget it. You okay? I know that's not really your style."

"Just tell me that it was the right thing."

"Without a doubt, they would have killed us all. Or, more likely, made a few of us kill everyone else. It would have been a game to them, something done merely for the entertainment value. You did exactly what needed to be done. Probably saved my life today as well."

"How so?"

"Tommy would have killed me while I tried to kill her. Speaking of which, where is he?"

"I think he went to the deck."

"I've got this. Get out of here. There's no sense in both of us getting scarred for life."

"I'd say it's a little late for that for at least one of us."

"Funny, go and check on BT. Make sure he's doing okay. He was pretty shaken up."

"What are you going to do with her?"

"Viking funeral without the boat."

17

MIKE JOURNAL 13

DENNIS HELPED ME GATHER SOME WOOD AND THEN WENT BACK in. When I placed her body on the makeshift pyre, Angel was the only one to stand with me as the body burned.

"She was a bad person," Angel said.

"Yes, she was," I answered.

"I miss Dizz."

"Yeah me too, kiddo." I grabbed her shoulder and pulled her in close. Even with the heat of the intense fire, it was still plenty cold inside my heart.

IT HAD BEEN A SOLID WEEK, and we'd heard absolutely nothing from the two vampires still out there. Tommy had stayed ever vigilant, as did we all, but where we were scanning with our eyes, he was using his mind. They'd gone dark. I'd like to think we had scared the hell out of them by putting the fear of God in its place, but I knew it was wishful and wistful, thinking. Vampires were bad losers, given they never really had to be accustomed with that end of the competitive spectrum. The problem with our enemy was that time meant absolutely nothing. They could seek revenge in a day or a decade. We could have all but forgotten about them when they struck. Sure, we were staying close to the house and always had to be in groups of two or more, but how long would that last? Another couple of weeks and most, if not all, of us would return to our normal routines. We'd become lax. Humans just can't stay on high alert forever. We can't handle that kind of strain. We'll invent safety and security, if we have to, just to feel better.

"Michael, I need some help."

"Why the formality, MJ?"

"Because I really need your help."

"Okay, I guess honesty is the best policy. What can I help you with?"

"I need some transformers."

"Don't we all. I would really love to have an Optimus Prime. Shit, even a Bumblebee would be great."

The blank stare I received back confirmed to me MJ had absolutely no idea I was talking about the incredibly successful cartoons and movies about beings from another planet that could transform into various pieces of equipment, like a truck or car, and then switch into their alter egos, capable of massive amounts of mayhem and destruction.

"We are not talking about the same thing."

"You're the smart one. Are you just figuring that out now?"

"I need the transformers on the telephone poles. They're roughly the size of a large trash can."

"How much do they weigh?"

"Five hundred to eight hundred pounds."

"Are you kidding me? How are you planning on getting them down?"

"The same truck you used at the post office and a series of cables and pulleys."

"Well, not that the utility company is going to give a shit, but how long do you think this whole procedure is going to take?"

"Should be able to safely get one down in under two hours, three at the most."

"And the zombies?"

"What about them?" he asked, clearly confused.

"What do you think they'll be doing for all that time?"

"I have no idea. I would imagine zombie-type activities though."

"What do you think would be a favorite zombie-type activity?"

"Eating people, I presume. I really don't see what this has to do with me getting a transformer."

"Nothing? Nothing at all? How in the hell did you make it for so long through life without falling through an open manhole cover or something?"

"I always watched where I walked."

"And a good thing, too. Listen, when I was getting that cherry picker, I noticed some of those transformers off to the side. I can't confirm whether they worked or not; I was a little busy."

"That's all right. As long as the main components are in there, I can repair them."

"Now, before I wrangle up some help to get these things, can you tell me what the hell you are going to do with them?"

"Fission bomb."

I think my mouth dropped open.

"Oh, my gosh, I crack myself up. You should see your face. I'm a few materials short of actually being able to do that, and this has absolutely nothing to do with that project."

"You're actually working on designs for a fission bomb?"

"Oh, I'm a little ways past the planning phase."

"I don't want to know. I'd rather be surprised with the bright white light of disintegration."

"I'll let you know when I'm ready to test fire one."

"Yeah, I'd appreciate that. We'd all appreciate that. How many of these damn things do you need?"

"Three would be ideal, at least two. Wait, no three, just in case I need to scavenge parts. Probably four. Wait, how many can I have?"

"You make my head hurt, and we're not even talking sciencey stuff right now. I'll round you up what I can."

"Can I come?"

I wanted to say no only because there was absolutely no doubt in my mind that he was going to go into great detail about exactly what he was going to do with these transformers. But I didn't want to go to the power facility to only grab the wrong stuff.

"Fine, it would be a pleasure," I told him instead. "Let me just go grab BT."

"And who else?"

"What do you mean?"

"The transformers are heavy. Who's going to move them?"

"Have you seen BT? It'd be like him holding a can of beer."

"Not really, Michael. It wouldn't be like that at all. The ratio of BT to the diameter of—"

"Okay, okay, I get it. I'm not taking too much muscle, MJ, because if anything happens here..."

"What would happen here?"

"You cannot be this clueless. You remember the whole war with the zombies and the added fun of the vampires? Remember all that?"

He waved it off as if that was no concern to him.

"You and Trip should hang out sometime."

"I really don't see what that has to do with anything."

"Just be ready in a couple of minutes. I'll let everyone know."

I know how my bread is buttered and who does the buttering. The first person I went to was Tracy. Without even looking up, she said we needed diapers. I guess she was all right with it.

I had to wake BT up. He was about as happy as you would expect someone that had just gone to sleep four hours ago would be after pulling a late night guard shift. The scowl he directed at me almost had me leave his room before I even asked, and then it just kind of went away. The scowl I mean.

"What are you in here for?"

"MJ and Tracy want me to run some errands."

"This isn't about his fission bomb is it?"

"You know about that?"

"Everybody does, damn near all he talks about. How could you not?"

"I start tuning him out the second he starts talking about his experiments."

"When someone starts talking about a bomb that can take out a city, it's generally a good idea to pay attention."

"You coming or what?"

"Bored already? Yeah, maybe it will do me some good to get out."

"Really? I figured for sure you were going to throw something at me. Although, I don't know how much that silk robe would have hurt."

"It's a kimono."

"Okay, man, no reason to get testy. It looks pretty on you."

He tossed a pillow at me with enough force to have ripped my head off if I hadn't moved. "Fuck, man. You're going to put holes in my brother's walls."

"How's he doing?" BT sat on the edge of the bed and wiped his hand across his face, trying to rub the tiredness away.

"The way you'd expect him to be."

"When we leaving?"

"Five minutes."

MJ, me, BT, and Justin, who unexpectedly wanted to come, were all in the truck. I realized halfway to the power facility that MJ never *really* told me what we needed the transformers for.

"They're for the zombies." He'd answered after I'd asked. "Well, I mean not *for* the zombies specifically. They're more for us. Well, in the abstract, they're for us."

"Oh for the love of God, MJ, what are the transformers going to do?"

"They're going to stop the zombies, of course." He seemed a little chuffed.

"I bet dentists have an easier time pulling teeth from patients trying to run away from them."

BT smiled.

"Let's just say for argument's sake I have no idea what you're talking about."

"Well, it's obviously clear enough that you don't," he said.

"You believe this guy?" I asked the other occupants of the car.

"Well, he is right."

"From my own son? That hurts more than you know." Justin had been working through his loss. Slowly but surely, he was coming more into his own. I think the biggest part of the equation was the love he had for his nephew. He would stay with the infant for hours on end. The baby was the balm that soothed his soul. Nicole had all the help she could ask for, and sometimes, even more.

"I can take some power off of Ron's generator and run it through the transformers to create a charge that I will apply to some fencing that will inhibit the zombies' ability to come closer to the house."

"Like an electric fence?" I asked.

"Something like that." He had dodged the answer again. Giving a genius access to materials and time was never a good thing. I swear MJ did half the things he did merely because he could. If we could have built him a lab off grounds, we would have. As it was, we had to check in on him from time to time just to make sure he wasn't going to get us sucked into a portable wormhole or something.

It looked all quiet as we pulled up to the fence. MJ started to get out.

"Hey cowboy, how about holding on for a sec." BT arm-barred his exit.

"Yeah, and I'm the one without a clue. All right, the last time I was here, there were a bunch of zombies up on the third floor. Let's just make sure they haven't found a way out and aren't just milling around."

"That would probably be a good idea." MJ said when he realized he wasn't going to be able to move BT's arm.

The parking lot was clear. We all peered up to the top floor. Seven or eight zombies peered down. Apparently, the rest had broken free or were just disinterested in the goings on below. Either way, I was happy for it.

"You have got to be kidding me." I pointed to a flatbed truck with six of the transformers parked on the back of it. The truck was even equipped with its own small crane to deploy the large cylinders. "This is too fucking easy." I looked around.

BT let Mad Jack get out.

"What's the matter, Talbot? The gods can't throw you a bone every once in a while without you getting suspicious?" BT laughed while he joined MJ outside.

"Their bones come with a heavy price." I was still looking around. Justin got out as well. My heart skipped when the truck roared to life. I got out of my ride. "There is no way the keys were in it."

"What? No," MJ stated. "I hotwired it."

"And the battery was okay?"

"It's running. I don't think we need one of MJ's hypotheses to prove that." BT said.

"What the hell did I bother bringing you here for?"

"I'm security, man," BT informed me.

"Naw, man. I just brought you for the muscle. I thought you were going to have to load those things into the truck." I told him.

"You're an asshole."

"Meh, I've been called worse by better, and I'm just talking about today."

"All right, smart guy, what do you want to do now?" BT asked me, but MJ replied instead.

"Well, I would like to get this equipment back to my lab where I can change the—"

"Sciency shit! BT, if you could take him back, Justin and I will go and get the diapers."

"You sure, man?"

"It's diapers. How hard could it be?" It's after the fact that you ever wonder why you uttered words like that out in the open where everyone can hear. "I'll take Justin and meet you at the house. We'll be right behind you."

BT looked at me. "Just follow us back, and we'll go out again."

"It's fine, man. It's diapers."

"Mike, I don't feel good about this."

It took me a couple of minutes to assuage him of his bad feelings. "We'll be right back, I promise."

BT waved as he drove the truck out of the yard. "Right back, man. No side stops."

"Of course," I replied. I waited until they were out of range. "Now we just need to figure out where to get diapers, and we'll be all set." The grocery store in Belfast was cleaned out. It had been orderly, but there wasn't much more than a memory of products being housed there. There were a few convenience stores, but they'd been just as empty.

"What about the hospital?"

I thought for a second. "That's not a bad idea. The drugs

will be wiped out and so will most of the medical supplies, but I can't imagine the maternity ward getting too slammed."

We pulled up. Ghost building didn't even begin to describe the feeling one got when looking upon the place. There was a chill in the air. Brown leaves were being hustled down the roadway on a wind that was beginning to pick up. Broken windows littered the front parking lot. The hospital looked just like a place you would expect to be ground zero for this area. A few of the windows showed the soot of a fire that had poured through the openings. Bullet holes were strewn across the front. Zombies in various states of decomposition were all around. Those humans that had died here had long ago been laid to rest by their loved ones or just those who were civic minded and still resided nearby.

"Maybe this wasn't such a good idea." Justin said while we walked closer.

"You catching the same thing BT had?" I wanted to laugh it off, but more than once, we'd survived merely because of a premonition, and if he was were tapping in to something unseen, I could not discount it out of hand just because I was not privy to the details.

"I'm good."

"Okay, hold up for a sec."

He did.

"Listen, this is no time to 'man up.' If you sense something, let me know and we'll figure something else out."

"I'm fine, Dad. I guess I'm just a little spooked. BT must have got to me."

"You sounded more convincing that time you said you hadn't eaten the cake and I found you with frosting on your head."

"I was five. I think maybe you should let it go."

"Hell no, that was one of the funniest things I've ever seen."

ZOMBIE FALLOUT 9

"There hasn't been a girlfriend of mine that you've failed to tell."

"That's what parents do. Now, be straight with me here. We'll keep using dish towels as diapers if we have to."

"Have you changed any of those?"

"Hell no, I'm the grandfather. That's one of the perks. It's not in my job description."

"Well, I have. It's horrible. Crap leaks out all over the place. We need these diapers."

"All right, let's do this then."

I think foreboding is a good word to use as we walked up to the main entrance. Wheelchairs, gurneys, blood, and a general sense of past mayhem were strewn all about the opening and into the large reception area. It was even worse off to the immediate right, which was the urgent care section. Brass casings and bodies made an entirely new type of flooring. The worst of the smell was gone, but there was still a persistent stink of death that would be present for a generation or two. I pointed to a hallway where I knew the stairs to be. We went around and over the dead as best we could, trying not to disturb them from their eternity. It was not always possible. These boots, like so many others before them, were destroyed. There wasn't a disinfectant powerful enough that was going to get out the stains I was imprinting on them as I stepped on and ultimately through body after body.

I thought the stairwell would be a relief of sorts. If anything, it was worse. The smell, which had been bottled up like a corked wine, released its essence like a stale breath once the door was opened. I swear the air sighed as it moved past, like the souls of the damned had been trapped in there as well.

"That was weird."

"You caught that too?" I asked Justin.

He nodded, his eyes wide. There were very little light making its way into the stairwell, and what it showed was definitely not worth its effort to reach those far confines. Bodies littered the steps. Skulls were smashed, brains were mashed, and bodies were broken along multiple stairs. Intestines and internal organs speckled the entire area. It looked like a psychopath with a penchant for interior decorating had spent the afternoon here. There had been a mighty battle. It was easy enough to see that this was someone's final stand. Otherwise, they would have left long before it had gotten this bad. I'd had to forgo holding onto my weapon to grab the handrail because of how my feet kept slipping on the aftermath as we ascended. Although now I was putting my hands on all manners of things, some slimy, some slick, most just plain gross. It harkened back to one of my days at the grocery store. I *always* wiped down that handle with the provided sani-wipes, and this is just one of the reasons why. I would love to say this is fiction; I'd be lying.

I'm going down the snack aisle and there's this lady, maybe mid-sixties, could have been mid-seventies. Shit, with all the sores on her, she could have been in her forties and looked the way she did because of her meth addiction and how it had taken its toll on her. Well, just her touching the handle would have been bad enough. Anyway, she's got a kid in the kid seat part. He's gotta be closing in on nine years old. He's clearly about four years too old to be in the thing. He makes Pigpen from Charlie Brown look like the poster child for Lysol. Kid is covered head to toe in dirt, and he has this hacking cough that reminds me of a TB clinic in Bangkok (don't ask). Anyway, the kid is literally (not figuratively), *literally,* spitting out long strings of phlegm *purposefully* on the buggy handle. She's laughing as he's doing this like it's the cutest thing in the fucking world! Can you imagine if you were the next one to use that cart? Especially if you were going to grab fresh fruit for your family? Have fun with that one. And just to add a small dollop of added grossness, I would swear that he may or may not have had a diaper on and it was leaking. Isn't that top part where most of us generally put our most delicate and delectable eateries? It was at this point I began to wonder if I could buy my own shopping cart and transport it around with me. It's shit like this that makes me like people even less.

Right now, there was a chance I would have licked that shopping cart handle if I could have let go of the handrail I was holding. All right, all right, we both know I'm lying, but that I even suggested it shows just how distressed I was. My hand was so slick from the material coating it that I at first mistakenly thought the door on the third floor was locked when I turned the knob and only my hand spun. There was a small well of panic as I thought about having to go back down the same way we'd come. I gripped it harder. I was rewarded with the sound of something squishing and popping in my hand. The heebies had started, and the jeebies were not far behind, but at least the handle turned this time. I stepped out onto the third floor without even bothering to take a look if I was alone or not. I wanted to wipe my hands on something, anything, to get the thick layers of goop off of them. There was a dead doctor zombie not more than four feet away. The shot that had killed him had only removed the top of his head; his scrubs were near pristine as I bent over and wiped furiously on his chest.

"I'm sorry, man, I really am." But I kept doing it.

Justin stepped into the hallway. He gave me a funny look, but he was beside me in a flash.

"This is so wrong, Dad."

"Don't need to tell me."

"Dad." Justin pointed, and I was figuring we had company. There was a large dispenser of hand sanitizer attached to the wall. I've wished for a lot of things in my life. An unlimited supply of candy in my youth, an unlimited supply of girlfriends in my late teens, an unending supply of health and happiness for my family later on … right now, the most powerful wish I think I'd ever had was that the bottle of sanitizer was still liquidy and had not dried out. Funny how your priorities change given the circumstances.

"There is a God," I said as I pressed the button in five times.

"Any chance you could save some for me?" Justin elbowed me out of the way. "Wait. Are you crying?"

"Um, I'm fine. Just so very, very happy right now," I said while I vigorously rubbed my hands together.

"It's the small stuff right?"

"I couldn't be any more proud of you than at this very moment." I turned the doc over to wipe on the other side of his smock. "Special place in Hell for doing this, but right now, it's so worth it." I waited until Justin cleaned up a bit, and then it was time to go exploring. I think I should have prepped myself a little more mentally than I had. We were going to a nursery. What should I have been expecting? It wasn't my first run through with infant victims. I guess I just do my best to forget I'd ever crossed their paths. Much better way to keep a grip. Know what I mean? I'm not going to go into vivid detail here even if I know I'm never going to read this again. To do so would be reliving the event, and I just don't want to, plain and simple.

There were zombie babies and human babies and all I could see was the destruction of so much potential, so much life, unlived. It was heartrending. Justin didn't even pretend not to see it; he heaved all over the hallway. Got some distance if I'm being honest. I saw what I needed. Sucked big giant spider penises that it was on the other side of the infirmary. Do spiders even have penises? That was not a question I was going to think long on. I strode across that room like I had blinders on. I may have heard a small groan or two but whatever made it was way beyond my help, and I in no way wanted to add its face to the long list of nightmares I already had. A quick check of the drawers yielded a laundry bag. This I stuffed with all manner of diapers from infant to pre-teen (made that last part up), but if there was a size, I was taking it because I was not coming the fuck back.

Another gurgled cry, something between a baby looking for its mom and a tortured soul looking for something to eat. It would find neither. Justin was busy holding a wall up outside in the hallway. I looked like a redneck Santa Claus as I came out of that room with a large sack over my left shoulder and my rifle slung over my right.

"How you holding up?"

"And they call me Captain Obvious."

"Sorry."

"Dad, I just keep thinking, what if that were Wesley in there?"

"It isn't."

"Yeah, but what if...?"

"It *isn't!*" I said with more force then I meant. "There are paths you want to travel down, that ain't one of them. Okay?"

"Yeah, okay."

"Come on, let's find another way out of here." No stupider words were uttered by me that day. Ended up going the wrong way. We went through some double doors. Directly to our front was a large, round desk that encircled the nurse's station. Like spokes on a wheel, there were birthing rooms for expecting parents all around. Three zombies, all pregnant, were on the floor eating a couple of rats that must have had the misfortune of finding their way up here.

"I don't think this is the way." Justin nearly walked into the back of me when I stopped. We hadn't been discovered until he'd spoken. It was too late now. I dropped the bag and got my rifle up.

The first woman was screeching as I placed a round in her head. She skidded to a death. Unfortunately, whatever she was carrying had not died. Her belly was all elbows and knees as whatever was inside her continued to move.

"Dad?"

"Yeah, I know." The other two zombies were hiding behind the nurse's station.

"What do we do?"

"What the hell are you talking about?"

"There's a baby inside of her."

"Doubtful." I scanned back and forth, wondering when they were going to launch their attack.

"It's moving!"

I took a quick glance down. It still was. Could it possibly be human? And if she had delivered it, would she have immediately started eating it? I'm not ashamed to admit I gagged with that thought. If there was even an inkling it was human, we owed it at least that chance.

"I don't know how to do an emergency C-section. Do you?" I was honestly asking; there was not a hint of sarcasm in my query.

"How hard can it be?"

"Did you really just ask that?"

"It's not like we need to worry about the mother."

"Dammit. I'll cover you. Pull her into that room." I motioned to the closest room. The door was open, and I could see in. Unless someone had on a cloak of invisibility, it was empty. I backed up with Justin, covering him. He dragged her along the floor; thick blood and brain left a meaty slime trail behind her.

I shut and locked the door, and we got her onto the bed. I stared at her belly like it was a hell mound.

"Now what, Justin? I'm a little out of my element. I was a Marine; we blew shit up."

"I need a surgical kit."

"Any in here?"

"Doubt it. Should be a cart around the nurses' station though."

"Of course."

"We need to hurry. The baby doesn't have much time. He's not receiving oxygen or nutrients."

"Or human flesh. Sorry that came out before I could pull it back in. Are you sure about this? And how do you know all that?" I looked out the small privacy window in the door. The two other zombies were not in view. That didn't mean they weren't close; that just meant I couldn't see them.

"We need to at least try, and I paid attention during the human sexuality classes."

I nodded. "Sometimes it sucks having a moral compass." I said the words just as I opened the door. I'd barely had enough time to pull the trigger, as one of the zombies pressed the hollow of her collar against my barrel. I'd just about split her slender neck in two, cutting her spine. Her head fell to the side. I moved the muzzle, placing it against her skull, and finished the job. Unlike the zombie we had in the bed, this one's stomach did not move. Whatever had been in there was long gone, and I could only hope to a better place. I saw the double doors still slightly swinging as the third made her escape. I hoped she wasn't going for reinforcements. I was not a fan of our current locale.

"Okay, it's clear. Get what you need." I stayed by his side while he searched. When he found a sterile, plastic-wrapped pack, he ran back to the room, oblivious that his bodyguard was struggling to keep up.

"Now what?" he asked after he tore the pack open. He was holding a scalpel.

I locked the door again and placed my rifle on the dresser that held a small television.

"Now we, and by we, I mean you, cut into her belly. Softly; this isn't a block of cheese. You go too deep, and you'll injure whatever that thing in there is." I pulled her dirty shirt up; thick, black-blue veins crisscrossed her gray abdomen.

Justin wasn't even touching the zombie as he ran the blade down.

"Umm, you need to make contact."

"I'm practicing." His hand was shaking.

"You want me to do this?"

He gulped and looked at me. "No, I need to do this."

I was going to ask why he needed to do it and what would it set right if he did. In the end, I didn't.

Her skin was stretched tight like a rubber band at its breaking point. When he finally let the blade slice into her, the skin pulled back and rolled up.

"You're going to have to go through her abdominal wall."

"You're making me nervous."

"*I'm* making you nervous? You think it has anything to do with what you're doing?"

He didn't answer as he once again ran the blade down the now exposed muscle. That also peeled away like a layer of an onion. Although when one cuts an onion, you generally only want to cry. There were way more bodily functions I wanted to do at this exact moment. There wasn't as much blood as I thought there might be. Probably because most of it was on the floor. A baby hand pushed up against a nearly translucent membrane, the last obstacle between him and us.

"Careful," I said as Justin once again moved in.

"I got this, Dad."

"Yeah, I seem to remember you saying the same thing when you went to get your driver's license; took you three times."

"Are you really bringing that up right now?" He looked over to me, fat droplets of sweat clinging to his forehead.

"Just trying to help you relax."

"So you say." He moved slowly but deliberately, cutting through that membrane. A small hand shot through the opening.

I pushed my son back.

"Babies don't have teeth, Dad."

"How do you know what this thing has? We don't even

know what it is. And just for the record, one in two thousand babies are indeed born with teeth."

"Mom was right."

"About what?"

"You are stuffed with a bunch of useless trivial information."

"Useless? That trivia might have just saved your life." I still had my hand on his chest.

"Can I get him?"

"Be careful." I don't know what I was expecting. Some campy B-roll movie and the baby goes all psycho and adheres itself to Justin's neck just as the camera fades to black. That seemed the most likely, at least in my head. The reality was much fucking scarier. The throaty scream of a penis-less baby echoed throughout the room. Yeah, it took me a second to realize the penis-less boy was actually a girl.

"She's beautiful." Justin had a full stream of tears coming down his face. I took the scalpel from his hand and severed the umbilical connection to the zombie. I wrapped the mother up in the blankets and carefully placed her on the floor against the wall behind me. Justin, in the meanwhile, placed the baby down on the bed and cleaned her off.

"What do we do now?" I looked down at the baby, who to my untrained eye, looked as healthy as can be. The baby was blinking slowly. She was looking pretty intently at Justin, her mouth open in what looked like the beginnings of a smile. I was extremely happy to note she was of the other one thousand, nine hundred, and ninety-nine, not one tooth showed. Can't be too careful.

"We get her home and show her off," he said triumphantly.

"Just so we're on the same page, I'm freaking out right now."

"I know, Dad, I know. I just didn't want to state the obvious."

"That's a first."

In addition to the diaper bag, I also filled up one with formula. It was going to be difficult aiming correctly, loaded down the way I was, but they were necessary supplies. The day had taken a turn I could have never expected, and we weren't done. The third zombie had a change of heart in regard to escaping, or maybe she was looking for a better place from which to launch an attack, or maybe she was just fucking horrible at hide and seek. She was standing in the hallway like she just plain forgot what she was doing. I mean, how many times have we all done that? Go into a room maybe looking for our keys or something as inane and then got in the room and completely spaced it out. Sure, she forgot she wanted to eat somebody, but pretty much the same thing. She quickly remembered when she spotted me; I shot a hole clean through her. I immediately went and placed my hand on her belly. We already had one miracle for the day. Would it be asking too much for another? The flesh was still and, more importantly, cold. I shook my head to Justin.

The baby was bundled up in his arms as he approached. I stood and went over to the windows just to see if anything had heard the shots and was even now coming to investigate. It was a yes and no sort of answer on that. There was indeed a group of six zombies in the parking lot, they had been running at full tilt but all stopped at the same time and began to look around. My guess was that they'd been hunting some-one, and the person had had the good fortune to get away, at least for the moment. One of the six zombies stepped out of the small, loosely formed circle. He stood straight up and rigid as if at the position of attention for a military formation.

"What the…?" Never got to the expletive, as a *ding* like a tiny bell had been rung inside my head; this was immediately followed by a quick flash of a zombie. Fear knocked through me, and then whatever had invaded my personal space was gone. A couple of things happened at the same time. The first, the one I thought delivered the pinging turned and looked up to the window I was perfectly silhouetted in; the second, from across the parking lot, a man stood up from his hiding spot behind a small van. The other zombies were in quick pursuit when he took off running.

Justin had a dazed look on his face, and the baby was in the midst of a full-throated cry. It was safe to assume they'd all just experienced what I had.

"We've got to get the fuck out of here." I grabbed Justin's arm. He didn't need much goading. We'd found a much cleaner stairwell down, and we were in the truck in under two minutes. Even with the windows up, I could hear the man scream as the zombies tore into him. Justin got the baby to calm down just as we were pulling up to Ron's. Neither of us had spoken at all about what we'd felt. I was too busy trying to figure out what it meant and how it affected us. The zombies, thankfully and unexpectedly, yielded us the roadway.

Tracy was the first to approach as we came in. She must have been in dire need of some changing material for Wesley, or she was going to give me hell for separating from BT. Whatever she was going to say changed, suddenly, when she saw me carrying two heavy bags and Justin one small parcel.

"That's just like you, Mike," she said. "I send you for diapers, you bring home a baby." She gave me a quick kiss, kissed Justin on the forehead, and escorted both of them into the house. Stephanie grabbed the bags, easily hefting them. Sometimes I forgot just how stout of a woman she was.

"You okay, man?" BT asked astutely.

"Well, I just watched my son perform a medical procedure on a zombie to save a baby."

"You need to tell me that story."

"Oh, I will brother, but we've got some more pressing problems we need to deal with." I called a meeting of the entire house occupants to let them know what I'd witnessed.

"LIKE DOLPHINS," Trip had explained to the clearly confused table when I was done presenting my new information about the zombies' ability to reach out for victims.

"Is there any defense against this?" It was Stephanie who asked.

"I've known all along!" Trip said almost gleefully. He'd pulled off one of his sandals and had his foot up by his nose. He took a big sniff and winced.

"He's talking those fool tinfoil hats isn't he?" BT asked in disgust.

"Those fool tinfoil hats saved your life," I reminded him.

"Thanks, asshole," was his reply.

"I think I can work on something that will be a little less conspicuous," Mad Jack stepped in.

"Maybe something without batteries," I said.

"Yeah, we don't want anything burning through our skulls." BT and I fist bumped under the table.

"Is it a priority yet? I mean the zombies know we're still here." Dennis had just come in from a shift on guard duty.

We all could only nod in agreement.

"I think if and when MJ comes up with something—"

"Or we use tinfoil!" Trip interrupted me by standing and blurting out with his finger in the air.

"Or we use tinfoil," I added. "We might want to start thinking about an exit strategy."

This was met with a chorus of disapproval, as I figured it would be. We were relatively safe here, we had supplies that a small third world country would be happy to have, and this was home. "Listen, I get it, that's just a suggestion. The zombies aren't going to go anywhere, at some point one of us has to leave. If any of you have noticed, every morning when we get up, there're more zombies." I could tell by some of the stares that most were not aware of this new development. "They're amassing. I think they're waiting to get to a number that we can't repel, that we have no chance in hell of repelling. They get a couple of hundred of those new bulkers and they'll take this house down."

There were murmurs, but no one doubted that.

"I, for one, am not leaving." It was Ron. I had the distinct feeling that if I said the sky was blue, he would have disagreed. This was exactly what we didn't need, divisiveness. Some would stay just because it was the easier decision, not because it was necessarily the right one.

"This isn't a game, Ron. We need to make intelligent decisions for the safety of everyone."

There was no heat in his voice. "Staying *is* the most intelligent choice, Mike."

Even if I swayed everyone and they agreed to leave, I would not go. Not without Ron, and he was not going anywhere. I toyed with the idea of kidnapping him. The thought passed soon enough. For good or bad, right or wrong, good or evil, this home would be the one written in the annals of the Talbot legacy where we made our final, desperate, doomed final stand or a miraculous come-from-behind victory.

I may have shown my utter disgust for the way the conversation went. I didn't give a shit as I let my chair fall back behind me when I got up and left.

The next morning, BT found me. I wasn't doing much of anything. He smacked me on my chest.

"Come on, MJ needs some help."

"I'm not test piloting his newfangled head scramblers. He'll probably make us all like Trip."

"No, it's for the transformers."

"Please tell me he didn't make some new high-powered ice cream maker."

"No, nothing like that."

"Wait … actually, that's not that bad an idea, not that soft-serve crap though; always thought of that as melty ice cream. First time I had it I was four; started crying because I thought it was going to get all over my hands."

"So you've had problems with your hands being dirty for a very long time?"

"Wow, I guess I did. You think maybe the ice cream was the root of my problem?"

"I think it goes much deeper than that, Talbot. Just come on, this has nothing to do with ice cream."

I followed BT outside. I was looking at a stack of four-inch-by-four-inch pressure treated posts.

"Why am I looking at these?"

"We need to dig some holes."

"Fence post holes? I hate digging fence post holes."

"Trust me, this is for a good reason."

"MJ tell you that?"

"I did." MJ said, coming over.

"You going to help dig these holes?" I asked.

"I invented this." He was using those words as a way of politely saying, "no."

"Fucking engineers. Okay, tell us what we need to do."

"You need to dig holes. I would think that part would be self-explanatory."

"He's kidding, right?" I asked BT. The big man merely shrugged.

"Okay, egghead, where do you want the holes? How far apart should the posts be and what is the layout?"

MJ merely pointed; there were small sticks in the ground with orange flags attached to them all around our perimeter.

"Shit, now I look like the asshole."

"Nothing ever really changes with you, man." BT said, grabbing the post hole digger while handing me a shovel.

If we were in Florida, we would have finished the job in five or six hours. After ten, we were about halfway there. One does not have a firm grasp on frustration until they have dug dirt in Maine, the birthplace of rocks, apparently. The first hole had been a set-up, I think, because of the ease with which we had dug it. Every one after that had boulders that needed to be removed. I had argued heatedly that we should move the hole; Mad Jack, who was supervising the labor, had told us, in no uncertain terms, that could not happen. I wondered a few times that day if he could survive a shovel strike to the side of the head.

Justin and Travis came out after a while to help. Justin looked like shit.

"How you doing?" I asked him, fearful he'd spent the entire night thinking about Jess.

"I'm okay." He had a smile. "Avalyn didn't sleep much. I stayed up with her."

"Avalyn?"

"The baby needed a name."

"I guess she did. She doing all right?"

"I don't want to get gross, Dad, but, umm, Nicole is helping out."

"With feeding?"

"Yeah, Dad, geez. You ever walk in on your sister breast-feeding two babies?"

"No."

"It was horrible."

On a fundamental level, I knew it was a beautiful act of nourishment and maternal bonding. That it was only a corporate greed that infused the unnatural aspect of this onto our perverse Western culture. Still though, I'm not ashamed to say I didn't want to watch my daughter breastfeeding. Maybe it made me realize she was no longer daddy's little girl. I don't know the reasons. I'm male. I don't dwell on my feelings much. Suffice it to say, I thought it was hilarious Justin was scarred and thrilled it wasn't me.

"You'll be fine. Watch out for the task master." I pointed to

MJ. BT and I pulled up a seat a few feet away from the work. My hands were raw, blistered, and in some spots, bleeding. I was about to ask BT how his hands were doing when I saw him take off heavy leather gloves.

"You been wearing them things the whole time?"

"You're fucking clueless, man." He set them to the side and took a long drink of water. "And don't even look at them. They'd look like boxing gloves on you, anyway."

He was right. Gary and Trip took a shift as well. By the time night descended, we were nearly done. When we'd decided to call it a night, Mad Jack had looked pissed that we were so close and not finishing. He actually picked up the post digger. When the first impact sent vibrations up his arms, he'd wisely put the implement down.

He cleared his throat then announced, "I think this is as good a stopping point as any."

Most of us were already in the house. The next day, we only had five holes to dig, and I almost couldn't do it, my hands hurt so damn bad. MJ was already having the old fencing removed a section at a time and was adhering it to the new posts. Luckily, the zombies just watched from a distance.

It was while I was helping move the old fencing into the new position I finally thought to ask why in the hell we were doing that. I initially had thought we'd be putting up more fencing, not just moving the old.

"The fence was grounded; I needed the wooden posts."

"The transformers, Mike. Remember those?" BT asked.

"Yeah, I remember them. So?"

"Pretend we're on Sesame Street. I'm going to give you two words and then you put them together, okay?" he asked in that condescending teacher to thick pupil way. "Electric." He paused then said, "Fence."

"Your mom must have been a saint, having to put up with you," I told him. "This going to be worth it?" I asked MJ. That was like asking the inventor of sliced bread if he thought it was a good idea. I could have not gotten a more biased answer if I'd tried.

"Sometimes I think someone has forgot to flip your pancakes." BT laughed.

"What the hell does that mean?"

"He thinks you're only half done!" Trip shouted, though he'd come up to my ear with his hand cupped around his mouth as if he were going to whisper that.

I had to pull back. "Better than being over cooked," I told him.

The fence moving procedure had gone much smoother than the digging, and more people could help out. We were done right around lunchtime. Which was perfect; I was starving.

"Aren't you guys going to stick around for the test?" Mad Jack looked distraught we were all leaving.

"I'll be back. I'm going to get a sandwich." All the thinking about sliced bread made me hanker for one.

When I returned with some food, I found Mad Jack by the side of the house. He had a huge lever nailed to a board stuck to the house, with a cable nearly as thick as my forearm attached to it.

"Don't touch that." I was insulted he felt the need to tell me that. As if the red signs painted with huge warnings weren't enough. I looked around him. The cable went to a bank of three of the transformers.

"You sure this isn't going to blow? I've seen what you could do with a nine volt."

"Should be fine."

"What should be fine?" BT had what looked like leg of cow and was gnawing on it.

"Mad Jack is pretty convinced this set up isn't going to blow up."

BT swallowed down hard on whatever had almost just got lodged in his throat.

"All right, flip the switch," I told him.

"Anybody else coming?" He was looking for a bigger audience.

"I think we're it for now." And the only reason I was there was because I wanted to see if all the tearing up of my hands had been worth it.

"Fine." He flipped the switch. I'll be honest, I didn't think anything had happened, then there was the buildup of a slight hum. "It works!" His face lit up like the angels had come down from the heavens and were singing just for him.

I turned to look at BT. "I'm going back in to finish eating," I said.

Trip had come outside along with Gary. "Hey, man." He hit my shoulder. "What are the lights for?" He pointed to small safety poles MJ had had us install that housed small red safety lights to let people know the fence was live.

I told Trip as much.

"Oh, I figured they were for an alien runway."

"Really? That's the first thing that came into your mind?" BT asked.

"Why wouldn't it be? Aliens are real."

"Nice job," I told MJ as I started to walk away.

"Nice job? That's all you can say?" He seemed pretty perturbed.

"Umm, it's a fence that hums. What else do you want me to say?" I took another bite of my sandwich.

MJ looked on the verge of exploding. He took two quick steps toward me, snatching the sandwich from my hands. "I'll show you nice job!"

"That's not cool, man. I'm eating that." My hands were still up by my face, maybe hoping the food would magically reappear.

He got within ten or so feet from the fence and tossed my sandwich at it. I don't even know if disintegrate is the right word. There was the *zzziiittt* sound like a bug zapper, and then there were atomized bits of my sandwich falling to the ground like some sort of strange protein snow shower.

"How's that for a nice *fucking* job?" If anything, MJ seemed to be getting hotter as he strode back and ripped out the cow leg from BT's hands. I think BT was just as shocked as I was. MJ once again tossed this into the fence. The *zzziiit* sound was a lot louder; the outcome nearly the same.

Trip fell to his knees, his head in his hands. "The horror! The horror, man! All that food, gone!"

"Holy shit. Sorry, man," I told MJ. "That's unreal!" That seemed to quell him a little. Good thing too; I don't think he would have stopped his demonstration until he started throwing people on that thing to prove his point.

"Yeah, it's unreal. I'm not using much more electricity than if I were running a hair dryer."

He started to go into the specifics of what he'd done and how it was being done. None of us moved. Honestly, he'd lost me at "invertor," but I was going to let him speak his piece, as it seemed he may have solved at least one problem. It wouldn't be long until we got our first test.

It wasn't a decade or even close to it, like I'd wanted. It was two more weeks, and just like I'd predicted, we'd started going back to our normal routine, to those things that made us feel more comfortable. I'd had to pull Gary by his ear to have him leave his personal bird's nest.

"We've been through this, brother, you can't go out there. You can't possibly have forgotten what happened the last time."

"Mike, you're hurting my ear. I'm your big brother!" He swatted my hand away.

"Then start acting like it. They're out there, just waiting."

"Tommy says he can't find them."

"That in no way implies they're gone. That just means he can't find them. Ever play hide and seek and not find someone?"

"Yeah."

"I think I just proved my point."

"It's just hard being in the house. Ron is so down, and he doesn't want anybody near him. Angel, Sty, and Ryan, too. It's tough. This is the only place I can hold on to a little of what life used to be like."

I sympathized with him, I did; still didn't mean I was going to let him stay.

"You smell that?" he asked as we traversed across the yard.

And I had. Smelled like sour milk and wet trash on a hundred-plus degree day.

"Run!"

We hadn't taken two steps when the cry of alarm rang out from the deck, and it wasn't from Justin, who was on duty, but rather Carol, her voice incredibly loud and clear though she was just coming off a serious bout of bronchitis. We'd used expired antibiotics to get her healthy. What were we going to do when even those were not effective anymore?

The ground began to rumble and bounce as if a stampeding herd of rhinos were heading our way. The ground was moving so much, it was impeding Gary's and my progress. It was like trying to run in a bouncy house. We'd go more to the side or up in the air than forward. Unlike the bouncy house, this wasn't fun. The sound of the fence being struck and the resulting *fzzzt* was overbearing. I couldn't even hear the blood pumping through my ears or my heavy breaths of exertion. The only thing louder was the intense arcing of electricity and then a massive explosion. Organic material of the most disgusting kind rained down on Gary and me as we made good our escape. Large lard-like jelly masses of yellow goo struck all around and on us. It looked like an old, decaying sperm whale had fucking blown up with large chunks of blubbery meat flopping wetly to the ground.

Gary retched, I turned to him to notice a reddish green mass was sliding down his head and onto his neck. I wanted to reach up and swat it away; I ... I just couldn't. He was on his own.

"Come on, man!"

He nodded while he was puking. That was as good a response as he was going to be able to deliver. Gunfire started; rounds were whizzing by over our heads. Justin was motioning for us to hurry. The more things change, the more they stay the same. There were more loud *fzzzzzts*. Luckily, we were not showered with any more debris. I didn't stop until I'd dragged Gary under the deck. I pushed him inside before I finally turned. Zombies were literally at the gate. Where the bulker had tried to get us, the fencing material was pushed inward, the normal diamond shapes were pulled so taut, looked more like slits. It had held and it had completely fried a bulker, but how long could it hold up to that kind of abuse? Along with the increase in head size, it appeared that the bulkers had also improved their brain mass. A solid ring of them surrounded us, yet none moved forward having witnessed the violent end to their comrade.

I would so love to end this chapter and say this was it; realizing their futility, they decided to pack up and go home. Yeah, that didn't happen. It got weird real quick, and then that changed to terrifying in a hurry. A couple of the bulkers in front of me started reaching behind them, not really looking at what they were doing, indiscriminately grabbing the more familiar zombie and then hurtling them at the fence. There was a downpour of zombie fragments as they threw body after body at the fence, looking for weak spots. Once the regular zombies finally got the picture that they were not going to be able to charge through holes left by the bulkers and were now being used as splattering rams, they backed up and out of range of the grasping bulkers. For a minute, nothing happened. The bulkers just glared at us as if they were pissed off that meat had the audacity to stay alive and well instead of inside of their bellies.

I don't know which of the smart bastards had the idea first, but it spread like wild fire. The bulkers did turn but not to leave. It was to grab at zombies who did not try to get out of their way, like they were all on the same page again. Personally, I was fine with them incinerating their buddies. Less we had to deal with, and unlike the brute force and weight of the torturous bulkers, the fence seemed to hold up exceedingly well under the assault of the much lighter zombies.

"Toss away, fuckers." I mumbled. Be careful what you wish for. Oh they tossed the zombies all right, but not *at* the fence but rather *over*. I mean not at first. They were having great difficulty judging the appropriate distance, so at first, the majority of the zombies were still being fried, but they were learning. I blew a hole into the first zombie that made it safely over the electrical impediment. Like a damn had been burst or the secret formula for force times trajectory had been discovered, it was no longer raining zombie parts, just zombies, whole, intact, ready-to-kill-and-eat zombies.

Gunfire was everywhere. I'd been moving closer to the fence to get better shots at the zombies coming over. I'd realized too late that I was in grave danger. Out in the middle of the yard, a lone solitary fighting station.

"Talbot, get your fool ass back here!" It was BT. He stood above and behind me, not exactly where I wanted or needed him to be.

An intense spray of bullets came up by my side; it was Dennis. "Come on, man!" He'd given me a precious few feet of free space to tactfully withdraw. The only reason we were still alive was that the zombies had to recover from their short flights. If they had landed feet first and hit the ground running, we'd have already been swarmed over. When my bolt stayed open, I clapped Dennis on the shoulder and pointed to the basement door. He got the message, firing off the remainder of his magazine quickly, leaving an acrid cloud of smoke in his wake and a rising zombie body toll as well. Gary was at a basement window, overseeing our withdrawal. I pushed Dennis through, closed the door, and barred it. I was confident it would hold for a reasonable amount of time against the regular zombies. Any sort of attack by the bulkers and they would breach the basement again.

"Thanks, man," I told Dennis.

"Anytime. I figured you resurrected me from the dead. I should help you out when I can."

I smiled. "Gary, I'm going upstairs. See about getting the kids in the shelter. You good?"

He nodded. He looked a little green around the gills but otherwise fine.

"I'll stay too," Dennis said as he set up shop in the window across from Gary.

Stephanie ushered Porkchop, Sty, Ryan, and Angel to the shelter. Nicole had Wesley and Jess's baby brother, Zachary, in her arms. Carol had Avalyn, and they were on Steph's heels. I kissed my daughter on the top of the head as they went by.

"Where's your mother?"

"On the deck with everyone else," a clearly tired Nicole answered.

I hoped everyone wasn't on the deck; that would be leaving two sides of the house vulnerable. BT, Mark, Meredith, and even my sister, Lyndsey, had a firing line going. It looked pretty impressive as they mowed through zombies. Steve, Jesse, and Melissa were reloading magazines as fast as their fingers would allow. Bullets were strewn all over the deck. This machine looked very well oiled, and I didn't want to gum up the works; plus, I wanted to find Tracy. I walked back into the living room. The damn cat eyed me warily. We'd not been on good terms since that feline got here. I'd not done anything to the animal. I'd also done nothing *for* the animal, and that probably irked it to no end. It scratched at the basement door.

"You going to the shelter? Probably, smart little vermin

that you are." She hissed at me. "Henry! Riley!" Of course, it was the psychotic lap dog that showed up instead. Ben-Ben had been running so fast he could not stop as he ran headlong into my legs. He shook his head a couple of times and started jumping up and down like mad. I won't swear it on a stack of Bibles, but that bark sounded suspiciously like the word "bacon," and he just kept saying it. Henry and Riley sauntered in at a much more subdued pace.

"Henry," I said as I got down on my haunches. "I need you to understand me, okay?"

He licked my face.

"I'll take that as a 'yes.' Okay mutt, you need to take yourself and your friends and the cat to the shelter. Understand?"

He licked my face again. I opened the door, and the cat bolted down and to the right. The others followed. I stood, and for a split second I swayed, almost as if I was dehydrated on a hot summer day. Zombies had made it inside. The smell was overwhelming. I had a coughing fit. I could almost taste the odor, it was so thick. On the tail end of the funky fragrance, I caught the distinct savoriness of peanut butter. "Fucking Henry." He'd left me a little present to remember him by.

I went into the kitchen. Justin was at the backdoor on the small porch. Zombies were there. They'd made it about three quarters across the yard. Mad Jack was at the kitchen window, doing his best to help. Not sure how successful he was going to be, though, since he constantly closed his eyes when he pulled the trigger.

"Get in the house, Justin!" This side was a lost cause. "Drop the stairs!"

Being one of the more vulnerable positions, we'd removed the normal stairs and built a set that was not permanently attached to the house. Nancy had not been a very happy camper when we'd drilled two large holes through her walls. These were used to drive thick rebar rods through and into hooks on the breakaway staircase. We'd attached large rings on the inside so there would be a good handhold to pull them loose when the time came.

Justin's look said it all. He didn't want to. I can't blame him. He was the one responsible for having to repair the stairs after every test run, and more than a few steps would invariably break each time. Plus, Travis loved messing with him and would sometimes pull the pins just for the fun of it.

"I'll help you fix them. Just pull the pins!"

Zombies had made it to the first step. Justin jumped in and slammed the door shut. More zombies were on the stairs. He couldn't pull the pin. We'd not taken into account the zombies' added weight putting stress on the bars. I ran over to help. The cords on my neck were pulsing out as I struggled to pull with all my might. We both went over on our asses when we finally yanked it free. We'd have a better chance of finding an honest used car salesman than we would getting that second pin free, now that all that weight was on it. I scrambled up just as the window to the backdoor blew inward from the force of the zombie that smashed into it. I started firing into the door and then higher up. I advanced as I shot.

"New magazine, Justin!" I kept firing and moving closer. I expelled the somewhat used up magazine and placed the new one in. I'd cleared the small porch. I aimed lower into all those that were trying to make it up. Blood coated the wooden steps and railings. Brains and bones were flying. Zombies were falling. When I'd got as many off as I thought we'd be able to, I went back to the ring. Justin was by my side in a heartbeat. I'd killed the closest zombies, but I could not get them off the steps completely. Their dead weight was still going to be a hindrance.

"Watch out!!" Mad Jack said, coming toward us with a huge plumber's wrench.

"What are you going to do with…" I stopped my question when he threaded the handle through the ring.

"Leverage!"

We pulled for all we were worth. The pin, which at first seemed frozen in place, subtly moved and then, as if the dam had been broken, pulled free. All three of us headed for the floor. The heavy end of the wrench collided with the ground not more than a half an inch from my manhood.

"Holy shit, Dad. You all right?" Justin laughed. We heard the wooden staircase come to a thudding crash with the ground.

"I'm fine. Sounds like you're going to have to rebuild the whole thing now." I got up, avoiding the wrench like it might still try to finish the job. "I'm going to find your mother. You stay put. Make sure these assholes don't find another way in."

"They can't reach the door now." Mad Jack said hopefully.

"Yeah, I wouldn't put it past them to rebuild the stairs or maybe even make a pyramid." I felt bad for dashing his dreams, but it was a reality he had to be aware of.

"We'll hold this spot," Justin assured me.

"All right, I'm going to track your mother down."

I exited the kitchen and headed into the living room. Travis, Trip, and Tommy were the only ones there. Unlike every other part of the house, it was relatively quiet here.

Quiet during a maelstrom is not necessarily a good thing.

"Boys?" I asked, coming closer. They were all staring out the windows. Well, sorry, two of them were. Trip was looking at the wall, an unadorned part, no less.

"Shhh, he's in France." Trip said, turning to me.

"Trip, I said no weed smoking around the kids."

"One does not simply call Maui Wowie weed!" He took a heavy toke. "Didn't they write a song about this shit? Forget it."

"And how the hell is Tommy in France?"

"Trance." Travis shook his head at Trip. "He says Payne and Charity are out there."

"Is that why you're not firing?"

"Nothing much going on here."

I peeked out the window. This was the only side of the house that did not have an obvious ingress, and the zombies apparently realized that and were concentrating their efforts elsewhere. I would have liked to send Travis to someplace else to help out, but right now, he was the only trustworthy one in that room. Tommy might as well have been in France for all the input he was offering. Trip was Trip and would do whatever the hell he felt like.

"All right, just stay here and make sure they don't start building ladders or something. Any idea where your mother is?"

Travis pointed upstairs. I took the stairs three at a time. Unlike in the living room, there was all sorts of gunfire going on up there. Ron was in the master bedroom. I could see his profile. He was shooting and crying and occasionally swearing. It was clear to see he was not doing great. I didn't ask him if he needed help because this was how guys worked through things. I mean, generally, it involved punching walls or destroying remote controls, but in this instance, annihilating zombies with intense intolerance seemed to be the best medicine. I left him to his own devices.

I backed out. If he took notice of me, he made no inclination. I took a hard right into what was Nancy's old sewing room, which previous to that had been my deceased niece, Melanie's, room. Maybe there was something about the room, the two prior occupants having passed on. With that thought being processed, I was not happy to see my wife at the window firing repeatedly.

"Took you long enough," she said without even looking over her shoulder.

"How the hell do you do that?"

She smiled as she turned around. She ejected her magazine and began to refill it.

"You've come a long way," I told her while she deftly reloaded.

"Everyone safe?"

"Define 'safe.' Fine, fine. Don't look at me that way. All the kids and the animals are in the shelter."

"What about our kids?"

"Justin's in the kitchen. Travis is in the living room. So far, we're holding the house."

"For how long?" She stopped loading to look at me. My guess was to see if I was going to bullshit her.

"We make it through the night, I'd be surprised."

I don't think she was expecting me to go the complete honesty route, and in reality, I hadn't meant to. If the vamps got into the mix, this could go bad a lot faster, and that was definitely a possibility.

Tracy let an uncharacteristic tear roll down from her eye. She was easily one of the strongest women I'd ever known or would ever know in my life, and for her to cry was unnerving.

"I just thought all of this was over." She sighed, then sniffed and brought her right hand up to wipe away the offending liquid.

I sat down next to her. There were times when I was supposed to offer advice. This wasn't one of them. She wanted my company more than my responses. Strange how quiet that room got in the midst of a full-scale invasion.

"Funny how before this started, I couldn't tell a magazine from a clip. What ammunition went with what gun or even how to load. Now I can load a thirty-round magazine with 5.56 ball ammunition in under fifteen seconds."

"Fifteen seconds? Holy shit."

"Shut up for a second," she said tenderly. "I can fix just about any jam, and more importantly, I can hit a zombie head at fifty yards almost all the time. I can do all of that, and I'm proud that I can. I just wish I didn't have to."

I leaned in. "Oh, honey."

She smacked my arm. "And I blame you, you male chauvinist pig, for not properly teaching Nicole and me all of this before it happened. Had to have an apocalypse before you could be bothered!"

"Is that how you see it?" I laughed. Not too heartily; I wasn't suicidal. "If I remember correctly, my beloved, you wanted nothing to do with it when me and the boys went to the range. You took it upon yourself to take your daughter out shopping. I think you thought you were getting me back for teaching them about firearms. And your daughter was not going to lose out on an opportunity to get a new outfit or pair of shoes just to go hit pieces of paper with bullets."

"Are you implying that I bribed my daughter?"

"Oh, I don't think I'm *implying* at all. To be truthful, I never really thought the end was going to come, anyway, I just used it as an excuse to get more guns."

"I knew that. All right, if we're being honest, I want you to know why I finally said yes to you getting that first rifle."

I perked up. This was news to me. "I thought my valid points made during our argument were the determining factors."

"Please. When's the last time *that* worked for you?"

"Don't rain on my parade, woman. I thought I actually won an argument."

"You remember that blue dress I bought?"

"Yeah, you looked fucking delicious in it."

"It cost more than fifty dollars."

"So you didn't find that at Marshall's, I take it?" Marshall's was a discount store where they sent either overstock or slightly blemished stuff to sell at deep discounts.

"Not even at the same mall."

"Do I even want to know?"

"It was five hundred."

"Five hundred!" I could feel my blood pressure rising as if monetary matters were still an issue.

"You yourself said I looked great." She was defending her position.

"For five hundred, *I* would have looked great in it."

"How much did that AR you *just* had to have cost?"

"Umm, a lot."

"One thousand thirty-two a lots."

"Well, if you want to get specific."

"I wanted that dress, and I knew you'd give me a hard time about the price."

"You lied to me."

"Relax, it wasn't the first time."

"What the hell is going on right now?"

"I was protecting you. Weren't you much happier thinking your daughter was going to study with friends rather than going out on dates?"

"Well sure."

"And Justin's car. Remember when that was hit and totaled in the parking lot where he worked?"

"Sure."

"He'd let his friend Mario borrow the car. He got drunk and totaled it."

"Why is no one telling me these things? So when Mario came over all busted up he hadn't been jumped by a motorcycle gang and robbed?"

"No."

"It's all lies. My entire life is a lie."

"You sure are melodramatic." She leaned in and kissed me. "Oh, and about your youngest…."

I got up quickly. "I don't want to know. Just let me live in peaceful ignorance. For God's sake, woman."

"We've had a good life, you and I." she said as I helped her up.

"Don't start down that road. This is the shit people start saying at the end of the movie when they're about to get killed. Their swan song. We've had a great life, and it ain't over yet."

"*Mike! Get down here!*" It was BT bellowing.

"He's almost as scary as you. Come on, I want you close. You're freaking me out a little bit with all these revelations and shit."

"What about your brother?"

"I think he needs a little more alone time."

"What is it with you males and your fragile egos that you can't allow someone to help you?"

"To need help is to imply weakness. When weakness is perceived, it is believed you are soft. When people think of you as soft, they will run roughshod over you."

"This is his family, for heaven's sake. Of all the places he should be able to turn to for help, this is it."

"Oh, hell no. You don't get it. Family is the worst because we will ride him mercilessly. Plus we have the added bonus of seeing him the most."

"If you didn't have a dick, you'd be useless."

I stopped. My foot hovered in the air between steps. By the time I got down to BT, tears were streaming out of my eyes and I was holding my gut.

"How in the fuck is this funny to you?" BT looked like he wanted to smack me into comprehension of the gravity of our situation, and that made it even funnier.

"I think he's finally snapped," Tracy said, coming up past me. "What's the matter?" she asked him.

"I think this is about to get messy. Come here." He looked over to me and then grabbed Tracy, pulling her onto the deck. I followed, still having some outbursts. What wasn't funny was that the bulkers seemed to be organizing something. They were herding the smaller zombies in front of them as they went ten or so deep rows back.

"What the…?" I had started to ask just as the bulkers began to push forward. They were trying to use the regular zombies as a barrier between them and the fence. Apparently, they didn't yet realize the properties of electricity. Once they completed the connection, they'd get fried as well. Or maybe they did. They were given enough space so that they could get a running start. The laugh and almost the remembrance of it were wiped from me. I along with everyone else was transfixed by this change in the game plan.

"The bulkers, shoot the damn bulkers!" I yelled.

That was easier said than done. They were far enough back as to almost be obscured. We couldn't stop them, but not for lack of trying. We gunned through the ranks of zombies lined up against the fence, maybe even halted their progress somewhat. The problem was we were just barely holding them at bay with six dedicated shooters and three reloaders. The rest of the house was severely undermanned in comparison. I honestly don't even know how to describe what was happening in the yard. It looked like the world's largest super soaker squirt guns had been filled with zombie guts and were forcibly being blown through the fence. Widespread Panic used to play this song called "Chilly Water" in concert, and when they sang the words, "gimme some of that cool water," the entire, and I'm talking the entire, audience would send showers of water into the air from squirt guns, water bottles, jugs, basically whatever they had. The water from ten thousand people would shower down all around us. It was magical. That would not be the word I would use when the water was replaced by zombie innards. The ground was beginning to overflow with the blood of our enemy.

Then, suddenly, it stopped. One second we were listening to what it would sound like if a T-Rex were stuck in a bug zapper, and the next a quiet so resounding as to be deafening.

"MJ!" I poked my head back into the house.

"The fence has been grounded!" he shouted back.

I was going to tell him to un-ground it, but there was no chance of that actually happening. We had to start moving to alternate plans. We were very much in danger of being cut off from the shelter, and much like the post office, was that where we wanted to be for the remainder of the apocalypse?

"I've got to get Ron," Tracy told me.

That was all great and fine. I was going with her.

"BT, we have to go get my brother." He grunted his reply as the battle waged on. With the fence out of commission, it would not be long until the press of zombies pushed it completely over.

Tracy was already on the steps by the time I got ready to join her. "When the fuck did she get so fast?" I asked as I pursued.

Tracy was by the window. Ron had stopped shooting. I couldn't tell from where I was standing, but I think he was out of ammo. Might have been for some time.

"We have to go now," Tracy said, gently extending her hand for him to take. I was pretty shocked when he did, no questions asked. No railings about how he'd lost a child, his wife, and now his house. I stepped back from the doorframe and into the hallway, hoping to prevent the mere sight of me sending him into a downward spiral. He didn't even acknowledge me. That was good in one sense, bad in others. I stepped in tow behind as they walked, anguished to get back into the fight but not enough to leave my wife. They were walking slowly enough this could have been a funeral procession. When Tracy got Ron onto the basement steps, she turned and placed a hand against my chest.

"Relax, Talbot. I can practically hear you trying to escape your skin."

"How in the hell do you do that?"

"You really don't need to follow me, you know. Go fight. Win." She pressed up as I leaned down. We shared a brief but intense kiss.

"Mike!" It was my sister.

"Go. I'll be right back."

This was that moment, that fucking portent moment. I

knew things were going to change right there and then. Every-thing had been building to it, and I stupidly chose to ignore it. There are regrets in life. There will always be a time when you look back on a particular situation and wish you had gone for it or looked before you leapt. That kind of thing. But every once in a while, there are monumental regrets, and those you have to live with the rest of your life and die knowing you fucked up.

"Dad!" This from Justin.

I'd like to say I was distracted by all those looking for me. That, at least, helps me to sleep at night. It was right there in front of my face. Tracy had turned. The door shut behind her, and I wept. Well not yet, but soon enough. I ran to the kitchen.

EPILOGUE 1

Iggy wanted to eat, but not only eat; he wanted to kill. In the wild, there were times he'd had to kill another animal either for his survival or sustenance, but it was different now. He wanted to kill just for the act of extinguishing another's life. Not for joy or food or to make sure he stayed alive, but just because anything and everything in his path needed to die. It was as uncomplicated as that. The gorilla chased the humans through the torture labs, wanting to separate limb from body, using his large canine teeth to rend body parts. He didn't know the word, but "revenge" might have been appropriate. He'd been taken by force from his home and shoved into small cages, most not large enough to even allow him the ability to stand, much less turn around.

They'd injected him with all manner of substances. Some making him so sick he wished he would die. Other times, they'd operated on him, cutting him open while he was awake. The pain had been so severe he did not think there could be anything worse. Then they'd injected him with sample number forty-four, and everything he thought he knew about the world had changed. He felt as if something deep inside of him had grabbed hold of his organs with metallic hooks and was slowly pulling everything within him to the outside. When it was done, he was convinced he knew what it felt like to die. He would return the favor to those who had shown him the way.

EPILOGUE 2

Conversation with God

POSSIBLY DRUG INDUCED, STRESS INDUCED, HARD IMPACT TO the head induced, or fuck, what do I know; maybe it's real induced.

"Hello, Michael."

"Seen any good movies lately?" I was nervous as all hell. Wow, what a bad turn of an expression, considering my surroundings.

"I don't think I brought you here to discuss my viewing habits."

"You can't fault me. You're the one that brought it up last time."

God actually paused for a second as he thought. To me, this was strange for an omnipotent being. Didn't He just know everything, always? Well, even a Cray computer needs a part of a second to figure a problem out.

"Things are not happening in your realm as I believed they would."

"You mean the shit show going on right now? Maybe you should have thought of that before you gave us that free will crap you seem so high and mighty on."

"I know you are in pain, Michael. You have suffered losses you will never fully forget, and for you, at least, time is not on your side."

Those last few words were charged with a couple of different meanings, and I was hesitant to get clarification. Was my time so short I would blissfully be let go from my pain or was it so long I would carry it for an indeterminate age? Neither response was good. Odds were He wouldn't answer it, and I didn't want to know. I went a different way.

"Are they..." I gulped.

"They're fine. Their pain is over."

I felt like a petulant child when I said it. Couldn't help myself. "What about my pain?"

"Stop, drop and roll will not work in Hell."

"Nice, so you're basically saying I still have things to do down there before I make my way here. I don't understand why you can't just tell me what I need to do. Certainly you know."

"I do." He nodded solemnly.

"Yet you can't tell me?"

He nodded again. "If I were but to give you a glimpse, it would wipe away the covenant of the free will."

"Covenant? An agreement? Free will is an agreement, like an arrangement?"

"Of a sort."

"So that's not done out of the kindness of your heart? Who is this agreement with? Between man and you?"

"You ever read the Old Testament?"

"That one is a little too preachy for me, full of fire and brimstone. Lots of kneeling and proselytizing."

"I agree, man can be somewhat overzealous in their depictions and descriptions of my actual message, but there is a kernel of truth hidden in there as well. It was never my intention for anybody to ever die in my name, yet countless millions have as they falsely fly my banner. I am not to be blindly worshipped, forced upon others, not even revered, just loved. That was all I have ever wanted. And not blindly loved merely because I exist but a mutual respect and appreciation of each other's existence. I knew there was going to be a problem when one of the first priests said there were certain ways that I must be loved and all other ways were wrong. It has been a long dark road since. The garden was a wonderful time. It was not quite the fairy tale it has been shown to be. Men and women still died. Life was a constant struggle. Yet it was beautiful in its innocence. I suppose in the end it was all my fault."

I didn't say anything. God was about to go all revelations and shit. I was curious.

"I had an affinity for man."

"Umm, because we were made in your image."

God actually laughed. "Not so much. I do not even believe your mind capable of understanding my true form."

"Do you look like a spider-centaur?" It was the first truly disturbing imagery I could come up with.

"Ah, I see the walls between your realities have come dangerously close. Let's hope they never collide. Let's just say we do not share very many traits. Early man was a very curious creature, always looking and wondering. It was the first time I saw one looking to the heavens that I wanted more for them. I gave a small gift, one so insignificant I thought it would go unnoticed."

"Gold?"

God sighed. "Not material things. You know nothing, Michael Talbot."

"You did *not* just say that."

God shrugged and continued on as if He had not just dropped a reference from a book I'd read. It was things like that which made me question whether this was all made up in my head or not. Or perhaps, if I wanted to go a layer deeper, He used the information I housed in my head to better be able to communicate with me. If He was as vastly different from us as He said He was, that might be the only way we could converse.

"Happiness, Michael. I gave that first man a small sliver of happiness for what he gazed upon. Had I known how things would turn out, I would have never done so. If we're being honest it was a female gazing upon a fruit. So there is some truth to the original Adam and Eve story, though she was not tempted, the gift was given to her without her knowledge or consent really. I wonder if she knew the cost, would she still have accepted?"

"Happiness? Not free will?"

"No, that came later and was born from that fateful decision of mine." He looked sad, immensely so.

"How could something like that cause you such misery?"

"It was the pursuit of this happiness. Happiness takes many forms. In a child, it can be something as beautiful and innocent as seeing a bumblebee land on a brilliant flower. For a man with no morals, it can be the dismemberment of his foes that gives him the greatest joy. For others, it is the accumulation of wealth at the expense of all others that brings the greatest joy."

"Wow, you really don't expect to hear God say He screwed up. Shit I thought when I … umm, forget it. Wait, the zombies aren't your way of scrubbing the playing field is it? Like a reboot?"

The look He gave me would have blasted my soul free from my body, well, you know, if I had one that is.

"Do you ever listen? Perhaps I should nominate your wife for Sainthood. Someone's idea of true happiness was having the ability to destroy all of their enemies."

"Why can't we be more like that kid with the bumblebee?"

"That was always my true intention. That wide-eyed stare

at something so natural and beautiful. That smile. It was almost immediately that I tried to take back my gift."

"Let me guess. This was when the covenant was formed? Do I even want to know who with? Forget it, that doesn't matter. What is my place in all of this?"

"Like many before you, Michael, you are a warrior. Though, I send you out without the benefit of a safe haven at your end. I ask everything of you without the ability to offer anything in return."

"I've had girlfriends like that before."

God smiled.

"As long as my pursuits of happiness are aligned with yours, like the safety of my family, we're good."

"That's all I could ever ask."

As I began to awaken—or be transported back or just fucking came back to sanity—I was shaken by one last disturbing image. There was a small black spot nearly the size of a soccer ball. It stuck out due to the vast whiteness that was this place. Red eyes gleamed at me out from that hole, then an incredibly long finger emerged and made the traditional come hither movement. "Psst, Mike. Over here, man." And then I fell off the couch I'd been on.

EPILOGUE 3

Conversations with my daughter.

NICOLE HAS A PROBLEM WITH SHARING. SO MUCH SO, THAT SHE is angry with me that Father's Day hovers at, or around, her birthday. I gently reminded her that without my celebration, she would not have hers. Dad one, Nicole zero. Although, in reality, she's up by about a hundred and twenty-seven thousand, six hundred and forty-six, give or take a thousand or so. For those who have raised a daughter, you understand the math. We welcome Wesley into the family with all of our hearts.

18

THE LOST CHAPTERS

Mike Journal Entry 14

"THE FENCE IS DOWN." JUSTIN WAS POINTING OUT THE window.

Mad Jack looked defeated. I had to believe he thought that this was going to be the best zombie deterrent of all time, and they had gone through it in much less time than it had taken to go up. My hands still ached from digging those damn post holes. Zombies were pouring into the yard. The obstacles that had done wonders for stopping the earlier versions of zombies were no more than a minor impediment now. They skirted around and over anything in their path. No amount of battling on our part was going to stem this red tide. I was about to tell everyone we needed to go when an explosion lifted me off the ground an inch, maybe more. The ground rippled from the percussions.

"That was intense!" BT screamed. He thought he was in a conversational tone, but there was a good chance everyone here had suffered some significant hearing loss.

He'd let loose an RPG into a small stack of used up five-gallon propane tanks. I'd wanted to use them for target practice. Mad Jack had informed me that would be a bad idea. Said that nearly empty cans were much more volatile than filled ones. Something about pressure and how the fumes were more flammable than the gas itself. I didn't want to believe him because they were good targets, but I wanted to blow myself up even less. I ran to the deck. The crater BT had created was pretty impressive. There was a clear twenty-five-foot perimeter around the blast zone, which was completely free from all enemies. I would imagine because they'd been blown apart or away. The dead and dying were laid out for another twenty feet from that point. Two hundred more explosions like that and we could win this war. We had one RPG round left and no more propane tanks.

Travis was tossing sparkler bombs, but those were like firecrackers compared to the grenade BT had launched. It was inflicting casualties, but not at a rate that they even acknowledged. This amassing was huge and was being directed. Payne and Charity had something to do with this, of that, there was no doubt. There were too many zombies, and they had bided their time for too long. Zombies by nature are not patient creatures. Glass all around us broke out as zombies reached into some of the lower lying windows, and even more unsettling, they broke out some that they had no business reaching. They had not yet quite figured out the mechanics of building cheerleader-worthy pyramids, but they had no problem climbing up and over the backs of anything in front of them. When one popped through the window in the kitchen, which was nearly fifteen feet from the ground, that was pause for concern. Pause for concern? Why the fuck am I trying to be so stoic? It was petrifying. Thousands of intelligent zombies were here. They were here to stay. They were pissed off, and they were hungry.

There was a moment where I was stuck. I didn't know

what to do. So many things were going on at once, and I could not process all of the information. I don't know if there's a term, but "battle burden" seems to work. I was needed in a half-dozen spots, yet I knew no matter where I went, I would be virtually ineffectual. There were a dozen things that needed to be done; any one of them would cost human lives if they weren't performed. Still, I stood in the living room. The only thing moving was my heart and my head as I swiveled it back and forth. Explosions rocked the house. At some point, BT had set loose the final RPG round. Sparkler bombs were going off, a couple every minute. Mini-explosions from bullets being fired were at the blistering pace of a few hundred a minute. Once upon a time in fairyland, I had written that most fire-fights lasted in the neighborhood of a minute. This was not one of those times. We were at an unsustainable pace, both in resources and stamina. I'd made my decision.

"Downstairs, Justin. Drag MJ with you!" He did not hesitate. "Tommy, let's go!" He still seemed relatively lost in some deep recess of his mind.

"This is my fault. All of it." He had tears rolling from his eyes.

This was war. There would be tears, but they would have to be reserved for the aftermath.

"Get downstairs." I grabbed his shoulder and tried to force him in that general direction. When he didn't even budge, I remembered that he was much, much stronger than I was. If the saying "God helps those that help themselves" was good enough for the big man, I would also need to adopt it. I couldn't spare the time. This was a case of weighing out the safety of one for the safety of many. And if he didn't want my help, there wasn't anything I could do about it anyway.

I went out onto the deck. "Let's go! Now!" I guarantee I shredded vocal chords. They'd have plenty of time to heal in the bunker. BT gave me a look as if to say he didn't quite think things were lost and past the point of no return. That faded the moment the house shook from the collision of bulkers against the frame. Gary and Dennis were still firing shots down below, but the war had gotten a lot quieter all of a sudden. Wood was being splintered and cement was being cracked under the assault. Everyone was running. That I knew. But still the events seemed to be unfolding in super slow motion, like the world wanted me to make sure I didn't miss any fucking detail. Mark had dropped some bullets, causing my sister to stumble. Trip reached out and caught her shoulder, keeping her from falling over. Meredith turned back, looking for her father.

MJ seemed to be more getting carried along than actually walking. BT had got down to the bottom and was nearly hurling people toward the shelter. I was at the top of the stairs, making sure our retreat was not being pursued. Oh, it was. I just happened to be in the wrong position. My head whipped back around when I heard Tracy's voice as she helped usher people in.

"Get the fuck back in...." Then my words were drowned out as bulkers crashed through. Nearly took the top of my head off as I jumped down the stairs. Decapitation by low hanging ceiling. Gary had been launched from his previous spot. He was a good ten feet away, unconscious. Dennis had leaned down. I thought to check my brother's condition. I'd find out differently later. He was firing his weapon. Even so, he had the time to find me. There was a strange expression on his face. I knew it for what it was: sadness. If he left his position, Gary would die. If he tried to drag Gary away, they both would die. BT was ushering everyone, including my wife, into the shelter. If I could, I would thank him later. I headed to my downed brother. If I thought things were going slow upstairs, I was now seeing life one frame at a time. I could track the trajectory of a casing as it left Dennis's gun. The thing seemed to take five seconds from ejection to floor.

Dennis was screaming, "Run, Talbot!" It was that low,

slow sound of a voice pulled over a long time and distance. I gripped Gary's collar and dragged him along the floor.

"Let's go, Dennis!"

I'm not sure exactly what he said, but it sounded a lot like "Can't." He was still blasting away. Bulkers and speeders had flooded into the basement, overturning furniture while they tried to get to us all. I wasn't going to make it. I turned so that I was backing up, then I placed the rifle up against my shoulder and started firing. Much like Dennis, I was screaming, my war face, my death mask, I don't know. I hoped it was as fierce as it sounded. I cried out as Dennis was dragged down, the muzzle of his rifle still coughing out plumes of fire as he kept shooting.

"*No!!!*" I started to move forward, dragging Gary with me. I was firing as well. A huge hand wrapped itself around my jacket, I was lifted up off the floor.

"No, Talbot, *No!*" BT was yanking me backward.

"*Ahhhhh!*" The pain I felt was both physical and mental. Dennis's rifle had finally stopped. I couldn't see him anymore as zombies were now in the short hallway with us. I almost let Gary go when my bolt popped open so I could reach for another magazine. I was willing to die right there and then, and I would have if another's life wasn't hanging in the balance. BT's eyes were wide when he whipped us in. Tracy had been at the door along with Stephanie and Steve. They slammed it shut and spun the dial just as something collided with the door.

"Where's Dennis?" Tracy asked, looking around.

I dropped my rifle and slid down against the door. My head in my hands, I cried until I felt as if my head would explode from the pressure. Another loss—they were piling up and we were far from out of the woods.

I DIDN'T MOVE MUCH. I looked up when Gary groggily came to. The shelter was a hive of activity as the women did their best to keep the children from being scared. I took note that the stronger sex seemed to be getting things done while us men were lost in our misery. Ron, Mad Jack, Justin, Travis, me —we were junk. We'd all taken up refuge, suffering in solitude. Gary had a bandage wrapped around his head. Looked like he should be playing a fife and reporting to General Washington. I was happy to see he was going to be all right, at least for now. My head pounded as I stared at the floor. I looked up when I felt a tap on my shoulder. It was Gary. He handed me a small piece of paper and walked away. It was a note from Dennis.

Hey Mike, I always knew it was going to end this way.

I sat up straighter.

Well, honestly I have no idea how I went out. Let's just hope it was heroic and I didn't take a header off a cliff or something.

"It was heroic, brother." I mumbled.

We both know something supernatural happened in your parent's basement all those years ago. Something I don't think was ever supposed to happen. You gave me more time though, brother, more time to watch my kids grow up, hell to even have kids! To enjoy this existence we call life … and how could I ever repay you for that?

"You did every day you were alive." More tears came out from a well I had thought was completely dry.

We cheated death, you and me. Somehow, someway, you found a loophole in the fabric of existence….

"I don't think it was me, my friend. I think we had help from someone who specifically said they could not help." God was playing a dangerous game. This was twice now that Gary had been pulled from the jaws of death. What part did my brother play in all of this? It had to be huge if all of these elements were being manipulated in such a way as to ensure his existence, right? I mean, what would be the purpose of placing him in the center of the maelstrom and not making sure he survived? What kind of grand writer would kill off a main character? And God was the most majestic designer of them all, wasn't He? A thought formed in my head. Dennis had been saved and used to save Gary because he was unaccounted for.

He should not have been alive. He was not on the giant game board being played out among the gods. No one else today would have been in a position to save my brother. We *had* been accounted for. Dennis was the wild card. I'd been used as a messenger to save him, and Dennis had been used as a sacrificial pawn. I went back to reading the page in my hand.

"*...and I thank you for that. Listen, man. I don't know why this happened, but I thank you. Whatever happens, man. No matter how I finally die, just a simple thank you, man. You bestowed a gift to me beyond recompense. I love you, Mike, and I don't even care who knows that. You are my brother no matter what the last name on the birth certificates say.*"

At some point, even the bottomless well of tears dried up, I canted to the side and fell asleep. I awoke some time later. Most of the lights were out, and the vast majority of bunker inhabitants were asleep. I had a blanket draped over me, but even that could not keep the cold out that was slowly drifting to my heart.

"Hello, Michael." I scooted to the side quickly as a voice whispered in my ear. "Wait, do not force me out. I will not delve deeply." It was Payne.

"Fuck you want?" I stood.

"I can feel the heat of your anger through this door."

"Give me a sec, you can feel the heat of my anger around your throat."

I reached for the dial. Tommy grabbed my hand.

"That would not be wise," he said softly.

"Yeah? When have I been known for my wiseness?"

"Wiseass, maybe. What the hell is going on?" BT asked.

"Apparently, we're having a party and the vamps are crashing," I told him.

"They're here?"

I nodded.

"What do they want?"

"I was about to find out before you two came along."

"He was about to open the door," Tommy ratted me out.

"What the fuck is wrong with you?" BT asked. "They aren't the welcome wagon. They don't have an apple pie with them."

"The welcome wagon? What is this, 1973? In Kansas? When's the last time someone brought a neighbor an apple pie?"

"You know what I mean."

"No, I don't. The last time I moved, my neighbor's dog shit in my yard. That was my greeting."

"Well, that should tell you something about yourself."

"Ahem." Tommy cleared his throat and pointed to the steel door.

"You're lucky," I told BT.

"Yeah, sure." He bumped into me with his chest, driving me into the wall.

"Real mature."

"You gave me your word no harm would befall Sophia." That came through loud and clear. So much so it even interrupted BT's retort.

"I meant to. Keep my promise, I mean." I told her honestly. "That was until I found out she would be able to, and most likely would, kill us remotely. I couldn't let that happen. Breaking an oath seemed the lesser of two evils." I wanted to laugh at my own words, didn't figure it was the right time. Maybe I do have some sage like qualities. Killing Sophia had rid the world of an evil. If anything, I was doing the planet a favor. "I'm going to take your silence as an admission of guilt."

"Her life was not yours to take."

"That's where you're wrong, Payne. I'll take anyone's life that threatens the safety of my friends and family. No questions asked."

"There are consequences."

"Of course there are. There would have been consequences had I chosen to let her live as well."

"Perhaps. Or maybe we would have left you all to your own devices."

"Doubtful, but if planting seeds of falsehood makes you feel any better, go for it."

"We've found that the living dead ones are very susceptible to suggestion." Payne said.

That I did believe, and wholeheartedly. Eliza had mastered that particular power, Tommy had some skill, and I could have a zombie pet puppet if I tried hard enough.

"I can feel you wondering right now whether or not this latest attack was caused by us or not. I can assure you that we are in complete control of the zombies."

There was at least some truth to her words or she would not be on the other side of that doorway.

"Have them eat Charity, and then I'll know you're telling the truth."

BT smacked my arm so hard I thought it was going to fall off. "Egging on a vampire. You need help, man."

"Michael, you cannot stay in there forever."

I knew she was right. "So what would you have us do?" I sighed. Not that I was going to do anything she suggested, but it would at least be nice to know my options, or lack thereof.

"I want to make you immortal, Michael, to have you by my side as we rule this world together."

"And what of the people here with me?"

There was deep silence before she spoke again. "I believe that you already know the answer to that question."

"So I come out, you convert me over, and then we dine

until our heart's content? Something like that? I mean it's tempting, especially with this big goon hovering over my head, that's for sure. Is there like a signing bonus or something? Just a taste of what it's like to be called up to the major leagues? You know what I mean?"

BT's head shook back and forth.

"Do not make me regret my decision to even offer you this."

"What could you possibly do that would be worse than what you have so generously *offered*?" I spat out that last word.

"Oh Michael, how naive you are. There are things much worse than death. I could erase all that you and your family are and replace it with anything of my choosing. I could torture them for millennia while you watched helplessly. I could easily make them go insane and then change them over. They would stay demented forever. Of all the things that our condition can heal, those of the mind are mysteriously absent. How would you feel, Michael, if your beautiful wife merely screamed constantly for hundreds of years? Or possibly one of your sons could not help but repeatedly stab himself? I have done these things merely for my amusement. Imagine what I could dream up as restitution for Sophia's death."

"Can she do what she says?" I asked Tommy, and he nodded sadly. "I think we'll just take our chances in here," I told her.

"Do you not think I can find people that will be able to open this door?"

I knew she could. It wasn't really a bank vault.

"We'll deal with that when it happens."

"Your family will die violently."

I could tell she was turning away.

"Wait!" Tommy said loudly.

I looked at him questioningly. He said nothing for a second as he seemed to be collecting himself or gathering courage.

"You are wasting my time," she hissed.

I felt like telling her, "What's the rush?" It wasn't like she was on the clock or something.

"What if I were to give myself up?"

She laughed. "What makes you think I care anything for you, Tomas, the sister killer? There is already too much broken within you. Your fall would not nearly be as enticing as that of Michael's."

"What the hell is wrong with you?" I put my hand on Tommy's shoulder. "And stop looking so sad; you look like you just received a rejection letter from Harvard."

"I want to try and prevent any more suffering."

"I appreciate that. We all do. But we'd no sooner let you out than I would anyone else here."

"That's the truth," BT chimed in.

"I've got this under control," I told him, placing my hand up.

"This is what you call under control? Man, I would have loved to have been one of your kids. They must have run roughshod over you."

"Anyone want one of these?" Trip said, coming up to us holding tin foil hats.

"I don't want your damn hats!" BT was about to swat them out of Trip's hands when we all reached our hands up to our ears. I'm not sure how everyone else felt, but judging by their reactions, I would say it was pretty close to what I was experiencing. Knitting needles shoved into and through my eardrums would have hurt less. The pain was sharp and severe and seemingly lasted forever. I was under the impression Payne was unleashing some sort of psychic event in my skull, maybe giving us all multiple aneurysms. I was reaching over to Trip and one of his hats when it stopped as suddenly as it had started. He was smoking a bone and had been completely oblivious to our suffering because, of course, he was already donning his.

Tracy looked over to me when it stopped. She was trying to comfort the kids. The pain did not linger, but the remembrance of it had.

"I don't know." Tommy answered before I could ask.

"Payne?" BT asked.

"She's leaving, and in a hurry." Tommy said.

19

THE LOST CHAPTERS

Tiffany

"I NEED TO STOP FOR THE NIGHT." SHE WAS LEANING AGAINST a sign that said "Searsport." Night was coming quickly, and she was wholly uncertain about exactly where she needed to go. A used book and antique store was not more than a hundred yards up and on her right. She could hear the sounds of battle, but it was far away and she certainly was not going to come up on it in the middle of the night not knowing which side, if any, she should be on. After a quick but thorough examination of the building, she found no one either living, dead, or undead, and for that she was grateful.

Tiffany read a lot those next couple of weeks. Foraging for food and water had not been difficult, as the store had a five gallon water dispenser with three untapped containers and the owner was apparently a fan of nut bars—he or she had an entire drawer stuffed full of them. An old bed that creaked loudly every time she moved had been the most comfortable thing she'd ever slept on. Even still, she couldn't stay here forever. She just had no direction to go in; the battle she'd heard previously had long ago ended.

"Maybe I should just get back to my car and go." Her hand was on the door handle when she heard the approach of a truck engine coming from her right. She moved away from the door and ducked down by a window. The truck rolled past quickly, so she couldn't be sure, but she thought it was the same people from the day she saw the heads on the road. She didn't know why, but she was glad they were still alive. Less than an hour later, a bigger truck rolled by, going back the way they'd come, the large man behind the wheel this time. She did not see the one with the goatee.

She'd got back on her bed and had been reading a first edition print of Moby Dick when she heard another engine. "Lot going on today," she said as she got back to her window. The same white truck as earlier was heading back, the man with the goatee driving. "I wonder if I can trust you?" she asked before going back to her book. It was another two weeks before she was forced to make a decision. Even with some serious rationing, she was down to the last of the candy bars and she was officially sick of the wild blueberries she'd been harvesting in the back.

"Forwards or backwards, what are you going to do Tiffany?" She was standing on the "welcome" mat looking up and down the street for some sort of sign. It was the prehistoric cry of a loon up ahead that made her move forward and helped shape Michael Talbot's fate. She'd wished she'd started off sooner in the day; by the time she figured she was in the center of town it was already getting dark. It seemed this part of the world had a penchant for losing light at an unnatural pace.

She was literally at a crossroad as she stared upon a small grocery store called Tozier's. She could either take a left onto Mt. Ephraim road or stay straight on Route 1. Whichever way she went, it would have to wait until the morning. The grocery store looked entirely too dark and foreboding to go in there. She figured the laundromat to her immediate left was the better choice. Not many people cleaning clothes during the apocalypse, whether like her, they really had wanted to. Two of the large floor to ceiling windows had been broken out. She could see in about halfway. Rows of washing machines were on her right and dryers on her left. Besides a small pile of discarded clothing and some shattered glass, the place looked as if it could open back up for business tomorrow morning. She entered. Tiffany pulled and pushed three of the large washing machines in the middle of the row away from the wall, far enough that she would have enough room to sleep and be safe; in theory, no zombie would be able to get to her while she did so.

"Oh, gross." At first, she thought she was looking at dead rats on the newly cleared space. Her view of the matter didn't get much better when she realized that they were dust bunnies bigger than actual rabbits. She brushed some of them away, then started checking machines, finally getting a better idea as she looked upon the hundreds of garments of clothing hanging in plastic wrap. She grabbed armloads of the cleaned clothes and lined the bottom of her makeshift bed, hiding the dirt and debris while also giving her a comfortable place to sleep. She felt relatively secure in her hidey-hole, although as tired as she was feeling, she thought she could have laid down on the street and fallen asleep. It was pure blackness out when she awoke. She felt as if she'd slept for a fair amount of hours, yet she was not completely caught up. She was uncertain as to what had disturbed her. When she realized what it was, she could not help but to hold her breath.

There was no sound. No crickets, no birds, not even the wind had the fortitude to stir. She had been convinced that the vacuum of space would be louder. She stirred just enough to grab her rifle, and even that sounded like a fire alarm in the stillness. She wished she'd checked her inventory of bedding a little better; one of the jackets was made of a nylon type substance, and every time she shifted, it sounded like the rustling of a large pile of leaves. She moved slowly at first, sitting up and then slowly rising so that her head was up over the lip of the machine. She could see nothing outside, although her other senses were letting her know that the danger was real. The smell was first, then the sound of clothes moving—of feet walking. The occasional soft moan of the dead as they passed. Zombies were walking by, hundreds, maybe thousands. She wasn't even aware when her knees began shake. She had to rest her elbows on the machine top to keep from collapsing back down.

A half-hour passed, an hour, and still they moved past. From time to time, a sliver of moonlight would break through the cloud cover and illuminate the nightmare. The zombies were within feet of the entrance to the laundromat. They were cutting through the parking lot and heading down Mt. Ephraim road as they got off the main drag. She did not believe her terror could get much sharper, then she realized just how wrong she was. Just as the zombies began to tail off, she saw two vampires walking in silence behind. She dug down for enough courage to sight one of them in, hoping that she would have enough time to kill them all before they could return the favor. She was applying pressure to the trigger just as the moon was blanketed over. The last thing she saw was the eye shine of one of the vampires as she turned her head to peer into the inky blackness of the laundromat.

Tiffany didn't know if she could handle any more adrenaline surging through her system. The vampire had somehow looked directly at her, somehow seeing her. But she knew that couldn't be the case or she'd already be dead. She waited until her heart had stopped beating like a hummingbird's and crawled over the machine to go outside. She didn't venture far before retreating back to her spot in the hopes she would ever be able to fall asleep again. She awoke to a small sparrow looking down upon her. After the horrors of the previous night, the inquisitive stare of the bird was welcome. She wondered if perhaps this was the bird's first glimpse of a human and it was trying to determine if the rarely encountered beast was dangerous. The bird flitted away as she arose. A quick glimpse of the roadway showed that she was alone. She could almost believe that last night was a dream if not for the bloody footprints along the roadway.

"Follow the red stained asphalt," she sang in mockery of the *Yellow Brick Road* song. "And then what, Tiffany? What the hell are you going to do when you get there? As if two vampires weren't bad enough, now there are a thousand zombies. You owe Pappy. You don't owe him that much, though." She was convinced now that the earlier truck she'd seen filled with people was the target of the vampires. It had to be. Where else would they be going? "Screw this." She turned to go back to the Mustang. "But." She paused. "If that much evil is gathering to oppose them, just how good are those people? No, you can't think like that. Odds are the vampires and the zombies are going to join up with them." She thought back to the inhabitants of the truck; there had been women and children and none of them seemed in distress. In fact, some were laughing. "The devil laughs. Get a grip, Tiffany. I'm just going to leave, find myself some little house to call my own." She was about to turn and go when the sun burst through the clouds and perfectly illuminated the roadway the zombies had gone down.

"Could you be any more obvious?" she asked the heavens as she followed the light. An hour later, she heard shooting. Sounded like a full-scale invasion. "I guess that answers the question about them being on the same side. Doesn't mean they're necessarily good, but they're enemies of my enemies, so that's at least good."

She stood in the middle of the roadway for a few minutes, figuring out exactly what she was going to do. She wanted to stay where she was, but the exposure was too great. "Awesome." She said as she looked into the thick Maine woods. "I just got my hair done." Tiffany hiked roughly a mile, in a more or less straight line, to get closer to the sounds of battle. She'd had to make a few detour adjustments around a small body of water and an impregnable briar patch. She thought she was getting close, but she couldn't see much more than fifteen feet in any direction. The concussion from an explosion nearly knocked her off her feet. Her ears were ringing when she stood.

"I think this might be close enough." She was in a small clearing under the umbrella of a large pine. The battle waxed and waned as the day wore on. Hunger, thirst, and the constant waving off of biting insects were beginning to take their toll on the girl. "Should I stay or should I go? And I definitely need to stop singing small snippets of songs." She stayed, gathering up as much of the pine needles as she could in an attempt to build a bed. She sat back and tried to rest while a battle ensued, then fell asleep just as it was dying down. She awoke hours later, once again to an unnatural stillness that blanketed the area. The fight was over. There had been multiple explosions and more bullets fired than at any time she figured wasn't a World War, yet still, she did not think the humans survived. Her first, second, and part of her third instinct said she should just leave, turn around and go. In fact, never even think upon this place again.

It was the damn quiet that got her moving. Unlike the previous night, the sky was cloudless and the moon bright. Within five minutes, she was at the edge of a clearing. She could see a house not too far off, and much like she figured, it was still completely surrounded by more zombies than she had ever seen in one place. *There's nothing I can do here except die*, she thought, looking out upon the field covered with zombies. "Why am I still here then?" she breathed out quietly. Movement on the deck above the zombies caught her eye. The being walked slowly along the length of the structure, sometimes pausing and looking skyward. "That's no zombie, that's for sure." Of that, she was convinced. She rested her rifle on a small branch. She had the being lined up perfectly in her sights. What she wasn't completely sure of was whether or not the person was an occupant of the house or not. All she could tell with a fair degree of reliability was that the figure was a female. That wasn't enough. She could not risk the chance of killing an innocent.

"Just give me a sign; you've been doing it for the last two days, so why stop now?" She was not expecting her request to be express delivered quite so quickly. The figure on the deck whipped her head around and stared directly at her. The moon had reflected off the creature's eyes, giving off a pale red color that nearly froze Tiffany's blood in mid-transit. It was eerily similar to what had happened the previous night. Tiffany didn't hesitate as she pulled the trigger. Tiffany thought she saw the bullet impact the vampire's head but she couldn't be sure as a blinding white spoke of pain bore its way through the center of her skull. She dropped the rifle, and in the process of falling to the ground, struck her head against the trunk and a large rock. She was unconscious before her head came to a complete rest.

EPILOGUE 4

It's amazing how your mind wanders right before you're about to fall asleep. Why it wandered to this recent passage I don't know. Must be the stress of being stuck inside a bomb shelter.

It was early morning. I'd gone outside to take a piss. Yeah, I don't know why I do it outside. I just like to. There's something back to nature about it, I suppose. I don't tell Tracy I do it because it absolutely drives her nuts, and I already do enough things that test the limits of her love for me, so why add another? Anyway, this isn't about what pisses my wife off (pun intended I guess), this has to do with Trip and Stephanie. I was walking into the house and Stephanie had just tossed a plastic cup at Trip, who was hastily retreating. It had hit him in the shoulder with enough force to spin him sideways. I keep reminding you that Stephanie is a big woman. This is just one more example.

"I can't believe you, Trip!" she shouted loud enough that if we still had neighbors, they would be calling in a domestic disturbance.

"Do I even ask?" I directed my question to BT, who was sitting at the kitchen table.

"You can, but you might not believe it. Maybe, wait a second and see how it plays out."

"Any more juice?" I asked as I sat next to him.

He picked up the cup that had fortuitously spun back into the kitchen. He placed it on the table and poured me some. Stephanie was ranting and raving. Trip was apologizing profusely. She had cornered him in the living room and was beating him mercilessly with a throw pillow.

"How could you!" she just kept repeating, over and over.

I took a nice, long drink. "Okay, man I need to know," I said as I placed my nearly empty cup down.

"He took a shit."

"What?"

"He took a shit," BT repeated.

"What, like on their bed or something?"

"No, in the bathroom."

"In the toilet?" I mean, it's a damn shame I had to ask for clarification, but with Trip, there's no real safe assumption. BT nodded. "Okay, just give me the whole story."

BT had a bemused smile on his face. "Trip goes into the bathroom about twenty minutes ago, I thought maybe a zombie or two had gone in with him because he was grunting and groaning like he was fending off the enemy. Know what I mean?"

"Yeah, I get it. Maybe if he stopped eating cheese snacks, he wouldn't be so stopped up." He'd been complaining about not being able to go for the last few days.

"Well, he went. And went, and went. His words, not mine. Said it was like a gravy train was shooting out his—"

"Okay, I get it. Did he stop the toilet up?"

"No, but he went and grabbed Stephanie, who was already coming down to brush her teeth. Said he had to show her something."

"No … he did not."

"Yup, said he was so proud of his food babies that he had

to show her. She of course didn't know what the hell he was talking about, at least until the pungent funk of three-day old colon-festering processed cheese food punched her in the nose."

"Is there really a need to be that graphic?"

"I gotta admit it was pretty impressive."

"You went and looked?"

"It was the color of a canary and the size of a small eagle. Of course I had to."

"What the hell is wrong with the people in this house? So basically Stephanie is yelling at Trip for taking a shit in the bathroom?"

"That's about the gist of it. Said she wanted to brush her teeth and now she wouldn't be able to for at least another hour because of the reek."

"This is why I piss outside."

"What?" Tracy had a look of alarm on her face as she walked into the room.

"Dammit." I mumbled.

THE LOST CHAPTERS #20

Mike Journal Entry 15

AFTER THE PSYCHIC STABBING IN ALL OF OUR SKULLS, THERE was nothing. Well, I mean my wife will argue that there is generally nothing going on in my head at any time. But I was referring more specifically to vampires or zombies. A day had gone by, and we could hear nothing. We were getting close to opening the door and checking when a soft knocking came on the door.

"Hey," a female voice called out.

We all stayed silent within. I held my hand up to keep it that way.

"Hey, is there anyone in there?" There was more knocking.

"Answer her," Tracy said softly.

"What if she's a zombie?" BT asked.

"Really?" the voice on the other side of the door responded. BT shrugged.

"Who's out there?" I called out.

There was a pause on her end. "Who's in there?"

"Fair enough, I suppose. My name is Michael Talbot."

"I'm Tiffany. Tiffany Churchill."

"As in Winston?" Trip asked.

"Yeah, of the Kentucky chapter." I could tell she said it sarcastically. She was endearing herself to me already and I hadn't even seen her.

"So there are no zombies?" I asked before Trip could start to question her about the famous leader.

"Well, I think I'd be dead if there were. They pretty much left after I shot one of the vampires."

So that's what happened. That made sense, to a degree. Charity seemed to be the one directing the zombies, and when she'd been injured, and hopefully killed, that connection had been removed. Zombies rely on smell and sight to hunt, and now, apparently, echo location, but if no food was present, these new zombies won't stick around long. They went in search of greener pastures. Or what the hell do I know? Maybe Charity's mind ripping scream had sent them off. In the end, who gives a shit as long as they were gone?

I keyed in the code, looked over to BT and Tracy, who both had their weapons ready. I pulled the door open quickly. There was a waif of a woman standing there holding a large hunting rifle. She looked a little worse for the wear.

"Are you good people?" She gulped.

"I am," I said pointing to myself. "He's an asshole." I looked over to BT.

"Put the damn guns down," Tracy told us. "Come on in. We'll get you some food and water." The girl, young woman really, looked pretty relieved.

BT, me, Gary, Travis, Justin, and Meredith did a complete sweep of the house, the yard, and a little into the surrounding woods. Besides the hundreds of bodies of dead zombies, there was nothing else. We knocked on the bunker door.

"They're gone." There was relief in our group. Tiffany

told us her story up to putting a bullet in Charity's noggin. "We didn't find her. You got anything?" I asked Tommy.

He shook his head curtly.

Tiffany looked over at him strangely. I didn't think now was a good time to let her in on Tommy's and my little secret. She had a very skewed version of what vampires were like, and she was never more than half a step from her rifle. I wasn't going to give her any reason to pick it up and start blasting shit.

"WHAT NOW, TALBOT?" BT and I stood on the deck. The yard and the house, and hell, even the family, were in a shambles. I consider myself a fighter not a runner, but right then my instincts and my desires both shared the strong wish to leave, to put this place as far behind us as possible. Maybe if the vamps came from England, we should go there. At least we'd know they weren't with us on the continent. Maybe our best course of action was to find a ship and just sail the seven seas. Although that held as much craving for me as walking on to the set of a BDSM movie respite with leather, whips, chains, and strap-ons. If I'm not making it abundantly clear, those were both things I did not want to do. The thought of all those ocean waves and petroleum jelly, respectively, freaked me out.

"We rebuild." I'd gripped the railing tightly, maybe to anchor myself so I wouldn't start running and never stop. Forrest Gump might have been impressed if I started. Zombies were out there. One, perhaps two, extremely pissed off vampires were out there. A giant zombie primate was out there, and just to put a cherry on the cake, Deneaux was still out there. And I knew, I just fucking knew, all of those elements were going to find their way back to us no matter where we went. Our fates, our destinies, providence, fortune, chance, and all that other karmic bullshit were so tightly intertwined, that it was an eventuality. We'd added two lives to our group and lost four. You can do the math, these were not sustainable numbers. We were on the losing end of the extinction event. We were the tattered remnants.

ABOUT THE AUTHOR

Visit Mark at www.marktufo.com

Zombie Fallout trailer
https://youtu.be/FUQEUWy-v5o

For the most current updates join Mark Tufo's newsletter
http://www.marktufo.com/contact.html

For more information: www.marktufo.com
www.marktufo.com
mark@marktufo.com

ZOMBIE FALLOUT THE SERIES

Zombie Fallout 1

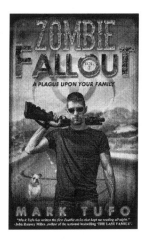

Zombie Fallout 2: A Plague Upon Your Family

Zombie Fallout 3: The End…..

Zombie Fallout 3.5: Dr. Hugh Mann

Zombie Fallout 4: The End Has Come and Gone

Zombie Fallout 5: Alive In A Dead World

Zombie Fallout 6: Til' Death Do Us Part

Zombie Fallout 7: For The Fallen

Zombie Fallout 8: An Old Beginning

Zombie Fallout 9: Tattered Remnants

Zombie Fallout 10: Those Left Behind

Zombie Fallout 11: Etna Station

Zombie Fallout 12: Dog Days

Zombie Fallout 13: The Perfect Betrayal

Zombie Fallout 14: The Trembling Path

Zombie Fallout 15: Sifting Through The Ashes

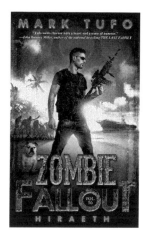

Zombie Fallout 16: Hiraeth

Zombie Fallout 17: The Lost Journals

ALSO BY MARK TUFO

Click here for other books by Mark Tufo

Lycan Fallout Book 1

The Book Of Riley A Zombie Tale Book 1

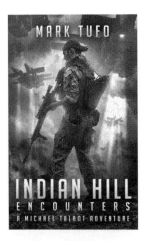

Indian Hill 1: Encounters Book 1

Distance Winter's Rising Book 1

Timothy Book 1

The Spirit Clearing

Callis Rose

ALSO FROM DEVILDOG PRESS

www.devildogpress.com

Burkheart Witch Saga By Christine Sutton

The Hollowing By Travis Tufo

Chelsea Avenue By Armand Rosamilia

"I don't come across books like Armand Rosamilia's CHELSEA AVENUE often. Beautifully dark, this book held me entranced." Joe McKinney, Bram Stoker Award-winning author of PLAGUE OF THE UNDEAD

CHELSEA AVENUE

Armand Rosamilia

Revelations: Cast In Blood by Christine Sutton, Jaime Johnesee & Lisa Lane

THANK YOU

Thank you for reading Zombie Fallout: Tattered Remnants. Gaining exposure as an independent author relies mostly on word-of-mouth, please consider leaving a review wherever you purchased this story.

Made in the USA
Columbia, SC
19 February 2025

54084669R00209